John Lathrop

After a four-year enlistment in the US Air Force, John Lathrop attended university in Los Angeles, and then spent time in the southern Philippines in the US Peace Corps. This was followed by almost a decade and a half in the Middle East, primarily Saudi Arabia. He is the author of *The Desert Contract*. While researching *The End of the Monsoon* he spent several months in Phnom Penh.

Also by John Lathrop

The Desert Contract

The End of the Monsoon

JOHN LATHROP

JOHN MURRAY

First published in Great Britain in 2010 by John Murray (Publishers)
An Hachette UK Company

First published in paperback in 2011

2

A CIP catalogue record for this title is available from the British Library

ISBN 978-0-7195-2341-0

Typeset in Monotype Bembo by Servis Filmsetting Ltd, Stockport, Cheshire

Printed and bound by Clays Ltd, St Ives plc

John Murray policy is to use papers that are natural, renewable and recyclable products and
made from wood grown in sustainable forests. The logging and manufacturing processes are
expected to conform to the environmental regulations of the country of origin.

John Murray (Publishers)
338 Euston Road
London NW1 3BH

www.johnmurray.co.uk

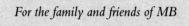
For the family and friends of MB

Author's Note

The action of the novel takes place today in Cambodia, mostly in the capital, Phnom Penh. Many locations exist: the Himawari Hotel; Sisowath Quay; the Foreign Correspondents' Club; Wat Lanka – and Martini's Bar. Banteay Chhmar exists, and is in fact under active conservation.

However, the details of the settings are filtered through the eyes of the narrator and defined by the needs of the story.

All characters are imaginary.

A flame is never constant; a fire lit at nightfall both is and is not the fire that still burns at daybreak.

Buddha: Karen Armstrong

PART ONE

I

The dream rose like an old friend's voice on the phone.

Our riverboat, stolen from retirement, its engine drowned and the hull one slow leak, was sinking by the stern. We drifted downstream with the current. I stood on the open deck in the bows; Zainab balanced barefoot above me, her heels on the edge of the upper deck, holding on to the railing behind. It was night. I don't remember there being a moon. It was the end of the monsoon and the river was high. We'd reached Phnom Penh, the smallest capital city I've ever seen, and the lights of the French colonial waterfront on the Mekong's muddy tributary passed by to starboard.

An arm waved over the water – one of our party had already abandoned ship – and a calm voice informed us that the stern was now awash. On cue the bow tilted and I lunged for support; I looked back as the river, now finally gaining speed, advanced towards me up the main deck.

Zainab shouted, not with alarm but with happiness, as if this were the highpoint of some party, or the successful climax of an adventure: 'Every man for himself!' She let go of the rail, raised her arms, and sprang in an arched dive into the river.

It was typically spontaneous. I hung back, hesitated, then dived in after her, into the ink-black water . . .

. . . and awoke clenching the sheet.

The dream was always the same: a remembrance of reality – but only a fragment, and only up to a point. I always awoke at the same moment. Isn't waking supposed to bring relief? The afternoon sun bathed my hotel room; cloudy bright, warm, full of life. But waking from this dream brought only numbness, a sense of absence: as if I were still numb from that ink-black water, or from something I'd forgotten, the answer to a question, maybe . . . or the question itself?

I swung my legs down, letting inertia pull me off the bed. I picked up my watch. It was later than I thought: past three in the afternoon. I padded in my bare feet over the scuffed parquet to the sliding glass door leading to the balcony, and looked out at the Tonlé Sap four floors below. The river, a tributary of the Mekong, was low and mud-brown. A ferry receded in the distance; near to shore an inland tanker, its deck nearly awash, chugged upriver in a river without a current, carrying oil or gas north to Siem Reap. It was June, the beginning of the monsoon season, and the Tonlé Sap, for months flowing south, had stopped for a day before reversing and flowing north. Puffy cumulus clouds filled half the sky; soon they would combine and the downpour begin. I slid the glass door open and breathed in the humid air. Scents rose from the hotel garden below; I recognized the odour of frangipani. The smell brought back a memory: a young Cambodian woman, Lim Sovan, Zainab's maid, telling me with absolute seriousness that in the countryside, spirits dwelt in the frangipani trees. Her voice was almost too soft to hear and her diction astray, but a sense of familiarity came through: for her, spirits in the trees were as natural as birds in the air. They just weren't as harmless.

I'd arrived at 6 a.m. on Friday, after twenty-six hours of air travel and stopovers, from Washington to Seoul to Phnom Penh. It was seven by the time I checked into the Himawari Hotel, and I'd gone directly to bed. It was not the correct thing to do. To alleviate jet-lag you should try to stay up the first day, try to get into a regular schedule. But I was wrecked. And I had no pressing business. The embassy wouldn't expect me to check in until Monday morning.

I shuffled back inside and stood under the shower with the tap turned on full. After that I pulled on some clothes, made coffee in the little kitchen and took it back out to the

4

balcony. I lit the first cigarette of the day. It was an old vice, and nowadays a private one, but it was a reminder of the past and a comfort.

When the State Department asked me to resume my assignment in Cambodia I'd agreed. Washington wanted to make it clear to the government – meaning the Prime Minister, the archetypal Asian strong man who made all the big decisions – that he couldn't get away with kicking out American diplomats: they'd just return. I had my own reasons for going back.

Six months in Washington had frayed my memory of Phnom Penh. The psychologist I'd seen (it was the department's mandatory post-trauma policy) wanted me to let go of anything that made for unhappiness. He told me that it was old-fashioned to see happiness as a result: happiness was a goal, a life goal, a goal to which we should all aspire, even claim as a right. I didn't buy it. It sounded like feel-good psychology to me – the stuff you read in women's magazines in dentists' waiting rooms (the advice column, written by Doctor Bob – or some such name – with a photo of the doctor: a young, well-dressed man with an open, vacant smile). Sometimes you want to hold on to something even if it is painful. Trying to forget your mistakes, your failures, other people's pain, only denatures memory, poisons it by degrees. If happiness meant forgetting – then I'd choose something less than happiness.

So I'd come back to recall the past. To revive memory, what I recalled and what I'd forgotten, maybe even questions I'd forgotten. Maybe I'd find some answers I never knew.

I hoped I wasn't too late. It's easy to revisit the past in the developed, western world. Change is slow, even resisted. What noticeable alteration can six months bring to Los Angeles, London, Toronto, Paris? Asia's different. A year is enough to refashion the skyline, and if most of your friends were there on six-month to two-year contracts, then the landscape of acquaintance will be refashioned, too.

The Cambodian elections, the demonstrations and assassinations, were all history. My colleagues in Washington pointed to jerky videos on YouTube the way an archaeologist holds up a shard (I didn't need the evidence – I'd been involved); but how could those smudged images compete with the cranes raising the city's second skyscraper, or the work crews widening the airport boulevard? The price of oil was going up again, there was hunger in the provinces and more poverty in the capital, but business was booming and the election campaign had been too short to disrupt the tourist trade. I was certain the hostess bars a couple of blocks west of the riverside hotels were still open, probably doing better than ever. I mention them as an indicator of economic activity. I work for the State Department, but am by profession an economist.

Between drags on my cigarette I breathed in the humidity and the scents rising from the garden. A flag flapped as a breeze rose and brought with it the faint stink of sewage. Maybe it was the mixture of scents and odour on the air that made me think of those bars (I only ever visited them on business), their curious mixture of vice and innocence, of ambivalence, both moral and practical. Who, in each transaction, would turn out to be the victim – or the greater victim? The recollection contrasted so utterly with the sterility of my hotel. No matter how tawdry the bars, they weren't as tawdry as my room, a room with zero individuality or atmosphere, where the only evidence of humanity was scuffs on the parquet floor and scars on the rosewood furniture, a 'luxury' room that could have been anywhere, in any luxury hotel anywhere in the world.

I hadn't come all this way, from Washington to Phnom Penh, for sterility. The afternoon was already advanced, but a few hours of daylight remained. I picked up my wallet and my keys and headed for the lift.

The Himawari was the first luxury hotel built in Phnom Penh after the Khmer Rouge, and the usual place for the US Embassy to put its temporary duty assignment personnel and its newly arrived permanent staff. At check-in it looked unchanged from my previous tour: a circular driveway leading to an open-air reception and lobby, a sofa and chairs and a central atrium. But as soon as I emerged from the lift I saw and heard what I'd missed that morning: a grand piano. Perhaps it was a move by management to bring the lobby closer to a Beijing or Hanoi standard. A Cambodian woman pianist (she must have been either a returned American emigrant or the product of one of the artier NGOs) was playing Bach. I'm not even remotely musical, but I recognized the piece – a Goldberg canon – because Zainab had played and explained it for me.

Of course it was just coincidence. I don't believe in some higher being ordering such things for our edification or enlightenment or direction. Coincidence exists. The only person ultimately responsible for our lives' order or disorder is ourselves. We have to make our own order if our life is to have any meaning at all – other than evidence of just another throw of the dice. But sometimes a happy chance gives us a clue, shows us the way. And at that moment I saw the place in memory to begin my search for what I'd forgotten and for what I never knew; where it all started: a classical concert at the British Ambassador's Christmas party, at his residence, a year and a half ago.

I strode through the lobby and down the curving drive to the street. The Friday afternoon traffic up Sisowath Quay was heavy, with more cars than I remembered pushing their way through the sea of motorcycles. A cab would be conspicuous and diplomats aren't supposed to ride on the back of motorcycles. So I decided on a tuk-tuk, a motorcycle-drawn, aluminium-framed rickshaw. There were always a few waiting for custom in front of the hotel; out of the four drivers who gave me a hail I picked the one who looked most careful, told him, 'Wat Preah Keo,' and climbed in.

He drove me to the nearby landmark and I directed him from there. The residence was only a few blocks from the hotel – nothing's far in Phnom Penh. I stepped out on to a tree-lined pavement in an older, high-class residential neighbourhood. Tall concrete walls lined both sides of the road. The slanting sun flashed off a brass plate; I crossed the street to read it and make sure. It was still the residence, but the guardhouse stood empty and one side of the double gate hung ajar. I looked around. No one in sight. The street held the silence that in Asian cities only privilege buys. I pulled the gate further open and slipped through.

A driveway without a car wound to the right; beyond the driveway stretched a lawn and garden. A cement walk led ahead along the side of the house to the front stairs. Opposite the stairs a veranda ended in a swimming pool. Cans of paint littered the poolside and the top of a ladder leaned against its rim – the pool was dry. The painters were gone, maybe on a mid-afternoon break . . . a break that, without supervision, had extended. I walked to the pool but saw no one and no sign of anyone at home. Very likely a guard loitered somewhere on the premises. Loitered or slept, stretched out flat under a tree.

A wave of irritation swept over me: what a failure of security! At an ambassador's residence! A familiar tide of anger, one of the bouts of fury that engulfed me daily for months (and that I thought I was getting over) rose again. My fists clenched. My eyes stared but I was only half aware of what I looked at, or even where I was. I wanted to fight back, to strike out – at whom, at what? These episodes of rage were divorced from what appeared to initiate them. I got a grip. The sane part of my brain pulled the handle back. I calmed down. I took a breath and looked around, reorienting myself. The heat rose from the cracked poolside veranda and the sun beat down on my head. I retreated to the shade of the front porch and sat on the stairs.

I thought: the security failed then, too, when it all started, right here on these steps. It was the early evening instead of the afternoon. I'd been standing, not sitting on the stairs, and water filled the pool. Christmas lights wound around the side of the house and party lights hung from the trees in the garden. I'd stood alone, looking out at the scene. Then, too, the grounds lay empty apart from me, but the house was packed with guests. It was the British Ambassador's Christmas party, and it began with a full programme of classical Christmas music, presented by a local expat amateur singing group, the Phnom Penh Players.

It was that excruciating music – that and the nicotine habit – that brought Zainab and I together. We both needed a smoke and we both needed to escape from the Japanese Ambassador's wife singing *Laudamus Te*. I dislike Latin church music; Zainab disliked the performance. Looking back, it was my first example of her finer discrimination – I use the word in its older sense. I didn't know she'd followed me out. The rainy season was past, the sky was clear and black, and the pool lights and Christmas and garden lights lit up the tropical night. I'd just pulled out my cigarettes when a young man in a neat grey English-cut suit leapt up the stairs, his arm held out like a spear. It was either take his hand or jump out of the way. I took it.

'We apologize, Mister Ambassador,' he said breathlessly (his wife, behind him, was panting), 'for being so late. The street's blocked off . . . the demonstration . . .'

I'm American, not British. It's true I worked in the American Embassy in Phnom Penh, but not near the level of Chief of Mission. I saw no reason to delay him with the facts. He was on a trajectory. I said, in as neutral an accent as I could, 'Quite all right. Please go in.' Nodding and muttering thanks, he withdrew his hand without stopping and sidled through the half-open front door. His young wife followed, dropping the hint of a curtsy as she passed. She must have been even more confused than her husband, investing my imagined position with the status of royalty.

They were still singing the Latin Christmas song inside and I thought it best to light up before another interruption. I had the cigarette out of its pack when I heard behind me a smothered laugh, and then a woman's voice: 'Impersonating the British Ambassador is a serious offence.'

I turned around. From the accent I expected one of those upper-crust, refined, bloodless Brits. Instead, I saw a tall, slender black woman in her mid-thirties. She had a long, triangular face, with eyes wide apart, an aquiline nose and a square but narrow chin. She had thick black hair but a hairline so high it was almost receding. I said she was black, but her complexion was lighter than Nigerian, more chocolate brown. Her shoulders were square and her upper arms full – features I've always found attractive. She stood ramrod straight. Her lips parted wide in a frank, open smile that her eyes agreed with. It was infectious. I smiled back and said, 'Only if it's premeditated.'

'Can I bum a smoke? I left mine at home.'

'Certainly.' So we both lit up, companions in a minor escape and a minor vice.

She said, 'Your suit and tie confused them. The invitation said "relaxed formal". That usually means an open-necked shirt and sports jacket.'

'Except for the ambassador himself.'

'Yes, especially if he's British. And you may have looked a little bored, too. Most diplomatic duties are boring, but you can't let on in public. Looking bored in a private moment probably looked very believable. Why didn't you correct them?'

'I didn't like to embarrass the young man in front of his wife.'

She looked at me and smiled again, but with less humour. 'Yes, you're right. It would have been unkind. It was a little white lie – you kept them in the dark – but it was good karma.'

I was brought up in the Midwest and worked most of my life in New York, on Wall Street. 'Karma' and so on was never part of my vocabulary – my economic speciality was technical analysis. But she evidently meant it as a compliment.

We introduced ourselves the way expats do. In two minutes we had the other's name, job, time in-country and marital status. Michael Smith, American diplomat, economics officer at the US Embassy. New in-country and relatively new in-service, just finishing my second month in Cambodia, my second assignment. Zainab Ambler, British dependent spouse (her expression, formally correct and spoken with an amused grimace), wife of Robert Ambler, British diplomat in Phnom Penh. Their third posting together.

She had the manner of a securely married woman: self-confident, relaxed, agreeable. The kind of woman you can spend time with without right away considering the possibility of an affair. I'd recently emerged from one, from my previous posting, an affair that had, emotionally, spun badly out of control – on her part. I didn't mind the idea of a short break from sex, and was not looking for an emotional entanglement. Zainab was companionable, as we smoked and chatted on the porch, and I cast a sidelong glance at her modest wedding ring with approval.

So I felt regret when we finished our cigarettes and she said, 'The next piece is by Vivaldi. I've heard them rehearse it and they're not bad. The conductor's a friend of mine. I should show her my support.'

'I'll go in with you.'

We turned back to the door but she stopped and said, 'Didn't that young man say something about a demonstration?'

I tried to remember. 'He mentioned a roadblock; it was an excuse. It looked quiet enough when I arrived.'

It wasn't quiet inside. The Phnom Penh Players sang the Vivaldi, a joyous Christmas piece, for all they were worth. From the foyer we peeked into the main reception room. Its chandeliers glittered over a wall-to-wall crowd. The musicians stood in a tight clump, as if for safety, at the far end; Zainab and I would never be able to squeeze much further in than the door. A wave of locker-room sweat drifted out and hit me in the face. I've never been a fan of male locker-rooms. I turned around, and noticed a door ajar across the foyer. I put my hand on Zainab's arm – I think that was the first time I touched her – and said, 'It's hot. The drink table's over there. Want to see if there's anything left?'

She only hesitated for a second.

The bottles on the table were all empty but the punch bowl was still half full. Next to the punch stood a well-dressed Khmer man, talking to a short, slightly built western woman.

They leaned in to each other, the man bending over a little, his head down; she held her head back, looking up. Their postures suggested intimacy, or at least warmth. It was a scene it looked a pity to disturb. But Zainab led the way. She knew both of them. After I poured a couple of glasses, she introduced us.

Hun Prang was a politician, the leader of the Reform Party. Speaking to Zainab, his manner changed to professional courtesy as fast as throwing a switch. I put him in his late thirties. He had the physical stature and sleek look that identified the Cambodians of his generation who as children had escaped the killing fields and made it to the States or Europe. Now back home in Phnom Penh, they stood out. They were physically larger than Cambodians the same age, who as children had suffered hunger – from malnutrition to semi-starvation. When Zainab introduced me as an American diplomat, he grabbed my hand and pumped it, telling me in an American accent that he was acquainted with my Deputy Chief of Mission, Noelle McQuiston. 'She's well informed,' he said, with an ingratiating smile; he seemed to have a separate tone for each of us. 'She's interested in local politics and supportive of my party. She believes strongly in the reform process.'

The 'reform process' was an NGO, aid agency and embassy mantra. There were several others, all on the same lines. The Cambodian government was rated the second most corrupt in Asia, and one of the most corrupt in the world. Hun Prang had probably been mentioned in one of the embassy's weekly political briefings, which I had to attend, but I didn't immediately recall him. There are clean politicians in the developing world, but in my experience they are thin on the ground. I thought Mr Hun (the Cambodians, like the Chinese, put their family names first), might be clean – he had been brought up in America. But I thought it more likely he was self-delusional.

I was about to say something anodyne – even minor diplomats aren't supposed to stick their neck out in public – when he said, 'Probably you already know that I have hired Mrs Ambler's NGO to assist my campaign.'

Zainab interrupted: 'It's not "my" NGO. I just work there.'

I said, 'No, she hadn't told me; we just met.'

'Then I'm pleased to tell you now. She will be my personal consultant. Her former career in the media will be invaluable, and she is an expert on transparency issues.'

It didn't sound like the description of a dependent spouse. I threw her an interrogatory glance but she just smiled and looked away. Mr Hun laid his hand lightly on the young woman's shoulder, and said, 'Deria is also helping, as an independent journalist. She's writing an article now, about my new party, for several American and European newspapers and magazines.'

The shoulder dipped slightly as the young woman promptly said, 'But I can't guarantee any of them will print it.' She sounded as if she'd repeated the message more than once, and still wasn't sure it was getting through. Zainab had introduced Deria Goldstein as a journalist from New York. I had not previously met, in my brief career as a US Foreign Service Officer, any American journalists abroad. There are few left. The American newspapers and television networks have closed down most of their foreign bureaus. So I had no one to whom I could compare Deria. Her appearance was not prepossessing. Childhood malnutrition seemed unlikely for a New Yorker, so I assumed anorexia. Her hips were narrow and her chest flat; her sleeveless top displayed thin, unmuscular arms. Her hair needed a shampoo. Her expression looked almost simple, until you noticed the guarded cunning in her eyes. She emanated sexuality. The overall impression was louche.

She went on: 'I might be able to place something. An American candidate for Cambodian Prime Minister – and Harvard trained. It's a good hook.'

'Yes,' he said enthusiastically. 'We need international press, well before the elections. We need to put the elections on the international map.'

Zainab started to say something, but we'd forgotten the music. It had ended. The door swung open. A heavy-set, middle-aged Englishman in a navy blue blazer and a white open-necked shirt stepped in, took one look at the empty bottles, and asked, 'That punch?' Mr Hun assured him it was. The words weren't out of his mouth before the Brit barrelled past Zainab and picked up the ladle. Two other members of the audience appeared and made a beeline for the punch bowl. In another moment the trickle became a flood. Mr Hun and Deria disappeared behind a fresh wave; Zainab gave me a panicked look, a lone chocolate-brown face among the white scrum. I pushed through, grabbed her arm and pulled her against the tide through the door, across the foyer and out the main entrance.

We were back where we'd started, on the front porch.

'Thanks for saving me,' she said wryly.

'Forget it.' And then we stopped and stared, at first not understanding, not alarmed.

A young Cambodian man ran across the lawn from the main gate towards the house. He must have come from the street. He ran a few paces then stopped, looked back and around, apparently uncertain or confused; then ran again a few strides. He continued this halting progression until he reached the pool. The sight of it stopped him dead – he couldn't go further without swimming. It seemed to give him confidence: he looked across the veranda at Zainab and me, still on the front porch, and waved and smiled.

We didn't wave back. Two more men, similar to the first, ran through the gate towards the house.

'Hello,' an English voice said, 'what's this, then?' It was the Brit from the punch bowl. Away from the scrum he gave the appearance, with his blazer and open-necked shirt and glass of punch, of a professional man gone slightly to seed.

'We don't know,' I told him. 'They just appeared.'

The newcomers joined the first. A fourth brought up the rear. The group by the pool shouted among themselves, one pointing to us, another pointing towards the gate.

Then two plainclothes police appeared. That's who I assumed they were. They could have been any Cambodian

men on the street, except for their truncheons and a determined focus on doing harm – a focus apparent in the way
they moved. Cambodians tend to be pacific, gentle people.
But there was nothing pacific or gentle about these two. They
sprinted like two disciplined football players on the same team
towards the laggard on the lawn. I doubt he had a chance but
when he stopped and turned that was it. He managed another
couple of strides before they were on him. In a one-two
movement the pursuer on his left took a swing at his ass, and
as the man's head jerked back, the other swung his truncheon
forward to meet his skull. We heard the crack across the lawn.
It was then I noticed the truncheons were lengths of pipe.

The man crumpled in a heap on the immaculately mown
grass.

The brutality shocked, revolted us. We could hardly
believe our eyes. This was a Christmas party at the British
Ambassador's residence in Phnom Penh, the peaceful capital
of a peaceful country. I lived in New York City for more
than a decade, but its era of casual crime was over before I got
there. I'd never seen such violence.

Two other men with pipes came sprinting across the mani-
cured grass. The four of them joined up and headed towards
the pool.

'The fuckers,' the Brit said.

'What's going on?' I asked.

'I don't know. But we've got to stop this.'

He started down the front stairs, and then stopped as he
realized he still held a punch glass. He laid it on the banister
and struck out purposely across the veranda. Although badly
outnumbered he looked resolute. I don't believe the assail-
ants – I now doubted they were cops – were yet aware of us. I
was very aware of standing with Zainab, hanging back, while
the only other male westerner pressed forward alone.

But I could have done nothing for the unarmed men at the
pool. It was over before the Englishman got halfway there.
Two lay on the ground, broken; one was treading water in the
deep end while the men with pipes looked on. Maybe they

couldn't swim. I heard our man in the blazer shout something. I think that was when they became aware there were *Barang* around – the Khmer word for any white foreigner, but literally meaning 'French', a holdover from their colonial days.

I doubt we looked impressive. A couple of white foreigners, one out of shape and belligerent, one hanging back, and an African woman. And the Cambodians with their blood lust up. So they went on the attack.

Two of them ran towards the Brit, but at the last moment swerved away on each side. I thought they'd decided to run past him, but it was a feint: as they passed, one swung his pipe against the back of the Englishman's knee. He went down bellowing in pain. The two Cambodians didn't break their stride. They ran straight towards us, swinging their weapons, their faces set hard and blank as masks.

I was certainly afraid. But I'm temperamentally opposed to turning and running, even, probably, when I should. On the other hand I'm not half-witted. I backed up towards the door, taking Zainab with me by her hand; she seemed almost paralysed.

Then the second Brit appeared.

We learned later that he was the ambassador's personal security detail – in other words, his bodyguard. He'd been biding his time among some trees bordering the veranda, observing, sizing things up. He made a dash across the veranda so fast the Cambodians didn't take in what was happening. Neither did we. In a moment he had one man down in a running tackle, then in a vicious headlock. Leaving him motionless on the ground, he bounced back on his feet like a jack-in-the-box, the pipe in his hand.

He wasn't more than thirty or thirty-five feet away. He turned to me and yelled, 'Take it!' and threw the pipe low in the air so it hit the ground with a bang just in front of the porch, just in front of me. I hesitated for a second. Then I released Zainab's hand, ran down the stairs and picked up the weapon. God knows what I must have looked like to the Cambodian facing me in the middle of the veranda. I was at least a foot taller, and trimmer than the westerner he'd brought down; without thinking of it, I made the most of my advantage by holding the pipe high.

The bodyguard saw me as an adequate deterrent – or at least the best he could hope for under the circumstances; he started running in a slight crouch to the Cambodians still by the pool. There were two of us and three of them. I was armed and the Brit didn't seem to need a weapon.

And like that it was over. They turned and ran.

I felt an extraordinary rush. The guard knelt by the downed Englishman, who looked conscious although still on his back. I ran to them and told the guard, 'Thanks, thanks for your help.'

He looked up and said calmly, 'You can lower your weapon now.'

I still held the pipe over my head. I lowered it and asked if there was anything I could do. He didn't answer at first, he was speaking to someone on his cellphone in acronyms I didn't understand. Then he said I could help him get the injured man into his apartment.

We pulled him up. He was heavy, clearly in pain, and could use only one leg. He swore softly but continuously as we half carried him, limping, around the house and through a modest door into a sitting room. We laid him down on a sofa. He told us he was a doctor and instructed us to put a pillow under his bad knee. That seemed to make him more comfortable. The bodyguard said that an ambulance was on the way, and then introduced himself: his name was Scott Simmonds. He had a quiet, well-mannered voice and one of those English accents that an American can understand without strain. I could see him properly under the overhead light: he was of medium height, wiry and muscular. He looked my age. I learned later he was older – but fitter. He told me, not as if he were apolo-gizing, but rather as if he were explaining the justifiable use of means that were normally deplorable: 'I had to use violence. They used it first, on their own, then on one of us. I had to stop them.'

If there had been an American cop around with an assault rifle, I'm sure he would have used it without a second's thought. I said, 'It was fine with me. You did what you had to do. It worked.'

He said, 'The embassy detail's on the way. They'll secure the area. Now I have to brief the ambassador, and tell him the party's over. There's going to be a mass exodus. You'd better get out first.'

I returned the way I came, back to the porch. Zainab was where I'd left her, holding tight to the railing. It was still the intermission and people were beginning to spill out of the house; a couple holding drinks stood behind her. I walked up and put my hand on her arm. 'How are you?' I asked.

'Fine,' she said, with a quick, tense smile. 'I hadn't realized economic officers were so aggressive.'

'We're not.'

'You look pumped-up.'

I didn't know what to say to that, so I said, 'The guard told me we'd better go – the ambassador's going to announce that the party's over. Now's our chance to get out before the rush. We'd better find your husband.'

'He's at home, nursing a broken leg.'

'Did you drive?'

'I took a tuk-tuk.'

It was probably safe enough, but it was already a night of strange incidents. I said, 'I drove. If you like, I can give you a lift.'

'I'd like that very much.'

Halfway to the gate, she said, 'Wait. I want to thank that man.'

'His name's Simmonds. He said he was going to brief the ambassador. I'm not sure we have time . . .'

'Where'd you leave him?'

'In his apartment. It's at the back of the residence.'

'He might still be there. It'll only take a moment. Come on.'

So we went back. I didn't notice that the body we'd left on

the lawn was gone. As we walked past some trees at the rear of the building, I heard a sound I couldn't identify, followed by a gasp or groan. I reached out and took Zainab's arm, and we slowly edged around a thick trunk.

It was Simmonds, kicking the hell out of the Cambodian. He must have dragged him back while we were walking to the gate. The man lay on his side, curled up. Simmonds stood over him. He aimed his kicks unhurriedly, methodically. Before each kick he backed off a few paces, enough space for a short run-up, as if it were rugby practice. We saw him kick twice, once to the man's face, once to his ribcage. Then I pulled Zainab back. Simmonds never saw us.

We resumed our walk to the gate. I said, 'I'm sorry you saw that.'

She didn't reply.

I continued, 'I'm surprised. He didn't look the brutal type.'

She said, 'I hope he kills him.'

I glanced at her. Her face was set, but not in a frown; there was a hint of a grim smile. And suddenly it struck me as a gutsy thing, a real thing, to say, ripping away that politically correct, maybe even morally correct veil that's supposed to hold us back, keep us on a civilized path. An assailant heading towards you, a sawn-off pipe in his hand, his blood lust up, meaning violent harm – who wouldn't want him, at the least, disabled? She'd seen four unarmed men brutally beaten for no apparent reason; wasn't it normal to want to see the assailant permanently out of the picture?

The truth is we were both high. The kind of high you get when you're involved in a sudden, violent crisis or accident – especially if it's suddenly, violently overcome. I couldn't realize then how out of character her remark was. I was high enough myself to admire it.

She gave me directions to her place. I was still new to town and needed to be told where to make a left, where a right. She directed me south on Norodom Boulevard, to the east side of what we called the 'expat ghetto'. A good area, where rents were still cheap enough for the more obscure embassies – the Bulgarian, Swedish, Myanmar missions. I was too busy navigating the traffic for small talk. The passing scene – the hundreds of motorcycles, many with whole families crammed on to them, passing so close they seemed to hang from my car like fish on a shark; the occasional moto-drawn farm cart, overflowing with produce, on its way to a local market; the courting couples standing chastely close in the light of the waterworks surrounding the Independence Monument – seemed to me more vivid, brighter, than usual.

Just past Wat Thann she had me turn off the boulevard into a narrow alley squeezed by concrete walls topped with barbed wire; it was like a maze, turning right, then left, then left again, until we emerged into one of those quiet, back roads that still exist hidden away all over Phnom Penh. The usual walls ran along both sides. She told me to stop outside a large green double gate. A guard box stood empty. There was no traffic.

I asked her, 'Where's your gate guard?'

'Who knows. They're Cambodian – the embassy hires a contractor. We're short of staff: we lost our housemaid-cook. But the house guard should be here.' We got out and she knocked quietly on the metal gate. No one answered. She knocked again, louder. And again.

I said, 'He's gone, too?'

She reached down and inserted her hand through a tiny rectangular opening, struggled for a minute, then managed to slip the bolt. She pulled out her hand and pushed the gate open enough to pass through.

I followed her.

We stood on a cement driveway that ran straight to a two-storey house. A single light burned on an upstairs terrace. A long lawn and garden stretched ahead on our right, ending at the house; it was too dark to discern much detail, but a wave of denser humidity, a smell of the jungle, suggested the garden was overgrown.

She said, 'Welcome to the House of Usher.'

'I beg your pardon?'

'Poe. I call it that because it's so big, and so empty.'

Stray light from the road spilled over the wall behind us on to an open hut for the house guard. We peered inside. Other than a neatly made bed, a chair and a table the hut stood empty. 'They're all gone,' she said. 'So much for contractors.'

'I'd better walk you to the house.'

'There's no need. Robert's a light sleeper; with his leg cast, a very light sleeper. We don't want to wake him.'

'Don't you think it odd, both your guards missing?'

'No. It's happened before. It's just coincidence.'

I almost didn't want it to be coincidence. We were both still tense, still high. Our blood was up more than we knew.

Neither of us made a move to leave, her to her house, me to my car; we just stood there in the doorway of the hut, next to each other. She turned a little away and murmured, 'I'd better go.'

I didn't say anything. I reached out my hand to her back, the small of her back, just a little caress, hardly even that, but something – we'd been through a lot together in a very short time. By accident, I caressed her ass. It felt rounded and tight under her dress.

She swung round and kissed me awkwardly in the dark, her lips hitting the corner of my mouth. The tip of her tongue skated across my cheek. We grabbed each other; I pulled her inside the hut. I turned her around, facing the bed, and unzipped her dress. She bent over and we made love then and there, with our clothes half on and half off.

I write 'made love'; some would call it aggressive fucking. But there's more than one way to make love – although I wasn't yet thinking of an affair. The signs were already there: the opposites that attract, the similar responses, the things in the other to admire. And chemistry, of course. But I only saw them in hindsight. Like the first signs of a fatal illness, the ones you missed but should have seen, should have recognized. By the time a diagnosis is made, it's too late to take effective measures.

21

Not that an earlier diagnosis would have made a difference. I wasn't interested in a cure. I don't think she was, either, even though love complicated her life more than mine. I don't think she believed in regret any more than she believed in guilt. She'd mentioned karma but only lightly, with humour. I was still ignorant of her religious convictions, that tangle of contradictions that caused so many so much trouble, through which only she saw any light.

But if (I present it as a hypothesis) one of the differences between lust and love is that in love, after the act, there's not the slightest regret, then our first sex that night in that steamy little hut was the beginning of love. I closed my eyes as we strained against each other, one of my hands cupping her breast, the other gripping her shoulder, as her ass pressed into me. I closed my eyes . . .

. . . and opened them, a year and a half later, as my tuk-tuk pulled up in front of the same green gate set in the same compound wall. Just as before it was dusk, and the narrow guardhouse stood empty. Just as before the street lay quiet, deserted, the green gate closed.

Eighteen months is a long time in Phnom Penh. There was no point now in knocking or in trying to withdraw the bolt.

You can spend too much time and go too far to reclaim memory. I felt lonely, alone. My recollections were as empty of comfort as the street was of traffic. Standing dumbly in front of that gate, I was seized with doubt. Shouldn't I be moving forward? Shouldn't I be trying to grab life, or make a life, in the present, instead of the past?

I wanted company. A flesh-and-blood woman – but safe, not threatening involvement. At least, not emotional involvement. And then I remembered Ann. She was part of the past, too, but she'd be nostalgia-lite: a professional companion who'd slip into the desired mood, preferring comfort and surface talk to emotional depth. I wouldn't mind that. She was a trained confidante, trained at keeping secrets – much more difficult than people realize. If I caught her alone, no one would ever know we'd met . . . or spent the night. She was always attractive and always lonely. A night with her would entail the minimum of emotional commitment and emotional damage. To both of us. Maybe she'd bring me back into the here and now.

She should still be around. She'd arrived in-country just before me, and Agency assignments tend to run in parallel with State. Ann was what they now called a Core Collector Operations Officer. It sounds faintly geological, but in fact it's the Agency's latest euphemism for 'spy'.

I climbed back into my tuk-tuk, and told the driver, 'Norodom.' When we emerged from the alley, I directed him to cross the street, deeper into the expat ghetto.

2

The American Embassy in Phnom Penh held a country team meeting every Monday morning at 11 a.m., chaired by the Deputy Chief, which every State Department officer – consulate, administrative, political, economic and commercial – would attend. The main purpose was to keep us up to date as to what everyone else was doing, because we might have to step into another's shoes at any time. Cambodia is no longer an important country from a geopolitical perspective, and as a result the embassy is chronically undermanned. At least during my short tenure, however, Ann had never been asked to fill in for anyone. This was no surprise to any of us. Ann ostensibly worked as a Commercial Officer for the US Commerce Department, not, like the rest of us, for State. But most of us suspected that Commerce was just a cover, and she was really CIA. In an embassy, only the Deputy Chief and the ambassador know who the spooks are, and it's strictly against regulations – and very bad form – to speculate or gossip. But it's difficult to hide the fact that you're holding down two full-time jobs, one overt and one covert. So we never expected the Deputy Chief to ask her to fill in for us, and similarly – and less logically – we never expected to be asked to fill in for her.

That was about to change.

Five months after the incident at the British Ambassador's residence, I sat with Ann in our conference room. Also around the table were Cynthia, the Administrative Officer, Helen, the Consulate Officer, Sergeant Higgins, the OIC Security, and

Sergeant Higgins, his wife and embassy Security Officer. The Political Officer was on emergency leave (a dying spouse in DC). Noelle, the Deputy Chief, sat at the head of the table. A guest, Sheila from USAID, stood at the opposite end, with a clicker in her hand. She was clicking through the monthly presentation which, on a rotating basis, gave us an in-depth look into different aspects of the American mission.

Looking around I noticed again that I was one of only two men in the room. It did not bother me. This group was a nice change from my previous set of colleagues on Wall Street, a set composed overwhelmingly of type A young men, cut from the same cloth and the same collection of top business school cookie-cutters. I'm from that set, too, but I prefer a little diversity – as long as we're all on the same page.

Sheila was an old hand at development work, and her presentation, although peppered with the development jargon with which I'd become too familiar – outcomes, sustainability, transparency, etc. – was at least more focused than most. Her theme: major government aid organizations were beginning to draw down their operations. America's USAID, the UK's DFID, Canada's CIDA, and others, after years of crying wolf, were reducing funding for some projects and pulling the plug on a few. The reason: continued government corruption and a lack of accountability. In plain English, most projects were poorly managed and their Cambodian partners stole too much money. Her final slide presented a graph showing projected disbursements from major agencies over the next three years. It was partly speculative, but the trend was clear. Descending.

After a few questions she sat down and Sergeant Higgins stood up to give us the weekly security briefing. He was a career army enlisted man in his early thirties. He kept an inborn tendency to run to fat in control by a ferociously disciplined routine of exercise. When I'd first arrived, he'd invited me to spend two hours with him, after work, in the gym. I've always tried to keep myself fit, but two hours with Sergeant Higgins nearly killed me. I saw his exercise routine as a symbol, or metaphor, of the man: a determined over-achiever, originally from the wrong side of the tracks (or nearby), who had risen to be the Officer in Charge of Security at the US Embassy in Phnom Penh by dedicated, ruthless self-discipline.

He was not a natural public speaker, but he'd studied the subject and practised. His style was to the point, even clipped. In the past week there'd been three robberies of expats at gunpoint on the streets. The MO was identical in all cases. Two young, well-dressed Khmer men on a late model motorcycle of at least 300cc – large by Cambodian standards – held up the victims with a revolver. They took purses and wallets. Two of the victims were tourists, one a couple working for an NGO. From their descriptions it appeared that the thieves may have been different in every case, although they belonged to the same socio-economic class. Higgins handed out the familiar charts, updated for every briefing, of armed robberies of expats in Phnom Penh. The trend line was documented, not speculative. Ascending.

As we stared glumly at our handouts, he said, 'As usual, there's been no attempt to apprehend the culprits. They may be the sons of well-connected business people, or government officials. However, it's also possible the police are not under direct pressure to ignore these incidents. We know they are short of resources. It's possible they simply want to concentrate on investigations likely to bear fruit.' It seemed a lot of possibilities for a man not given to speculation. I felt his audience suppress a smile. Sergeant Higgins was a career non-commissioned officer. It went against his grain to suggest that security services were corrupt or incompetent.

He continued: 'As most of you know, there was also an attempted robbery. Since Sergeant Higgins was involved – she foiled the attempt – she will present the case.' He stepped back a metre and assumed the position of parade rest. His wife stood up.

A uniform on a woman often has a contradictory effect. It both accentuates and represses her figure, her attraction. Mrs Higgins was a good-looking brunette, but her uniform's knife-edge creases and cinched belt held her attraction in check. She consulted a clipboard and gave her report.

'At 7 p.m. on Friday night I left my apartment on Thirty-fourth Street to buy . . . to go shopping. As soon as I opened the gate I saw Mr Smith and Mrs Zainab Ambler, on her Vespa, pulling up to Mr Smith's house. We live two doors down.

'Before they could disembark, a moto — a typical, small motorcycle taxi of about 150cc — approached from behind and stopped beside them. The driver, a middle-aged Khmer, pulled out a knife. I ran to their assistance. The assailant dropped his knife, gunned his moto and sped off.'

Her husband stepped forward to take over and his wife sat back down. He thanked her, then straightened to attention. He looked more comfortable with his spine rigid.

'My strong advice to all mission personnel remains on record. Vary your route to work and home on a daily basis. Avoid patterns. Do not frequent empty streets at night. Practise situational awareness. If you become aware of an incident nearby, do not investigate. Withdraw from the scene of political rallies and demonstrations. Carry your cellphone at all times. Do not hesitate to call embassy security. Remember: we are your first responders, not the police.' He did not ask for questions. He sat down.

Noelle, the Deputy Chief, slid back her chair to take the floor, but I forestalled her. I said, 'I'd just like to express my thanks to Mrs — to Sergeant Higgins. Her own "situational awareness", her quick thinking and her bravery, saved me and Mrs Ambler from robbery — or worse.'

Noelle said, with a quiet smile, 'We would all like to thank her for a job very well done.' Then she stood up.

Tall, slender and fit, she wore her forty years as gracefully as she did her impeccable suits and skirts. She was a career Foreign Service officer, already as Deputy Chief of Mission just one step below the ambassador, and already developing the authoritative expression that such a career develops and such a position demands.

She thanked everyone for their presentations. She then informed us that Bill, our Political Officer, had had his emergency leave extended; it was now bereavement leave. The exact length of bereavement leave was determined by regulation, but could, at the embassy's discretion, be extended if the applicant had sufficient annual leave accrued; Bill had significant annual leave accrued, and his return date was uncertain. Noelle did not have to spell out what this meant. It was likely that one or more of the three State Department officers at the table would be handed some of Bill's duties.

Finally, she told us, 'I think all of you remember last December's incident at the British Ambassador's Christmas musical. One of us, Michael, was actually involved.' She gave me a brief nod and continued. 'Our investigation is finally finished; it took so long and is still incomplete due to a lack of cooperation from the Ministry of Interior.

'The incident started when a peaceful anti-government demonstration a couple of blocks away was violently broken up by a gang of thugs. Who hired them is still unknown. Naturally it was caught, amateurishly and obscurely, on someone's video camera, and by the next morning had made it up on YouTube. Four members of the gang, enjoying their work, chased a few of the fleeing demonstrators into the grounds of the British Ambassador's residence. I doubt they were aware that it was the residence. I imagine they were poor men hired to do a job; that would not be incompatible with their being affiliated in some way with one of the security services. The demonstrators were younger and more educated. There may have been a class distinction. We are all used to the Cambodian temperament that we see daily: invariably polite, pleasant, quiet, pacific. This incident displayed the other side of the national cultural coin.

'The police made one arrest, after everything was over: a member of the gang disabled at the residence. The Minister of Justice himself informed me yesterday that the whereabouts and status of that prisoner are unknown.

'The elections are still months away, but I believe we

should see this December incident as the first pre-election demonstration. We can expect more. Please, everyone, follow our OIC Security's recommendations to the letter. Unless you have been assigned to cover a rally or demonstration, avoid them. That's all I have to say. Are there any questions?'

'Yes,' I said. I admired Noelle, but four years as a young man in the US Air Force left me with an ingrained scepticism of authority. 'Should we also avoid ambassadorial social invitations?'

You do not become Chargé d'Affaires by rising to such bait. Noelle gave me a smile, thin but devoid of malice. 'No,' she said. 'No matter how conscientious our precautions, sometimes incidents are unavoidable.' She opened a folder on the desk, and said, 'Our guest speaker next month will be Dr White. He will give a presentation on dengue fever.' She sat down and closed the folder. It was the sign that the meeting was over. We all stood to leave. I had just left my place at the table when Noelle looked up, and asked me to accompany her to her office.

I followed her there. The US Embassy in Phnom Penh was the first American embassy built using the Standard Embassy Design criteria brought in after 9/11. As a result our offices were functional and, if not always roomy, at least not cramped. Noelle's, in keeping with her position, was the second largest private office in the building. The State Department furniture was heavy but chaste. The glassed and framed photographs on the walls, by a well-known photographer, of standard Cambodian scenes, had been selected and purchased by the American contractor. A large American flag hung from a tall pole behind and to the right of her desk; a flat-screen monitor stood unobtrusively on a side table to her desk's left. The office was distinguished by an almost complete lack of personal touch. Since she had been in-country for a year, I assumed it was because she enjoyed an undiluted official ambience.

She asked me to sit down. She said, 'Two incidents in less than six months. In a posting generally considered peaceful.'

'Bad luck.'

'Yes, it looks like bad luck.' Two of her fingers tapped the desk. 'I see you're keeping up friendly relations with the Amblers. It's always good to strengthen connections with our British colleagues.'

I had no special interest in my British colleagues, but I'd tried unsuccessfully to strengthen my connection with Mrs Ambler for months. Phnom Penh is not a big city; the professional expatriate community, although large in proportion to the population, is small; the diplomatic community, a subset, is tight-knit. Our problem was finding somewhere discreet. We hadn't repeated that first sex in the abandoned guardhouse. It was too risky; we both had too much to lose. Although we'd met at several functions and parties during the past few months, we were fortunate to steal a caress. The previous Friday night, out of sheer desperation, we'd tried to spend an hour at my place. We never made it to my front door.

Noelle said, 'Riding a moto, however, was careless. You know it's against department policy.'

'It was Mrs Ambler's Vespa.'

'The policy is aimed at commercial vehicles but a motorcycle's a motorcycle. I want you to be more careful.'

'I'll try.'

'Good. Now, I'm afraid, Michael, I have some bad news.'

In the embassy, only Noelle called me Michael. It is in fact my name, but everyone, except my mother, has always called me Mike. From Noelle, at least in private, it sounded slightly affectionate. It made me wonder. At forty I was her contemporary and a decade older than most junior officers. We had never socialized privately, but I knew she was unattached. She was not casually attractive but rather good-looking and highly competent. I felt certain she was much too competent and much too correct to initiate a romance with a junior officer . . . but how would she respond if I took the first step? I had no intention of finding out. In my experience, office romances, unless they lead to marriage (they seldom do) are a bad idea. I was intrigued, however, by the possibility of her holding me in some affectionate regard, and I was as friendly with her in private as our difference in rank permitted. I admired and liked her, and I think she liked me. I was not concerned when she told me she had some bad news.

'I'm listening,' I said.

'You know we're very short-staffed. Between you and me, it's now impossible to say when, or even if, Bill will be back. The death of a spouse frequently knocks the survivor off the rails. Sometimes they just resign from the Service; often they go through the motions for six months or a year, then resign. At the very least we have to assume that he'll be gone for the maximum time allowed. In his case, that's nearly three months. There are some political reporting jobs that we can't just drop. I imagine your annual country report is going well?'

She meant the embassy's annual Cambodia country report. Normally the Commerce, Economic and Political officers all had a hand in its production, but one officer was in charge – the primary writer and editor – and that was me. I did not expect more than a token contribution from Ann, and Bill of course was absent. However, this wasn't a report on some powerhouse like Germany or China. Cambodia was one of the smallest and least developed countries in Asia, in some ways less developed than Burma. Last year's report was there; it had to be revised and updated, but this was a very doable project.

I said, 'Yes, it's going okay so far.'

'Good. In that case, I'm going to ask you to pick up a little job of Bill's. It might even help you with the annual report. He won't be able to make his contribution, and this job might give you some insight into the country's political development. You might kill two birds with one stone.'

'What, exactly, is the other bird?'

'Hun Prang's election rally in Siem Reap. We need a political report.'

'When is the rally, and what exactly do you need?'

'It's in three weeks. Go up a couple of days before. Make a few appointments with some of the leading expats – I'll give

31

you names and numbers. They'll be your prime informants. Ask questions. We're not interested, of course, in what the expats think: we're interested in what the Khmers think.

'Siem Reap's a small city but it's the fastest growing in Cambodia. The airport's twice as busy as Phnom Penh's. Tourists, especially the better heeled ones, go there to see Angkor Wat, not to Phnom Penh to see the Genocide Museum at Tuol Sleng. Two-thirds of the country's hard currency earnings come through tourism, and arrive through Siem Reap. The place is booming. People will vote, and they won't be bought as easily as voters in the provinces.

'Ask your informants how they think the street sees the main candidates, the main parties. If public opinion is divided, into what groups, and why. The report doesn't have to be more than two thousand words long. I'll give you some of our old political reports that you can use as templates. You'll be able to fold most of it into your annual report.'

Siem Reap for three, maybe four days. A few interviews. Two days to write the report. It sounded like a nice change of pace. It would take time away from my regular work, but I had enough fat in my schedule. I said, 'Of course, I'd be happy to do it. After all, everyone has to help out.'

'Thank you, Michael. I was sure that would be your reaction. You're a politically astute member of the team. That's the kind of person this assignment needs.'

'I'll do my best.'

'It's not often one finds a member of staff who combines political awareness with training – and years of experience – as an economist. It makes you a natural candidate for a politically sensitive job . . .'

'You know I'm ready to help in any way I can.'

'. . . a job that combines political sensitivity with Commerce.'

'Naturally I'll look into the economic aspect in Siem Reap.'

'I wasn't thinking of Siem Reap.'

I blinked. 'You weren't?'

'No. I'm afraid I have another assignment for you. A more challenging one. I need you to give Ann a hand.'

The alliteration at first confused me. Then I got it. 'You want me to help her out on some Commerce job?'

'I want you to take it over.' Noelle got up and walked past her flag to the window. She was normally a direct woman and it was odd for her to be addressing me while peering across the street at the hill leading up to Wat Phnom. There was little to be seen from the embassy except the tops of trees and perhaps the wat's elephant, known affectionately throughout town.

She said, 'Ann, as you know, is a very busy officer. She has a full plate. We've received an order by Commerce – and State – to be of assistance to the Westin Oil Company. We have to help them firm up their contract with the Cambodian government.'

'I thought it was firm. Wrapped up years ago.'

She turned around. 'The status of their contract is unclear. At least, to the department. That's one of the things I need you to find out.'

I said carefully, 'This could be an involved job. I imagine I'll need to be briefed by Ann, and probably by the oil company's representative. It may require direct involvement by the embassy, with the appropriate Cambodian government ministry.'

'I want you to handle the whole thing. As I said, Ann has enough on her plate. And frankly your age and experience should be an asset for this job – that's between you and me, Michael, of course.'

'Of course. It could be time-consuming.'

'Make it your first priority. This, then Siem Reap, then the annual report. I want a status report every Friday. Washington wants the contract wrapped up, signed, sealed, delivered, before the elections.' She walked over to me. She was a very tall, very erect woman, with a face surprisingly open, given how often she had to try to keep it closed. She said, 'I appreciate your taking this on. I won't forget it.' She held out her hand to me, almost tentatively. I stood and took it. She let me hold it lightly for a moment, then withdrew. 'I've asked Ann to give you the file.'

The interview was over. I said goodbye and left for Ann's office.

It wasn't far. The professional staff were all on the same floor. But she wasn't there. I went back to my own office and found a note from her on my desk:

Mike,
The Westin file is a mess – I'm straightening it out tonight at home. I'll have it ready for you first thing in the morning.
Ann

Her handwriting was the unformed scribble of the new generation, who grew up from infancy using laptop keyboards instead of pens and pencils. I doubted she was more than twenty-three or -four. This was her first assignment, and much of the time she looked tired. She had the attraction of youth and health and displayed the confidence that was the result of good training. But she also looked inexperienced, and smart enough to know she was inexperienced. I'd seen her at a couple of embassy parties, and she'd never brought a date. She was going to spend part of this evening working a file that I could probably straighten out in half the time.

In the end I wasn't sure of my exact motivation for deciding to visit her. I'd time it for shortly after dinner. Before she'd had time to open the file, but late enough for her to be alone.

That night I took a tuk-tuk down Norodom, then right, past the Russian restaurant, deep into the expat ghetto. Despite the neighbourhood's nickname it was a pleasant area, full of mostly renovated and new apartments and houses and small compounds, but still enjoying an old-fashioned, leafy ambience. This was where most of the NGO, aid agency and second-tier diplomatic personnel lived. I lived nearby. Noelle and the ambassador belonged to a higher echelon and lived further south, past ministry row and the headquarters of the ruling party (as big as some of the ministries), in a new development with cul-de-sacs, huge houses, high walls and uniformed security at every gate. Noelle's neighbours were ambassadors, Cambodian politicians and the very rich. Ann's and mine were staff from the Deutscher Entwicklungsdienst, the Center for Disease Control, and World Vision. Along with a goodly number of more or less respectable adventurers in local business.

I had the driver stop in front of Ann's stretch of wall and stepped down. I wasn't expected but I was a self-confident American − another *Barang* − and the obsequious guard, in uniform from the waist down, opened the gate with a smile. Inside was a small, well-clipped lawn and a three-storey concrete house that managed to appear tall and squat at the same time. Ann opened the front door wearing shorts and a short-sleeved shirt. She looked surprised but invited me in, apologizing that she hadn't yet finished work on the file.

She offered me a beer and I accepted. While she retrieved it from the kitchen I looked around. Embassy housing came so well furnished, even decorated, that it was tempting for some of us to just forget about making the place homely by adding a personal touch. We made do with what we'd been given. You could call it the hotel approach. Others went all out, even sending the government furniture back into storage and replacing it with their own. Ann belonged to the hotel approach category. The only personal items I identified in the living room were two framed photographs. One was of an older couple, smiling and affectionate − I imagined her parents. The other was a snapshot of Ann, a little younger, with a tableful of girls the same age. It looked like a restaurant or bar, and they were all having a good time. Her girlfriends, maybe from grad school. There wasn't a boy among them.

She returned carrying my beer and started apologizing again about the file, so I told her to forget it − I'd come on purpose to take it from her. I'd clean it up myself. She asked me why, I thought a little defensively. I didn't want to tell her that I thought I could do it in half the time, so instead I said, 'Just to give you a hand. Noelle told me you had a full plate.'

'Did Noelle ask you to take the file?'

'No. She just told me you were busy, that's all. I'm not – or at least, I wasn't until this morning.'

'I volunteered for this assignment. It's Commerce work, after all.'

'Don't worry about it. Everyone knows you have a double workload.' She threw me a sharp glance. I realized too late the suggestiveness of the remark. I cast around to change the subject, and saw for the first time (she'd turned the volume right down), that the television was on. One look and I recognized the film. I said, 'You're watching *On the Beach*.'

'Everyone needs a little down time.'

'It's a good film. One of my favourites.'

'I like the actors. Peck plays an American in a foreign country, like us, in a way. He belongs to a service, too. But it's not a happy story, is it? No matter what he does, what any of them do, they're all going to die.'

I thought it a depressing take. I said, 'Shute, the author, was a flyer as well as a writer.'

'Really? What do you think of Ava Gardner?'

'She was considered a beautiful woman in her time.'

'She'd still be considered beautiful. Did you know she was of mixed blood? Her father was half Native American.'

I looked at Ann as she peered intently at Gardner on the government-issue flat-screen TV. Ann's skin was whiter than milk, her hair was blonde and her eyes blue. She could have been a poster girl for Ski Canada. 'No,' I said, 'I didn't know that. I don't think it's obvious.'

'She was an extremely dark brunette. It's one of those things that's quite clear, once you know.'

I thought it an obscure remark. I knocked back the beer and apologized for interrupting.

'Oh, that's all right. I have to thank you for taking that file off my hands. Stick around another minute. Care for another beer?'

'No thanks.'

'I understand there were only four people – four westerners – involved in that incident last year at the British Ambassador's residence.'

'I'd have to think about it, Ann. It was last December.'

'I've read the report. It was you, the British Ambassador's bodyguard, a Dr White and Robert Ambler's wife.'

'I'd say only the bodyguard and White were actively involved. I was just there.'

'With Mrs Ambler.'

'She was on the front porch with me, yes.'

'She's an interesting woman. Do you know her well?'

'That was the first time we met. No, I wouldn't say I know her well.'

'She's British, but of African parents. I think Sudanese. She trained as a lawyer and worked, before her marriage, as a television presenter in London. She's working here for a good governance NGO. She's published.'

'I'm impressed. You seem to know a lot about her.'

'Oh well, it's important to get the details right. Last Friday's incident, for example. The MO doesn't really fit a robbery.'

'What does it fit?'

'I'm not sure. Maybe an attempt to intimidate.'

I smiled. Her line of work probably inclined her to such theories. I said, 'I'm not sure how much importance we should give, over here, to our idea of an MO.'

'It's a tool – not the only tool.'

I put down my empty glass on a side table. 'Thanks for giving me the Westin file.'

'Thank you. You're the one helping me out.'

We stood there, facing each other, uncertain as to how to part; I was wondering if I should kiss her. Finally she held out her hand, and I took it. She pulled it away suddenly, as if just avoiding an indiscretion. It occurred to me that all day, in a country where every expat adopted the custom of kissing the opposite sex on the cheek, I'd been gingerly shaking hands.

She escorted me to her gate.

I climbed back into my tuk-tuk and reached out to wave goodbye. She called after me, 'Bring her over some time for a drink. You don't need an invitation.'

I called back, 'Who?' But the driver gunned his engine and slipped his clutch, and I didn't hear her answer . . .

. . . a year and a month later a different tuk-tuk drove me down the same street through the steamy Cambodian night, back to Ann's house. Little had changed. A guard wearing a complete uniform stood in front of her gate; maybe the embassy had changed contractors. He was more officious as well, insisting on calling Ann on the intercom. I wasn't expected, and he was making sure.

She met me before I got halfway across the little lawn, throwing her arms around me and holding me tight. It was a hell of a surprise – she'd never been demonstrative. But I could feel it was just affectionate concern; although who am I to label that 'just'? What more should I have expected, what more should she have displayed? Her face looking up at me (she was a short woman), vivid under the harsh light of the motion detector, was like a reality check: a little slap in my own face, pushing away the illusions and delusions brought on by the heat, by jet-lag, by memories of someone else's sex.

She questioned me as if I were a recently released invalid, still just ambulatory. I hadn't known I looked that rough. She took my hand and led me gently inside, a patient newly frail, liable to break. I hate being patronized, even by good intentions. I stepped into the living room through a wave of irritation, insisting I felt fine, trying to regain a vestige of male authority. When she asked if she could get me anything, I said a beer; she looked doubtful and I had to consciously try to force my blood pressure down. I said, steadily, 'I'm feeling fine. Just a little jet-lag. I know it's short notice – or no notice – but I came over to ask you out to dinner.'

'I'm sorry, Mike. I can't tonight. I have a date . . . in fact, she's going to be here shortly. But we have a few minutes. Here, sit down, and let me get you that beer.'

I sat down and made an attempt to relax. I looked around. The room was almost unrecognizable. Most of the heavy, government-issue furniture was gone. I sat on a sofa with green linen upholstery and bamboo arm rests that had definitely been manufactured locally, perhaps custom-made. The chairs matched. Colourful little pillows designed by the arts and crafts NGOs lay scattered around. The heavy sideboard had been replaced by a light table made of a thin plank of some local, reddish wood, on slender metal legs. It carried several framed photographs.

Ann returned with the beer. She noticed me examining the photos. She picked one up, looked at it fondly, then handed it to me. 'My dinner date,' she said evenly.

I put my glass down on a side table and studied the picture. It showed an attractive young black woman, perhaps thirty years old. She stood on the stairs of some public building – maybe the national museum. Her expression, her clothing, her carriage, all suggested an American or European professional staff member of one of the more serious NGOs. Her bearing was confident, feminine. Ann stood next to her, a good half-head shorter. The two women had their arms around each other easily, comfortably, as they both smiled into the camera.

I thought I saw something more than just affection in those smiles. It reminded me of the look of love, something I no longer felt and sometimes even no longer felt capable of. Envy motivated my first, uncharitable reaction. We'd ceased pretending before I left that I didn't know for whom she worked. I said, 'I hope she's not an agent. There must be a regulation against photographic evidence. Poor security. It could be used against you.'

'She's my lover, my partner,' Ann said.

I held the framed photograph without speaking. After a moment she sat down next to me on the sofa. 'It was something that Zainab told me,' she said. 'I invited her here, one night, before she went on that trip north. I advised her against pushing things any further. She was appreciative, but not concerned.'

'I didn't know the two of you ever met.'

'Only that once. You know she was perceptive. She figured me out immediately – but I don't mean that. I mean she said something very simple, something I've never forgotten.'

'Which was?'

She stared down at her hands, concentrating. 'I told her that this was a very small town and a very small community, and that everyone knew about your affair.' She looked up at me. 'I told her that the men at the top – the old Khmer guys – had held off because she was the wife of a diplomat, but he was only a British Second Secretary, and she was becoming a threat. I wanted to make her understand that she wasn't immune.

'She just smiled that quiet smile of hers. Then she said, "No one's completely immune. We all have to do what we think is right." And she told me that I must believe that, too. I guess she thought my work had some importance. She said, "The two most important things are love and compassion. Love's the most important thing in life – and the least important. But compassion's essential. If we didn't feel compassion, you and I, we wouldn't have chosen our jobs." I have to admit, I never thought of my job, before, as being in any way compassionate. Finally, she said, "You have to keep some back, keep some in reserve. For yourself."'

I supposed this was part of what I'd come back for: to reclaim memory. But Ann was an informant I hadn't expected. Certainly not to hear some of Zainab's more elevated quotes – that was part of her, all right, but only one part. I sat there, cradling my beer, and thought: they aren't even that elevated, more pop psychology. Zainab might have been talking down to her. Or maybe Ann only remembers what meant something to her; it's almost impossible to recall exactly what anyone said.

She continued, 'It gave me a sense of comfort. And confidence. So . . . I haven't exactly "come out", but I don't hide anything, either. I suppose the embassy knows, but no one's said anything to me – at least, not yet. My career's important to me, but Helen's more important.'

'Helen?'

'The woman in the picture. My date.' She looked at her watch and said, 'She's going to be here in a minute to pick me up. I've still got to change.'

'I'll go.'

'You don't have to. You can stick around and meet her.'

'I'll have plenty of time for that. I'm sorry to have disturbed you.'

'It wasn't a disturbance.' We got up and I headed towards the door. She held it open for me, and said, 'Mike, why did you come back?'

'The department asked me.'

'I know. Is that the only reason?'

It was turning into an evening of sharing, and no one was more expert than Ann at unearthing – and keeping – secrets. 'I came back to remember.'

'Remember what?'

'Everything. And something . . . something I've forgotten.'

She said, 'Everyone's still here – almost everyone you knew,' and I thought, she was keeping tabs on me – part of her job. She added, 'Even the oil guy,' and with a grimace, 'probably at Martini's.'

'Thanks, Ann. I suppose I'll see you at the office.'

'Sure. Take it easy. Get some sleep.' And she reached up and kissed me on the cheek. 'Welcome back,' she said.

I turned and walked out. A light rain was now falling, light by Phnom Penh standards, but already heavy enough to darken the night. As I climbed into my tuk-tuk I heard a car door slam across the street. A tall, slender black woman stood by it, struggling with her bag. The rain and the night obscured her features, but her figure and stature reminded me of Zainab.

I shrank back on to the tuk-tuk's plastic cushion. I didn't want to meet Ann's girlfriend, or even see her. I didn't want to see how much she resembled Zainab. I wanted something serious to drink, and something to eat, somewhere with life, maybe even with a girl. And Ann had reminded me of where I could find it all. I leaned forward, one knee on the opposite bench, and told the driver: 'Martini's.'

3

I didn't have far to travel. The oldest and best known pick-up bar in town was just a few minutes further west. We crossed Monivong, which might as well have been a rail track instead of one of the busiest main streets in the city, for we were now, in one sense, on the wrong side of the tracks. The expat ghetto lay behind us; ahead was what would once have been called the native quarter – an archaic expression, obsolete and politically incorrect, but weirdly suited for the aid-fuelled colonialism of this old French colonial town.

We drove down a commercial block lined with restaurants that neither tourist nor aid worker frequented, and bridal shops where mannequins strutted elaborate and garish bridal gowns behind plate-glass windows. We turned right at the first intersection and already down the road I could see the private security guards and the tuk-tuks scattered under the bar's neon sign. My driver made a left in front of the entrance and stopped but kept his engine running. Ahead of him stretched his escape route: a quiet, respectable street lined with newish two- and three-storey houses. The neighbourhood had moved up into the urban middle class but the bar remained, an undesirable feature that wouldn't go away. I paid off my driver and thanked him in Khmer, but I could tell I'd gone down in his estimation. He slipped the tuk-tuk into gear and drove off. I walked past the slouching guards and through the open door.

The establishment was open-plan. A vestibule led into a cavernous lounge which in turn led to two game rooms with card and billiard tables, and at the far end to a raised, banistered platform carrying the actual bar. Recent Hollywood movies, pirated, were projected on to a screen hung from one wall – the soundtrack drowned out by the hum of conversation. It was Friday night but still relatively early; it was busy but not packed. I sat down at a table in the lounge where I could watch the movie, a British action film, and immediately a young Cambodian waitress appeared with a menu. I didn't need it. I remembered what worked and what didn't, and ordered Chicken Kiev and a whisky sour.

I looked around. The scene was so familiar I felt half in the present, half in the past. The clientele was mixed: most were westerners but there were Cambodian businessmen and Asian tourists. Each group had one thing in common: they were all men.

The hospitality girls (that was the correct term, and it was not a euphemism, for there was no rule that they had to go to bed with you), outnumbered the customers. One or two girls hovered at most of the tables, keeping the men company – in the first two minutes I'd waved off three – and groups of girls hung around the gaming rooms and the bar. But there was still a surplus, a line-up, sitting on little hard chairs against one wall of the vestibule. After a glance in their direction I returned my attention to the lounge, where at least the girls had found someone to talk to, to buy them a drink and maybe dinner – and maybe something more. They were better off than their companions in the vestibule. That surplus line-up always depressed me.

The waitress refreshed my drink before I realized I'd finished it, then dinner came and I had another. The action movie flickered on, from car chase to explosion to shoot-out. I casually observed my fellow expats. They ranged from an ancient gentleman, shrunken and bent with age, wearing a suit of what I believe used to be called white ducks, sitting companionably with two hospitality girls, to a very young British accountant (only a British accountant would wear a British accountant's suit to a Phnom Penh bar) standing by a nearby pillar, and 'chatting up' a bemused and amused girl whose head barely came to his chest. Overhearing him, I don't think he realized that she didn't need chatting up. He was a very fresh-faced young man, and I recalled I'd met his double, almost his identical twin, a year before. The resemblance was so marked I almost thought it the same guy, until I realized that no one could possibly stay that innocent in Martini's that long.

The ancient gentleman in his white suit got up, supported on each arm by a girl, and with their help and the help of a cane shuffled out. The logistics and in fact the whole point of having two women at once had always perplexed me, but he was beyond those considerations. A party of Russians took his table. They could have been Israelis – the look is similar – except that Israelis frequent higher-class bars. To confirm my identification, when the waitress came to take away my empty plate and refresh my drink – you never had to ask at Martini's – I asked their nationality.

She said, 'Russian NGO.' I must have looked astonished, because she laughed, ran off for a moment to the vestibule, returned and laid a flyer on the table. She leaned down and said, 'Even Russians send NGOs.' She had to go.

I pulled it over and read:

Russian Centre of Science and Culture (RCSC) in Phnom Penh, representative member of the Russian Centre for International Scientific and Cultural Cooperation:

To maintain positive potential of the sisterly Russian–Cambodian cultural relations through the promotion of joint positive activities in Education, Arts, Science and Technique . . .

This continued for several more lines, and ended with a list of several of King Sihanouk's films, which the RCSC intended to screen, apparently to maintain positive potential. The retired Cambodian monarch had written and directed a number of movies in his youth.

My waitress was nearly right. The Russians weren't members of an NGO, they were attached to their embassy. But the flyer's prolix language belonged to the NGO world. Every professional field has its own jargon, but there's something about Third World development that promotes theirs to a higher level, a more rarefied and incomprehensible altitude.

I'm an economist, not a writer; I deal in numbers, statistics, quantities – and of course favourable or unfavourable trends, causes and results. But the discipline of dealing with quantities leads to discipline in using words, and economists, in my experience, are less wedded to jargon, to the pompous, the prolix and the plain illiterate than most professions. Jargon irritates me. Anything that appears to explain, to clarify, but which in fact obscures, irritates me.

Looking down at that ridiculous flyer, I recalled the worst example of obscurantist jargon I'd ever seen. Standing outside the Cambodiana Hotel a year back, I'd looked up at the banner two metres high and stretched right across the hotel's broad front:

> Welcome, all Attendees, to Westin Oil's Second Annual Conference on Extractive Industries Transparency Initiative, Supporting IMF Guide on Resource Revenue Transparency, Promoting Aggregation and Disaggregation Disclosure, UNDP EITI Guide Document, Paragraph 4, and Bill 6066.

It was a week after I'd picked up the Westin Oil file from Ann. The company's American representative was in town to host a conference, and had asked me to attend; he called it 'preliminary background'.

'All bullshit,' he told me later that night. It was my first visit to Martini's. He'd suggested it for our meeting, insisting it served the best Chicken Kiev in town. But observing him, I thought he had a wandering eye. To give him credit, he was at first acquaintance an impressive representative of Westin: not yet forty, a geologist by training but now involved in the business end, moving up in the organization. We'd started by discussing the conference. I thought it a model of its kind, with presentations by two high-profile NGOs, speeches by Cambodian government ministers and an interesting if self-serving presentation by the representative himself (his name was George Silk, from Texas), on Westin's own transparency initiatives in West Africa. It was only after his second drink that Silk interrupted me, asking me if I'd heard, at any time during the conference, a single hard fact about Westin's Cambodian contract, about the terms of the concession, or about local legislation necessary to make all the transparency talk a reality. It was while I was trying to remember any facts I might have heard that he told me the conference was all bullshit. That's when I started observing him more closely, and noticed the wandering eye.

His eye wandered away from the girls at the bar to his colleague, Julian, the company accountant from the London office. He stood against a nearby pillar, nursing a drink, in conversation with a hostess. He looked maybe twenty-five, and George had told me this was his first time away from the UK. 'A numbers guy,' Silk said. 'It was premature to bring him out here. I'm sending him back tomorrow. I thought I'd at least show him a little night life before he heads home.' He said resignedly, 'I'm not sure he knows what to do with that girl.' He turned to me and asked how long I'd been in-country.

'About nine months,' I told him. 'This is my second posting.'

'Really? You had a career before.'

'I was a technical analyst on Wall Street.'

It took a moment for it to sink in. Then he grinned. 'One of the big money boys?'

'Not that big. I'm an economist, not a salesman.'

'I'm sorry to hear it. A salesman's what I need.'

'I'm here to find out how I can help you wrap up your contract. Before the elections.'

He didn't immediately reply. He looked around, I thought wistfully, at the bar, taking in the crowded scene. Finally he said, 'This is my third visit to Phnom Penh. Four years ago we signed a deal with the government, on favourable terms to us. They asked for a little money – they pretended it was for

47

a charitable institution. We said we'd support it once the oil started flowing. Then two years ago the price of oil tanked, and we withdrew. Now the price is back up, we'd like to start drilling, but the government's no longer satisfied with its slice of the deal. They want to renegotiate the contract.

'Our competitor's the Chinese. They're offering a good up-front deal. We're offering a better long-term deal. But the Cambodians don't get it.

'We have advantages. Our technology is better than the Chinese; we can get more oil out, at less cost per barrel, and less cost to the environment. I wish I could explain that to the Minister of Oil in a way he could understand. Unfortunately, his English is just OK, and I know maybe three words of Khmer.'

'Well, I'm sure I can find you a first-class translator.'

'Have you ever met the Chinese Ambassador?'

'No.'

'A very nice lady. Speaks perfect English. Also perfect Khmer. When she talks to the minister, she speaks his language. In every way. She's his single point of contact for CNOC, the Chinese oil company. She's it. And the Chinese don't have anything like a Foreign Corrupt Practices Act.'

'You said you have technological advantages.'

'We have others as well. Westin has a good reputation. We're reliable. There's something to be said for a straight business relationship – although some cultures have a little trouble with that.'

I remembered the file I'd read. There was a section in it on the Chinese oil company. I said, 'Don't the Chinese already have a block?'

'Sure. Same as we do. But blocks can be reapportioned.'

I wanted to cut to the chase. 'What do you need to go ahead, to make you confident you have a deal?'

He focused on me. 'We need the top guy to sign off on an agreement we write in Houston. In this kind of country, it's the man at the top who counts. We need his signature on our dotted line. That's what we need.'

'What do you think it will take to get that?'

'Most likely, his own self-interest.'

'Meaning?'

'A bribe.'

I sat back. 'You know I can't get involved in—'

He interrupted: 'Neither can I. At least, not without the kind of protection that the British government gives its company executives when they dole out bribes. If it comes to that, I'd prefer it go through Julian over there. I wouldn't even want to know about it.'

I looked towards the pillar against which I'd last seen Julian leaning. He was now several feet further away. The little hostess was pulling him, half-unwilling, towards a dark alcove.

Silk asked me, 'Know anyone who needs a housemaid?'

'Did you say housemaid?'

'Yes. I can recommend one. My first tour in Phnom Penh lasted almost four months. I rented an apartment and got a cook-housemaid. She came from here – from Martini's. Now she's between clients, and having trouble finding a job. There're still plenty of expats in this town, but not as many as there used to be. Wouldn't want her to have to return to this place.'

'I'd be happy to ask around.'

'Would you? Good. Here's her name and number.' He took out a business card and scribbled on the reverse. 'I'd be much obliged.'

There are so many unintended and unforeseen consequences in life. I took a brief look at what Silk had scribbled, the name: Lim Sovan, and a local cellphone number, before slipping the card into my pocket. I doubted I'd ever use it. The US Embassy people would never hire a servant who'd worked at Martini's – why not call a spade a spade: who'd been a prostitute (now even that's politically incorrect: I should have written 'sex worker') – and the NGO people, even though some worked for outfits trying to get women out of places like this, wouldn't themselves care to hire a former Martini's employee . . .

. . . someone was massaging my leg. I looked down to see who, and discovered my eyes were closed. I opened them – I'd been half napping on memory lane – to find a young Cambodian girl, a hostess, short and with a face like a doll, sitting next to me and smiling an innocent smile while her hand, discreetly beneath the table, kneaded the inside of my thigh.

My glass for once was empty, but I waved off the waitress on approach. I picked up the girl's hand and gently laid it down on her own leg – unlike mine, bare.

I'd started off the evening wanting to remember. Now maybe I just wanted to forget. To live in the present moment.

I asked the girl her name, and she said, 'Anna.' It was absurd but practical: she'd picked a name her clients could at least pronounce and remember. I liked her at once: she didn't have the hard expression, or the chronically worried expression, that so many of those girls develop. She looked happy, and as if she wanted me to be happy. When she asked if I wanted to go to bed with her (such an old-fashioned expression – she was the more attractive for it), I didn't hesitate.

It was the alcohol, of course. I'd been a teetotaller for months, and my tolerance was gone, or nearly gone. So it was the alcohol and the heat and the jet-lag – and no longer wanting to remember. Anna and I had our short business discussion. It wouldn't have been discreet to take her to the Himawari, and Martini's had rooms for that purpose in a separate building reached via a passage behind the bar.

She led the way, holding my hand as soon as we were alone, which I appreciated, because the moment we left the public rooms all attempt at light and cleanliness disappeared. We walked through a narrow, dim, dirty Third World alley to a dim, narrow, uneven stairway. I began harbouring regrets before we reached the first landing but Anna didn't stop climbing until the third. When she finally opened a door off a hallway, pulled me in and switched on the light, I was relieved. 'My room,' she said, and I could see the pride she took.

It was small but large enough for a double bed and a dresser and side table and even a chair. The walls were bare but freshly painted, and the bedclothes clean. The room smelled fresh. There were no windows but I didn't feel the lack. It gave the impression of a cell, but not a prison cell, more like a monk's cell: a small, clean, private space in which to be comfortable, to be alone, to be one's self. Although she was hardly alone now.

A doorway led to a bathroom. She asked if I wanted to take a shower and I said no, so she proceeded to take one herself. I took off my clothes and folded them over the chair, and then lay down on the bed. She joined me presently, still a little damp.

Short but full-figured and well-muscled, she obviously came from a hard-working peasant family. She was perfect in bed: more than compliant: expert and enthusiastic. She gave the definite impression of enjoying herself. What was the psychological truth of this young girl from the rice fields and river banks? Was it some extraordinary level of pragmatism, or a saintly level of equanimity, or just a clinical simplicity that allowed her to smile at me afterwards, as we lay together in bed, that allowed her to feel content, happy?

We lay on our sides, facing each other, while I asked her the empty questions – what province she was from, and so on – the questions basic humanity makes us ask, to try to create some fleeting meaning from the raw sexual act. She asked me, in her basic English, who I worked for, but of course I couldn't tell her the truth and I just answered, 'An NGO.' It was easy for her to accept: it was the correct answer for thousands of *Barang* in Phnom Penh.

Then she reached over and held the ring finger of my left hand in hers. I thought she was going to pull it, playfully, but instead she said, 'You not have wife . . . not married?'

I've never been married. At my age, admitting that sounds like an admission of failure, even more so to a Cambodian than an American. But I've loved, and I wanted to explain that to her. That's why I said, in my execrable accent, '*Dtao.*' It's the Khmer word for 'go', and it stumped her for a moment: their verbs don't have tenses; the meaning depends on context, and I didn't remember enough Khmer to say, 'She's gone.'

It didn't matter. She got it the moment the tears appeared on my face. They were context enough. I lay on my back with her on her elbow beside me, looking down. The tears were out of character and certainly not intentional and I resented them, although I expect my department's psychologist would have approved. Nowadays self-control is as out of date as the word 'prostitute'.

My sex worker looked down on me with such compassion I was afraid I'd caused her to suffer, and to try to mitigate it I told her, 'She was Buddhist.'

I don't know if she understood; she simply brushed the hair back from my forehead, as if I were a child, while repeating, 'Do not cry.'

As soon as I recovered my composure I got up and put on my clothes. I left the girl a good tip. She walked with me right through and out of Martini's, only releasing my hand when I got into a tuk-tuk.

As the driver pulled away from the bar I thought: she's the first woman I've been to bed with since I left Cambodia. Had I betrayed the dead? Is it even possible?

The tuk-tuk drove down the now dark, empty street, the wheels jarring over the potholed surface as we pushed through an evening wind blowing from the river, the dust and ashes of a neglected neighbourhood in our face as we headed, from the wrong side of Monivong, back to the hotel.

4

I woke the next morning with the images from the previous day flitting through my mind like ghosts. At least it wasn't the usual nightmare. I got up, made some coffee, had my morning cigarette and took a shower. I still felt tired and stale and I dislike being unfit; it was Saturday so I decided to spend at least part of the day in the hotel's weight room and in the pool.

I got to the restaurant downstairs just in time to make breakfast – there were hardly any diners left, even on a weekend. But when I sat down to scrambled eggs and bacon and toast, my stomach turned over. I couldn't face it. If I couldn't eat, at least I could swim. I took the lift back upstairs to change, and then descended again to the outdoor pool. It was Olympic-sized, surrounded by tropical trees and deck chairs. The sun shone down on my white skin, and I decided to work a little on a tan before going in.

I laid down and surreptitiously took in the scene. My companions lounging around the poolside in their bikinis were all in their twenties and thirties. Most would be married; there were a few children in sight. The hotel's facilities were the best in Phnom Penh, and open to membership; many of the women would be dependent spouses ('trailing spouses' was another expression). They were all physically attractive and some were desirable. They reminded me of a similar, although younger group of women around a much smaller swimming pool in an apartment complex in the forgotten central California town of Merced. I used to gaze down upon them admiringly from my second-storey apartment. I was a second lieutenant in the US Air Force and they were my buddies' wives. It was right after the

53

First Gulf War and Clinton's economic boom hadn't yet taken off; getting married as a junior officer meant you were probably going to be a career man, and I already had doubts about my suitability for a military career. But staring down at those fit, tanned young women, their cute little sun visors shielding their faces from the central Californian sun, it occurred to me that a junior officer's rank in the air force did attract desirable wives.

I closed my eyes. The sun beat down. I heard a woman's voice, dimly, telling her daughter, 'Mary, take a shower before entering the pool . . .'

. . . and a more recent memory, only a year past instead of almost twenty, took over: I was under the open-air shower just behind the row of deck chairs, my back to the pool, rinsing off before taking a dip, when I heard a familiar voice ask, 'May I?'

I turned around and stared through the falling water at Zainab. Her rather long, triangular face carried an ambiguous smile: I could interpret it as harmless or conspiratorial. She wore a red one-piece bathing suit that showed off her chocolate skin. I stepped out of the shower; she stepped in.

'Do you come here often?' she said, the water bouncing off her shoulders.

'I've just become a member.'

'We're members too. I try to get here two or three times a week.' Her voice was soft, conversational. I had to concentrate to hear her over the sound of the shower. She said, 'Robert tries to come on Saturdays. Come and say hello.' She stepped out, the water running from her hair and face. A glint of humour flashed in her eyes as if she were giving me a dare. Behind the humour I thought I saw an appeal.

I followed her, both of us dripping, to the far side of the pool where her husband, also in a bathing suit, reclined on a lounger under a sun shade. He was my age or a little older. He had one of those refined, boyish, British faces, with an unruly mop of hair over his forehead. His white, almost hairless skin hung loose over a modest frame.

'Robert,' I said, 'I didn't know you used the sports club.'

'Zainab's the swimmer. Dr White told me to use the machines in the gym to strengthen my leg.'

His wife said, 'Dr White removed your cast last January.'

He smiled. 'Just walking around does it. It's amazing how quickly the strength comes back.'

I looked down at his bare legs. They were both the same size, slender and white.

Zainab, fit and black, asked her husband, 'Why don't we invite Michael to our party? I don't think he's been to one of our concerts.'

'Of course. Good idea. It's a week on Saturday. You'll come, won't you? I don't know if a musical soirée's your cup of tea, but there'll be plenty to drink and an interesting, mixed crowd. Not all embassy types, for a change.'

'I'd love to.'

One of the Cambodian waitresses came up and asked Ambler if he wanted anything to drink. He asked for a lemonade, and after she turned away, said, 'I wonder if we could steal one of these young women away from the hotel. I don't know if Zainab told you, we lost our housemaid-cook just when we needed her most.'

'The second one we've gone through,' Zainab said, 'in six months.'

I thought of George Silk's offer, and his card, which I was sure I still had in my room, in a little pile of business cards. Of course it was inappropriate to suggest that a British diplomat hire as housemaid a former Martini's hostess. But the girl might not choose to share with him that period of her employment, and if need be I could subsequently deny prior knowledge. I don't know what made me suggest her, other than pure devilry. It didn't occur to me that she'd pass an interview.

I said, 'I know of someone – a housemaid-cook – who might be available.'

Zainab said, 'Give her our number. Or, better still, give us hers, and we'll call her.'

'Yes,' her husband seconded, 'the sooner the better.'

Zainab turned to face the pool and said, over her shoulder, 'Robert, you don't mind if I grab him for a race, do you? Michael, you can swim?'

Ambler smiled and nodded. Zainab pushed off in a graceful, low dive. I sprang to the pool's edge and dived in after her.

We were about the same age, she was only four or five years younger, and I was heavier, which can give an advantage in a pool. And she only swam the breaststroke, whereas I swam freestyle – it should have been her handicap. But she was strong and she had a lead. For a time I thought I was gaining. I thought if I could just catch up I could pass her. After two-thirds of the length – it was a long pool – I was breathing so heavily I had to struggle to keep my rhythm, but I was sure I was getting closer, and she must be tiring, too: I'd catch her before we reached the end. Then I heard her whoop of triumph, and I gave in, finding the pool's bottom with my feet, standing, gulping air . . .

. . . and woke up on the deck chair, breathing heavily, blinded by the sun, feeling faint, weak, trying to get off, to stand up . . . then coming to, with the concrete deck in front of my face – in fact, my face flat on the concrete deck. People were talking behind or above me and a hand gently raised my shoulder. I planted my palms on the ground and attempted to stand but only fell over on my back. The sky flashed out of focus and the concrete didn't feel so bad. I decided to just rest for a moment.

Some strength returned but I still felt ill. The pool attend-ant and a waiter helped me to my feet while a group of the bikini-clad beauties stood around. I was probably the most interesting thing to happen in their lives that morning, maybe for the entire day. I rested one hand on the waiter's shoulder and together we walked back inside. I left him at the door of the changing room, but he was still there, waiting for me, when I emerged, now joined by a young man who introduced himself as the assistant manager.

I just wanted to go upstairs and be left alone. There was

nothing wrong with me other than a little too much sun on top of jet-lag. But I only got halfway across the lobby before I had to sit down on one of the hotel's Empire chairs. I'm sure the assistant manager thought he was being reassuring when he told me he'd called the doctor, and I hardly had time to display irritation before a heavy-set, middle-aged man carrying an old-fashioned doctor's bag – I think they used to call them a Gladstone – walked up to us through the open-air foyer.

'Hello,' he said, 'I'm Dr White, the hotel doctor. They just called me. You must be the chap who fainted.'

'Hello, Doctor. I'm Mike Smith. We've met. There's nothing wrong with me except too much sun.'

'You're pale and perspiring. You're sitting hunched. We should go to your room, where I can make a proper examination.'

In my room I lay on the bed while he listened with his stethoscope; when he sat back and pulled it from his ears, I said, 'I believe this is our first professional meeting.'

He smiled a doctor's humourless smile. 'You're right. Neither the bust-up at the British Ambassador's residence nor the Café Musicum count as consultations.'

He wasn't exactly hail-fellow-well-met. I thought I understood why. Before I'd left Phnom Penh he'd been publicly disgraced, exposed in the local English-language newspaper as a convicted paedophile. The conviction occurred years previously during the period when Hun Sen was consolidating his grip on power, before any local English-language press had been revived, and the doctor had managed to fly under the radar. But the retrospective exposé in the *Phnom Penh Post* brought a kind of delayed justice. At least, that's how nearly everyone in the NGO community viewed it. They shunned him, and his private practice collapsed.

But he'd stayed on. Working as an on-call hotel physician, most, maybe all of his patients would be transients. It was a step down but he'd survived. He couldn't be pleased to have me as a patient, even temporarily. He would want to be forgotten by the expat community, not remembered. I might talk.

57

He surprised me by saying, 'You were connected in some way with Zainab Ambler.'

I said nothing to that.

'You've been away, haven't you?'

'Six months in Washington. It feels longer.'

'When did you get back?'

'Yesterday.'

'I want you to spend this weekend in bed. At least all the rest of today, and half of tomorrow. You may, if you insist, spend a little time outside tomorrow, but only in the early morning or late afternoon or evening. Avoid physical exertion.'

'For Christ's sake, I've never spent a weekend in bed in my life. I'm just a little run down – and jet-lagged.'

'You've had a syncopal episode. It may well be as you say; it may be more serious. You're at one of the best hotels in town. Order room service. You're with the American Embassy, aren't you?'

'Yes.'

'They don't have a medical officer, but I'll have a note delivered to you later today. Give it to your Chargé. She'll arrange for a complete check-up, either here or in Bangkok.' He put a small phial on the bedside table. 'These pills will help you sleep, if you have trouble. I'm only giving you a few. Don't take more than two at a time.' He got up, snapped shut his doctor's bag and turned to go, then paused. He asked, 'Why did you come back?'

I don't know why I thought the disgraced physician deserved a serious answer. Maybe I needed an answer myself. All I could come up with was: 'I'm not sure. I thought I came back to remember, but maybe I came back to forget.'

He smiled again his humourless doctor's smile. He said, 'Then you can relax. You're in the right place for both.'

After he left I took off my clothes – even that was an effort – sat back down and picked up the remote control. I still felt drowsy and weak, but I wanted some entertainment. There was the usual crap on, but the French TV channel had just started an old art-house film with English subtitles called *Les*

Enfants Terribles. Years ago I'd had a girlfriend in New York who dragged me to that kind of thing. The opening title music sounded familiar. I lay back to watch, but almost immediately sank into an intermittent doze. Every few minutes a few bars of the music would play and I'd half wake before dozing off again. The music was familiar, not the film. The plot revolved around an incestuous relationship between a brother and sister, but the details escaped me. After an hour of slipping in and out, the music's increasing, insistent beat caught my attention at the climax: within an empty mansion the siblings, now a young man and woman, have recreated their childhood bedroom by pushing beds and scraps of furniture together within a wall of Chinese screens. The boy, his love sabotaged by his sister's jealousy, commits suicide by eating opium; the sister, driven mad by guilt, blows out her brains with a revolver. Dying, she falls against the screens, which appear to open as they fall, like the petals of a giant flower.

Then I remembered where I'd heard those final descending chords, the music of that last take: while looking down from the half-landing of Zainab's house, looking down at the crowded living room, with four pianos – three uprights and one baby grand – pushed together, the string players of the chamber orchestra around them, Zainab at the baby grand and only God knew how many guests squeezed in all over the house and grounds. It was Bach's Concerto for Four Harpsichords, played in the old French film with pianos and played with pianos again, last year, in Phnom Penh. The first half of the concert at Zainab's Saturday night musical soirée.

The concert caught me on the landing on my way to see Ambler. Zainab had insisted that I go upstairs and see her husband; he'd had another fall and re-broken his leg. It was painful for him to move around and he didn't plan to make an appearance until later. I didn't know why she was so intent on treating me like a family friend, unless she'd come to the conclusion an affair would be easiest carried on *en famille*.

It seemed rude to disappear while they were playing so I stayed on the landing for all three movements. It wasn't the dutiful act of courtesy I expected. The music was dramatic and easy on the ear; it was so rhythmic one almost wanted to swing along, and the final movement grabbed you viscerally, the four pianos pounding away together, running towards the end. I was surprised. I'd always associated classical music, especially baroque music, with a level of refinement to which my musical ear was not educated. But this was accessible – even to me.

I joined in the applause and then, while it still filled the house, resumed my ascent to the first floor. An open door on the upper landing led down to a sunken combination library and TV room; Zainab had told me that this was where she and her husband spent most of their time together. It was comfortable and informal and lived-in. It was also empty. I called out, 'Hello, Robert.' I felt it insulting to call him, a man whose wife I'd had sex with, by his first name; on the other hand, calling out simply 'Ambler' seemed pompous. I heard an answering, 'Hello – in here,' and proceeded across the room through another doorway.

It led to their bedroom. Oddly proportioned, like so many of these older Phnom Penh mansions, it was much longer than deep, stretching the length of one wing of the house. The matrimonial bed filled one end. A set of hinged Chinese screens half enclosed and separated the room's centre, furnished as a sitting room with a table, a standard lamp and two chairs. On one, a recliner, sat Ambler, a tumbler in hand. His broken leg, encased in plaster, jutted out.

'Sit down and pour yourself a drink,' he told me, as we shook hands. A decanter stood on the table. 'I'm afraid this leg restricts my mobility. But I heard the concert without any trouble. It won't be a long evening; once the rains start people will want to leave before the streets flood. I'll head down presently to say hello.'

I enquired after his injury.

'It's these stairs,' he said, with more than a hint of the irritable invalid. 'Not one of them is exactly the same height as another. Not one is exactly level.'

'You tripped?'

'Going down. But the whole place is a safety hazard. Did you notice the floor downstairs?'

'I'm afraid I didn't.'

'Slick, pitch-black artificial stone. And the living room's sunken – a sheer drop. Imagine what that's like in the dark, or even low light! And try to find a light switch in this house, in the dark. Not one's exactly where you'd expect.'

Their house, a semi-colonial mansion rebuilt after the Khmer Rouge and now leased by the British government, was typical of its kind. Huge, roomy, comfortable, with many quaint features – or too big, impossible to manage, uncomfortable, with many awkward and unworkable features. It was what you made of it.

I said, 'Well, it is the Third World.'

'One of the more extreme examples. I've forgotten: how long have you been in the Service?'

'Not long. This is only my second assignment.'

'Where was the first?'

'Riyadh.'

'I remember. Third World lite. This is the real thing. Its status is its explanation. It explains everything.'

I thought of all the couples I'd known who were walking examples of the old adage that opposites attract. I wondered if the Amblers belonged to that category. In my experience that kind of attraction rarely lasts. As I and those couples progressed through our thirties, more and more of them broke up under the strain. I asked him, 'How long have you been with the Foreign Office?'

'Since '91.'

'That's a good career. You and Zainab must have seen a lot.'

'We've only been married six years. I was late getting married – my first few assignments weren't conducive. And Zainab had her career as well. We met at a concert when I was in London on leave.'

'You're musical, too?'

'Not in the least. It was a blind date. I'm not really a liberal arts type. I took an engineering degree at Oxford, but it was the post Gulf War – the First Gulf War – recession, and employment in the private sector had dried up. I had an uncle in the Foreign Office, and he suggested I apply. In those days, a connection still meant something.'

His uncle in the Foreign Office, his obsolete accent, his frame, his pallor, all suggested a previous generation: the class-ridden and underfed post-war Brit. He was out of time. He came across as someone masquerading as a relic . . . or was he a bona fide relic, really obsolete?

I said, 'I enjoyed the concert. Bach, wasn't it?'

'Yes. Zainab's favourite composer. I heard the applause. There's precedent. Didn't the passengers on the *Titanic* enjoy the ship's orchestra, as the boat went down?'

'Are we sinking?'

'You'd never guess it, would you, from the party downstairs? But the writing's on the wall and many of the bigger NGOs are already winding down. Phnom Penh will continue to do business as a consumption hub, but the rest of the country, with the exception of a couple of tourist towns, is going down the drain. There's no coherent plan for rural development. It's trickle-down economics, Third World style.'

My job is economic analysis and I'd been doing it since I arrived. Our assessments were identical. Professionally, I was pleased at the confirmation. Personally, I would have preferred him on a different page. I said, 'Do you expect Prang's Reform Party to make any difference?'

'Prang. You know his name's British World War Two slang for a crash, a smash-up? No. Mr Prang will prang – his party will not make any difference. Although Zainab disagrees with me. I'm sure she thinks they have a chance. You know she's their transparency consultant.'

'Yes.'

'She's doing good work. She's published some well-researched exposés of high-level corruption – at the very top – on her website. Of course, no one pays much attention to that, but Deutsche Presse-Agentur accepted an article and placed it with several European papers. I know because I got a call from the Deputy Minister, a Mr Sok. He insisted, in an almost pro-forma way, that the Prime Minister was upset.'

'What did you say to that?'

'I invited him to the soirée downstairs. Always try to co-opt the opposition whenever you can.'

'From what I've read, elections here are generally fair – as fair as can be expected. Ninety per cent of the population lives in the countryside. What if they decide to throw the bastards out?'

'The ruling party will use a combination of vote buying and intimidation. It's already begun. That's what the incident at the British Ambassador's residence was about. It just got out of hand.'

'It certainly did.'

'A one-off. We have to use a bit of care, of caution. None of it will affect us.' He paused to take a drink. 'Unless,' he added, 'you're the type who can no longer stand living in a place like this.'

A tentative knock made us both turn. A young Cambodian woman, not more than thirty, stood by the open door. She was slender and short and would have looked almost childlike but for her expression: sweet, but heavily guarded.

She said, 'Madam asks you to come down.' Even the tenor of her voice was sweet but guarded. Life had trained her not to overstep.

Ambler said, 'Tell her we're coming down now.' She spun round fast as a top, then disappeared. For the first time I saw on Ambler's face an uncritical smile. He said, 'Our latest addition. We have you to thank.'

'Me?'

'Yes, your recommendation. Our new housemaid-cook. Lim Sovan. She was a bit of a risk; her recommendations had all left, back to Australia, the UK, the US. But we took her on. So far it's working out, although this mansion's a bit much for her. It'd be a bit much for anyone. Zainab calls it the House of Usher.' As if on cue, someone downstairs hammered out one of those baroque chords (I later learned the correct term was arpeggio) that suggest a stagey menace. 'Come on,' he said, 'we'd better put in an appearance.'

He got up on his crutches and together we walked out to the landing. He asked me to descend first: 'In case I fall,' he said. I assumed he was being humorous. It's time-consuming going down stairs on crutches, and we stopped for a breather on the lower landing.

A light but steady rain fell outside, emptying the garden and filling the house. The crowd was massed, cheek by jowl, below. 'There they are,' Ambler told me, 'every kind and type of NGO expat, as God created them. Do you see that tall, skinny man over by the concert grand, the one with the Hitler moustache?'

I picked out a figure from the crowd. 'Yes.'

'A New Zealand lawyer. An expert on the legal code bequeathed by the UN Transitional Authority. Does a good deal of work monitoring land ownership issues. If you ask him, what is the one most effective answer for the country's ills, do you know what he'll say?'

'No.'

'Birth control.' Ambler grinned. 'Cambodia has one of the lowest population densities in Asia.' He pointed out a figure I recognized from the Christmas party, Hun Prang. 'You know him?'

'We've met.'

'Prang's Cambodian-American. Has a foot in both camps. Over here, he's really an expat, masquerading as a Cambodian. His party has opened offices in eighteen out of twenty provinces. There's a rumour, which may be true, that he's getting some funding from the International Republican Institute. His party's main plank is transparency and good governance.' Prang had seen us on the stairs, and waved; Ambler waved back. 'He's in a wonderful position to enrich himself and his family. Zainab thinks he's clean.'

'What do you think?'

He shook his head. 'It all depends on how averse he is to accepting bribes. Does he know?'

We continued down. Several guests spotted Ambler and surrounded him as soon as we reached the glossy, black floor. I'm a lover of fresh air and there was none in the room; I pushed my way through the crowd to a door that looked like it might lead out, opened it and slipped through.

I stood on a long veranda facing the garden. The lights from the rooms above picked out trees surrounding a central lawn and, dimly through the rain and the dripping leaves, a gazebo. The veranda's roof was not weatherproof and I wondered if the gazebo was a drier bet. A path led between the trees in the right general direction. I set off carefully, trying to use the trees as shelter but avoiding low hanging branches.

I was halfway to the gazebo when I saw it was inhabited. What I'd assumed was a central support was in fact two figures clasped in an embrace. I'm not one to disturb lovers but the woman's figure looked familiar. I crept a little closer. It was Deria, the American journalist. She stood in the arms of Dr White, the British doctor who had tried to help at the Christmas party, and been clubbed. From Prang to White: she evidently got around, but within the same set.

I retreated into the darkness, back to the house.

Somewhere I stepped off the path. A maze of shrubs as high as my head surrounded me. I blundered on but in deeper dark-ness: someone had turned off the upstairs lights, or maybe I'd penetrated to a different side of the house. I pushed through the branches and leaves and, stumbling over a root, fell to my knees in front of the veranda.

Ahead was a double door. I turned the handle and stepped inside. It was pitch black. I felt over the wall for a light switch, found one, pulled the door shut and turned on the light.

A single overhead bulb showed an almost empty room. Woven mats lay scattered on the floor. Folded prayer benches leaned against a wall. A wooden Buddha and two candles stood on a low table to my right. Although unfurnished the room felt comfortable, welcoming. Someone kept the place clean; the walls were spotlessly whitewashed.

I heard a lock turn. On reflex I turned the light off. A door opposite opened. A woman stepped in, backlit, and closed the door behind her. The light blinked back on.

Zainab and I stood staring at each other. She was quick to humour. She grinned and said, 'Michael, what are you doing here, alone, in the dark?' She came closer. 'You're wet – drenched.' Her red lipstick against her white teeth and black complexion was more like body paint than make-up. Her hand brushed the rain off my cheek. I pulled her close and kissed her; without effort I opened her lips.

But she pushed away. 'It's not safe,' she said. 'I didn't lock the door. Anyone could come in.'

'You could lock it now.'

'I'm the hostess.'

'Why did you come in?'

'Oh, for just a moment or two of peace and quiet; instead, I got you.'

She was right: we had to maintain discretion. We both took a step further apart; I took a deep breath. She asked, 'What do you think of the room?'

I shrugged. 'It's curious. It's about as bare as can be.' I looked around again. 'Not even a proper chair or table. But you get the impression you could sit on one of these mats, and get some serious work done.'

'You're perceptive. That's exactly what meditation is: work. And this is a meditation room. That's what we do here.'

'You and your husband?'

'No. Me and some of my women friends. Robert isn't involved.'

Through the door we heard someone call out her name.

She said, 'The party's breaking up. It's the rain; people want to get home before the streets flood. I'd better go back in.'

'I'll go with you.'

'No, stay here for a few minutes. Keep the light on.'

'All right.' It made sense, but I thought, it's not yet even a proper affair, and already I'm taking precautions.

She sweetened the pill: 'We can have a drink after the others have gone.'

In half an hour the monsoon was in full flood and the crowd was history. The house was a wreck, empty glasses and plates everywhere, but when Sovan started to clear up, Zainab told her that tomorrow would do and she should go to bed – she had her own room near to theirs. Zainab told her husband that she was going to take advantage of having a baby grand in the house (it was on loan from the Intercontinental – the manager was one of her guests), and play for me a little. He took the opportunity to excuse himself. Sovan helped him up the stairs. His last words were to ask his wife not to play too loud.

We were alone in her living room, with her husband and her maid upstairs. She turned out some of the lights and asked me if I wanted another drink. I declined. She sat down at the piano.

I don't know how to play an instrument, I'm not musical, I'd never been around musical people – at least, not anyone who was as serious about it as Zainab. With her chocolate skin and ironic expression, her tall, sexy figure – she wore a backless dress and her bare back seemed to go on for ever – she didn't fit any idea I'd ever had about someone deeply into classical music.

This evening was the first time I'd seen her at a keyboard. She knew I was ignorant. She said, 'I'm going to play you something by Bach. It's called a canon at the fifth, but that's not important. It probably isn't a kind of music you'll recognize – you may not even recognize it, at first, as music. Its theme is abstract and its construction rigid.'

I said, 'It sounds pretty dry.'

'I know.' She laughed, then put her hand on mine. 'But it's the furthest thing from dry imaginable. The focus on the abstract produces a melody that flows and develops right through the song, and the rigidity is the backbone to the song's freedom. Listen.'

And so, surrounded by dirty plates and glasses, all the detritus of the party, with the rain pouring down outside, Zainab played for me, for the first of many times, the fifteenth variation of Bach's Goldberg Variations. The piece is in two parts, and she repeated each part once. High baroque music is not a subject in which I have a background. I'd be lying if I said I understood it, or even if I said I found it profoundly musical. But somewhere towards the middle of the repeats, I began to catch a glimpse of what she was getting at. For a few bars I felt I was listening to music, as opposed to a series of notes. In the very last measure, the melody in the left hand descends as the melody in the right ascends; the left hand finishes, while the right continues upward, solo, for a final three notes. It gave me a contradictory feeling: that the music had come to its natural end – but also that it continued . . . where, when, how, I didn't know.

My face must have betrayed some confusion. She rose and said, 'Yes, it's a mystery. End of lesson number one.' She glanced quickly up the stairs – all clear – then came closer. She wore an unfamiliar scent, more bitter than sweet. Her dress showed off her figure. She said, 'Thank you for coming.'

'You're welcome. Thanks for inviting me.' We were alone. She was out of bounds, trouble with a capital T, but we'd already crossed the boundary line. I lightly caressed her smooth arm with my fingers, and said, 'I hope we can meet again.'

She whispered, 'I'm heading north next weekend to Siem Reap. Prang wants me there for his rally on Sunday – he's giving a major speech.'

My heart leapt. 'I'm flying to Siem Reap on Friday. I'll be there on Sunday to cover the rally. The embassy's short-staffed.'

'I could go up a little early . . . where are you staying?'

Local politics had solved our problem. I said, 'Call my office on Monday, and I'll tell you which hotel the embassy's using. We may as well get rooms in the same place.' I caressed her hip, but she shook her head.

'The maid,' she whispered. 'Sovan sleeps like a dog, ready to jump at anything.'

I thought, there's always the guard hut. But the monsoon rain still poured down, and the hut was at the end of the drive – too far away.

I'd parked my car on the street. Zainab lent me one of their umbrellas, but the ribs collapsed halfway to the gate. The city had cut off electricity to half the street lights to save money and I reached the car in the dark and drenched for the second time that night. None of it mattered. I had something to look forward to. Siem Reap.

5

Six days later I took the 7 a.m. flight north. I checked into my hotel, had a late breakfast, then looked over my notes before taking a tuk-tuk to my only interview. Noelle had three contacts but two were unavailable: one had transferred out permanently, the other was on leave.

My informant was an American doctor in her early sixties working as an A&E specialist – a trainer and mentor for Cambodian staff – at the German Clinic. She'd worked there for two years. Most of her colleagues and all her patients were Khmer. I interviewed her over lunch. She was pleasant but brisk; she had little time in her busy schedule for me. We kept our introductions brief and almost dispensed with small talk.

'You'll have to excuse my office,' she said. 'Ours is a charity clinic and we spend our money on drugs and equipment.'

'No problem. You're aware the Reform Party is planning a rally the day after tomorrow?'

'Yes. The rally's being held on clinic land: the field and car park on your left as you walked in the front door.'

'So the clinic supports the party?'

'The clinic's director, Herr Bülow, supports Reform. The population here is a natural electorate for an opposition party. This is a go-ahead place with a lot of foreign influence, better than average local education, but still a lot of poverty. And the town and the province give more – much more – to Phnom Penh than they receive. We expect a big turnout.'

'Is Reform well established here?'

'For a new party, without much money, they have a good organization. Of course, the police and security services are controlled by the Prime Minister's party. We're trying our best to be prepared for trouble.'

'Trouble?'

'Trauma injuries, gunshot wounds – we're taking precautions. We'll be fully staffed and we'll have volunteer blood donors on call.'

'You sound like you expect the worst.'

'We don't expect it, Mr Smith. We just recognize the possibility.'

She went back to her patients and I went back to my hotel. At two I picked Zainab up at the airport and checked her in. A maid was cleaning our rooms so we went exploring. By sunset we'd 'done' Siem Reap.

Not, of course, Angkor Wat – that takes days to do properly. Nor the floating villages, which are an afternoon to themselves; more, if you want to include the Tonlé Sap Lake. But Siem Reap itself is small, a provincial French colonial survival that's grown to service the tourists – Asian, Australian, European and even a few Americans – who come to view, in the dusty jungle north of town, the remains of temples built over entire reigns and ruined over centuries.

We walked from our hotel, La Lumière de l'Angkor, through the grounds of the neighbourhood wat and along the river, then down the main street. We inspected the dark and odorous covered market and breathed a sigh of relief as we emerged into the late afternoon sun. We toured a small museum, and we each bought a print in an art gallery. The number of art galleries in Phnom Penh and even in Siem Reap is extraordinary, considering these towns' size and level of development. Artists fleeing New York and Arizona are thick on the ground – the climate is easy and expenses reasonable – and indigenous artistic development (using oils and water colours on framed canvas, suitable for the western market) is fertile ground for NGO local capacity building.

Night falls quickly in the tropics and it was dark on the inadequately lit street when we took seats in an Indian restaurant recommended by the guidebook. The streets, the restaurants, the art galleries – everything and everywhere was full of *Barang* and Asian tourists. The local Khmers, slim and elegant, were by far the most attractive ethnic group.

Over dinner Zainab and I talked like two tourists ourselves, two tourists who had met by accident in front of a canvas in one of the galleries (I'm sure it happens), who hit it off and who decided to further their acquaintance.

We gave each other our personal histories as if we were on a first date, which in a way we were. But it's not the standard, first-date biographies that tell you what you need to know about a person. What did she learn about me? That I'd started my career as a transport pilot, left the military a decade and a half ago, and become an economist – a technical analyst – on Wall Street. That I'd joined the Foreign Service after the Wall Street meltdown. That I'd had affairs but never been married . . . she asked why not, and I told her, lamely, that Wall Street was a honey pot for gold-diggers. That's true as far as it goes.

I learned about her that she'd been born in the Sudan, but at the age of two moved with her family to the UK. Her father was an academic and she'd done well at Oxford, had studied law but became a television news presenter, then an activist for developing world causes. She'd married upon turning thirty. They had no children. Quite casually she mentioned that, having been brought up a Catholic – her parents were both converts – she'd become a Buddhist. None of it explained why she was so open to having an affair, or at least why she was so open to having an affair with me.

It had been a long day for us both and we agreed to return straight to our hotel after dinner. Zainab visited the Ladies; I went down by myself to the street.

It was late and most of the tourists were gone. A young Khmer man leaned negligently against a lamp-post. He would have looked out of place during the day, but at night, on the shadowy, nearly empty street, he looked comfortable, part of the scenery. A Khmer woman walked towards me down the pavement. She had the stature of a child but a pronounced figure. It was easy to see because she wore so little. She walked past the lamp-post and I thought the man nodded at her. She stopped an arm's length away and scanned my face with an expression that combined a frank invitation with assessment, as if she were asking herself: is he a good bet, this foreign stranger? I smiled at her – there was no point in being discourteous – but said nothing. She looked like she'd made up her mind and was going to give me the benefit of the doubt. I was pleased to think I'd passed.

'Hello,' she finally said, and cutting straight to the chase quoted a figure ridiculously low even for Siem Reap. I shook my head, said, 'Sorry,' and she glanced back at the young man below the lamp-post. She quoted me another figure, this time a few hundred riels less. I was about to explain my position when Zainab appeared, rendering explanation unnecessary. As far as the girl was concerned I just vanished; she resumed walking up the pavement. If I'd been in her way I think she might have walked right through me.

'Did she proposition you?' Zainab asked.

'I made the grade, but I turned her down.'

Two doors up a young man staggered out of a shadow, reaching for the girl. I didn't catch his exact words – he had some kind of regional British accent – but his meaning was clear. He was falling-down drunk. The girl performed an evasive manoeuvre neat as a pirouette and continued on undisturbed, unperturbed.

'The drunken Brit abroad,' I said.

'He's not typical.'

'He's one hundred per cent typical. He's just a little further off the beaten track than most.'

He fell to his knees in the gutter and bent over. Down the street the girl was negotiating with a middle-aged Asian gentleman who'd stepped smoothly out of his own shadow. He may have been Japanese.

Zainab said, 'That girl's barely a teen.'

'She may be older than you think.'

'No wonder this country attracts paedophiles.'

'I'm sorry?'

'Look at that old man.'

'I'm not sure he fits the profile. At the embassy we pay for their deportation weekly. They have the complacent, harmless presentation of Protestant missionaries.'

'He fits my profile. That little girl. Wouldn't it be like going to bed with a child?'

'I doubt it, Zainab. Maybe in terms of her height.'

We caught a tuk-tuk back to La Lumière de l'Angkor. It was a rustic but comfortable three-star hotel off a dirt road on the edge of town, where the jungle, although tamed, still lapped at the walls of the wats and the paddy fields and, for that matter, at the perimeter – poorly defined – of the hotel itself. A footbridge led over a dubious stream to the two-storey central building, with an office and foyer and lounge downstairs and a restaurant and bar above. In three nights I never saw a customer in the bar.

Accommodation was scattered around the hotel's central feature, a long, winding swimming pool. All construction (save the pool) was of native wood, and the grounds were heavily treed and ornamented with bougainvillaea and heliconia and God knows how many other tropical plants, many of which, stretching their branches and winding up walls and balconies, seemed on the verge of engulfing the property.

I hoped it wasn't the beginning of paranoia that made me opt for discretion, even in Siem Reap. Our building, like them all, boasted two rooms on the ground floor and two upstairs; I'd booked both above. We shared a balcony and a set of wooden stairs in an evolutionary stage not far removed from a ladder. I told Zainab to climb first; if she fell, I told her, she'd be better off falling on me.

On the balcony we paused and looked out over the treetops. It was too dark to see much other than the stars and the flicker of the party lights strung beneath the trees. I said, 'Your room, or mine?'

'Do you snore?'

'I'm not sure. If I do, I'm unaware of it.'

'Your room, then. At least for tonight. If I have to escape I'll do it without waking you.'

She took my arm and led me in. I shut the door and closed the wooden shutters in the unglazed windows.

By mutual consent we decided to shower, one after the other, before making love. Was it fatigue, or a reaction from the manner of our first coupling, or the slight revulsion of the street scene, the prostitute and her pimp; or maybe an effect of our dinner conversation, superficial as it was – the realization that we were having an affair with a real person, a person with a life moulded by a past – that resulted in our making love like a couple long married? She was a beautiful woman, but I found myself making an effort at arousal. It didn't take much of an effort, but any was unexpected.

Afterwards I felt a little alone, although in the same bed. It felt ridiculous to be in bed, after all this planning, with someone distant, someone perhaps barely inclined to be there at all. In a bed in a primitive hotel on the edge of a tiny Third World town, in a country remoter than remote. It was a cold thought. It suggested personal failure, something I've always tried hard to avoid.

I asked her, 'Why are you doing this? Why are you cheating on your husband?'

She answered evenly: 'Do you object?'

'No. I don't. I just wonder why.'

'Robert isn't much interested in sex. He was in the beginning. But, just as some men get to an end of sex, usually in their sixties or older, Robert got to an end – in his thirties.'

I didn't understand her. 'You mean, he's incapable?'

'No. I mean he's no longer interested. Not in me. I think, not in anyone.'

'For how long?' I asked.

'Years.'

The memory of an English woman I'd once loved, over a decade ago, when I was still new to New York, came back to me. She'd also lost interest. I said, 'Don't the English – a lot of them – have a reputation for being cold, or at least, not very sexual?'

'That's such a cliché.'

'There's a reason for clichés. There's usually something to them.'

'You really don't like the Brits, do you?'

Instead of answering, I asked her, 'Why haven't you left your husband?'

'Partly upbringing. I wasn't brought up to divorce my husband. And Robert has qualities you're unaware of, as an American you may not appreciate. He's upper class and was brought up upper class, but completely without colour prejudice. He's no notion of it. You have no idea how refreshing that was to me. But it's more than that. You said you've never been married.'

'That's right.'

'I think there are some things you have to experience, to understand the truth even of clichés. Marriage is about a good deal more than sex. I still love him. I'm not in love with him, in love romantically, any more than he is with me. But we're part of each other's lives. We're even part of each other's careers. He's an asset to mine. To a lesser degree, I'm an asset to his.'

The opposite of an asset is a debit; I wondered where I fitted in. Maybe as yet I didn't appear on the balance sheet. An unearned and so far unvalued item. I might have felt sorry for myself but I didn't, I felt sorry for her; or, to be more exact, I regretted being a disappointment: due to her husband's lack of passion, she was having an affair with a man, who had, that evening, displayed a lack of passion. Rather awkwardly I complimented her on her beauty.

'That's what he still says,' she told me, 'when he remembers.'

We'd progressed from being lovers by accident, but not very far. Was she wondering if she'd made a mistake? I wasn't. We had two nights ahead of us, and passion might return. I hadn't felt so comfortable in bed with anyone for a long time. I held her hand, closed my eyes and slept.

The next morning we rose before dawn for our balloon ascent.

I'd kept Zainab in the dark, simply telling her that I had a surprise for her. We drove off in the dark, literally, before sunrise. I'd ordered a taxi since timing was important and you never knew when something on a tuk-tuk – a wheel, an exhaust pipe – was going to fall off. I don't know what Zainab expected. I know for a fact it wasn't what she saw, as the taxi turned off the main road to Angkor Wat, down a beaten earth track and through a stand of trees to the biggest balloon either of us had ever seen.

She climbed out of the cab gaping. I paid the driver enough to keep him there for an hour, and joined her.

The balloon, seventy feet in diameter, tethered to a circular gondola in turn tethered to the ground, hung motionless in the still air. The sun just cleared the horizon, lighting up some scattered low cumulus in the distance.

'What's it for?' she said, her eyes riveted to the giant envelope.

'It's for us. We're going up in it. We're going to see Angkor from the air.'

'What if I don't want to see Angkor from the air?'

'Come on. Of course you do.'

'Are you sure this is safe?'

'If I wasn't, we wouldn't be here. I'm ex-air force, remember?'

'Did you ever fly one of these things?'

'No . . . I only flew fixed-wing aircraft. However, I'm familiar with the theory.'

'The theory. Great.'

Another taxi drove up and stopped beside us; a party of three Japanese emerged and headed towards a palm-roofed shack near the balloon. 'We'd better get aboard,' I said. 'It's first come first served. I picked the first flight of the day.'

'Why?'

'The light: Angkor should be at its best. And the wind. It's nearly always calmest at dawn.'

'It's past dawn.'

'Stop stalling.' I took her hand and together we walked to the ticket office.

I had no doubt it was safe. I'd researched it in as much depth as I could from the website of the German manufacturer, the last in the world of large, man-carrying gas balloons. If you want to carry only two or three people, hot air is fine. But if you want to lift, say, thirty people at once, even only five hundred feet into the air, you need the greater lifting power of helium. You need a gas balloon, like the one on which we were about to fly.

It's true the ticket office and its staff – a couple of Khmer girls with limited English and I believe no Japanese – was not confidence-building (Zainab needed reassurance, not I). But the motorized winch was impressive and impressively German, as was the balloon. The envelope was fully inflated and perfectly spherical. It loomed above us, straining at its attachment: a massive net tied at the bottom to a load-distributing hoop. The gondola itself, an aluminium-framed observation platform designed to hold thirty standing passengers in discomfort, hung suspended beneath the hoop.

I'd timed our arrival perfectly: we had only a couple of minutes before the first scheduled lift-off. Two young Khmer men busied themselves at the winch. We bought our tickets and started towards the platform. One of the young men left the winch and, beckoning us forward, opened a fragile-looking aluminium gate in the gondola's side.

The five of us stepped up and climbed in.

We stood on a circular walkway built around a load-carrying frame. Waist-high barriers prevented you from falling out and discouraged you from clambering on to the interior frame. The gondola was big, about fifteen feet in diameter, but the walkway itself was narrow, just big enough for two to pass abreast.

The young man who'd ushered us in climbed aboard, shut the gate and sat down at the pilot's station – a monitor and switch panel. He gestured to his companion by the winch. I heard the hum of an electric motor. The gondola rocked gently, slid a little to one side – then jerked level. We were airborne.

The winch paid out the tether. We ascended slowly and steadily through the fresh, early morning air. Soon the only sound was the creaking of the rigging. Our goal, I knew, was five hundred feet, a dangerously low altitude for any type of aircraft other than a tethered balloon, but high enough for a good view. Pilots are usually too busy to take an interest in the scenery that passes below; when they do take an interest it is analytical. My early training had not completely vanished. As I scanned the landscape to the horizon I noticed the green treetops and paddy, and the towers, burned red by the morning sun, of Angkor Wat. But the scattered cumulus I'd noticed earlier held my attention. The sun's heat and the tropical air's humidity pushed and grew the clouds into rising columns before my eyes.

Our ascent was smooth, well-managed. The balloon itself, from the fabric to the rigging to the gondola, looked in perfect condition. Zainab stood beside me gripping the railing like grim death.

I asked her, 'How do you measure this country's or these people's development? What metrics do you use? Are they mostly political?'

'That's a strange question to ask as I'm holding on to this thin-as-nothing aluminium rail.'

'It'll take your mind off the altitude.'

'All right. I suppose, for now, they're mostly political. That's what I'm involved in after all: local politics.'

'And my metrics, in my job, are almost all economic. Numbers. But there's another metric: who flies and maintains their aircraft?'

'Is that a question?'

'In the Gulf Arab states, from Kuwait to Yemen, there's hardly a single Arab pilot flying commercial passenger aircraft. Their pilots are mostly Brits and Americans. There's not a single Arab mechanic working on a passenger aircraft. They don't have the education, the skill, the work ethic. Asia's better but mixed. Vietnam has its own pilots and a great safety record; Indonesia has its own pilots but you'd be nuts to fly Air Garuda if you could avoid it.'

'What's your point?'

'The point is that maybe, just maybe, we can see evidence for actual development, not in the corrupt politics, not in the rise or fall of per capita GDP, but in something real: the locals' ability to maintain and fly their own aircraft.'

'I never thought I'd hear you give such a ringing endorsement for local capacity building. I'd like to point out that we're not on a 747.'

'You have to start somewhere. Maintaining this thing isn't trivial.'

My rant had one good effect: Zainab relaxed. She left my side and walked right around, taking in the ascent from every angle. I let her circumambulate by herself – I figured it was confidence-building. I was interested in the mechanism and in the flight characteristics on tether.

Looking down, I saw we were still almost directly above the launch platform. I turned and leaned over the inner railing to inspect the tether attach point. The underside of the aluminium felt rough and damp against my fingers; I gave it a scrape with my nails and then inspected my hand.

Flakes of rust spotted my fingers.

I inspected the railing more closely. The inner supports looked to be part of the load-bearing structure. I wasn't certain, but I thought they were probably steel alloy. The supports were covered in aluminium sheet forming a narrow ledge at waist level and a barrier from the waist to the knees.

I stood there, leaning on the ledge, facing in to the tether attach point, feeling under the ledge with my fingers. I tried to remember what I'd ever learned about galvanic corrosion.

Zainab was on the opposite side of the gondola, chatting, or maybe just exchanging exclamations, with the Japanese. She probably had a lot of experience in interviewing people during her television career. She managed to be classy and approach-able at the same time. Her smile drew people in. Attractive features, neither required nor common among pilots – or economists.

Galvanic corrosion results when two metals of differing electrolytic properties come in contact in the presence of an electrolyte. An historical example is copper hull sheathing and iron nails in sea water, but there are innumerable contemporary examples. It is of course something that designers try to avoid. I was surprised to find possible evidence of galvanic corrosion on our gondola. The German design team would have aggres-sively tracked down areas that could produce such corrosion, and either eliminated or taken steps to mitigate them.

We were still ascending, and a sudden breeze blew the balloon slightly to one side; the rigging creaked and the gondola swayed and tipped a few degrees. One of the Japanese laughed.

Corrosion is not unknown in fixed-wing aircraft. It is regu-larly inspected for, and metal fatigue and corrosion are the two main factors that determine an aircraft's designed service life. This is sometimes expressed in the number of take-offs and landings, sometimes in total flight hours.

A balloon had to have a designed service life as well; I won-dered how far down that road this balloon had gone. I'd done the necessary research at my computer in Phnom Penh. What were the relevant design specs?

'Turn around, Michael, stop looking at the mechanics and observe the view! There's Angkor Wat, and beyond you can see . . . I think, Bayon! It's fantastic! Take a look!'

Zainab had rejoined me. I turned around. We were higher; we must be approaching our flight altitude of five hundred feet. According to the company's website, the balloon's designed maximum altitude was one thousand feet, but that would be on tether; with a light load, such as our current load, the balloon if set free might conceivably ascend to thousands of feet. By itself that wouldn't be a problem. The problem would be descending safely. A descending balloon loses buoyancy. The principle is straightforward: the further you descend, the denser the air, and as a result the more compressed the gas in the balloon. Practically, this means that the further you descend, the faster you descend. In order to reduce speed – in order to avoid hitting the ground like a rock – you reduce the balloon's load by throwing off ballast. Ballast is generally either sand or water.

But this was a tethered balloon. We would have no ballast.

Zainab threw her arm around me and gave me a hug. 'What a wonderful morning surprise,' she said.

'I'm glad you like it.'

'You know, you look terribly in your head.'

'I'm sorry. Old habits die hard – sometimes they even get resurrected, after death. Certain design features of this balloon interest me.'

'But you're enjoying yourself?'

'Very much.'

A tethered balloon's service life could be expressed in numbers of ascents. I did not recall seeing that, but I did recall reading the balloon's estimated lifespan in years, and the manufacturer's suggested number of daily ascents. Potential clients were informed that their purchase would last from four to five years, and they could expect to take customers up, if weather conditions were favourable, a maximum of ten times a day.

I did the maths. Fifty-two weeks in the year, times five years, times ten ascents a day, times six days a week, came to 15,600 ascent in five years.

Designers always factor in a safety margin. Suppose it were fifty per cent. That would indicate a service life of 23,400 ascents.

'Oh,' Zainab said, 'there goes the sun.' She was right. The stones of Angkor Wat had dimmed to dull grey, rising over the green treetops. Beyond them the scattered low cumulus I'd observed earlier had built significantly; they were still growing, the cloud tops ascending visibly and simultaneously combining, blotting out the sun.

How could I compare the balloon's designed service life with its actual life so far? I held the ascents schedule in my hand; I read it again, more carefully. If they followed the schedule strictly, they'd make twenty-three ascents a day. I hadn't noticed that before, perhaps because it was so improbable. Schedules were seldom strictly followed in Cambodia; we'd already been up nearly our allotted time, and hadn't yet started to descend. Let's settle on eighteen. They operated seven days a week. Looking at the fine print at the bottom of the flyer, I noticed a date: it had been printed six and a half years ago. So the balloon had probably been in service about six years.

Again, I did the maths: 39,312 ascents. It was such an enormous figure, I did the calculations again. The result was the same. I had to concentrate a little harder to figure out the percentage difference, but I've always been good with numbers.

The tethered balloon in which Zainab and I were flying had sixty-eight per cent more ascents and descents on its clock than its estimated designed service life – and that with a fifty per cent safety margin.

The gondola swayed sharply. I gripped the railing and again felt the rust under my fingers. I heard Zainab say, 'Whoa.' On the opposite side the Japanese were exclaiming in Japanese. Zainab asked me, 'Michael, what's going on?'

'Turbulence,' I replied.

'From where?'

I looked again at the building cumulus beyond Angkor. 'You see those clouds?'

'Yes.'

'They're creating an updraught – I expect a strong and growing updraught.' We faced the ruins. 'The air they're sucking up has to come from somewhere. Some of it's coming from behind us, hence the turbulence.'

'But we're safe, right?'

'Yes. I'm sure the balloon is rated for much stronger winds than this, on tether. But, to be on the safe side, they'll winch it down before it gets much worse.' I glanced at my watch. 'They're due to start winching us down now.' I looked over the rail, down to the winch housing. I saw no staff nearby. In fact, I didn't see a living soul.

The gondola began to rock, back and forth and side to side simultaneously. The effect was of a roughly circular motion at an increasing angle, with abrupt accelerations and decelerations in speed and direction. It was exactly the kind of movement associated with sea- and air-sickness. I noticed the Japanese gripping the railing hard.

It was the rust that worried me. There was an interesting case several years ago of an American jetplane losing a significant strip of its skin in flight. It simply peeled off at altitude. The pilot managed to land safely, but not before explosive decompression sucked a flight attendant out at twenty thousand feet. Investigation showed that corrosion caused the failure, despite the airframe being well within its service life. The plane had spent its entire life flying in and around the Hawaiian islands – a hot, humid, flying environment.

But not nearly as hot and humid as Angkor Wat.

We could be in a worse position than that jet aircraft. Not only had the balloon operated for its entire service life in a tropical environment – far away from the design team's environment in Germany – it was also almost seventy per cent over its design life, as far as I'd been able to estimate.

A weakened, because corroded, structure, which is also over-age and fatigued, can fail under stress.

The wind sang in the rigging. The balloon leaned under the strain, swaying and trying to right itself; the gondola swayed and leaned with the balloon. I tried to take in everything: the envelope, the netting, the net attachments to the load ring, the load ring's attachments to the gondola, the gondola structure itself and finally the tether attach point. Which part, or parts, were most likely to be weakened due to corrosion, to fail due to fatigue under stress?

The rigging had many attach points and therefore many places to spread the load. The tether had only one. The cable from the ground was anchored to the bottom of a vertical metal tube in the centre of the gondola. A hole pierced the top of the tube, through which ran a cylinder, which in turn rode within a U joint. What caught my eye was the cylinder's only anchor to the U joint.

A single cotter pin.

Over the wind and the gondola's creaks and groans, I heard our Khmer pilot yelling into his microphone. He stood half over his monitor, waving to the ground like a shipwreck victim to a passing vessel. I swung to the outer railing and peered down. One man stood by the winch; another ran towards him from the ticket hut. Five hundred feet had never looked so high; we seemed a long way from the ground.

'Shouldn't we be doing something?' Zainab asked me, shouting over the wind. 'Shouldn't we be trying to get back down?'

'Stay here,' I told her, 'and hang on. I'll see what the pilot's trying to do.'

I struggled to the pilot's station. He bent over the rail. I looked down beside him. Two men huddled over the winch. I grasped the pilot's shoulder and said, 'What's the problem?' He looked at me uncomprehending, panic-stricken. I repeated my question. He looked down, then back to me, and said, 'Winch stuck.'

That's when the gust hit, and the cotter pin snapped.

It was what meteorologists call a sustained gust. The gondola tilted further, the wind screaming in the rigging, every wire and rope stretched taut. Then a sharp clang as the lower half of that U joint hit the structure a glancing blow – on the joint's way down.

I was looking overboard when it happened. I just had time to see the steel tether descend in a coil, like a stretched spring let loose, before we all had to hang on for dear life as the balloon leapt towards the clouds.

The gondola's swinging lessened and the wind dropped. In a minute you could almost have held up a newspaper. I was too busy observing and trying to figure it out to realize the need for immediate action. I'd read of many free, untethered ascents. In the real world, this was my first.

Zainab approached from one end of the walkway, the Japanese from the other. Zainab reached me first. She said, 'Michael, what's happened?'

'We're off tether,' I told her. 'The cable snapped.'

'But there's no wind. It's gone calm.'

'The wind's still blowing. We're just moving with it. We're part of it now. Look.' I pointed down. The treetops below raced by – and were getting smaller. I looked towards the towers of Angkor. We rode the wind to them, but we were higher, further away. We were gaining altitude. At this rate, in a few minutes we'd be beyond the ruins and barely beneath the cloud base. Soon we'd be within the clouds.

'We've got to release helium, and fast.' The Japanese were trying to ask me something, but I didn't have time. The pilot was sunk into his chair, staring at his screen. I crouched down and stared at it with him.

It wasn't hard to figure out. A digital altimeter blinked by too fast to read; we were definitely going up. 'The valve,' I asked him, 'where's the control for the valve?'

He didn't respond.

I scanned the display and the controls. The controls for the valve were easy to identify; below were the controls for the rip panel. Those I didn't want to touch. Instead I threw the switch to activate and turned the knob to open the valve at the very top of the balloon. Immediately a light blinked red and a bar indicator jumped up to max. There was nothing else I could do. I gently pulled the pilot out of his seat, away from the controls.

We'd started with a lot of positive buoyancy, we were in an updraught, and we'd built up inertia. The altimeter began to slow, but we were still ascending. We passed fifteen hundred feet. I looked down. I could no longer identify the site of our ascent. We'd floated too far away. The ruins, however, were nearer – as was the line of cumulus. The clouds were still building.

Zainab tried to calm the Japanese – none too successfully. I sat at the controls and monitored the altimeter. Our rate of ascent continued to decline, and I started to slowly close the valve. My goal was to seal it when we'd reached the slightest level of negative buoyancy: when we'd just started to descend.

I think I came close, as close as I could, considering I had no experience of the balloon's flight characteristics, and we were in a pretty turbulent updraught. I had the valve closed tight shortly after the altimeter started to unwind, at just over two thousand feet.

I threw the switch to deactivate the valve and rejoined Zainab. The three Japanese stood by her along the walkway. I addressed everyone: 'We've started our descent – we're going down. We have no ballast, nothing to throw overboard, so we'll pick up speed as we descend. I expect we'll land pretty hard. Try to keep calm, and follow my instructions.'

The balloon rotated gently; I walked to the bow or the prow or the front or whatever you call that part of a circular gondola that represents the point of direct forward movement. I wanted to estimate our landing site. Zainab joined me. 'Isn't there any way we can slow it down?' she asked.

'No, I'm afraid not.'

'How hard do you think we'll land?'

'I don't know. I think hard. If we're lucky, we'll land in a moat – in the water – or in the trees. I hope we don't come down on any of the ruins. I don't want to land on solid stone.'

'Isn't there any way we can steer it?'

'Do you see propellers, an elevator, a rudder?' I took a breath. She was an intelligent woman. She just didn't know anything about aviation – or aeronautics. What percentage of the population does? 'I'm sorry,' I said. 'No, there's no way for us to steer. There's nothing we can do, except brace ourselves before landing.'

There wasn't much to say for the next couple of minutes. Two thousand feet, from the point of view of an ordinary aircraft, is quite low. From the point of view of a free balloon, accelerating as it descends, it's a significant altitude. It gives you distance to gain speed. Travelling with the wind, we were only aware of an occasional breeze, but as we got lower the trees sped by beneath, and it occurred to me that we had two things to worry about: our rate of descent, and our airspeed. It promised to be a rough landing.

We passed almost directly over the central temple complex of Angkor Wat, although I was too busy trying to estimate our landing site – or impact point – to admire the architecture. We flew over the temple grounds and approached the outer walls. We cleared them easily but now we were descending fast. Would we come down in the lake (a wide moat, crossed by a stone causeway), or on the bare ground of the opposite shore, or in the trees beyond?

In a few moments I had the answer. We'd just clear the lake and crash on the opposite shore. It was better than the ruins, but not much. I thought it probable that most of us would survive, maybe all of us. But we would all sustain injuries.

I turned to Zainab. 'I think we're going to hit just beyond the lake. This will be a violent crash, there's no other way to describe it. We have to figure out the best positions to take; we don't want to be thrown out.'

'Wouldn't it be safer to come down in those trees?'

'Yes, but we aren't going to get that far.'

'If you had enough ballast to throw, do you think you could reach them?'

'Maybe. We've got a lot of inertia built up. We'd have to throw it overboard immediately. But there's none.'

We could see our shadow racing across the lake's surface towards the shore. As it raced it grew larger. I said, 'We'd better tell the Japanese to brace.'

'How deep is the lake?'

I thought it a pointless question. 'I don't know.'

I turned to the other passengers and so I didn't see Zainab pull herself up by the rigging, and crouch insecurely on the top of the outer rail. The Japanese saw what she was doing before I did. They yelled and pointed and I turned around.

'Michael,' she said, and I thought for a moment, incredibly,

88

that she was laughing, 'here's your ballast: nine-and-a-half stone!' She sprang from the railing, up and out, her arms in the air and her legs together. She fell straight, feet first, her dress billowing up, covering her face and arms. As she fell her forward motion slowed; we all ran to the rear of the gondola to follow her down. Just before she hit, I thought: at least she can't see it coming.

She vanished in a splash of water, about two-thirds of the way across the lake.

We concentrated so hard on where she went in, trying to see her surface – any sign of life – that we didn't at first realize our rate of descent was slowing. We crossed the shore almost neutrally buoyant and just above the ground, but with a dangerously high airspeed.

A line of trees stood straight ahead, the advance wall of a thick jungle. I thought it the best outcome we could hope for; branches would slow us easier than just hitting the ground and would break our fall. Then an updraught from somewhere grabbed us. It was like being in an express lift. The walkway pressed into our feet and the ground fell away. We were going to clear the trees.

I yelled to the others to hang on as tight as they could, and ran to the panel. I scanned the controls. A treetop whipped by underneath. We didn't have time for the valve. I disengaged the rip panel's safety, and threw the switch.

Batteries set off two seam charges at the top of the balloon. An entire gore blew open. Gas rushed out. Our buoyancy disappeared in an instant. The lift's cables snapped: the trees rushed to meet us. I crouched down and wrapped my arms around as much of the structure as I could reach before we hit.

We cut a downward swath through the trees, the branches breaking our fall, slowing us down before the gondola hit the ground. I remember the sound of wood smashing all around, then something must have hit my head. I opened my eyes and looked up at bent metal, broken trees, crazy rigging and the envelope torn and flapping wildly in the wind.

It's common, after a smash-up like that, at first to be unaware of your injuries. But I could walk and as far as I could see I only had a few cuts. Two of the Japanese weren't so lucky: the fall threw them clear and they suffered broken bones. The third Japanese and the pilot escaped almost without a scratch. I left them to help the others and started scrambling my way through the forest, back to the shore.

The characteristic that made the forest a life-saver in which to land, its density, made it miserable to get through on foot. As I neared its edge I passed two Khmer rescuers beating their way in to the crash site. I urged them on and continued in the opposite direction. It started to rain lightly.

By the time I reached the shoreline it was a downpour.

The sheets of rain obscured the towers beyond. I scanned the lake but didn't see Zainab. Then I saw her head – she swam breaststroke – several yards out. I hailed her and waved my arms, and she rose to her waist and waved back.

I ran into the lake as she walked out; we met up to our knees. She held her arms up, triumphant. Her dress clung to her every curve. She looked like a sea nymph come from the sea and if she'd had any wind left she would have been laughing.

Instead she fell into my arms. I told her I couldn't believe she was in one piece, and after a minute she said, 'I came first in the high dive in the sixth form.' We both laughed at that. She asked about the others and I reassured her. Then she said, 'I'm all right, too, I know I am. But if the police find us we'll wind up in the local clinic with IVs in our arms. I'm certain of it. Do you think we could disappear?'

It went against my grain. Survivors of a crash don't just melt away. They volunteer information to the accident investigation team. But, I considered, what pertinent information could I give, that such a team wouldn't already have, or be able to find? And what kind of team would it be? It certainly wouldn't be the US Federal Aviation Administration and I knew the Cambodian government had nothing similar. Any team would most likely come from the balloon manufacturer.

They'd discover as much as I did, in less time, without any input from me.

'There wasn't a passenger manifest,' I said. I turned around. More people were arriving, some now with machetes, hacking their way in to the crash site. There was even a tuk-tuk nearby. 'Come on,' I told her, 'let's just go.'

In twenty-five minutes we stepped through the doorway of my room at La Lumière de l'Angkor. We'd stopped off at a little pharmacy nearby and bought a box of assorted Band-aids, and Zainab patched me up. She was in good shape, except for her neck: she'd suffered a slight whiplash upon hitting the water.

Neither my Band-aids nor her neck held us back. We made love passionately. We'd dried ourselves off from the rain and the lake when we came in, but soon her chocolate-coloured skin glistened with sweat. It was as if, having escaped death, we were celebrating life, being alive.

We rested during the afternoon and decided to eat dinner in; neither of us wanted to go back into town. We ate and had a couple of drinks in the hotel restaurant and bar. Halfway through the second drink the proprietor showed up, perhaps alerted by his staff that he had customers. He was a pale, slight Frenchman, a long-stay expat holding on to sobriety by his fingernails, and he bought us a third round. He told us there had been an accident with the tourist balloon, and two passengers were missing. There had been little embellishment to the story so far – maybe the bare facts were embellishment enough. We acted suitably astonished, and declined another drink.

I woke up in the middle of the night and she wasn't beside me; the door was open and I saw her smoking outside on the balcony. I joined her. It was so late even the fairy lights were turned off. We smoked in the dark in companionable silence. After a couple of minutes I heard her chuckle. I said, 'What's so funny?'

'In the future, when discussing development metrics, perhaps we should stick to politics and economics.'

I was about to object, to say that it was the fault of the climate. Then I remembered that aircraft maintenance is supposed to take climate into consideration, and my estimates, and how far the balloon might have exceeded its service life.

In the end I laughed too – at myself. 'At least,' I told her, 'it hasn't been boring.'

She smiled. 'No, not boring.' She smoked for a minute, then said, 'Do you know what I'd be doing, typically, on a Saturday afternoon – that is, if I didn't have some obligation?'

'No.'

'I'd probably be doing meditation practice.'

'Well, I hope you don't regret missing your practice.'

For a moment she didn't answer. Then, 'No, I don't. Not at all.'

The next morning we just wanted to spend the day in bed, but we both had an appointment to keep. After a late breakfast we took a tuk-tuk into town to the grounds of the German Clinic, where the Reform Party's rally was to take place.

This was Hun Prang's day, his moment in the spotlight. Everyone already knew the main points of his party's platform. He and his party's other candidates had stumped through villages, given television interviews and been the subject of magazine and newspaper articles. But today was his first major, pre-election rally, in the second most important city in the country – and probably with the most sophisticated electorate.

Prang and several other party members sat on a platform about five feet high under a colourful canopy. On one side stood tables covered with gifts – money, textiles, even soup – that the party would hand out to the audience after Prang's speech. Zainab and I kept our distance, standing behind some local worthies under another canopy a little away to the other side. She was a party consultant and I was there on official business, to write a report, but I wanted to keep a low profile. State Department regulations discourage American diplomats from appearing too close to foreign politicians during election contests. In any case I doubted Prang would want me on stage with him. This was strictly a Khmer event. He was campaigning against the sale of vast tracts of government land to foreigners, and, standing a foot taller than anyone nearby and looking American from head to toe, I was definitely a foreigner.

The rally began with a recording of the national anthem, followed by several minutes of chanting by a seated row of orange-robed monks. Then Prang rose from an ornately carved hardwood chair and took the microphone.

There was no teleprompter. Khmers expect a speech to be funny, dramatic, moving. I don't think they mind it being a little rambling, as long as it appears spontaneous. It also has to be fluent, and I wondered about Prang's Khmer. He'd been brought up in the States from childhood. Even if he spoke it at home, it was certain to be at least a little rusty. I was pretty sure that this crowd would be able to tell immediately if Prang was one of the lucky few who had spent the Khmer Rouge years abroad, or, like almost all of them, had spent it on some ill-run commune, where not starving was a victory.

Maybe due to the journey north (the drive can be exhaust-ing, even for a passenger) or maybe due to the heat, he'd managed to shed some of the western sleekness I'd noticed at the ambassador's Christmas party. He gave the impres-sion of a prosperous local, instead of a prosperous expatriate Cambodian-American. I glanced around at the Cambodian faces. They looked willing to give him the benefit of the doubt. When he started in on the meat of his platform the audience listened. One of his promises was that, if elected with a major-ity, his party would sign the UN Transparency Agreement. It's a mistake to underestimate the sophistication of a developing world urban audience – even of a very small town. The locals understood what he was talking about, what it meant. The pledge went down well in Siem Reap.

It was just after eleven, and Prang had been talking for about twenty minutes with the audience leaning into his speech, when the shots were fired. There were only three, in rapid succession, as if the assassin were as interested in escape as he was in murder, although there was subsequently some doubt as to whether murder or just chaos had been his intention. The shots all went wild. What the first two hit, if anything, no one discovered. The third ricocheted off an iron drainpipe on the wall of the German Clinic, then penetrated the skull of an eleven-year-old Khmer girl standing nearby.

That was the end of the rally. Pandemonium broke out. Prang's bodyguards hustled him off the stage. Most of the crowd ran for their lives. The police response, from the edge of the crowd, was ambiguous. Newspaper reports by eyewitnesses suggested that some of them allowed the assassin to escape by blocking his pursuers. I was an eyewitness myself, and stood a head taller than anyone else there, but all I could see or interpret was a confused crowd running in all directions, through and past a few bewildered-looking police.

I would never have noticed the wounded child – most of the crowd did not – if it hadn't been for Zainab. An observant woman, in the midst of the panic she zeroed in on the small corner of quiet.

We fought our way through to the family huddle; that's how you distinguished real trouble: the people who weren't yelling or screaming or rushing around. It was only a partial family unit, a boy and two young men squatted around an older sister holding the dying child. She was almost certainly beyond help, but the clinic was right there, and Zainab took charge, telling me to carry the girl inside. After so many years of UN tutelage, and an NGO on every street corner, many Cambodians, in an emergency, defer to the *Barang*. So I carried the girl as gently as I could up the front stairs and into the clinic. The staff took the child from my arms as soon as I walked in the door, laid her on a wheeled table and rushed her away down a hallway; this was what they'd expected, what they'd prepared for. Her family ran after her, but Zainab and I, schooled in western hospital etiquette, stayed behind, alone.

There was nothing there for us to do. Zainab was concerned about Prang, and it occurred to me that Noelle would expect my political report to be a little longer than originally planned, so we headed back out. But Prang was gone and the crowd dispersed. The local police milled around, filling in time. I'm sure they would rather have been enforcing traffic regulations on the airport road. At least there'd be the opportunity of obtaining bribes.

We took a tuk-tuk to Prang's hotel – a much fancier establishment than ours – and gained admittance to his room. He was excited, elated, a man without fear.

'Zainab,' he said, 'do you realize what this means? Free publicity! And excellent publicity! Is there any doubt that the Prime Minister is behind this? It's typical of his tactics. Cambodians were willing to look the other way when the economy was booming. But now . . . this will remind them of the bad old days – at least, it will remind the older Khmers. But even the young generation will be disgusted. We could not have asked for a better outcome!'

Neither of us mentioned the child in the clinic. In any case his Khmer coterie of fellow candidates, consultants and hangers-on grabbed his attention. We left and returned to the clinic, but the girl, as I expected, was dead. A nurse pointed out a few spots of blood on the right arm of my shirt. They weren't mine. The child hadn't bled much.

I think we were, without knowing it, on an adrenalin rush. But there was nowhere else to rush to. So we went back to our hotel. The clouds were building again but hadn't yet broken; the air was heavy, humid, charged. We went to my room and I pulled off my shirt. She came to me. The chemistry between us was electric.

We weren't just passionate, we were aggressive. We dominated in turns. At the end, I took her in what my grandfather might have called the Italian fashion, but even then she pushed against me, wanting me deeper.

It was too hot to lie entwined, so we dozed side by side on my bed through the long afternoon, with the rain pouring down outside. She awoke first, with a sense of playfulness, whispering in my ear, pretending to be me, expounding pompously on how totally safe were tethered balloon ascents. I couldn't help but laugh.

Before dinner we took a shower together in my bathroom. She didn't want to put on her soiled clothes and her suitcase was next door, so I lent her one of my shirts, and she darted in that across the balcony to her room. In three days she'd hardly used it.

After dressing I walked over. It was near dusk and she sat on her bed under the weak overhead light, looking at a wooden Buddha she'd brought with her. She said, 'There's a school of Tibetan Buddhism that holds that sex can actually help you achieve enlightenment.'

'Really?' I sat down next to her.

'Yes. However, I'm Theravada, not Tibetan.'

'You never know. Maybe the Tibetans have something. I'm feeling a little enlightened, right now.' I put my hand between her legs.

She shook her head. 'You have a long, long way to go.'

'Are you feeling close?'

'I've never been close. I just wonder how much further away I am.'

I was very ignorant. I asked her, 'Why do you think you're further away?'

'Adultery is not considered good practice – an example of correct living.'

I had nothing to say to that.

Maybe she wanted to reassure me, for after a moment she said, 'But I don't regret it.' Then she kissed me on the mouth.

We got up to go to dinner, again at the little hotel restaurant, but before we climbed down from the balcony, she asked me who I thought fired the shots and what they hoped to accomplish.

I said, 'The government can't be happy that Prang's promised to sign the UN Transparency Agreement. It's throwing their corruption in their face. Probably someone in the ruling party hired someone to break up the rally, to scare Prang. I don't know if these things have to go to the top, or not.'

'But a child was killed. Murdered.'

'An accident.'

'An accident caused by a political decision. A decision I initiated and pushed for. Successfully.'

I said, 'An accident caused by someone shooting a gun. Come on, let's eat.'

She made no reply and if I thought of it at all I assumed that we'd avoided going down the pointless road of guilt and blame.

The sun was nearly gone and someone had forgotten to turn on the fairy lights. We started down the stairs ducking and weaving to avoid the branches; the native trees and ornamental plants, so long unpruned, were out of control, engulfing the property. The grounds were reverting to jungle. We descended into deeper darkness, the trees, the shrubs, the vines, even the flowers obscuring the failing light.

PART TWO

6

Zainab asked me: 'Did it come from the top, the decision to send the gunman? Even if it was just to throw a scare, if the murder was accidental – did it come from the Prime Minister?'

This time I knew the answer, but I took a drag before answering. It was a month later and orchids and bougainvillaea again surrounded us, but tonight they posed not even a psychological threat: they'd been domesticated. They grew out of pots at eye level. Our eye level was low because we lay on a low bamboo platform on the terrace of our new apartment, on the third floor of a three-storey building half a block down from Martini's Bar.

Ornamental gardening at altitude was the American occupant's passion, but she was on a seven-month visit to the States, and Zainab had agreed to take care of the apartment and the terrace garden in her absence. It was convenient. The Khmer owners lived on the first floor with their extended family, and as far as we knew had no close or distant relatives associated with either the American or British Embassies. They kept themselves to themselves, as did we. The street was middle-class Khmer, ascendant in a questionable neighbourhood, with the bar on the corner. Westerners came to get drunk or get laid. A street that no one wants to admit visiting is bound to be discreet. We'd found, by accident, the perfect place in town to pursue our affair.

It was dusk, the time when the creatures of the night emerge, and a large bat flitted overhead, hanging first from one potted tree, then another. Perhaps it objected to the occasional cloud of smoke: we both had a cigarette and a glass of wine. We'd made love inside on the bed but the AC had failed with the electricity, and the heat outdoors where there might be a hint of a breeze was preferable to the heat within.

This was only our third time together after Siem Reap, but already we'd fallen into a pattern; or rather, I'd fallen in with hers. Upon meeting we'd make love, with few if any preliminaries. The discussion began afterwards. I was having an affair with a woman who was starved, not only of sex, but of sharing her ideas, her feelings, her doubts.

She asked me again, but without impatience, understanding that the heat, the night air heavy with scent, the nicotine and the wine and even the bats all conspired to slow one down: 'Do you think it went all the way to the top?'

'Yes,' I said, remembering that morning in Noelle's office. I'd asked her the same question. I'd just handed in the annual country report and the political report on the Siem Reap rally. The latter had gone through several revisions. Political reporting was not my forte and both Ann and Noelle had provided their input. Noelle told me to stick to the facts: 'Leave the speculation,' she said, 'to some analyst in DC.' So I had. But the final revision struck me as unsatisfactory. There was not a word as to a result, because it would have been pure speculation: would the people of Siem Reap, cowed by the violence, vote for the ruling party, or, inflamed by the attempt at intimidation, vote for Prang's alternative? But even important facts were missing (although I'd included the little girl's death): the gunman had escaped, and as yet he had neither an identity nor even an unequivocal motive: intimidation, or assassination? Was he acting alone, or was he the hireling of some low-level, or mid-level, party functionary – or did it come straight from the top?

Noelle stood, as before, looking out of her office's second-storey window, towards Wat Phnom. She answered directly, but didn't meet my eye, didn't even turn around. State Department body language, maybe, for keep it off the record. 'Yes,' she said, 'we can be reasonably certain it came straight from the top. The Prime Minister was originally installed by the Vietnamese. He learned politics from the communists, and he was their eager protégé. He's a believer in centralized control. Every important political decision comes from his office, every sensitive decision directly from him.' She turned to face me; perhaps we were back on the record. 'I'm afraid,' she said, 'that I'll have to ask you to keep an eye on the political situation. I don't expect you to make it your major activity – at least, not yet. I'll tell you, as far as I'm able, when I think something's coming up that you should observe and report on.'

'Why don't I just liaise with Ann?' As soon as it was out of my mouth I regretted having made the suggestion. It was a smart-alecky thing to say, and a breach of department etiquette. I would have apologized, but I was out of practice and the moment passed.

Noelle sat down at her desk. She said, 'I realize political reporting is an irritating extra duty. It's only because we're so short-staffed, and we're coming up to the elections. And of course, because you're unusually competent. Please continue to liaise directly with me. I'll try to keep my requests to a minimum. Now, how about Westin Oil?'

'I met Silk again last week, for an update on his negotiations. They're going nowhere.'

'Did he suggest anything we could do, to expedite the process?'

'He suggested that if we could convince the government that we – the embassy – speak for the company, the government might be more open to negotiation.'

'Anything else?'

'Yes. He thinks it's going to take a bribe.'

She sat back. 'That's distasteful. And illegal. However, it wouldn't be the first time. I expect you're aware of the Foreign Corrupt Practices Act?'

'Yes.'

'It's enforced, although not with regularity. You could be forgiven for assuming that when indictments do emerge from the Department of Justice, they do so because they managed to slip through, or under, the process.'

'Process?'

'The political process. The vetting process. The cost-benefit process.' She relaxed a little in her chair; her body language, always correct, took on a more friendly demeanour. 'This is only your second tour in the Service. I don't know how interested you were in foreign policy when you were on Wall Street.'

'We were mostly interested in exchange rates and interest rate differentials. We tried to stay out of markets where foreign policy could be a serious factor.'

'Of course. Well, for most of the Clinton presidency Saddam Hussein was supposed to sell oil only through a tightly regulated UN programme called Oil for Food. The purpose was to allow only humanitarian goods into the country – nothing that could be used for rearmament. Every major power, including ourselves, backed it one hundred per cent.

'As far as I'm aware, nearly everyone on the Gulf, and everyone involved either in intelligence or the oil industry, knew that western oil companies, major and minor, were paying bribes to Hussein for extra shipments of Iraqi crude. It was a completely open secret. I don't remember reading a single newspaper article about it during that time. Perhaps it wasn't considered newsworthy.

'It all exploded after the Second Gulf War. It became a handy bat for the Republican administration to use to beat up the UN. Everyone in the government expressed surprise and indignation. How could this have gone on? In the end, I think one American businessman was indicted for bribery. That was it.'

Noelle stared down at her desk. She blinked and re-entered the present. 'I'm sorry,' she said. 'I must sound cynical. All I meant is, the Foreign Corrupt Practices Act is not enforced consistently. Now, did Silk give you any definite suggestions?'

'No.'

'Then this is what I want you to do. Tell Silk to get you a copy of a contract that Westin can live with. Tell him also to give you a simplified explanation of the contract, in both English and Khmer. Put together a presentation, then make an appointment with the Deputy Minister.'

'The Deputy Minister?'

'Yes. His name's Sok. The Minister of Oil's in hospital. Sok's his stand-in. See how far you get. Here's a couple of selling points: intimate to him – don't tell him directly, just intimate – that the Prime Minister could add the UN Transparency Agreement to his platform.'

'You mean, adopt part of the Reform Party's platform.'

'You don't have to spell it out. He'll get it. I suppose you've heard the latest?'

'What latest?'

'In this morning's *Post*. Reform's going to insist on outside auditors for the agreement. An excellent idea. Tell him we'd be happy to help his government implement the agreement. The Chinese won't, they wouldn't know how to begin. He'll get the quid pro quo.'

'And if he intimates that he needs a bribe?'

'Then walk away from it, Michael. Be polite, but walk away. Of course, Silk will be interested. He'll want a full report.'

'Will you?'

'Yes. Give me your draft. I may want to edit it a little. Then we can both sign it, and send it up to the ambassador, and to Washington.'

Up to Washington, up the chain of command . . . an ascent to the higher regions, like a note going up a scale, one step, one key, after another. I could hear it, it halted on a trill – I hadn't even known what a trill was, until Zainab showed me . . .

. . . I opened my eyes. Night had fallen, but light came from what we'd dubbed the music room, an unused bedroom off the living room, into which Zainab (with the help of five Khmer labourers) had shoe-horned an upright piano. I could hear her playing and nowadays I even recognized the piece, the canon at the fifth in contrary motion, the fifteenth variation of the Goldberg.

I waited until she finished, then got up off the mat and walked in. The apartment was full of heavy, dark, ornate furniture. The usual American occupant was sympathetic towards eastern philosophy, and light from the music room glinted off the smooth surface of a Buddha on a plinth in the corner.

Zainab wanted to play one more piece and said she'd join me after, so I went back to our bedroom which had cooled almost to the temperature of the night air. Ambler was out of town, spending the night in Kokong, so we had our first full night together in Phnom Penh. I lay alone on the borrowed sheets on the borrowed bed and thought: at least it's not their bed – or even mine. I was sleeping with Ambler's wife but I wasn't insulting his house, and my own was still sacrosanct. But I missed her and I was happy when she came to bed, wearing only a slip. She was a professional woman of her generation and worked out regularly; she had long legs and arms, muscular but still womanly, with an African's fullness of figure. As she climbed in over me I thought: a black British solicitor, TV presenter, journalist, now transparency consultant – and beautiful to boot. She was as dissimilar as possible from the professional women I'd met on Wall Street. They generally fell into two types: technical specialists like myself, who were even more technically proficient than me and even narrower in interests, or saleswomen – brokers and so on – determined to outsell and out-male their male colleagues. Maybe that's a little rough, but a decade on Wall Street had left me with few happy memories of romance.

I'm not completely unaware, unself-critical, and I knew my lack of success in love had to be partly my fault. I asked Zainab, as she hovered over my chest, 'What do you see in me? Why are you here?'

She said, 'I've always been attracted to serial savers.'

'Serial savers?'

'You've been saving me, serially, one save after another,

ever since we've known each other. I find it an attractive feature.'

She had a British sense of humour, and it sometimes took me a while to figure out when she was joking. 'Seriously,' I said, 'one: I'm American. I know what that means to you Brits. Two: I'm not even remotely cultivated the way you are – your music, all that. Three: I'm just a duty-oriented civil servant overseas; I'm not into reforming Cambodian politics. I'd be happy to help, of course, if it turns out to be part of my job, but I'm not about to resign a pensionable third career and become Prang's clean election – or whatever – consultant. Finally, I'm not and never have been a spiritual type. I'm not into Buddhism, Christianity, Judaism or any other "ism". So, why me?'

She said, 'I admire men who are redeeming themselves.'

'What on earth do you mean?'

'You spent ten years getting rich on Wall Street, thinking only of yourself and your bank balance – '

'Wait a second. I was a technical analyst, not a broker. I may have had a few lapses of judgement, but I'm not responsible for the financial meltdown. And I put all my own money in super-secure, blue-chip insurance and bank stocks. In other words, I'm now broke. When I retire I'll be almost completely dependent on my State Department pension.'

'As I said, you were thinking only of yourself and your bank balance. Then, you started thinking of others. Of how you might spend the rest of your working life in service to your country.'

There was just enough – barely enough – truth to it to keep me from objecting.

'And,' she said, 'I felt the first time I saw you, that I could trust you. And you've proved it.'

'In that case . . .' I started to pull her slip up, over her hips. But she wasn't finished.

'Wait. Remember what you said, earlier, about Siem Reap, that it had to come from the top?'

'Yes.'

'Then that must mean the Prime Minister feels threatened.'

'By what?'

'By the Reform Party winning.'

'Zainab, at the most, they'll win a few votes. They won't threaten the regime.'

'Then by being shown up as corrupt.'

'That's hardly news to anyone.'

'Then by being pushed. Pushed to clean up the government's act, to sign the Transparency Agreement.'

She knew nothing, yet, of my activities with Westin, and I wanted to keep it that way.

'We have to keep up the pressure. To go on the attack. We have to make some sense of that little girl's death.'

'You'll never make sense out of that.'

I'd never before known a woman who got sexually turned on by politics. She lowered herself on to me and said, 'We can't do it their way, with bullets; we'll do it the Buddhist way. By pressuring them on to the right path.'

'How?'

'We'll appeal to their self-interest.'

I was tired of the subject: it was like being in bed with a business competitor. One selling a more enlightened product. 'You could appeal to mine,' I said.

'How disgusting.' But her lips smiled as they skated across my mouth before slowly heading elsewhere, and I was able to forget work and Prang and conflict, and just enjoy being with her the whole night through.

A few days later I was sitting in an overstuffed chair with a high winged back at a table in a remote corner of the foyer of Raffles Hotel. It was the most up-market hotel in town and had the best bar. It was also the most expensive. Not that I was drinking. The Deputy Minister had asked me to meet him here because his own office was being repainted. I looked around at the thick carpets, the ornate furniture, the sturdy columns, the expensive-looking paintings on the walls. No matter how fancy the Deputy Minister's office, I doubted it looked as good as the foyer of Raffles. It was of course a British institution, and I observed with interest a British couple, guests of the hotel, who belonged to a type of upper-crust Brit almost unchanged in appearance or manner for at least fifty years, and which, incredibly, Britain still produces. Her dress and his suit were so formal, out of date, colonial, they could have been costume, but both wore them as easily as if they were a second skin. When speaking to Khmer staff (I overheard them twice while waiting), they were correctly courteous and polite, but not even faintly friendly. Their accents were classy and educated, the type that any American or other English-speaking foreigner can understand at once, but which the BBC, for reasons of political correctness, will now only allow on the air if issuing from the mouth of an English man or woman of colour – such as Zainab, for instance.

If I was critical it was partly because it had already been a long day, and I was not feeling well. In the mid-morning I'd driven to the airport to pick up a new embassy staff member, Noelle's new secretary. But the plane was delayed. I was hungry, and the most familiar-looking thing to eat was a bright pink hot dog sold at a hot dog stand outside the airport restaurant. It was a recognizable hot dog with a recognizable bun and a familiar jar of mustard. The stand looked clean enough. I was in the mood for some comfort food. I bought and ate one.

Two hours later, waiting for the Deputy Minister at Raffles, I felt the first stirrings inside. Cambodia was a clean posting and I was very seldom ill; if it was to happen now, the timing could not have been worse.

I was just wondering if I had time for a preliminary run to the Raffles bathroom when the Deputy Minister, Mr Sok, appeared. I stood and introduced myself. We sat down.

Picking Raffles at short notice meant that the formal presentation I'd put together was out; however, I'd printed the slides, with notes, and bound them quickly in a folder. That, and the material that Noelle had told me to obtain from Silk was what I had to offer.

I figured the Deputy Minister was a busy man, but this was Cambodia so I asked him if he wanted a drink. He declined. His demeanour was pleasant but businesslike. I'd researched him. He was about ten years older than Prang, but like him had left the country for the States just before the Khmer Rouge moved into Phnom Penh. He'd stayed in the States, like Prang getting a good education and becoming an American citizen. But he'd returned earlier, as soon as the UN took the administration of Cambodia over from Vietnam. Sok and Prang were on opposite ends of the political spectrum. Prang was on the outside trying to get in, using reform as his platform. Sok was on the inside, and I was sure he intended to stay there, using any means he had.

I had my opening spiel all figured out and rehearsed. He listened politely. I handed him my papers, explaining the most important points. I pointed out that Westin's revised contract actually presented more favourable terms to his government than the original Letter of Intent. He continued to listen politely. Finally, I told him that, as soon as his government signed the contract – even before the elections – the embassy would publicly offer to help them implement the UN Transparency Agreement.

My bowels by this time were churning. It's possible that I rushed the presentation.

He thanked me and said that he would make sure that all the points I had made were passed on to the Prime Minister. Then he said, 'Mr Smith, I appreciate your embassy's offer of help with the Transparency Agreement. An announcement will be made soon, but I can tell you, in confidence, that the Prime Minister is seriously considering becoming a party to the agreement.'

'Really?'

He smiled. 'Yes. Our party is determined to stamp out corruption where it exists, and where it does not yet exist, prevent it from occurring.'

This high-flown sentiment, coupled with the surprising suggestion that the government might actually sign on to the

UN agreement, had an unfortunate relaxing effect. A sudden rush seized my bowels; my sphincter tightened.

I croaked: 'That's admirable.'

'Thank you.'

I couldn't resist adding, 'I understand that at least one of the competing parties has already promised to sign it.'

'Yes. Mr Prang's party. I think you know him.'

'I've met him.'

'Do not overestimate the conflict between Mr Prang and the Prime Minister. Their ideological differences are exaggerated. Both are pragmatists. You may even see him in the next government. In a minority, junior role, of course. We have no wish to leave Mr Prang out in the cold. But we will win the election on our platform, not his.

'This oil business, Mr Smith, is just that: business. It has nothing to do with party politics. You know, just last week I was talking to the Chinese Ambassador about these contracts. Have you met her?'

The foyer of Raffles was well air-conditioned, but I could feel the perspiration on my forehead. Wiping it with a paper napkin would only draw attention. I needed to act cool. 'No,' I said, 'I'm afraid not. Not yet.'

'A remarkable woman. She speaks Khmer better than I do! Her English, also, is excellent. It is very straightforward, dealing with the Chinese. Am I to understand from this meeting that from now on I am to deal directly with you, or with your ambassador, instead of with Westin's executives?'

'I wouldn't say that, no. My role today is that of an interested, and I hope helpful, intermediary.'

He picked up the folder. 'You'll have to excuse me, Mr Smith. I'm afraid I'm already late for my next meeting. Please tell Mr Silk that the Chinese are being extremely generous. They, too, are sweetening their offer; their new terms are similar to yours. But they are also offering to help underwrite a project dear to the Prime Minister's heart. You've probably heard of it: the proposed new bridge over the Tonlé Sap.'

'I had not.'

'It is a major project. We have barely entered the design phase.'

'May I ask how much the Chinese have pledged?'

'Of course. So far, they have pledged forty million US.' He paused. His eyes appeared fixed, for some reason, on my chest. A little off-centre, perhaps on my lapel.

I looked down. There was nothing there but my lapel pin, a small, even tiny, brass American flag.

He said, 'Is it State Department policy for diplomats to wear those?'

'No, it's not.'

'Are you concerned there may be some doubt about your nationality?'

'No.'

'In Phnom Penh an American wearing an American flag on his lapel is usually a professional salesman. I see them in my office. They are selling various investments, and often real estate in more developed, but remote countries, such as Switzerland. You, however – I hope you do not mind me saying this, Mr Smith – you do not strike me as a professional salesman.'

'I'm not. I'm an economic analyst. I'm just filling in for our commercial officer; we're short-manned at the moment.'

'Then why the flag?'

I had to think for a moment. 'I guess because I started my career in the US Air Force. Foreign Service officers don't have a uniform, we aren't a uniformed service. But it is a service. I suppose I wear this little flag out of respect.'

The Cambodian-American Deputy Minister nodded. He said, 'I understand. I never served in the military, but I am an American, too.' He let the folder fall open in his hand and glanced at a couple of pages. 'I have no desire to see Westin Oil lose their concession. The Chinese advantages are primarily on the business side; Westin's advantages are technical. And it need not be a zero-sum game. Westin could keep its current block, which in any case is the most challenging, technically; the Chinese could keep theirs.' He leaned over the table towards me. 'If Westin could just make it a little easier for us.'

'How?'

'First, by matching, preferably by raising, the Chinese contribution to the bridge project.'

I said carefully, 'I'll pass that along.'

'Second, the American Justice Department does not always operate . . . transparently.' He smiled. 'Yes, it is an expression often flung at us, used to describe our failings: a "lack of transparency". But it also describes the enforcement of the Foreign Corrupt Practices Act. Who knows if a contribution by Westin to the bridge project would even be on the department's radar? Or if it is, how it would be construed? Compatible, or incompatible, with the Act? Think of the publicity. Westin could be indicted. I might be named. Even the Prime Minister.

'If the embassy could give us some assurance – a formal, written assurance – from the ambassador to the Prime Minister, that, along with a contribution to the bridge project, would go a long way to helping Westin's application.'

I wasn't sure how to reply. Finally I just nodded, and said I'd pass that along, too.

'Good. Goodbye, Mr Smith. It has been a pleasure.'

I stood and shook his hand. I waited, still standing – I'm afraid slightly bent over – until he'd passed behind a pillar, before I headed stiffly but with controlled haste towards the Raffles' Gents. I made it just in time. Seldom have I voided explosive diarrhoea in such marbled luxury.

Afterwards I crossed the hallway to the long bar. In the middle of a weekday the place was almost empty. I took a stool at the bar and ordered a Coke. I felt the need to rehydrate. I took a sip and swivelled around – and spied Ann at a corner table, facing me. She was with a companion, another woman, whom I didn't recognize from her back alone.

It was pleasant, after the Deputy Minister, the suggested bribe, and the diarrhoea, to lay eyes on a colleague as cleancut, as squeaky-clean as Ann. For some reason, working for the Agency made her seem even cleaner. You couldn't doubt her sense of mission: whatever she did, it wasn't for personal gain, it was for the greater good of the country, the country's security and foreign policy goals. Just looking at her cheered me up. I raised my glass in a salute, and caught her eye, and stepped off the stool, but to my surprise she shot me a cold glance, as if to say, 'Stay where you are.' She appeared to excuse herself, got up and walked towards me.

I said, 'I hope I'm not disturbing you.' It finally occurred to me that the woman at the table might be one of her agents.

'It's bad timing but not a disaster. Concentrate on me and just ignore her. What are you doing here in the middle of the day, anyway?'

'A meeting with the Deputy Minister. The Westin Oil contract.'

'Right. Sorry about that.'

It was really her job, but she sounded and looked sincerely apologetic. I said, 'Don't worry about it. We're on the same team.'

She looked at her companion. 'Yes,' she said, 'but I'm not sure we're playing the same game.' She turned back to me. 'I'm sorry the file was such a mess. You know, it was originally a British concession. You should talk to Ambler.'

I'd forgotten about the old British connection. 'I'll give him a call.'

'Talk to his wife while you're at it.'

'His wife?'

'She's making enemies.'

I just stared at her. She'd floored me. How much did she know? I said, 'She can make all the enemies she wants. She's the British Second Secretary's wife.'

'This isn't the States or the UK. Just tell her to be careful. I'll see you later.'

She returned to her agent and I stepped out into the dense humidity of the early afternoon. I stole a look back before the door closed. I couldn't be sure but I thought I glimpsed Deria, the New York stringer, at the corner table.

Outside, heavy clouds already pressed down. I thought with a sense of oppression what disagreeable characters we both had to deal with: Ann with the local expat hustler, and me with the Deputy Minister on the take. We both worked for the US government, for the good of the country, but we would have had a better class of client with AIG or Lehman Brothers.

My oppression did not lift when I thought of Ambler. I had to talk to him about oil. Why not tomorrow – Saturday? I was picking up Zainab after lunch; we were spending the afternoon together, supposedly on a tour of Wat Lanka. I could fit in her husband before we left. My spirits began to lift. I didn't mind seeing him as long as it was on business.

I pulled out of the hotel driveway as the first raindrops hit the windscreen, my spirits still rising, almost as if I had some reason to expect, against all experience, that the rain would actually cool things down.

7

'It was only a few years ago,' Ambler told me, 'but in those days there was no oil ministry. They didn't have one yet. For that kind of negotiation you went straight to the top. The Prime Minister wasn't yet nuts; he wasn't an isolated megalomaniac. But he was already greedy.'

Ambler sat opposite me in the same room in which we'd first met: his bedroom. The folding Chinese screen behind him hid the matrimonial bed. His leg hadn't yet healed completely and although he was ambulatory – the cast was gone, replaced by a tensor bandage – he still used a cane. During the week he worked normally but the effort exhausted him. Directly after our interview he was going to take a nap.

He'd started off by telling me he couldn't just slip me the file: against regs. But he'd give me a summary.

'Our previous ambassador,' he said, 'was a man with scruples. That's rarer than you think in Her Majesty's Foreign Service. Since Thatcher we've paid off whoever we had to pay to get contracts. That's why we have less prestige, in countries like this, than the Yanks. That's why the English spend more jail time for the same infractions in Asia, Africa, the Middle East.'

'I don't understand.'

'If I ask you for a bribe, and you pay me, and make it clear – oh, so subtly – when you pay me, that you've lowered yourself, then you lose my respect.

'The Prime Minister wanted five million US dollars. It was supposed to be for a charity he patronized, but of course that was a front. Five million for that concession was a joke – the

Prime Minister didn't know any better. It's not surprising. He started out as a Khmer Rouge functionary, then deserted to the Vietnamese communists. In those days he didn't have experience with multinational corporations. All that came later, with capitalism and democracy and dealing with the west. Even then it took a few years to get used to the money. Five million would have seemed a lot.

'Maybe the ambassador should have taken the Prime Minister's offer. Whitehall would have been pleased. But he was a very old-fashioned man; this was his last assignment before retirement, and the story is that he told the interpreter to tell the Prime Minister that he could put his request for five million where the monkey put the nuts.'

Ambler chuckled. I chuckled along with him. But I'd learned nothing new.

Probably Ambler was telling me everything he thought could be of use; maybe everything, period. But there might be more. A confidence on my part could recall a detail to his mind; his take on the deal might prove useful. I said, 'Can I speak confidentially?'

His eyebrows rose to a prim altitude and he said archly, 'No need to ask, old boy. Special relationship, you know.'

I thought, what patience it would take, to live with him. I said, 'The amount's gone up considerably.'

'Yes?'

'The Deputy Minister told me that the Chinese have offered him forty million US. Ostensibly a contribution for a project: a new bridge across the Tonlé Sap.'

'Forty million is still small beer. The Chinese are trying to low-ball it.'

'That's not all. The government's taking a leaf from the opposition's book: it's signing the UN Transparency Agreement. But here's the kicker: he practically assured me that Westin could keep its block, if they bettered the Chinese offer and, somehow, got the US to give the government immunity against prosecution under the FCPA.'

Ambler reached over and poured from his antique shaker a

little more gin and tonic. Then he said, 'It's probably ignorance that gives them their nerve. It's a kind of innocence. The
opposition's upped the ante, and they've had to respond. I'd
call it the snowball effect if it weren't an absurd simile in this
climate.

'The UN agreement means they'll be under pressure to
get cleaner with the oil revenue. Probably you've heard that
Reform has promised to hire outside auditors. If they go along
with that the opportunity for rake-offs will decrease. So they
want more money up front – it's still cheap at the price. As for
immunity . . . they have cause to be a little worried about the
Americans. It's rare, but every now and then some crusader in
the Justice Department does actually bring a case. There was
Chevron in Nigeria. I'm certain the Prime Minister would
rather go with the Chinese than get involved with that.'

He pulled gently on the top of his tensor bandage and made
a face. He said, 'But no matter what UN agreement they sign,
life's getting harder for them. Has Zainab told you her latest?'

'No.'

'Land appropriations. Last year she wrote a couple of articles
for her little NGO. They were only published on their website,
which is not exactly inundated with hits. The topics were land
grabs and the Prime Minister's collusion with shady business
figures – by no means just Asian. He's sold government land to
Russians, Europeans, even British "consortiums". She named
names. Now the *New York Times* has picked them up. Just in
time to peel votes off the ruling party.'

Ann was right: talking to Ambler had been moderately
worthwhile. He'd confirmed my take on the oil deal, and
brought me up to date on Zainab's latest efforts. But there was
something about him, other than his feebleness, that irritated
me. Maybe it was the amusement he gained in knocking his
own country in front of a foreigner – me. He sat there smiling
with a tall drink in his hand, more ironic than proud, an uninvolved man. Uninvolved in business, uninvolved in politics,
uninvolved in his marriage. I said, 'I want to thank you for
your take on all this. I appreciate it.'

'Not at all. My pleasure.' The room had darkened a little while we'd talked. 'It may start raining soon. You and Zainab had better get started on that tour of Wat Lanka.'

The temple complex was less than a mile away, just on the corner of Norodom and Sihanouk, but the threat of rain was real, so we took my car.

I hadn't realized, when agreeing with Zainab's idea of a 'quick tour, then your place', that she'd meant a real tour. We even took Sovan along as an interpreter. She sat in the back as I drove. Now and then I glanced at her in the rear-view mirror. She belonged to the class of Khmers (the vast majority), who do not and will not ever drive or own a car, and she was as taut as a spring with delight and excitement. It was a pleasure to see her, to see what pleasure a little drive in a car could give.

I parked across the street from the temple, in front of the restaurant where I often ate breakfast before heading to work. It was British-owned; the spelling of its sign was British: Flavours. I knew the menu by heart and the waitresses by sight: all Cambodian. Now two of them struggled and laughed, erecting the awning over the terrace. Across the street, along the temple wall, the newspaper vendors were putting up their awnings as well. You could smell the approaching rain in the air. An old lady not much higher than my waist appeared, as they often did, out of nowhere, and held out her hand with a quiet smile. She was giving me an opportunity to earn karma, and I handed her a few thousand crumbled riels – perhaps a dollar. She nodded and moved away, and I caught Sovan looking at me with the curious, inward look you sometimes catch on Khmer faces when they're critically observing the *Barang*.

The double gate leading to the temple's rear entrance stood open and as we started across the street a ragged column of police cars and motorcycles appeared around the corner. They pulled up in a cloud of fumes. The police exited their cars and climbed from their motorcycles without urgency, as if they'd arrived at a picnic, but they were on a job and around every man's waist hung a holster and revolver. Neither as an American nor as a diplomat did I want to get involved in police action. Sovan pressed against Zainab's arm; I gently took Zainab's other arm and the three of us turned and walked back at a normal pace until we reached the terrace of Flavours. We sat down, facing the scene. I ordered fresh-squeezed juice for everyone, and lit a cigarette.

Two officers who must have been in charge walked into the temple complex; the others stood around, joked among themselves and adjusted their uniforms. Cambodian police do not as a rule look threatening. They don't have to. The relationship between the police and the populace in the developed west is governed by detailed, written rules; in the Third World the rules are unwritten. Their authority is unquestioned, but they must still exist in society. They can do more or less what they want as long as they discriminate.

None of us knew why the police were there or what was going on. Few if any of the men in front of us would know much English. Not one American at my embassy, including myself, spoke more than a few words or phrases of Khmer. Zainab probably knew less than me: she worked for a western transparency NGO on contract to a political party headed by a Cambodian who spoke better English than Khmer. Sovan belonged to the generation and class of Cambodian that instinctively steers clear of any involvement with the police, the authorities. It was one of those moments when you realize you really are in a foreign country. In it, but out of it.

Our ignorance didn't last long. Sovan turned to Zainab, said simply, 'I find out,' and approached the closest cop. He looked down at her as she spoke to him; at one point she gestured to us. He threw us a passing glance. His manner was non-threatening, almost avuncular. She returned. Her English was such that Zainab had to ask several questions to clarify her meaning, but we finally got the message.

It was all about Burma. The military junta in Rangoon, reacting to political demonstrations, had imprisoned several prominent monks. The monks at Wat Lanka planned a public demonstration demanding the freedom of their Burmese colleagues. This was not as unobjectionable as it sounded, for Cambodia has friendly official relations with Burma. The police were there to make sure the demonstration did not take place.

I didn't think there'd be any trouble. From what I understood, in Cambodia the government had the clergy under control. I asked Zainab, 'Have you heard of any of this?'

'Everyone's heard of the demonstrations in Rangoon, and the government crackdown.'

'I hadn't.'

'Well, you're an economist. But I hadn't heard of a demonstration here.'

Zainab asked Sovan if she thought it would be okay to enter the wat. She replied, 'You *Barang*, it okay.'

So we crossed the street, nodding to the police, and passed through the open double gates.

We walked into a flagstone-paved courtyard. It was empty. At the courtyard's far end stood the temple crematorium, a hulking iron oven surmounted by a chimney as high as a pagoda. A breeze blew through and scattered scraps of paper and dust over the flagstones, bare save for a naked, wood-frame bier – the white cloth gone, the mourners departed, the straw baskets of offerings taken away. The oven's iron doors were shut. Grey smoke trailed from the chimney.

This was Cambodian territory: Sovan took Zainab's hand and the three of us started down the temple complex's main street.

The wat was like a miniature town, or miniature, model village; it could, I thought, also be likened to a developing world army or air base, minus the open space required for drill. Here no open space existed; every square foot was occupied by something practical: school buildings secular and divine (the wat helped educate the poor of the neighbourhood, as well as monks from childhood to adult); dormitories, guest houses and dining rooms; administrative offices, libraries and storerooms. Although one can hardly walk a block in Phnom Penh without seeing a group of yellow-robed monks, or a monk hitching a ride on a motorcycle, we did not see one on the main streets of Wat Lanka. But we heard them. They were all inside, working, eating, studying, chanting. It was a hive of activity. Sovan led us down the streets, pointing out each building and telling us its function. Over many a door hung a painted sign; Sovan told us with pride that the signs were written in Pali, the language of the Buddha, and she could even read them; what little formal education she had, she'd gained at her village's Pagoda school.

At one point we came across a line of stupas – towers twenty feet high that house the ashes of the dead – and I saw dozens of strips of paper tied on each, and on each strip of paper a streamer of gaily coloured fabric. It looked like some kind of primitive adornment. I asked Sovan what they meant. She told me that on each paper was written the name of a deceased (I looked closer and, sure enough, saw the Khmer lettering). I said, 'And the strips of cloth: what do they mean, what are they for?'

Sometimes she had a curious, almost deadpan way of speaking. She said, 'They are clothes for the soul in the next world. Some people believe that.'

Her tone suggested it was a piece of superstition too far even for her, a Cambodian Buddhist to her bone marrow, to swallow. I cast an amused glance at Zainab. But she met my eyes seriously and said, as if correcting the sceptic: 'It's like architecture or ritual, Michael. Every faith, every belief system, has its architecture, its art, its rituals – I'm not sure which exact category these strips of cloth belong to, but they're one of the little things that help and console. In a small way, they support faith.'

We continued our tour. Sovan led us ever inward, moving towards the temple. In a corner behind the temple's concrete foundation, on a street almost submerged under standing water and mounds of wet sand and concrete blocks, stood the oldest building we'd seen, a wooden two-storey house, complete with balcony and high, unglazed windows. Nearly all the buildings so far (save for the temple itself) were modern, sterile, functional. But this little home was old, perhaps ancient; its design suggested a pre-French, pre-colonial period. It looked human, comfortable. You could imagine yourself at some distant period happy to be living there. But it was falling down. The wooden walls were grey with age, crumbling; jagged gaps in the roof exposed the rafters; half the balcony's balustrade had disappeared.

Nevertheless its appeal held us. Unlike the other buildings this was silent. Its silence bred silence in us; we crept along one side, observing, peeking surreptitiously into a dark window, trying to imagine ourselves within.

Then, just before rounding the back, through an open lat-ticework of boards all askew, the three of us surprised a young monk bathing.

Monks are ubiquitous in Phnom Penh. One sees them everywhere, every day. They are a uniformed order with rigorous grooming standards and are always dressed in their yellow robes, and are always clean-shaven, with shaven skulls. Other than head, face and neck, and perhaps a hand and foot, a monk is yellow fabric. Cotton, I believe.

Perhaps for this reason the sight of a young naked man – a monk – evoked in us all not just surprise and embarrassment, but also curiosity. We froze. We held our breath. We stared. He looked about twenty-five years old and was tall for a Khmer. He was lean and muscular. His back was towards us as he emptied a plastic bowl of water over his head. He had wide shoulders and a narrow waist, strong legs and prominent, muscular buttocks. I cast sidelong glances at the two women beside me. They stood entranced.

I don't think we made a sound but the young man picked up on something; he turned his head in our direction and, as one, we stepped backwards and back around the wall, silent as mice.

None of us said a word as we walked away, Sovan leading us again up to the front of the main temple. She was much shorter than Zainab or me, but she walked briskly – she was a farm girl from the provinces – and soon she was away ahead. I asked Zainab, 'I'm right, aren't I, in thinking that these monks are all celibate?'

'Yes. They're supposed to be, and I believe they nearly all are.'

'The monk back there looked a pretty virile specimen.'

She said nothing.

'I wonder,' I continued, 'how someone that age can sign on to it? Is it really necessary? To reach whatever level of spirituality they're trying to attain?'

'The Buddha taught that celibacy is not necessary to attain insight, spirituality. But monks are supposed to be trying for a higher level of insight than I, for instance, can reasonably hope for. They have a higher goal.'

'So celibacy is necessary.'

'For them it is. They're trying to break out of the cycle of desire leading to suffering leading to rebirth. I'm making this as simple as I can for you, Michael; if it sounds over-simplified, it is. If they can eliminate desire – in the scriptures, it's usually translated as "craving" – then they're going to be further along the road.'

'So sex is a hindrance.'

'Yes. Even love – romantic love – is supposed to be a hindrance, at that point.'

'That's a lot of renunciation. I'm glad you haven't yet reached that point.'

'I haven't reached any point, Michael. I'm going backwards, not forwards.'

She said it sadly, looking down at the steps we were ascending, climbing up the platform on which the temple stood. She was speaking of herself, not of me, but we were in a relationship together, in an affair. Her remark stung me like a criticism. She was going backwards because of me, because of her attraction to me, because of mine to her; because we'd given in to it – how low did the bottom line go? How low did I go, had I gone? I looked up. At the top of the stairs little Lim

Sovan looked down at us, smiling her slightly equivocal smile. She had her hands on her hips, like a miniature, Cambodian female version of Gary Cooper in the last scene of Ayn Rand's *The Fountainhead*, the master architect looking down from his morally elevated perch of self-realization (as an economics grad student I'd been exposed to some of the sillier pop psychology behind American capitalism). The movie scene was absurd and although I couldn't accuse Sovan of pretensions to moral elevation, I could certainly accuse Buddhism. I didn't believe the souls of the dead needed fragments of cloth to hide their nakedness and I didn't believe in spirituality through renunciation. I resented the suggestion that I was an enabler for Zainab's spiritual aridity and I didn't want any part of anyone's guilt – hers or mine.

In silence we joined Sovan. She led us up the final flight of steps to the high, open doors of the temple of Wat Lanka.

A Buddhist temple is a place for meditation. That's its function. Wat Lanka is a very old temple, one of the oldest in the city; it was built of wood and although it has been repaired and restored over and over again and is still in daily use, it speaks its age. Its architecture is simple. Although the roof is elaborate, the building itself is a high but simple oblong box, with doors on the east and west sides. Today the doors on both sides were open, allowing the breeze free entry to help cool the meditators, worshippers and supplicants within.

Two rows of columns supported the roof rafters. There was no ceiling. The floor was tiled. Prayer rugs lay scattered here and there and more were available in piles thrown in the corners. The columns were painted a dull red. The only light was natural, coming through the doors, and although there was enough light to see it was not bright. Many Buddhas sat or reclined along the north and south walls, but the main and by far the largest Buddha dominated the north wall. It sat in the lotus position and was covered in gold and myriad tiny mirrors. As such statues go I thought it unusually vulgar, but I'm sure mine was a minority opinion.

We halted just inside the door, taking it all in, and presently out of a shadow a man sidled up to us. He looked like a fellow American and the second he opened his mouth he confirmed his nationality.

'Greetings, friends,' he said, and for a confused moment I wondered if he could be a Quaker. 'I and a small group of fellow Buddhists are here today to meditate and pray for a member of our group who is terminally ill. Are any of you Buddhists?' Addressing us, he held his hands together with his shoulders slightly bowed, in the Cambodian way of addressing an elder or superior. Although not above average height, he was heavy, and the effect was incongruous.

Zainab said, 'Yes, I am. I mean,' she said, glancing at Sovan, 'two of us are.'

'We would be very happy if you would pray or meditate with us. Our group is right there.' He nodded in the direction of the large Buddha. In front sat a group of five western women of different ages, all in the lotus position on prayer mats. Their eyes were closed and they appeared to be concentrating. 'Here is the name of our ill friend.' He handed Zainab a piece of paper. 'We are very grateful for your contribution.'

In the modern world it is rare to find someone whose manner can be described as unctuous. The man repelled me. Zainab pulled us away. She took Sovan's hand and mine and led us to the periphery of the little group. She gave Sovan the piece of paper and pronounced the name for her (it was a woman), and asked her to say a prayer for the lady because she was dying. Then she turned to me.

'Michael, I know you're not familiar with this, and don't much care for it, but please, just for a few minutes, sit down here, in any way that's comfortable for you, and just rest for a moment. We'll only be five minutes, that's all. Sovan's going to say a prayer, and I'm going to meditate. It will be over before you know.'

Prayer rugs were scattered all around; we each picked one and sat on it. Since most people had assumed the lotus position, so did I. Zainab leaned over and whispered to me, 'You don't have to sit that way – you can sit any way that's comfortable.'

But I just nodded. I've always been able to sit with my legs crossed and knees bent without any trouble. I could sit like that for an hour if I wanted to.

I did not, at that time, know anything about meditation (I know little more now). So the experience of sitting quietly with a group of meditators was new to me. I examined them. Their ages appeared to span from the early forties to the mid-fifties. They looked like NGO workers, or the wives of executives of the various relief-based organizations. In short they looked respectable, agreeable, temperamentally pacific. Zainab and Sovan stood out. Sovan because she was the only Cambodian there – the five ladies were all westerners – Zainab because she was black (or at least dark), and also because there was an intellectual angularity about her face and expression that the others lacked.

As soon as Zainab and Sovan sat down, they assumed the posture of the rest: clearly they were both practised meditators. They sat with their backs straight and their hands folded easily in their laps. Their heads were erect and their eyes closed. Except for muffled chants from a group of monks in a far corner, the hall was soundless. There wasn't much to see, and, once seen, there wasn't much to ponder. I relaxed and closed my eyes.

I have never been one of those people who is hyper-sensitive to an intuitive environment. As a pilot of US Air Force cargo planes I had seldom had the urge to fly by the seat of my pants; the inputs coming from that region were confused, ambivalent and without clear priority. I preferred concentrating on the instrument panel. As a technical analyst on Wall Street I'd specialized in making short-term predictions of price movements based on historical trends and mathematical models. That worked fine for a good many years.

So I was surprised, after just a few minutes, to realize that I might – I could hardly believe it, and it was in any case faint – that I might be picking up something: a feeling, or aura (a word which, outside meteorology, is ill-defined and which I hesitate to use). The best description I can give is a feeling of intensity: as if I were surrounded by a silent, impalpable, but definite field of concentration.

Shortly after I became aware of this, several of the ladies opened their eyes, took deeper breaths and unwound their legs. They were either calling it a day, or taking a rest. Zainab and Sovan did the same, and stood up; I followed them. Together, silently, we left the temple.

Outside the clouds were lowering and darker. Sovan suggested we start back along the temple wall. If it started to rain, the overhanging roof would protect us. She led the way at a little distance.

Zainab and I walked side by side. She took my hand lightly, surreptitiously. She whispered, 'We can drop Sovan off at home, and tell her that we're going shopping. That should give us a couple of hours.'

It was what I wanted, sexually, but it was such a contradiction: first, the guilt – religious guilt? – over our affair; then the Buddhist meditation, a serious religious scene, it looked to me, which she slipped into as easily as slipping her hand into her glove; followed by the suggestion that we could, just as easily, drop off Sovan and retrieve our original plan: sex at my place. The pendulum was swinging too far and too fast. The motion confused me. I thought, how well do I really know this woman by my side? I felt her give my hand a squeeze and heard her whisper, 'Michael, is that OK . . . is it enough time?'

The ground exploded in front of us. Shrapnel peppered our legs. We stood stupefied. And in an instant I was back at the controls of my C-130, just a young kid, a second lieutenant, banking into final approach to the apparently liberated Kuwait airport in February 1991, when anti-aircraft fire shattered the cockpit's starboard lower window – by my right foot. I was lucky: we landed safely and a few minor cuts in my leg got me a Purple Heart. It could have been worse. We lost twenty-eight fixed-wing aircraft to Iraqi forces in the First Gulf War.

Sovan heard the smash, whirled around and ran to us. She looked at the ground and then up to the roof. 'The roof fall down,' she said, and, grabbing our hands, pulled us closer to the temple wall.

It was more than I could handle. I freed myself from Sovan's surprisingly strong grip and examined the shards. 'It's a ceramic roof tile,' I said. 'Christ Almighty. We missed being brained by a foot.'

Zainab joined me and looked down. She said, 'It would have been a good time and place.' She spoke as if in a trance.

I asked her what she meant.

'Under the roof of Wat Lanka, right after meditation. A good time and a good place to die.'

Sovan slipped in front, staring up at her (Sovan was nearly two feet shorter) with the most intense expression I'd ever seen on that little Cambodian face: part hurt, part pure anger. She said, 'Don't say that! Don't ever say that! Don't say good time to die!'

I lost it. Who wouldn't? Well, maybe some new-age, passive-aggressive type could handle it better than I did. Maybe someone into reiki or crystal pyramids. Someone more tuned into spirituality.

My married lover had suggested our affair was partly to blame for her recent spiritual lapse. Then, after coming out of a trance, she propositioned me. Two seconds later we just missed being killed, or at least seriously injured by a chunk of roof half the size of my leg falling from a dilapidated Buddhist temple. Her first subsequent remark: it would have been a felicitous moment to die.

It was too much. I told them roughly that we had to move, had to hurry, any moment the sky was going to open. I took Zainab's arm and practically dragged her along, as if I could drag her out of her foolishness. Halfway to the car the rain hit, a solid wall, the full-scale, instantaneous monsoon. We splashed back through the crematorium gates drenched to the skin, unable to see more than a few yards in any direction.

The demonstration hadn't materialized. The police cars and motorcycles still cluttered the road. The police sheltered in their cars, the motorcycle cops under the awnings.

I put Sovan in the back seat of my car and Zainab in the front, and splashed my way around the corner to a third-class tourist hotel. There was always a tuk-tuk parked in front. I told the driver he had a fare. A fare was worth getting drenched; he drove me back to my car.

I transferred the women into the tuk-tuk. I told them I was sorry, but I couldn't take them home; I had an appointment I'd forgotten. Sovan looked confused. Cambodian culture must be among the most courteous on earth. Among expats it's an unwritten rule that you didn't show anger or discourtesy around servants. (Probably even the white men she'd had at Martini's hadn't been too rough; if they were anything like Silk's young Brit associate, they'd probably been too embarrassed to perform.) Yet here was I, an American diplomat and friend of the family, being rude as hell.

Zainab looked crestfallen. It was an expression I didn't recall seeing before on that confident, intellectual face. As the driver engaged his gear, she looked at me as if asking humbly for some kindness, and reached out her hand, tentatively, towards mine. I snatched mine away and they drove off into a sheet of rain.

I almost always feel regret too late. Staring at that developing world conveyance – a motorcycle hitched to a rickshaw – disappear, and thinking of Zainab's face, her expression, I felt a stab of regret. But I crushed it. Someone once said that a man always kills the thing he loves. I was ahead of that game. I didn't yet realize I loved her, but already I was trying to end the affair.

8

But of course I didn't kill it off. I just gained a three-week hiatus.

The Monday following the escape from sudden death at Wat Lanka, I submitted my report to Noelle. It was my third report in a week: first the annual economic report, then the political report on Siem Reap, and now the report I titled, 'Result of Proposal to the Deputy Minister, Ministry of Oil, Concerning Westin Oil'. She revised it that afternoon, asked me to sign the revised copy and then sent it 'upstairs'. She told me to hold off calling Silk until we'd heard back from Washington.

They must have thought Cambodia was important, or maybe Westin had more pull than I thought. We heard back within the week – a record-breaker for the State Department. Noelle called me in and told me my instructions were to report my conversation with the minister to Silk verbatim, except for any mention of concern regarding the FCPA. I asked her if that meant that I should pass on the proposed amount of the bribe. She just nodded.

So I did. Silk and I met, again at his suggestion, at Martini's. I followed Noelle's instructions to the letter. Then I got out. The line of little girls in the foyer, sitting side by side in their hooker outfits, looking both bored and anxious while waiting to be called on to the floor, depressed the hell out of me.

I thought then that I'd washed my hands of the Westin Oil deal. But I was wrong. Three days later Silk called again. He needed some more official help. He didn't want to tell me what kind of help over the phone.

That's how I found myself at the Shaker, a very small hostess bar a few blocks in from the quay. There were two pool tables; Silk was playing at one with a house girl. Silk and myself, and an almost unconsciously drunk Brit at the bar, were the only customers. It was early in the afternoon but I doubted it was going to pick up much. There were a hundred bars just like this, or better, within a square mile. The girls were probably the best judges of the business environment; they all looked despondent.

Silk hit a ball, missed, swore good-naturedly, then looked up and greeted me. I greeted him back. He introduced me to his partner, a short, round-faced Vietnamese girl named, absurdly, Debbie. She didn't have time for me, she was intent on playing. 'A dollar a game,' Silk told me. 'The best and cheapest entertainment in town. Take a seat. I'll be with you in just a few minutes.'

I took a seat at a table in a corner and waved off the bar girls. Sooner than I thought, Silk handed over his dollar and joined me. 'Hope you don't mind the place,' he said. 'There's so little to do in this damn town.'

'Really? I thought there was a fair amount going on.'

'Like what? Tuol Sleng? Yeah, the Genocide Museum's a great draw. Once done, you don't want to go there again. Then there's the National Museum. A lot more attractive, but let's face it, how many stone Buddhas do you want to see? As for the temples . . . one wat's a lot like another wat. The town has one elephant. I've seen it twice.' He cast a quick smile at Debbie, now back behind the bar. 'At least here you get a little entertainment. And they like making a little money without putting out. I don't blame them. I like it too.'

'You said you needed some kind of official help?'

'Yes, Mr Smith, I do. I went and talked to the Deputy Minister. I told him that Westin Oil had no problem beating the Chinese contribution to the bridge project. In fact, in countries such as this, we generally build all kinds of schools, clinics and so on. We'd leave the Chinese in the dust. He pointed out that the contribution to the bridge project would be in the form of cash, and I said no problem.' Silk paused and took a gulp of beer. The bar's air conditioning – if there was any – was broken or turned off (electricity in the city was more expensive than rent) and the overhead fans turned slow enough to count the blades.

'The minister was all smiles. He was still smiling when I told him that our embassy – you – would be happy to help his ministry with the compliance paperwork for the UN Transparency Agreement. That's when I asked him if there was anything else he needed clarified, and that's when things started to go off-track.' Silk leaned a little towards me. 'Why didn't you tell me he wanted immunity from the FCPA?'

'Sorry. I wasn't authorized.'

'Weren't authorized?'

'No.'

'Is there anything else you "weren't authorized" to tell me?'

'No.'

'OK, listen. The Deputy Minister was not impressed that I was in the dark, and I wasn't impressed, either. Westin Oil does not deal in letters of immunity from federal prosecution. You do understand that?'

'Yes.'

'Can you obtain such a letter?'

'I don't know.'

'I hope you can. Without that letter we don't have a contract.'

'I'll see what I can do.'

'Houston's eager to sign. Before the fixed costs go any higher.'

Debbie came out from behind the bar and hovered beside him with a pool cue in her hand. She said, 'You want play another game?'

'Sure, hon, just a second.' He turned back to me. 'By the way, how's Sovan working out?'

I'd almost forgotten she'd come from him. 'She's fine,

she's working out fine. Her employers like her, and she likes them.'

'It's a married couple, right?'

'That's right.'

'I'm glad to hear she landed on her feet. Try to get back to me with an answer as soon as you can.'

I gave an oral report to Noelle the next day. She said she'd do the rest and I thought that would, finally, be the end of it – at least for me. I was fed up with Commerce work. I wanted to get back to economic analysis. At least there, there wasn't any dirt.

Twice during the next few days Zainab left a message on my answering machine. I didn't return them. But I had read her stuff in the *New York Times*. I read the *Times* online every morning in the office. She'd dug up some serious dirt on the Prime Minister and his cronies, and the articles were being picked up and printed in the Phnom Penh papers as well, both English and Khmer. They were hard-hitting and were bound to have some effect on the elections. When Noelle called me in at the end of the week, I was afraid she was going to ask me to write a special political report on the subject.

Instead, she asked me out for a date.

Despite her apparent fondness for me, I was still surprised. It wasn't protocol. But we were pretty far from Washington – about as far as we could get – and she'd been in-country longer than me. I don't mean to suggest that she was dying for a date. I simply mean that protocol was getting a little remote, a little dusty, a little thin on the ground.

She had, she told me, two tickets for a performance by a troupe of disabled Chinese dancers. She told me this with a completely straight face, so I kept mine straight, too. The King of Cambodia would be in attendance. The king, before ascending the throne, had been a ballet dancer in Paris, and still held a keen interest in the performing arts. Noelle handed me an invitation. It was a heavy piece of cardboard with three official stamps, and read:

The show was that night at the National Theatre. She said, 'I have to tell you that this could be a long and tedious evening. But there's so little to do here. I'm hoping for the best.'

'Thanks very much,' I said, 'I'd be happy to go. I should probably wear a suit.'

'I think that would be a good idea. I thought we might have dinner afterwards at the FCC.' That was the abbreviation for the Foreign Correspondents' Club, which, despite its name, was a restaurant open to all.

I said, 'Shall I pick you up?'

She had to consider that for a moment. She was my superior officer, and she'd asked me out for a date – although I'm sure she wouldn't, in an official report on the incident, have used that expression. On the other hand, on a date it was customary for the man to drive the woman. She smiled. 'Sure,' she said, 'pick me up at six.'

So that evening I did.

Driving up Sisowath to the theatre we passed under a banner hung right across the street. It was obviously a government job. Huge Khmer and English letters, red against white, announced North Korean-Cambodian Friendship Week. No sooner had I read it than we passed under another, welcoming the North Korean leader to Cambodia. I asked Noelle what on earth it meant.

'This is Asia,' she said. 'The evil hermit kingdom of Washington is our neighbour. The two countries have long had friendly relations. Their former leaders faced similar challenges. They didn't have debates on the free market versus socialized health care. They fought wars of independence. Even in their leisure they had common interests: the king father and the former North Korean leader were both cinephiles.'

This was a royal affair and as we approached the National Theatre the police presence became noticeable; they closed off the smaller side streets and checked invitations. The theatre is on the river, a two-minute walk north from the Himawari Hotel. A fairly new construction, it's one of those showpiece edifices that every country feels it wants or needs in its capital. Cambodia's example manages to be opulent but also sized or scaled correctly for its status as a developing country. It is unfortunate that a municipal outfall pipe dumps raw sewage into the river next to and below the theatre. The guests arrived in their suits and gowns (Noelle was dressed in an elegant but severe suit), with many of the women holding perfumed handkerchiefs to their faces as we filed in.

A group of Cambodian children in costume, some of them clutching traditional Cambodian instruments, played and sang the national anthem. Then the king made his appearance. He looked about fifty. Although not tall he was clearly fit, and for the first time in my life I saw what a 'regal bearing' looks like. He had it, and it was impressive. One felt that, if ever a man was a symbol for his people, and above politics, this was he. The king gave the traditional greeting to the audience, bowing slightly with his hands pressed together as if in prayer, then sat down on a modest throne that faced the stage. He did not move a muscle for the next two hours. Later when I mentioned the feat to Noelle, she told me that he'd been a monk for some years.

The Chinese Disabled People's Performing Art Troupe is just that: a group of Chinese performers who, in one way or another, are disabled. Thus you have dancers who are mute, singers who are wheelchair-bound, a blind pianist. Their disabilities only served to showcase more vividly the Chinese passion for excellence through remorseless training.

Chinese performing acts such as these are always cleaner than clean. They make Donny and Marie look daring, up to date; they make the Beatles look risqué. I can't remember seeing a Stateside act so aggressively clean, pure and happy since I was a kid in the seventies. It's at first refreshing; looking around I couldn't help but notice that hardly a member of the audience did not have a smile on their face. The smiles became fixed after about an hour. Even purity eventually becomes tedious.

Act followed act with no break for an intermission. Although the overall tone never changed, great pains had been taken to maximize variety: singing, dancing, acrobatic, instrumental; solo, soloists, group, choral. It was like watching a kaleidoscope of changing images, one after another, and as a result after a time the mind, or at least my mind, felt numbed, barely able to register.

By the end of the final curtain call I was comatose. The Cambodians loved it. Standing, applauding, I glanced at Noelle. She showed little, if any strain. Her stamina impressed me. It was almost as strong as the king's. After the last of the applause, the children's orchestra played the national anthem again and the monarch made his exit as regally as he had entered hours before.

The audience broke up. On the way out so many people recognized Noelle and insisted on paying their respects, our exit became a kind of receiving line. Her professional carapace descended. She shook hands, made small talk, smiled, always gracious but slightly distant. I was so far in the background I could have been an early lesson, a training video, for Ann. As far as I know, no one recognized me except, towards the end, the Deputy Minister. He stood near the door, but when we approached he just smiled and nodded and melted away.

Outside, with the king safely back in his palace, the police had also melted away. But in the car park a loose crowd had formed, staring up the quay. They stared at a column of monks, chanting and walking slowly in their yellow robes, some holding signs in Khmer. They walked down the road in our direction.

Noelle said, 'Michael, find out what's going on.'

'How?'

'Ask somebody.'

Her tone was not unfriendly, but I felt like an idiot. I looked around for anyone I might know, and spotted, standing under a street light next to his 4x4, the Deputy Minister. I walked to him, waving to catch his eye – I didn't want him to disappear again.

He shook my hand. He said, 'Hello, Mr Smith. I see you are in good company. I hope you enjoyed the concert.'

'It was very long.'

'We have more time, here, for these entertainments, than they do in the States. What did you think of our king?'

'I thought he had a regal bearing.'

The Deputy Minister smiled. 'That is true; he does. When his father first chose him as his successor, with the approval of course of the government, many thought he would be weak. But he has become a strong figurehead. The people hold him in regard. It is a pity that, due to his inclinations, he will not have descendants.'

We were straying far afield. I asked him, 'What's the demonstration about?'

'I believe they are monks from Wat Lanka. Their placards say . . .' He paused, trying to read them. 'They are protesting against the imprisonment of monks in Yangon. They are calling for the release of those monks.' He turned to me. 'I must leave, now, Mr Smith. I suggest you and Ms McQuiston do the same. Cambodia has friendly relations with Myanmar. I expect the police here shortly. I doubt there will be conflict; we are all Buddhists. But you never know. It is not desirable to witness.'

I thanked him and returned to Noelle. I'd given her the keys and she was already in the car. I drove us south to avoid the demonstration, then turned into a couple of side streets and headed north again, to the FCC. She showed no surprise when I told her what the demo was about.

'You will have to include it,' she told me, 'in your next

political report. Burma is also part of the neighbourhood, like North Korea.'

I parked across the street from the restaurant and we climbed the stairs to the dining room and bar, both open to the air. Noelle had some pull: a waitress showed us straight to a table overlooking the river. We both ordered the fish special of the day – you can't go wrong with the local fish in Phnom Penh – and I ordered a bottle of wine. I tried it before buying it; what with the sea voyage and the climate, wine doesn't always travel well to Cambodia. But the bottle was all right.

After we discussed the concert and I refilled our glasses – it was a hot, humid night – Noelle said, coolly, 'Michael, I asked you out tonight mainly for your company. In fact, after we've finished dinner and you take me home, if you aren't too tired, I'd like to ask you in for a drink.' She ended her sentence with just the hint of a smile. I was concentrating on the 'mainly'.

'However,' she continued, 'I also had a small, ulterior motive.' She reached into her bag, and pulled out a slender, letter-sized envelope. It was one of ours: it carried the embassy letterhead. She put it on the table between us, next to the bread basket. 'This,' she said, 'is the letter that the Deputy Minister wants from the embassy.'

'That was fast work.'

'The ambassador put it together last night . . . with a little help from Washington.'

'And you want me to deliver it to Silk.'

'Yes. I'd appreciate it. As a favour.'

'Not,' I said quietly, 'as an order?'

'No. The ambassador signed it, but he gave it to me to deliver. Frankly, I'd prefer not to myself. I haven't much cared for what I've heard of Silk.'

I was sure that wasn't the real reason, but I said nothing. The envelope contained a letter that, whatever the exact language, at least suggested immunity from prosecution for bribery to Westin and to ministers of the Cambodian government. It was on embassy notepaper and was signed by our ambassador. He was a political appointee, a former businessman and a big party fundraiser – Noelle ran the day-to-day embassy show – but he was far from being a fool and he must have known the letter was potentially toxic. So he'd given it to Noelle to deliver, and now she'd offered it to me.

She said, 'You don't have to, Michael. Let me take it.' And she reached out her arm to pick it up.

But I snatched it off the table first, and slipped it into my inside jacket pocket. 'I'll do it,' I said.

'You don't have to.'

'I know.'

Our fish arrived. It was after ten and we were both hungry. Soon I poured us each another glass of wine. I wanted to know more about her. I asked her about her career. She'd been in the Service for a decade. Of course I'd read her State Department biography, but the department's officer biographies are incredibly dry. I wanted some insight.

Maybe it was the favour, maybe it was the wine, maybe it was just the night out. She opened up. She jumped backwards in time and told me how she'd been brought up in upstate New York in the kind of little town where you stood out if you were brainy, and where, if you'd been given that label, you also had to be tough. The town had only one high school and she'd been its valedictorian. Unlike every high school valedictorian I'd ever known, she'd actually gone on to make something important out of her life. At least, it seemed pretty important to me.

Noelle joined the Service right out of college and immediately stepped into the kind of assignments reserved for young officers with leadership potential. A stint in Bosnia and another in the UN. A secondment to an international organization in The Hague. Then time out for a second master's degree, followed by an assignment in Bangkok and now second in command in Phnom Penh. She could look forward with some confidence, in another year or two, to an ambassadorship in one of the developing countries where the US has some strategic or economic interest. Some place too important for a political employee.

She'd always struck me as a woman of character, of integrity. And I had had to snatch the letter away from her. It made me wonder how far she was prepared to go. I asked her.

She mulled it over for a moment, swishing the wine in her glass. The restaurant was emptying out. The shouts rising from the street, from the tuk-tuk drivers and moto drivers looking for fares, and the touts selling anything and everything, were tapering off. It had cooled down a little (from hot to mildly hot) and there was a hint of rain in the air.

'It's not always,' she told me, 'a simple calculation. At the beginning of your career in the Service your job is to implement policy. Realistically, most officers do not rise above that level – no matter what their grade code. Some officers, however, do. In their case, there is the possibility, usually at mid-career, of influencing policy. A few officers at a senior level help make policy.

'Inevitably you're called upon to implement policies with which you disagree. But even there it's not always clear-cut. In some cases implementation is left, within boundaries, to the officer's judgement; in other cases it's rigid. So, how far do you go? At what point do you feel you have to resign? I think there are two considerations.

'One: it's an equation. Even in implementation, you are often doing good, as well as bad. You can create opportunity; you can help people; you can further policy goals you believe in. And it's possible that the opportunity for sound implementation, for influencing and eventually even making policy, will grow the longer you stay in.

'But the second consideration is your own red lines. Nearly everyone has them; if you don't, in my opinion, you shouldn't be in the Service. Here the question is: how many red lines do you have to cross, before you decide you can't, in good conscience, remain? And are there some red lines that you simply can't cross?' She paused.

I said, 'And you, Noelle, have you ever been called upon to cross a red line – one that you simply can't cross?'

'Not yet.'

'If you were ordered to?'

'I've always been prepared to resign.'

The certainty of her answers discouraged cross-examination. I signalled to the waiter for the bill, and asked her if she was ready to go.

'Yes,' she said, 'let's head to my place for a nightcap.'

She lived much further south on Norodom than Zainab, further south and in a tonier quarter. The guard in front of her door looked like he was there for a little more than show, and saluted smartly before opening the gate.

It was my first time in her house, a large, very modern two-storey villa, complete with a small swimming pool in the front garden. Inside it resembled her office in one respect: there was almost nothing personal. The furniture was all US government-issue, and solid (and heavy and dull) as a rock. The pictures on the wall were, without exception, government-issue – impossible to misidentify. I finally found one personal photograph, framed under glass on a sideboard. A candid shot, it showed Noelle with a small group of similar-aged women outside on a lawn, under some trees. A breeze blew their dresses against their legs, and, with the exception of Noelle, they all looked happy, smiling into the wind. Noelle looked in the same direction, but severely at someone out of the frame. It gave the impression that, in the group, she was the one on the alert for potential problems, proactively ready to tackle anything or anyone likely to become a problem. I asked her where it had been taken, and she replied at a hotel in the Dominican Republic, at a family reunion.

She asked if I cared for a drink and I asked for a beer. In that climate I preferred it to a cocktail. She brought me the beer and poured herself a glass of white wine. We sat down on opposite sides of a medium-sized sofa, our legs crossed towards each other. Eschewing small talk – perhaps she thought our previous conversation qualified – she asked why I was still unmarried.

I gave her my standard answer, told chronologically. My undergraduate major, engineering, did not attract women. In the air force I observed that, once a young officer got married, he tended to stay in the services. The salary, although initially modest, rose regularly and the benefits were exceptional. After you made captain, few wives wanted you to leave the air force, and few officers at that point in their career did.

Graduate school offered more opportunity than college, but I was an assiduous student and economics was almost as male-oriented a discipline as engineering. Wall Street was more difficult to explain. It was true that women were under-represented at the trading desks and in the chart rooms where I worked, but I was there for ten years. A long time. This was always the most difficult period to justify, or rather, explain, and I explained it by saying that although I'd had the occasional affair, which was true, I never found the right one. I hinted that I'd been the victim, more than once, of unrequited love. This was not actually true (like most men, I'd been the victim of unrequited lust rather than unrequited love) but it usually went down well with women.

The Foreign Service was not so far an improvement. My first assignment was Riyadh, where romance, western-style, was officially banned as un-Islamic. That lasted three years. Then Cambodia.

In short, I'd been the victim of circumstance.

Noelle listened attentively. When I finished, she said, 'And was there nothing else, no other reason?'

'Not that I'm aware of,' I told her. 'And you? What about you?'

'I'm a career woman,' she said, 'much as you are evidently a career-oriented man. My first assignment in the Service, Bosnia, was not, like Riyadh, congenial for romance. In any case I was much too busy. Later on, as I rose in the Service, I found the circle of possibilities shrinking. It's now shrunk to almost nothing, at least within the embassies where I'm assigned.'

'What do you mean?'

'Ideally one would find a partner within the embassy, with similar interests and background, at a not too distant grade code. But I'm now the Chargé d'Affaires. There is no one at my level. The only staff member above me is the ambassador. He is married with two children. Every other member of staff in the embassy is below me, and I have to supervise and sign, and in some cases write, their performance reports. They would have to resign from the Service.'

'Well, there are people outside the embassy.'

'Yes, but the right calibre of man, particularly in this kind of station, is not easy to find. They'd have to be willing to follow me all over the globe. That doesn't mean a man willing to take the standard woman's role. I'm not interested in marrying a dependent spouse. Whoever he might be, he would have to have a career that's portable. A writer perhaps. Or someone with your background in finance: you'd be able to find work almost anywhere in the world.' Pensively, she took a sip of her wine. She said, 'I know one woman who wound up marrying her Brazilian tennis coach.'

I felt flattered that, at least in terms of my background and former occupation, I could be a contender. It was a pity about my grade code, but if I resigned I might make the shortlist. Looking at her I thought, not for the first time, that she was an attractive woman. Her main drawback, for me, was her severity, but I suspected that was an occupational mask that would shed in a more intimate setting. I said, 'It sounds to me like we share many of the same reasons for having stayed single.'

She said evenly, 'Yes, I agree. But there's at least one more reason in my case. I have had opportunities; I've even had suitable relationships with suitable men. Not many – a couple. But in both cases I had difficulty making the necessary commitment. I mean an emotional commitment.' She looked down. 'I'm not certain why.'

It was an evening of self-disclosure, although more for her than for me. Her first had been inadvertent: by trying to palm off the delivery of that letter she had shown a willingness to pass the poisoned chalice, to possibly compromise a fellow officer rather than herself. Of course she was my superior and that was her prerogative. But I thought it showed a moment of weakness. I didn't mind. It softened her severity, her certainty.

Her second was her hesitation to make an emotional commitment. I recognized the problem.

She'd ended on a questioning note. An invitation to explore further? I'd gone as far as I felt comfortable. I looked at my watch. It was getting on towards midnight. I made some remark about the time, thanked her for the evening, and got up to go.

At the door she said, 'Michael, do you mind if I give you a little personal advice? Off the record. As a friend?'

'Of course not.'

'Have you ever heard the phrase, "corridor reputation"?'

'It rings a faint bell.'

'It's departmental slang. It refers to an officer's reputation in the department, apart from the formal performance reports. There are always things, even objective things, that can't go into those reports.'

'Yes?'

'One's love life, for instance. You can't believe how much havoc I've seen officers create, within our embassies, in the community, even in other embassies.'

I said nothing.

'I'm the last person to tell anyone how to manage their love life. But this is a small town. It's almost impossible, in a town this size, to be completely discreet. To be certain of discretion. That's all I wanted to say. Thanks so much for taking me to the concert, and for dinner, and for our talk. I enjoyed the evening.'

I returned her thanks and left. On the drive home I wondered who'd tipped her off. Ann? Did she inform on her fellow officers, as well as spy for the Agency? I hoped not. Noelle was right: it was a very small town. I'm sure she thought she was doing me a favour, but it rankled.

I walked into my own government-issue villa – I hadn't been there long enough to personalize it much, even if I'd wanted to – and reflected on the evening. Sterile, nearly as sterile as my four walls, and as lonely. I looked to the ancient fax-answering machine I'd owned for years and had the department ship over. Its little green eye blinked. I played the message. It was the third from Zainab. She asked me if I'd care to escort her to an evening of Brahms at the Café Musicum on Saturday night – tomorrow.

I recalled that our third-floor apartment was still free. Noelle was right: my love life was my own affair (an unintentional pun) not hers. Or was it more exact to call it my sex life?

It was too late to return Zainab's call now, but in the morning I'd call her on her cellphone, to accept her invitation. And I'd make it clear that I expected to end the evening with her – on the third floor.

9

I picked Zainab up at six the next evening. She wasn't quite ready so I sat down to wait. After a minute Ambler appeared, hobbling down the stairs with a crutch, one leg at a time. Instead of a tensor bandage he wore a full leg cast. I asked him what had happened.

He didn't reply until he finished his descent. He said, 'It was the day you were last here. I was feeling pretty perky – I only had a week to go – and after my afternoon nap I decided I'd come down and take a stroll, or a limp, in the garden.

'It's always dark on the ground floor in the afternoon – you can see why: the place was built to keep the sun out, to keep it cool – and on top of that it was raining. Anyway, I didn't realize that Sovan had, a few minutes earlier, mopped the floor.'

I looked down. The shiny black fake marble was slippery even when dry.

'I got to about here,' he said, pointing with his crutch to the point where the split-level floor dropped down, sharp as a knife. 'That's when I slipped. My knee cap came down right on the edge. Dislocated.'

Zainab appeared in the doorway to a spare room. She said, 'It's a miracle it wasn't broken. I was asleep in here. I heard his scream—'

'It was a yell.'

'Well, I heard him, and rushed out. Sovan was ironing and she rushed to help, too. We splinted his leg and carried him out to the 4×4. Thank God we have a large vehicle. We took him straight to Dr White's office. It's like an old-fashioned surgery – he lives upstairs.'

Ambler continued: 'He gave me a shot of morphine – they give out opiates here as if it were World War Two – and then took me to the hospital. They X-rayed and set the knee and cast the leg.'

I asked, 'How long, this time?'

'Six weeks. Then physical therapy.'

I expressed my commiseration. Silently I thought: I've never met a more accident-prone individual.

He thanked me for taking his wife out: 'Poor thing, I'm not much good to her right now,' he said.

I told him it was my pleasure, which was true.

The Café Musicum was a ten-minute drive, a few blocks down the street from the FCC and around the corner. Zainab and I didn't talk about how we'd parted last. Instead we talked about our work. I had little to say – I'd never told her about Westin Oil, and I didn't now. But she was excited about her latest coup: the *Phnom Penh Post* and a local Khmer-language paper had picked up her articles about government corruption. I congratulated her, and asked, only half facetiously, if her gate guard had seen any strangers hanging around her compound. 'I don't think he'd notice if there were,' she said, and laughed. 'Do you think the Prime Minister wants me under surveillance?'

'There's an election coming up. Anything's possible. Someone might send a member of the goon squad over just to case the joint.'

'How exciting. Goon squads, "under surveillance": it sounds like one of those forties movies that Robert likes to watch on the French television channel. Come on, let's get in-role. Lower the windows and we'll have a cigarette.'

So I lowered the windows, she put her feet up on the dashboard and we each lit a cigarette. She was in one of her up moods, which was fine as far as I was concerned. It was better than spiritual guilt.

The café was on the northern edge of the tourist area. I parked in a dusty patch of ground. It was a stormy night and the wind whipped up the dirt behind us as we walked, me in my sports jacket and Zainab in her sleek black dress, across the potholed road and broken pavement to the café's front door.

The restaurant/recital hall was a small, not conspicuously clean ground-floor room, narrow but long; there was space for tables and chairs on each wall and enough space down the centre to allow a waiter and a diner to pass. They'd just squeezed in a bar and a baby grand piano at the far end. The owner arranged dinner recitals on an irregular schedule. For tonight's recital the 'hall' was half full.

A waiter showed us to a table and we ordered an appetizer and drinks. We planned to have dinner afterwards at the FCC. Zainab pointed out to me the proprietor, a retired Dutch professor, now a Phnom Penh restaurateur and impresario, and various guests with whom she was acquainted due to their mutual interest in classical music. A heavy-set man walked in with a date and Zainab formally introduced me to Dr White. We'd last met at the British Ambassador's Christmas party. It seemed years ago. He in turn introduced his dining companion, Deria Goldstein. She was still thin, still unprepossessing. She smiled, but there was no actual smile there.

We were just served when the pianist, an Englishman in a dark jacket but without a tie, introduced himself and spoke briefly about the music he was going to perform. Although he was not far away and the other diners were silent, I was unable to understand him clearly; I had the impression he was slurring his words, and wondered if he had a slight speech impediment. Fortunately each table had a programme. I examined it. It looked to be a large number of short pieces: intermezzi, ballads, waltzes, etc.

He played. To me, each piece sounded the same. Melodies that never quite coalesced, and climaxes that never quite came to a climax, despite crashing chords. I was hungry, and by the second intermezzo I was digging into the calamari. When Zainab picked up her fork and joined me, I suspected there were problems with the performer's execution to an educated ear, not just to mine.

We reached the intermission. The applause, within the

narrow walls, sounded impressive and must have felt reward-
ing to the pianist. He rose from the piano bench and bowed
deeply; I noticed he kept one hand on the piano as if to steady
himself. He was perspiring freely and took out a handkerchief
to mop his brow.

Zainab said, 'Let's hurry and finish our drinks. Do you mind
if we leave for dinner before he gets going again?'

'I'd prefer it.'

The proprietor led the performer down the narrow aisle,
introducing him to the regulars. They made good progress
and it became evident that we had no hope of leaving before
they reached our table. They reached Dr White's table first.
The former professor introduced the doctor, who held out
his hand; the pianist shook it perfunctorily. His attention was
taken by Deria.

There are women who, despite being physically plain, or
even downright unattractive, nevertheless emanate sexuality.
Such was Deria. She held out her small, bony hand; the pianist
grasped it and was loath to let it go. He asked her about her
career and he told her how much he admired foreign correspondents. He told her he was amazed that one so young
as her had risen to such a position of responsibility. She was,
after all, the source of so much that so many people around
the world read about the Far East. He hoped that she and her
friend could stay on after the concert, so that they could have
a chat.

Seen and heard up close, the pianist was, in his way, as
unprepossessing as the foreign correspondent. He looked in his
late forties, but his outdated, tousled haircut and jerky manner
suggested an attempt to hold on to youth. His white shirt was
heavily stained with perspiration and the elbows of his black
dinner jacket shone with wear. He was also, clearly, drunk. I
recognized the type. My old securities firm had laid off several
over the years. It takes time to become a high-performing
alcoholic. The pianist looked a little younger than those I'd
encountered in business. He must have started early.

The proprietor looked at his watch and pulled him away

and across the aisle to us. We had never met so he simply ignored me and introduced Zainab as 'the leader of Phnom Penh's amateur musicians'.

The Brit held out his hand automatically and opened his mouth, but no sound came; Zainab took his hand, said coolly, 'How do you do?' and then withdrew hers.

He just stared at her, a puzzled expression on his face. Then he smiled broadly. He said, 'Zainab Mohammed!'

Zainab nodded her head almost imperceptibly.

'The black BBC girl! I've watched your show often, always with pleasure! Imagine you turning up here! Bloody hell, we're not even in the Arab world.'

'I'm British.'

He laughed. 'Of course you are! As British as the queen! In any case' – here he leaned towards her – 'I'm a great believer in what the Yanks call "affirmative action". Give them a chance! You're the Beeb's answer to Condi Rice – maybe even Michelle Obama! You look great on the tube, dearie; you look even better here, tonight.'

I should have got up at that point and knocked him down. But his offensiveness was so sudden it took me a moment to catch up. I believe he meant to offer her some kind of toast. He laid his left hand familiarly on her bare right arm, and picking up his glass, swung it towards her. At the same time she reached over with her left hand to try to dislodge his paw. His glass and her arm collided violently. Red wine splashed on to her face and down her breasts.

Zainab froze, stunned. The Brit recovered first, apologizing heavily; he picked up her cloth napkin from the table, shook it open and pressed it against her breasts.

At that point I started to get to my feet. I pushed my chair back, but Dr White was way ahead of me. Before I could stand he was beside the pianist, pulling his hands off Zainab. 'I think you've done enough,' he said. 'You'd best head back to your piano.'

A drunk, at a certain stage in an altercation or crisis, can just lose it without warning. They may become hysterical.

They may enter, in the blink of an eye, a world or reality of their own. The pianist lost it now. He swore at the doctor; he picked up my glass and threw the contents on to the doctor's suit; he slapped his face with the back of his hand.

Dr White turned and took two strides back to his table. He pulled Deria to her feet and away – he was a big man and she was a small woman. Then he grabbed the tablecloth and yanked it off. Plates and glasses smashed but he ignored them; he turned back to us, wrapping the cloth tight around his right hand. He stepped up to the pianist and delivered an almost surgical uppercut. The pianist, I'm certain, never knew what hit him. He bounced back against our table and recoiled forward, heading down; the doctor caught him as he fell. Although a dead weight the doctor carried him across the aisle without difficulty, and sat him down in his own chair. After a brief examination he laid the pianist's head down on his arms.

The Dutch proprietor, not one hundred per cent sober himself, alternately apologized to Zainab and asked the doctor what he thought he was doing. Dr White suggested that Zainab might want to clean herself up at his surgery, which was just a block away. She accepted gratefully. The two of us followed him and Deria out.

His surgery was on the same side of the street but further down from the river. It consisted of a foyer and a hallway with a couple of examination rooms leading off; at the end was his office and a bathroom. He escorted Zainab there, ran some water and gave her towels and then closed the door. He showed Deria and I into his office.

He sat us down, pulled glasses and a bottle from a cupboard behind his desk, and poured us all a small shot of whisky. 'Sorry about the way that ended,' he said. 'I can't stand drunks, especially British drunks, especially British racist drunks.'

'But you're British yourself,' Deria said. I thought I detected a slight slur in her speech.

'That's probably the reason. It disgusts me when my fellow nationals make spectacles of themselves. It lowers the reputation of the whole country. Of course I mean Britain.'

Deria said, 'Then I'm glad I'm American.' This time she definitely slurred.

The doctor stared at her. 'Yes,' he said. 'I'm glad you are, too.'

She didn't reply, but from her expression I think it dawned on her that his last remark could be interpreted as uncomplimentary. Had I traded one conflict for another? I decided to change the subject. I asked him if he'd been in-country long.

'Since UNTAC started up,' he said. 'The city was almost deserted when I first arrived. It didn't stay deserted for long. I opened this surgery in '93 and I've been here ever since.'

'That's a lengthy stay,' I said. 'You've never thought of moving back to the UK?'

'Once or twice. Now it's probably too late.'

We heard a door swing open and Zainab reappeared.

The doctor treated her like a favourite patient, congratulating her on her repairs to her appearance, insisting on taking her pulse, proffering a shot of whisky – 'Medicinal,' he said – and finally giving his opinion that the evening would have been far more satisfactory, and more musical, had she performed. They both laughed, and criticized the pianist's performance in the way that musicians or people knowledgeable about music can. Finally he congratulated her on her recently published articles in the local press. 'Corruption's been endemic here since UNTAC left – if not before. The whole society's rotten with it, from top to bottom. And it's getting worse, not better. The man at the top sets the tone. Your articles show exactly what kind of tone he's set.'

I thought we should leave on a high note – Deria, the stringer, sat silent and sullen – so I took Zainab's arm and announced that we had a dinner date at the FCC. Dr White showed us to his front door. His last words as we left were uttered to me, I thought humorously: 'Keep an eye on her back – she's making enemies in high places.'

It took us less than five minutes to drive to the FCC; I was lucky and found a parking place across the street. A serious storm on the opposite side of the river moved towards us;

as we pushed between the touts, beggars and drivers, distant flashes of embedded lightning lit up the cloud base.

We walked upstairs. It was earlier than the night before and the restaurant was busier. The FCC was well advertised on every Cambodian travel website and was packed with Australians, Kiwis, Canadians, Brits, Europeans. Ages varied, but the majority were in their twenties and thirties. As usual, Americans were poorly represented. Fewer and fewer of my fellow nationals any longer have the money or interest for international travel.

We ordered. I'd noticed before in an affair that relations were often much smoother, more trouble-free and easy, after either a shared crisis or the first serious quarrel and break-up. A crisis started our affair; now, after breaking up, it had resumed even easier than before.

As we ate I cast a glance now and then around the room. Many of the young women had come with a girlfriend. I don't think most were gay. They hoped to find a young man. They'd come on their holiday to Phnom Penh, probably with their best girlfriend, to find excitement, hopefully sex, maybe even love. Most were heavily made up and dressed as if to advertise the fact they were a ready pick-up. They were so young that my first instinct was to feel protective towards them. Most were a little too plump or too thin, with too much or too little figure; they gave the impression of having already been in town for two or three days without luck, and were on the verge of losing hope. I wished I could have put them on a plane home, wherever 'home' might be.

'Taking in the scenery?' Zainab asked me.

'Yes. And congratulating myself, no doubt in a self-satisfied manner.'

'On what?'

'On you.'

She smiled . . . and a flash of light exploded over the river, painting the ceiling, the floor, the tables and every face flat white, for a second painting out every shadow. The crack that followed shook our bones. Silence settled over the restaurant on blank faces. Then cries and exclamations rose from the pavements.

People stood in a general movement to see what had happened. The restaurant was open to the air; Zainab and I sat next to the parapet overlooking the river. We were the first to peer over the concrete ledge.

An oil coaster, of a type that steams up and down the Tonlé Sap every day, rode at anchor not far offshore, still loaded, decks nearly awash. A communication mast rose from the stern deckhouse, and from the truck of the mast a ball of electricity radiated like a ball of fire, illuminating the vessel and the river around.

Zainab asked me: 'What is it?'

'I'm not sure. St Elmo's fire. Or maybe ball lightning. It's a known phenomenon, but this is the first time I've ever seen it.'

Every eye in the restaurant fastened on the ship's mast. The fiery sphere gradually descended. It reached the roof of the deckhouse, expanded – and then vanished in the blink of an eye.

The crowd drifted away and we sat back down. Neither of us wanted to linger and I had to get Zainab home at a reasonable hour; we ate enough to kill our hunger and I called our waitress and paid our bill. She'd given us a good table and I gave her a good tip. She thanked me, and said, 'Storm mean monsoon's end. Rain almost finished. Now river slow. Soon turn back.'

Outside it was peak hour and we had to push our way through the beggars and touts. It was too much for Zainab: she opened her purse for a beggar without legs and they mobbed us. I told her to hold on to her purse and I kept one hand over my wallet pocket, while pushing through with the other. They followed us right across the street to the car, like flies after a piece of meat.

The scene affected her. On the way to our apartment she told me how, every month, the numbers of homeless, of beggars, of the destitute grew – kicked out of their homes, off their land, by the Prime Minister and his cronies, selling the country off, selling government land off, for a million here, a million there, to Russian and British and Swiss and Chinese speculators, hoteliers, developers. I knew it all, of course. Tidied and sanitized with the aid of statistics and the passive voice, it had gone into my own annual country report. But I didn't tell her that. She needed or wanted to let off steam. I concentrated on driving.

We turned past Martini's. It was a busy night. Tuk-tuks crowded the bar's entrance and little girls with more paint than clothes darted in and out like minnows around the stolid, private security guards. So many cars lined our street that I had to park at the next intersection, next to the open drain that flowed in a street-level viaduct north to the river.

We walked back to our apartment, rising gusts from the storm at our back. Away from the bar the street was empty and poorly lit: the city turned off half the street lights and dimmed the rest to save power. The residents belonged to the landed Khmer middle class; they owned the neighbourhood during the day. At night, especially on weekends, they stayed inside.

Our building's gate was closed and bolted. Zainab had the slimmer wrists; she reached through the hole cut for that purpose and started jiggling the bolt open, our usual procedure. I looked down the block at Martini's, and back, gratefully, to our little oasis of peace and quiet. A flicker of distant lightning lit the shadows of the house across the street.

And picked out the watcher.

I knew the type of Khmer to expect in this neighbourhood. The man flattened against the wall opposite, trying to squeeze deeper into shadow, wasn't the right type. A string of flashes exposed him clearly. He didn't belong to the landed middle class. His clothes – his print shirt and cheap trousers – were wrong: property owners here dressed either further up or further down. He might have been a driver, but there were no tuk-tuks or motos nearby. Besides, drivers weren't furtive; they often pushed themselves upon you. This man was trying, unsuccessfully, for invisibility. He was too far from the right neighbourhood for an addict: addicts haunted Tuol Sleng, blocks away. And he was too healthy. Or at least, he drank too well.

He didn't belong.

There's a school of thought that says good expats wink at occasional drunkenness in servants. They take in their stride government clerks asking for bribes, local contractors taking rake-offs. They admit it's too bad that the government is a dictatorship or a monarchy or an oligarchy, but that's the state of the culture's political evolution. They'd prefer it if women were not discriminated against but that's an ingrained part of local culture. They consider spies across the road part of the scenery. They shrug their shoulders.

It's called cultural subjectivism.

I was tired of shrugging my shoulders. Three years in Riyadh inclined me towards cultural objectivism.

'Stay here,' I told Zainab, and crossed the street, my blood pressure going up with every stride. I didn't have a plan, other than to confront the bastard. He'd squeezed himself into his corner but I pushed him in deeper, just by intimidation. He was thicker around the waist but I stood a foot taller. I was older but in better condition.

I assaulted him with questions, accusations – but of course his English was elementary. He couldn't have answered if he'd wanted to, even if he'd known the answers. The experience of being confronted was too much. He cringed and grinned and tried to sidle out and away. There was an etiquette to spying: he stayed in sight but unobtrusive; his victims pretended he wasn't there. I was breaking the rules. I blocked him in, but only for a minute. The pleasure palled fast. He was so obviously the low man, the lowest man, on his particular totem pole – probably too far down to even identify the pole: party security, government security, the police. I let him go with a final, 'Beat it.' He scurried down the street towards the bar.

Zainab had the gate open. 'It was just the neighbourhood spy,' I told her. 'I got rid of him.'

'Was that wise?'

'What can they do?' We climbed the narrow stairs to our third-floor borrowed apartment.

We had under two hours before I had to deliver her home. No time to waste. The apartment had been closed for days; I turned on the air conditioning in the bedroom and then opened the double doors leading on to the balcony. I didn't mind being extravagant with electricity. It wouldn't be long.

A rising wind wanted to blow the doors closed; I propped them open with piles of books. Lightning flashed over the river and the curtains flapped like loose sails. One of them caught a hand-sized Buddha on a pedestal and flipped it over but Zainab, by a lucky chance, caught it. She placed it on a low table away from the curtains, and said, 'If Sovan saw that, she'd say it was a spirit that guided my hand.'

It was an electric night, a nervy night; I wanted her but I didn't want Sovan's spirits or Buddhas, I didn't want to be reminded of Zainab's efforts to expose Cambodian corruption and I didn't want to think about my own efforts to enable it. 'Come on,' I said, and took her hand.

I left the bedroom light off but kept the door open – her skin was dark but not as dark as night; enough light came in from the street through the balcony doors to see her clearly. I pushed her up against the wall and kissed her mouth. She responded with a thrust of her tongue.

We'd followed the Cambodian custom of taking our shoes off inside the door; now I unzipped her dress and pulled it over her head. I undid her bra. Her skin was fine-pored and smooth. She was firm but womanly; she was one of those women who keep themselves fit without looking like a steroid-fuelled body builder. Her breasts, like her figure, were slender; they were well-defined and became fuller as they fell, jutting forward. I cupped them and pulled her to me and kissed her again, pushing her head back, then I put my hands on her shoulders and pushed her down to her knees.

We'd both had a fair amount to drink in a short period of time, what with the abortive concert, the doctor's office, then dinner. It was a lot but not too much, not too much to perform. Just enough to let the inhibitions down: to let us each take what we wanted to take, and give what we wanted to give.

I'm not normally an introspective type; perhaps this narrative is a breakout for me, in that sense. Particularly regarding the act of love, or of sex. Outside bed, we were still moving in opposite directions, but only I knew all the details. Her moral purity (except for sex), was a constant reminder, an affront; it made it easy for me to want to humiliate her, although of course in sex that's a word open to wide interpretation. As for her . . . she gave herself willingly, even aggressively. I think she saw it as a proof of love; I hope she didn't see it as some kind of expiation. I don't think so. That's Christianity, not Buddhism (although I admit I'm not theologically qualified to pronounce).

Looking back at that night (the background so melodramatic, in such a Third World way: the lightning, the wind and the squalls outside, and above us the Chinese-made air-conditioning unit clattering like a gun on the wall), looking back, I think our love-making, our sex, mirrored our anxieties, our frustrations, our needs. In her case, maybe even her love.

On her knees, she performed the act expertly. But I didn't want to come in her mouth. I pulled her up and told her to lie down on the bed. She was one of those women who, in passion, like their breasts sucked; after that I knelt over her, her arms above her head on the bed, and she accepted me again.

I rolled off and turned her over, spread her legs and pulled her up on her knees and entered her from behind. She arched her back and kept her head low, pressing into me as violently as I pressed into her. I don't know how long we kept that up; by this time despite the Chinese air conditioning we were both covered in sweat; when I felt myself near, I pushed her down flat on the bed, withdrew, then, in one movement, thrust myself in to her as far as I could.

She moaned and gripped the sheets with her hands but never told me to stop; on the contrary; as I slammed in she pushed back to meet me. There was nothing passive about her. I never thought, and I still don't, that she was masochistic, certainly not expiatory. I think she received pleasure by giving it to me. I think it was love.

10

Nine days later, directly after our Monday morning staff meeting, Noelle and I stood in her office, looking out of her window in the direction of Wat Phnom. A huge crowd, still growing, pressed at the base of the hill. The wat's elephant was lost among it.

Ann had announced the demonstration the previous week. Anti-government, anti-appropriation and anti-corruption, it was organized by the Reform Party, with thousands of participants bussed and taxied into town in small groups from the countryside. The assembly point was Wat Phnom; the march would pass the US Embassy, then to Sisowath Quay to the rallying point: the royal palace. There Hun Prang would give a speech. Ann said he was expected to present challenges the government would have a hard time answering, much less meeting.

'Thank God,' Noelle said, 'we've put some distance between the US administration and the Cambodian government.'

'Yes, in public.'

'And in private. We've raised many concerns. Including every concern at the root of this demonstration.'

'Including corruption?'

'Yes, including that.' She turned and walked back to her desk, and I followed her. She motioned me to a seat, and asked if I knew Deria Goldstein. I admitted I did.

'I admire her,' Noelle said. 'You know, there's not a single foreign news bureau in this country. There're fewer and fewer newspapers left in the States, and less space in those that remain for foreign news. If a story about Cambodia does appear, it's probably hers, and she's not only had to write it, she's had to sell it as well.'

I said, 'Zainab Ambler just got published – abroad and locally.'

'Yes, they were good articles. She's to be congratulated. But it's a sideline for her. She's married to a British diplomat. Deria's making a living as a stringer. It's not an easy thing to do.' She picked up a copy of the *Phnom Penh Post* from her desk. 'This is today's paper. Have you read it?'

I made a point of reading the *International Herald Tribune* every morning over breakfast at my regular restaurant opposite Wat Lanka. I saved the *Post* for the office. 'No,' I said, 'I haven't seen it yet.'

'There's an article in it by her. She's branching out, placing stories in the local press. This story's fundamentally of local interest. You remember the British physician the embassy has contracted?'

'You mean Dr White?'

'Yes.'

'I'm acquainted with him.'

'I doubt you knew he's a convicted paedophile.'

I could hardly believe I'd heard correctly. I said nothing.

'I can imagine it's a shock. Deria dug up the facts. He was convicted by a Phnom Penh court in '94. The scandal is, not only didn't he serve any jail time, he wasn't even deported. In less than a year he'd reopened his practice. For that matter, he's still practising.'

'Deria and White were dating just over a week ago. Are you certain there's not been a mistake?'

Noelle paused only a moment. 'She has her details and dates all down. It's not the sort of thing you'd publish unless you were sure of your facts. Of course, we can't close his practice or expatriate him. But as of this morning he's no longer on the approved embassy medical list, and I intend to make sure that, as long as I'm here, he won't be issued any kind of visa to the US.'

It seemed pretty summary justice, based on one article in

the local paper by Deria Goldstein. But at least it was action; you could even call it 'anti-corruption' action, of some sort. And maybe it made her next job a little easier.

'However,' she said, 'that's not why I asked you here.'

'The demonstration?'

'No, no . . . It's Westin. Michael, have you handed Silk the letter yet?'

'Not yet.'

'When do you plan to?'

I'd been putting off the small but disagreeable job. I couldn't put it off any longer. I said, 'The embassy monsoon party.'

Noelle looked surprised, then the professional carapace settled back. 'That's Friday. Have you sent him an invitation yet?'

'Not yet.'

'I'll have my secretary send him one today, by messenger. With an RSVP.'

My cellphone buzzed. I said, 'Excuse me,' and flipped it open. It was Zainab. She sounded excited; she asked me if I could meet her at the little shrine on the quay, two or three blocks north of the National Theatre. I'd have to come now – the streets would soon be impassable due to the demonstration. She had something important to show me. I said I'd try, and hung up.

'I'm sorry,' I told Noelle. 'That was Mrs Ambler. You know she works for an NGO advising the Reform Party.'

'Yes, I know.'

'She wants to meet on Sisowath. She has something she wants to tell me, regarding the demonstration.'

'I'm glad you're taking your assignments as a political officer seriously enough to develop informants.' She paused. Then as if recalling a passing doubt, she said, 'But, Michael, it's all one way, isn't it? I mean, you aren't giving her any information?'

'It's one way. I don't discuss work with her.'

'Good, good. It's just that I've heard that one of her recent articles included some sensitive information. Information that normally she wouldn't have access to.'

'She is married to the British Second Secretary.'

'That's true. Come on. Let's see what the crowd looks like so far.'

We went back to the window. The march, if you could call such an undisciplined movement a march, had begun. An advance line only a block away, spanning the street, approached the embassy. The elephant lumbered down the middle of the road a little ahead. It was in the lead.

Noelle said, 'If you want to reach Mrs Ambler any time soon, I suggest you go now.'

We never figured out the exact meaning of the little shrine along the river. It was the size of a single car garage and looked like a Buddhist concession stand. Inside on a plinth stood a statue of a deity. It was pre-Buddhist, probably Hindu, or maybe one hundred per cent Cambodian – no one seemed to know for sure. From the shrine's windows young ladies sold various small devotional objects. Outside, older ladies sold lotus flowers and jasmine and the like. Two or three ladies held wicker baskets full of tiny birds; the birds were very cheap, only a few hundred riels; you bought one and released it, thereby earning good karma. (It was the intention, not the bird, that counted: young boys with nets caught the released birds almost immediately and returned them, for a minuscule fee, to their baskets.) Here and there people knelt and prayed on prayer mats that they'd laid on the grass, but mostly they sat and chatted, on the lawns or under the acacia trees.

Across the street an undeveloped, open area actually did hold concession stands. It was a Cambodian market where dozens of vendors sold various types of fried, steamed, raw and lightly salted insects. It was amusing to watch a young wife and mother walk up to a stand and closely inspect, for instance, a basket of freshly fried spiders. Picking one up carefully by a fried leg, she would take a delicate, assessing nibble.

Beyond the market ran a wide boulevard; beyond that rose the royal palace.

I reached the shrine by moto – it was the only certain way –

ahead of the advance line of demonstrators. I jumped off, paid the driver and started looking for Zainab. It didn't take long. Tall and dressed in a sleeveless green cotton blouse and slacks, she stood out. She waved to me with her bare arms and I joined her.

'Come here,' she said, and pulled me with her under a broad, thick-trunked acacia. The trunk was shaped such that you could sit not uncomfortably on one part. We took a seat together. She said, 'I expect it's going to be a long demo, and I wanted a place with some shade.'

'How many people . . .'

'Easily a thousand, maybe two. Maybe even more. No one's sure. The party went all out. It's a clever strategy: the demonstration's under the aegis of the party, but the destination is the palace, and a delegation will try to present a petition to the king. You know the monarchy's still held in high regard. Prang's going to give his speech just before the petition's delivered. I have a copy here, translated. I've highlighted the parts I pushed to include.' She handed me a slim folder.

I was grateful for the highlights, because it was a very long and prolix speech – pages and pages of it – and the translator had not been a native English speaker. Zainab's contributions were mostly concerned with the anti-corruption and land-appropriation drive, but there was something new, towards the end, which after reading twice I still didn't completely get the gist of. It was hotter than hell outside and the acacia but feebly protected us against the sun.

'What's this,' I said, 'about Burma?'

Zainab grinned. Sitting on the knobby acacia trunk, she looked cool as a cucumber. I'd often noticed that the Cambodian heat did not bother her as it did me. 'Care for a cigarette?' she said.

'No thank you.'

She lit one up. 'You remember the afternoon we spent at Wat Lanka.' It appeared to be a statement rather than a question.

I said, 'Yes,' and then, 'I will have a cigarette, thanks.'

She handed one over and lit it for me. 'The police were there to stop a demonstration. A demonstration by the monks in support of jailed monks in Burma.'

'An official translation should probably read, "Myanmar".'

'I disagree. It's a mistake to give the junta any legitimacy. The Burmese monks organized last month's pro-democracy demonstrations, and the junta jailed hundreds of them.'

'I read about it.'

'So have the Cambodians. Most have little time for what we call foreign affairs, but the common man and woman here are more sophisticated than you might think. And they don't like monks being thrown in jail.

'China's the only country in the world that has real influence on Rangoon, and there's a rumour that our Prime Minister is going to double the size of the Chinese offshore oil concession.'

'That's a new one on me.'

'Prang will state today that the Reform Party, when elected, will rescind any Chinese oil concession until the Burmese junta releases those prisoners.'

The chutzpah of it floored me. 'Zainab, the Chinese will never accept that.'

'How can you know? Has it ever been tried? I'll tell you this: it's going to be a winner for the Reform Party.'

She was high as a kite with excitement. It made her even more attractive. I thought: this is what she would have looked like, just a few years ago, hosting *Hard Talk*, right after landing a telling blow on some pompous, stuffed, Third World autocrat.

While we talked, Wat Phnom's elephant, no longer leading the pack – the marchers moved faster than the pachyderm – shuffled ponderously past. In front of the palace wall workers put the finishing touches to a prefabricated stage. Attracted by our shady tree men squeezed around and into our acacia; we abandoned it and retreated towards the river. At least Prang would be safe: in such a multitude an assassin would have to be suicidal.

The sun beat down on a thousand heads, including ours, as

the crowd pushed us further from the palace, further from the stage. I said, 'Zainab, you don't really want to stand in this heat through this whole thing, do you?'

Together we scanned the scene. The only escape route left lay to the south: to the National Theatre and the Himawari. There it might still be possible to find a moto or a tuk-tuk to get out.

'No,' she said, 'I don't. Let's go. Now. To our apartment.'

She grabbed my hand and led the way. We had to pass one of the Cambodian ladies holding a basket of birds; she'd been taken by surprise and was wondering what to do and where to go, herself. Zainab stopped, halted by an inspiration, and pulled a wad of dollar bills out of her wallet. She pressed them on the woman while indicating that she wanted the whole basket.

'Zainab, what are you doing?'

'I'm buying these birds. I'm going to free the lot.'

'Don't be ridiculous. You know they'll just be caught and returned.'

'No bird wants to be in a cage, Michael. They'll only need freedom for an hour or so – then they'll never go back.' The old lady took the wad of bills hesitantly – I expect she was unused to sudden changes of fortune, to unexpected runs on birds – and handed the basket over. Zainab ran the few steps left to the river's edge, opened the little wicker door, and started to pull the birds out, one by one, throwing them into the sky. I noticed some of the locals looking at her curiously, half smiling. I didn't blame them. It was a curious sight.

When the last bird had flown, she swung the cage out into the air, past the narrow river bank below, into the river. She swung back to me, laughing, with an expression of pure happiness, a look I recalled: it was how she looked when, to save our lives, she'd leapt from the rail of the gondola into the moat of Angkor Wat.

She grabbed my hand again and we ran through the heat and the humidity and the crowd, down the river's edge to the theatre and the hotel and air conditioning and escape. When we reached the outflow pipe I looked back. The old lady had climbed down the bank. Up to her knees in the muddy water of the Tonlé Sap, she was trying, with the aid of a long stick, to retrieve her half-drowned basket.

The embassy monsoon party the following Friday night was not, as its name suggested, in honour of or to mark the start of the monsoon. The party celebrated the monsoon's end. It was fancy dress.

Although Phnom Penh was not an official State Department hardship post, it was far off the beaten track, and also distant from the traditional Foreign Service idea of a desirable posting, such as London, Paris, or Madrid. As a result the embassy spent a fair amount of time and money on social events. Some in the embassy thought it money wasted; after all, what was Phnom Penh – from the expat perspective – but one big party town? But others pointed out that most public social activities were oriented towards the backpacking crowd, or the slightly better off cosmopolitan youth crowd, spending their bar-hopping month in Asia, or towards one of the vast number of niche NGO groups (HIV/AIDS, legal aid, eco-tourism development, etc.). These were not types with whom most embassy employees mingled. The embassy was a self-centred community. Although many members had outside connections, they tended to be with other embassies or operations like the IMF. The monsoon party was an example of an embassy social event which all employees were encouraged to attend, for which invitations would be extended to the British and French Embassies, and to which everyone could invite one or two suitable friends and acquaintances.

It was held on the *Mary Deare*, a large and well-equipped riverboat, recently refurbished in Thailand by the new American owner. The boat rode at anchor a few blocks north of the FCC on the edge of the tourist area. Coloured lights hung between bow and stern masts and along the roof of the deckhouse that covered almost all of the main deck. The deckhouse included a dance floor, bar, buffet and lounge, and featured air conditioning, a luxury on the Tonlé Sap.

I brought Zainab and Ambler as my guests. Ambler, still in his new cast, was going stir-crazy spending every night at home, and although he had to leave early to attend a governor's reception in a neighbouring province, wanted to at least make an appearance at·a night out with his wife.

The US military does not promote fancy dress parties and I do not recall an invitation to one during my career as a Wall Street technical analyst. Zainab bailed me out by deciding what identity I should assume and preparing my costume. I boarded the boat wearing an outfit of black dress slacks, a black, short-sleeved shirt, and a white clerical collar, hand-made, of cardboard covered with linen. It was meant to be humorous, and from most people's reactions, especially if they'd already had a drink or two, I suppose it was. Zainab wore what she described as a 'bewitched costume', a black, low-cut dress, ragged at the hem, with jagged red stripes and a high, scarlet-lined collar. Ambler was dressed as usual due to the official reception he would soon be attending.

We boarded the stern deck. The gangway's slope and cross-planks made it difficult for Ambler; he winced trying to gain a purchase with his crutch. Once inside, surrounded by embassy staffers and their friends filling the long deckhouse, he smiled broadly. He suggested we all head to the bar.

Music blared out of a massive stereo system and couples danced on the dance floor. By the bar I recognized Sergeant Higgins, our OIC Security, by his Batman costume. He looked credible but his wife eclipsed him. I had seen her seldom and always in uniform; she'd struck me as preferring the background. Now, dressed as Wonder Woman, she stood erect as a flagpole, hands on her waist, her feet apart, bare thighs rock-solid but inviting, bare arms bulging with sexy Michelle Obama muscles, her expression wild with fun. I must have stared; she met my eyes with a mischievous grin and, adopting a boxing attitude, threw me a one-two punch.

I turned to Zainab but she was already gone, on the dance floor with someone I didn't recognize in a black cape and mask. I turned back to the bar to Ambler but he'd moved off too, leaning on his crutch in animated conversation with a woman, not in her first youth but still attractive and showing a lot of barely covered behind under the short skirt of a French maid outfit. I ordered a drink.

A familiar voice asked me, 'Are you hearing confessions before Mass?'

It took me a moment to recognize Ann. She was hidden within a nun's costume, under cover, complete with cowl. I said, 'The collar's for old time's sake. I was defrocked years ago.' Then I complimented her on her outfit. She smiled. She looked pleased and looking forward to having fun. 'It's remarkable,' I said, 'how thoroughly a cowl can disguise you.'

'I'll have to wear one more often.'

'Can I get you a drink?'

'Thanks. Just a Coke.'

I did not recall her being a teetotaller, and I wondered if she could possibly be on duty. It seemed an unlikely venue in which to field or find an agent. It was in any case not a subject I could raise, even if I had the opportunity, which I did not.

On my other side an outstandingly built blonde in a dress with no back and little front nudged me in the ribs. I turned to her and she said, 'How about buying me a real drink, cutie?'

Ann recognized her first. 'Sheila! You're stunning as a blonde!' It was our embassy veteran from USAID.

I could hardly believe my eyes. The buttoned-down, starched brunette, a dedicated development worker with years of experience, at least in her late forties, had come, from her blonde wig down to her high-heeled shoes, as Marilyn Monroe. She pulled it off.

She put her arm around my waist and told me, 'I've always been attracted to men of the cloth.'

Wonder Woman appeared before us with a camera. 'Pose!' she ordered. I draped my arm around Marilyn and leaned into her, my head affectionately turned towards hers; I couldn't help but notice her cleavage, which appeared to be thrusting up, straight up, to me. The camera flashed. Wonder Woman peered into the display and let out a howl of laughter. She showed the picture to Marilyn. Her face fell into an expression of distaste; Marilyn morphed back into Sheila. Her new-found humour was only wig-deep. I remembered I had business and left the bar to search out Silk.

Revellers in costume packed the dance floor; I headed towards the door to get a better view. The crowd thinned out at the edges and near the companionway I found myself alone except for Robin Hood, dressed in green tights, a short green skirt and tunic and a jaunty green cap. The outfit came complete with a bow slung over one shoulder and a quiver of arrows. I took another look. It was Noelle.

We complimented each other on our costumes. I'd had just enough to drink, and felt familiar enough, or loose enough, to compliment her on her legs as well. She accepted the compliment with a calm smile. She was keeping an eye on the proceedings and I asked her if she'd seen Silk. She had – dressed as himself.

'What do you mean?' I asked.

'He's wearing a three-piece suit, a white shirt and a red tie. I wouldn't be surprised if he's wearing garters over his socks. In short, he's dressed like an American oil company executive. The strange thing is, it works. In here, it looks like another costume.'

She thought he might be upstairs, on the upper deck. She asked me to come back and tell her if the river reversed. I said I would and headed for the door.

Due to the length of the deckhouse the main deck was just a short platform in the bows and stern. This being Phnom Penh you could smoke inside; out on the stern deck I was alone. The silence was balm to my ears. A ladder led to the upper deck; I had just put my foot on the first step when a man's voice said, 'Mr Smith, I did not realize you were a religious man.' The voice came from a shadow by the bulwarks.

I'd grown tired of the running joke, and replied, maybe too bluntly, 'I'm not.'

Two figures stepped forward into the light: Hun Prang and

Deria. It was like a magic trick: they emerged from a shadow so small I could hardly see how it held Deria alone, much less the two of them together.

The yellow robes of a Buddhist monk hung from Prang's shoulders; Deria wore a costume I could not identify: a tight black leather jerkin and short, tight, black leather pants. Her legs were so white they gave the impression of phosphorescence.

Prang said, 'Please forgive me, Mr Smith, if I upset you. I did not mean any disrespect. As you can see, I too am in my national religious costume, although I am certainly not a monk.'

'Forget it,' I said. 'You both look great. I'll catch up with you later.' They stepped back into darkness and I resumed my climb.

Sofas and chairs were scattered over the rear of the upper deck, making a kind of open lounge; further forward, ornamental walls and arches divided the deck into semi-private cubicles. I lit a cigarette and ambled towards the bow, looking for a man in a three-piece suit. I found him halfway up, sitting by himself on a sofa, smoking too, nursing a drink and facing the quay.

I hailed him; he hailed me back. He said, 'Pretty toney party.'

I took a nearby chair. 'It's not Martini's.'

'You've had a career in business. Which would you prefer? Your old firm's crowd, say, at a Christmas party, or this bunch?'

It wasn't a question I expected. I gave it some thought. Government work, rock-solid pensions, occasionally work that was worthwhile, but much of the time a lot of bureaucracy, a lot of work that might, or might not, eventually prove useful. Versus the profit motive, shareholder value, growing the business, market penetration, bonuses. There was no question which group had the stronger focus. And as a result, more camaraderie, more fun. I said, 'Maybe the old firm's crowd – if the old firm still existed.'

'Went to the wall?'

'Yes.'

'Sorry to hear it. We may be going to the wall, too.'

'What do you mean?'

'Oh, just the boat. The monsoon's over. The Tonlé Sap's reversing course right now.'

'How can you tell?'

'Look at the stern.'

I did and saw immediately what he meant. Anchored by the bow, the boat rode pointing south. Now the stern had swung out into the river, not much, maybe ten degrees. I didn't see at first what it could mean. Then I heard a whoop, a yell and a splash. We got up and looked over the rail.

The boat had pulled its gangway across the pier, so gradually that no one on the pier noticed. A young man and his date were halfway across when it finally pulled free. The plank, the young man and woman fell together into the river. Fortunately the current was slow and the water warm. Already half a dozen eager hands stretched down to pull them out.

Silk said, 'So much for the stern line.'

'Once the boat's turned, they can just reset the gangway lower down the pier. It'll be on the opposite side of the boat, that's all.'

'Sure, that's the way it ought to work.'

I think we both felt the possibility of doubt. At any rate we stayed by the rail, observing as the stern swung out further until the current grabbed it and pulled the boat right around, the bow pointing north. A crew fished out the gangway and replaced it, now on the port side.

'I think I'll head down,' Silk said. 'Before the anchor chain goes.'

I pulled the embassy letter out of my pocket. 'This is for you,' I said quietly. 'It's the letter the Deputy Minister wants. It's all official and above board.' I held it out to him.

He took a step back. He said, 'Immunity from prosecution?'

'From the FCPA. That's what it amounts to.'

He held his hands up, palms out. 'No thanks,' he said. 'I don't want it. It's not for me, in any case. Give it to the Deputy Minister.'

'It's directed to all parties to your contract. That includes Westin.'

'That's fine, Mr Smith. It's good to know the Department of Justice isn't going to make trouble for my company over this small-beer oil concession. But administrations change. I don't want anything in the company's files that could surface and create problems in a future investigation.'

I put the envelope back in my pocket. 'We went to some trouble to get this,' I said. 'I hope the Deputy Minister isn't so fastidious.'

'I doubt he is. You can ask him yourself. He's on the boat.'

'On the boat?'

'It's a pretty mixed party.'

I wondered who could have invited him. 'Is he in costume?'

'Yes. I'm not sure, but I think he's supposed to be a World War One flying ace.'

A vision of the Deputy Minister in a Spad or Sopwith Camel rendered me speechless.

Silk said, 'Thanks, Mr Smith, for your help. I appreciate it. Hopefully we'll get that contract signed. I think Mr Sok is up in the bows. I'm headed to dry land. Goodnight.'

We shook hands. Then I started again towards the bow, now pointing north, up river.

The upper deck was almost deserted. I passed under arches and by empty tables, chairs, settees. A solitary drinker dressed in what may have been a toga sat alone. I didn't disturb him. I peered into mostly empty cubicles. Two held costumed couples making out. Neither of the men fitted the bill.

Then, just as the deck began to narrow, I glimpsed in a cubicle on my right a cowled nun in a white habit. She was having a drink with a Cambodian wearing an open, black leather jacket.

A white silk scarf hung carelessly over one shoulder. A pair of antique aviator goggles rested on top of his head.

It was Ann and Mr Sok, the Deputy Minister.

We all said hello. I told them I was just heading to the bows to have a cigarette, but I had some information for Mr Sok, after they'd finished. Ann surprised me by standing up and insisting that they had finished, and it was time she headed back down, and 'contributed' to the party. She left the Deputy Minister and me alone.

I sat down in her place and pulled out the envelope. I told Mr Sok what it was and handed it to him. He slipped it into an inside jacket pocket, and said, 'An unusual time and place, Mr Smith, but it is discreet. I see we are, after all, dealing directly with the US Embassy. The Prime Minister will be pleased.'

I only wanted to leave, but I didn't wish to be rude. I complimented him on his costume. He smiled.

'Influences can be curious. I was fourteen years old when my family escaped to America, just before the Khmer Rouge entered Phnom Penh. I was a good Cambodian and a royalist. The US was at first a strange environment. I knew that King Sihanouk was much interested in film. Probably to feel closer to him I studied film history and watched old films – the ones I thought might have influenced him – whenever I had the opportunity.

'That is how I saw *Grand Illusion*. It is a moral film about World War One. A German pilot – in those days they wore goggles, like mine, and a scarf – treats the men he shot down with compassion, courtesy, honour. Unusual qualities for war! Qualities I learned as a temple boy. So different from those we heard later, from our own country.

'So I came to idolize, as a teenager, those First World War airmen. They represented the virtues the monks taught me as a child. And I loved to watch them flying, high above our troubles on earth, in their aeroplanes so small they were like sport cars with wings.'

The flood of nostalgia surprised me; I wondered how much the Deputy Minister had had to drink. Some reply was necessary. I said, 'Mr Prang also came in a costume that represents Buddhist virtues. He's come as a monk.'

Mr Sok stared at me. He said, 'A monk?'

'Yes.'

'I hope for his sake there are no press photographers on board.'

'Why?'

'No Cambodian could imagine someone masquerading as a monk. It is too disrespectful. Prang does not know that. It must be because he left Cambodia when he was only four years old.' He thought for a moment. 'One of his party's slogans is "A Man of the People". What do you think of that, Mr Smith?'

I didn't want a political discussion. I said, 'I only vote in American elections,' and rose to go.

'You came with the Amblers?'

'Yes.'

'I spoke to Mr Ambler briefly downstairs. It is a pity about his leg. Do you think it makes him impatient?'

'He's had a cast on it for most of the year.'

'You know his wife is becoming a thorn in the Prime Minister's side.'

'I'm sure a very small thorn.'

'But painful. It's been suggested that you and Mrs Ambler might have an intimate knowledge of each other's work.'

I didn't know where this came from or was going to. I started to ask him, but he interrupted.

'Oh, it does not matter.' He stood up. 'I told Mr Ambler that his wife could find herself in difficulties with the authorities. I don't think he took me seriously.'

'He is the British Second Secretary.'

'He pointed that out. He has great faith in the Vienna Convention. But the English have few economic interests in this country, and his wife is a woman of colour.'

'I don't understand what that has to do with anything.'

'Neither does he. The Khmers are less experienced with foreigners than the Thais, for instance, or the Vietnamese. It would be wise for Mrs Ambler to stay in Phnom Penh, away from the provinces, until after the election.'

He'd barely finished his sentence when we both felt the deck shudder under our feet. It focused our attention on the here and now. We weren't far from the port rail; we walked together in that direction.

At first nothing looked amiss. The quayside was deserted except for two Khmers near the stern. Something about the stern drew their attention; presently one of them began to shout towards the bows but neither Mr Sok nor I could see anyone on duty there. One of the men started running up the quay in our direction. Mr Sok hailed him in Khmer as he approached, and he stopped to reply. I asked Sok what he said.

'He thinks the anchor has got loose . . . You know, these boats are poorly regulated. Accidents are common. Fatalities are rare. Our five-year plan includes stricter regulation of vessels. Probably we should go ashore.'

We headed forward together, then Sok stopped and laid his hand on my arm. 'We should leave separately,' he said. He patted his inside jacket pocket. 'We do not want to give the appearance of collusion. Please, after you, Mr Smith.'

I descended the stairs to the front deck and re-entered the deckhouse. Stepping inside I hit a sonic wall of Patsy Cline. It was like a speaker against my ear: every southern syllable loud and clear. Waltzing costumed couples filled the floor. I pushed through as politely as I could, trying to find Zainab, but halfway across Noelle found me first.

'We're sinking by the stern,' she told me. She still wore her green Robin Hood costume. 'We have to abandon ship.'

'Sinking?'

'The boat slipped its anchor and the stern crashed into some pilings. We're holed and taking on water. The crew's already on shore.'

'We'd better make an announcement.'

'The sound system's controlled from shore and there is no PA. In any case, we want to avoid a panic. I'm trying to inform first our own staff.'

'I escorted Mrs Ambler. Have you seen her?'

'I saw her near the buffet. Have you been on the upper deck?'

'Yes. I didn't see any of ours. In any case, the river's shallow this close to shore. If the boat sinks, the upper deck should still be above water.'

'Unless it capsizes. If you see any of our people on your way out, tell them to get on shore calmly, but immediately.'

We parted in opposite directions. I headed towards the stern.

I found Ann and Deria by the bar, looking like they'd come from an English vicars and tarts party (or perhaps a nuns and tarts party). They each held a drink and looked locked in close conversation. I broke it up, gave them their marching orders from Noelle, and continued on.

Zainab had moved from the buffet to the stern; she was waltzing with Prang: the Good Witch of the North in the arms of the monk. Cline warbled out 'That Old Tennessee Waltz', and when I took Zainab's arm, Prang objected: 'Oh, my friend, I hope you are not going to steal my sweetheart from me?'

'I'm afraid I must. The boat's taking on water. We're sinking.'

Zainab said, 'Sinking?' She threw her head back and laughed.

Prang looked down at his feet. 'I see no water. This is the *Mary Deare* – it's just been rebuilt. I know the owner.'

'Nevertheless, we've got to go.'

'I am sorry, but if you must . . . Mrs Ambler, it was a pleasure, as always.'

Leading her up the short companionway, I noticed a thin stream of water running down the stairs, as if someone had forgotten to turn off the tap and let the bath overflow on the landing. Outside, the stern deck was just awash. A new gangway rested on top of the low bulwark. Expecting to lead the way, I climbed up, steadying myself by holding tight to the deckhouse roof, and had just put a foot on the gangway when

Zainab landed on it with one jump. I lunged to steady her but she was already across, laughing and saying something about 'walking the plank'. I disembarked after her.

We found Noelle on the quay. With a borrowed pad and pen she checked off staff safely ashore against staff still on board. Her expression was grim and did not lighten when a group of young people, Australians by their accent, and almost certainly not invited, decided nevertheless to board what was clearly, by this time, a sinking ship. What the hell, it was a party. I wished Noelle luck and took Zainab up to the road where a row of tuk-tuks waited.

We drove straight to our apartment half a block from Martini's, and, as soon as I turned all the air conditioners on, went straight to bed. She was still pretty high, pretty happy, I thought from just having a good time (I didn't yet know what plans she had afoot). She was a pleasure to be in bed with, to make love to. Maybe somewhere in the back of my mind I even knew I loved her. We made love passionately but conventionally, if it's conventional for the man to concentrate on pleasing the woman. Unless a rock-solid, contemporary academic study exists, I expect it's a matter of opinion.

After sex I poured us both a glass of crème de cassis and we went out to the balcony for a smoke. But it was too hot to stay and as soon as we finished our cigarettes we went back inside. Zainab told me it was time for a piano lesson.

I refilled our glasses. She sat down at the upright and I sat down on the couch.

Throughout the monsoon I'd had several 'lessons', which is how we both humorously referred to them. We early determined I was not musical. But Zainab wouldn't say die; tenaciousness, not grim but pleasant, hopeful, even funny, was one of her many strong points. She would play, asking me now and then if I heard this or that, or asking my opinion of something: whether a passage sounded dissonant or consonant, disagreeable or agreeable, emotionally up or down. If I admitted I was at sea (which was usual) she would just laugh, shrug her shoulders and continue on. She was not a pedagogue. She was a performer who wanted to share with me as much as I was capable of sharing.

Save for one piece by Haydn, the F Minor Variations, all the pieces she'd played me were by Bach. For me Bach, at his easiest, is at first difficult to appreciate, and Zainab tried hard to make it accessible for me. But tonight, for some reason, she was gripped by a theme that she became recondite in her desire to illustrate.

She played a few chords to warm up, then said, 'Michael, you're a numbers person, you see truth in numbers, you believe that numbers can represent truth, don't you?'

'Two plus three equals five. No one will dispute that. Yes, selections of numbers – which after all are just quantities – carefully selected economic quantities properly computed and correlated, can represent the truth about something. It can be almost anything, depending on the selection criteria.'

She said, 'Bach believed something similar. Of course, he was a musician; he believed that music could represent truth. In his religious pieces, his masses and cantatas, he used music to represent, in a way that his listeners would immediately have understood, what he believed to be literal biblical and spiritual truth.

'But he also believed in the truth of numbers, in what we now call numerology, although these days it's not respectable. It belonged to his spiritual view of the world. As a Lutheran he believed in the trinity, so he believed that the number three and its multiples were spiritual, were significant.

'Bach used numbers as basic architecture for his music. Take these variations you've been hearing the whole monsoon! You've listened to some of them individually, but consider them as a group. There are thirty in all; each third variation is a canon – I've taught you what that is – and each canon's second part is successively at a greater interval: the first canon's is at the unison, and the ninth canon's is at the ninth.'

I said, 'I'm sure this means something for a Lutheran. I thought you were Buddhist.'

'I am. But there are many paths, Michael, that lead to a spiritual life. In Bach's numerology, the number three stood for birth, life and death; but also for the thinker, the thought, and the subject of the thinking. This sounds, philosophically, like someone stumbling towards Buddhism. And do you know what nine stood for?'

'No.'

'It stood for rebirth.'

I was reaching the end of my tolerance, but I nodded.

'Let me play you three pieces from the Goldberg. Variations three and nine, then variation twenty-five. The first two are canons; the twenty-fifth is not a canon, it's a sarabande, but it's also the third and last variation in the minor key: G minor.'

It usually took me a few minutes to get into what Zainab played. I have to admit the first piece meant nothing to me. The second tried to be cheerful but kept falling into dissonance. But the third piece, the twenty-fifth variation, gripped me.

It was like a song, but for piano, not for voice. It was slow, but intensely dramatic. It had what Zainab called chromatic passages, which almost assaulted the ear; there were two climaxes which left you on the edge of your seat, and a final climax, the melody descending and descending further, which to me, at any rate, seemed to represent death. That's what I told her when she finished.

'Yes,' she said, 'but in Buddhism death is just the moment before rebirth. It's not a depressive or pessimistic subject for meditation; it's not depressive or pessimistic at all.'

It seemed pretty pessimistic to me, although I didn't tell her that. I suggested we finish off our crème de cassis with one last cigarette outside. I wanted us to spend the night there – we seldom had an opportunity for a full night together – and asked when her husband was due back.

She said, 'Tonight, I'm afraid. You should drive me home as soon as we finish our cigarettes. But we'll be together again soon, although maybe not as soon as you'd like. I'm leaving town over the weekend – just for a few days.'

I remembered Mr Sok's suggestion, and said, 'Elections are coming up. It might be a good idea to avoid rallies. They could turn into demonstrations.'

'Don't worry. I'm not planning on attending any. But I hope to have something exciting to tell you next week. Something that's almost a kind of rebirth.'

I asked her what she meant, but she wouldn't tell me. She wanted it to be a surprise.

The night was overcast and dark. Although the monsoon was officially over, lightning flashed far to the north. I made my cigarette last as long as I could, then I drove her home.

I I

On Monday Ann told me that she'd talked to the Amblers the day before at the Himawari's pool. I assumed Zainab's trip had been cancelled or delayed. I did not call to confirm. She was the one with a spouse to work around, so I generally let her initiate our appointments.

I rang Silk on Thursday for Noelle's Westin Oil update. He told me he'd seen the Deputy Minister the day before. Mr Sok informed him that the government had agreed to award Westin a concession for block C – the block for which they'd negotiated – and that he hoped to have the contract signed before the election. Silk was satisfied. He was flying back to his office in Bangkok over the weekend, and had no plans to return to Cambodia until after the election. He was too discreet to mention the letter over the phone. It looked like Westin and the Prime Minister were on course towards a solid business relationship. Both were getting what they wanted, and both had the same thing to hide. It reminded me of certain classes of deals in my old Wall Street investment bank – just before the collapse.

On Friday night I attended a dinner hosted by the World Bank representative, at the most upscale restaurant in town. The diners were top-tier financial people: the IMF representative and his staff, the Cambodian Minister of Finance, the head of their Central Bank, etc. The Americans all had twenty-year-old economics degrees from Chicago. The conversation was like going back in time to the medieval period – the Age of Faith. Free markets, deregulation, comparative advantage. I felt like a newly minted atheist, or at least an agnostic, in a sea of believers. The food was as out of date as the degrees: haute cuisine, miniature but artistic portions in four courses spread over three hours. By the time I got home I was hungry. If you ate that way every day for two or three months you'd be in danger of starving.

The next morning I had breakfast on the terrace of my regular breakfast restaurant opposite Wat Lanka. It was a fine day, already hot. Across the street the stupas rose in a line behind the wat's high wall, and higher yet white smoke streamed from the crematorium chimney. I'd heard a rumour that the city authorities were going to close the wat crematoriums on public health grounds. I wondered what threat such minor portions of ash could pose to the population of Phnom Penh.

I was not yet alarmed or concerned, but I wondered what had happened to Zainab. I called her cellphone. But I only reached the automatic message. I tried again after lunch, but still nothing. So I decided to drop by her house on the pretext of inviting them both to the Himawari gym and pool.

The gate guards all knew me by this time, and let me in without question. I walked down the drive and saw Ambler reclining upstairs on the terrace, with a long drink. He asked me up.

He turned down the offer of the Himawari – he didn't feel up to it – and told me that Zainab had left that morning for Siem Reap, to cover another Reform Party rally. I was surprised and must have shown it. Ambler asked me if anything was wrong.

'No,' I said. 'I just didn't know there was a rally there this weekend. Usually my Deputy Chief keeps me informed. But there are so many rallies now that we're down to the wire, she probably didn't think it worth mentioning.'

He said he didn't expect Zainab back until Monday or Tuesday. He invited me to dinner after the pool, but I told him I had a previous engagement with a member of staff. We parted amicably.

That night I ate a solitary meal at Phnom Penh's only Russian restaurant. Their stroganoff is excellent but I was tired of dining alone. I finished the evening with an old movie, a pirated video I'd inherited from the house's previous occupant. It was called *The Small Back Room*, and was about the relationship between a crippled engineer and his girl, an English actress named Kathleen Byron who had a weird resemblance to Zainab, even to the high hairline, except that she was white. The man's in pain and the girl has a hell of a time keeping him off the bottle. In one scene she's late coming home and the strain of staying sober by himself is too much; he can't take it and flees the house. She catches up with him and asks, 'Where were you going?'

'I don't know.'

She says, 'A woman?'

'Maybe.'

She says simply, 'How about me?'

The man didn't resemble Ambler, except for his leg, and the woman, as I said, was white, not black. I went to bed in my big, American government-furnished house, alone.

At nine next morning the telephone rang. It was Ambler.

'Mike, I think I may have lost my wife.' His tone was jokey.

I said, 'What do you mean?'

'I woke this morning with a presentiment.'

'A what?'

'I know it sounds absurd. A presentiment. I never have such things, so I didn't know what to make of it. I woke with a strong feeling that Zainab was lost . . . hello – still there?'

'Yes.'

'I started calling her around eight but her cellphone didn't ring. I thought of calling her hotel, but I couldn't remember the name of the one she uses in Siem Reap. Then I remembered that you'd stayed up there with her during another rally, at the beginning of the monsoon.'

'Yes, we stayed at the same hotel.'

'Can you tell me the name?'

'It was La Lumière de l'Angkor. But I'm afraid I don't have its number.'

'I'll get the number. Thanks.'

'Call me when you reach her.'

But Ambler didn't reach her. She wasn't at the hotel and they didn't have a reservation. When he called to give me the news he didn't sound jokey any more. He told me he was going to try to find Prang to see if he knew anything, and asked me if I could try to reach him, or get some information about the rally through my embassy. 'You've got more staff,' he told me, 'more contacts. You can help.'

I told him I'd try but it might take a little time. I'd call him back. Then I gave it some thought: should I ring Ann directly, or go through Noelle? I decided on Noelle. Protocol.

I reached her at her home. I explained the situation but left out the presentiment. She was not impressed. 'The embassy is not a missing spouse agency,' she said. But she'd make enquiries.

No one then had any idea how far this would go.

She called me back just before noon, and asked me to get hold of Ambler and bring him to her office at the embassy.

An hour later, Ambler, Noelle, Ann and I sat together in Noelle's office. It was Sunday but Noelle looked just as professionally turned-out as if it were a regular work day. She started by introducing Ann as the embassy's Commerce Officer who, due to under-manning, did double duty as a political officer. She'd done most of the legwork for us that morning, and was here to make sure Noelle got everything right.

Ambler still walked with his crutch and I thought he already looked like an abandoned husband. Noelle told him evenly, 'We've been pretty busy on our end during the past couple of hours. What we've learned may indicate that Mrs Ambler has unwittingly put herself in a compromising position.' She paused. 'This is all about politics.

'As you know, the Prime Minister has, over many years and by many means, from assassination to bribery, destroyed and co-opted the political opposition. Based on his record, in the unlikely case that the Reform Party wins the upcoming elections, we do not believe that the Prime

Minister would allow them to assume power. He'd simply arrange a coup d'état.

'Both parties see which way the electoral wind is blowing. Neither is likely to win an outright majority. US policy is to promote democracy in this region, and we have been working, behind the scenes and at the highest levels, to promote the formation – should it be indicated by the election results – of a coalition government.

'To overcome mutual distrust, the embassy suggested a confidence-building measure. Both the Prime Minister and Prang signed on.

'You may be aware of the latest Reform Party demand, that Cambodia use its influence with China to persuade Burma to release some of the recently detained Burmese monks.'

Ambler said, 'We'll communicate more clearly if we avoid euphemisms. Burma did not detain monks. They imprisoned them. I am aware of the Reform Party's demand, because it was my wife's idea. What was your "confidence-building measure", and how does it affect my wife?'

Noelle was unused to correction; she paused momentarily. She said, 'The Prime Minister is arranging the release of a high-profile Burmese monk. The monk will appear publicly in Phnom Penh before the election. Both parties will share credit. Reform for initiating the idea and the Prime Minister for execution: for effective, "soft" diplomacy. The Thai authorities are arranging the monk's passage across their borders to Cambodia. In fact, we believe he is already near or over the Cambodian border.'

'Where does my wife come in?'

'The government insisted that Zainab pick up the monk.'

'Pick up the monk?'

'Take possession of him, near the border.'

Ambler looked incredulous. 'Why?'

'We aren't sure. We only presented the idea; we left the planning and execution to the parties. She chose the monk to be released – that could be one reason. Another may be the Thai government's disinclination to be seen dealing directly on such a sensitive issue with the Cambodian government. However, we've learned that there may be another, more sinister reason. This morning a squad of the Prime Minister's bodyguards flew north, to Siem Reap. They are flying on to Banteay Chhmar.'

Ambler interrupted, 'There is no airport at Banteay Chhmar.'

'That is true. But apparently there is a runway, or airstrip of some kind.' Noelle paused again. 'This is where we enter speculation. One of our informants suggested that the government intends to have Mrs Ambler meet with an accident.'

Silence descended upon the office.

It was my turn to ask, 'Why?'

'Our informant is close to the Prime Minister. He reached Ann this morning, on his own initiative, to tell her about the bodyguards, and his suspicions. Mrs Ambler has a history of publication. The Prime Minister suspects' – here she cast me a glance devoid of friendliness – 'that she has access to a document that could put him in an unfavourable light, regarding bribes. We all know the Prime Minister has long shown signs of paranoia. According to our informant, he is also convinced that Mrs Ambler is the source of most of Prang's campaign initiatives.'

Noelle sat back in her executive chair. 'Now, the informant does not know why this squad of the Prime Minister's personal security force is flying to Banteay Chhmar. They might have nothing to do with Mrs Ambler. They could even be there to help with the handover. Our informant himself may be subject to paranoia. However, he is a dual national, an American–Cambodian, and has been useful in the past.' She turned towards our Commerce Officer. 'Ann thinks we have to at least consider his interpretation.'

Ambler said, 'You mean your informant thinks that the Prime Minister intends to have my wife assassinated?'

'He thinks it's possible.'

'It is implausible, to say the least. She's a British subject and the wife of a British diplomat.'

Ann said, 'Mr Ambler, colour makes a difference. We've had problems, just since I've been here, with black American tourists who wind up in jail. We have a lot of pull with the government, and it's very rare for an American to spend any time in a Cambodian jail, unless we think he belongs there. But the locals just don't see a black American as a real American. *Barang* literally means "French", but what it really means is "white". To Cambodians, Mrs Ambler isn't really *Barang*. She married a *Barang*, but that doesn't make her one. There are virtually no blacks on the street, in the embassies, or with the NGOs. From the Cambodian perspective, they don't belong to our class – the class that has influence, that you can't torture, that you can't jail without good reason. That you can't assassinate.'

'She grew up in the UK.'

'It doesn't matter. The locals don't get it. The Prime Minister, I'm sure, doesn't get it. My informant does get it, because he was brought up in the States, but he's also a Cambodian. He understands the way the Prime Minister thinks. Or at least he thinks he does. I believe we have to take his analysis seriously.'

Ambler said, 'Then we have to contact Zainab immediately. She must abandon this mission and return home.'

'How?' I said. 'Do we even know where she is? Or where the handover's supposed to take place?'

'We know she left town yesterday morning for Siem Reap. At least, that's what she told me. She said she expected to be back early next week.'

Noelle asked Ann, 'Do we know when or where she's supposed to pick up this monk?'

Ann shook her head. 'The bodyguards are flying to Siem Reap today. I don't think they'll fly on to Banteay until tomorrow. That would make the pick-up Monday or Tuesday. Banteay's close to the border, both remote and easy to find – there's nothing else around you could even be sure of finding. It's where I'd choose.'

Noelle said, 'It would be best if we could reach her before she got to Banteay.'

Ann said, 'May I make a suggestion?'

'Go ahead.'

'Mr Ambler, try calling all the main hotels in Siem Reap this afternoon. There aren't that many – a few out at the airport, a few in town. If you don't have any luck, then start on the guest houses that have phones listed. I'm certain you can cover them all in a couple of hours, at most.'

Ambler said, 'All right, I will. What's the plan if we can't find her?'

Noelle said, 'Your wife is a British national. What you do next is up to your own embassy.'

'I'm sure you're aware that both my ambassador and the First Secretary are out of the country, on leave. I am Chargé d'Affaires.'

Noelle nodded. Ambler sat there, I imagine going through his options. I went over them myself. If he couldn't reach her on the phone, I didn't think they looked very good.

Eventually he said, 'We're a very small embassy. If I can't reach her I don't see any alternative to going up to Banteay myself and trying to find her.'

I had never been to Banteay Chhmar but I had heard of it. Deep in the jungle not far from the Thai border, it was a day's hard drive from Phnom Penh, partly on dirt roads. It was an overgrown, unrestored Angkor-era ruin and only with difficulty could I imagine Ambler, with his crutch, getting out of his car after such a drive and hunting through the jungle, the ruins and the undergrowth for his wife. I admired his intention, but it did not look to me like a practical plan.

'Noelle,' I said, 'I think I know what the Prime Minister is worried about – the document he thinks that Mrs Ambler has access to.'

Ambler was too much the diplomat to make a remark. Noelle looked at me without warmth. 'Yes?'

'It seems to me that, as a result, the embassy is involved in this.'

She said nothing.

'Mr Ambler's suggestion that he go is admirable, but not

very practical, considering his condition. I suggest that I go up there myself. If I can locate her tonight in Siem Reap, I'll bring her back. Otherwise, I'll push on and try to find her tomorrow.'

'At Banteay Chhmar?' she asked.

'Yes.'

'As a one-man rescue party?'

Put that way it sounded both vain and ridiculous. 'Unless,' I said, 'you can send one or more of our security people with me.'

'I can't do that. Embassy security have a well-defined mission: the security of embassy documents. The security of our personnel is the responsibility of the host country.'

Technically she was correct. But it was an example of the kind of bureaucratic position for which the department is famous.

Ambler said, 'As Chargé I have a personal bodyguard. Simmonds. British. Ex–SAS. He goes where I tell him. I can send him up with you.'

'Excellent,' I said. I hadn't yet considered the implications of needing a bodyguard.

'This is damn good of you, Mike. I appreciate it. I'll have Simmonds give you a call right away. He'll probably want to drive you in the embassy Land-Rover.' He asked Noelle directly, 'Are we set, then?'

It wasn't the kind of thing that a second-rate Deputy Chief of Mission would want to make a snap decision about. But there was nothing second rate about Noelle. She said, 'Yes, we're set. However, I'd like to remind everyone here that the fewer people who know about this, the better.'

Ambler said, 'Quite right.'

'Now, we all have a lot to do. Michael, Ann, I'd like you both to stay for a minute.'

Ambler thanked everyone, shook my hand and hobbled out. After the door closed behind him, Noelle said, 'There is a departmental protocol for almost everything. I do not recall, however, ever seeing one for a case like this. Michael, you know who Ann works for. I think it best we be frank with each other. Ann, you'd better tell Michael your sources.'

'My primary source is the Deputy Minister, Mr Sok. Hun Prang and Deria Goldstein are secondary. They're all on the payroll.'

I said, 'You mean, they're all your agents?'

'Yes. It's unusual for an American journalist to be on the payroll. Both the Agency and most journalists see it as a conflict. But she's only a stringer. And she does get around.'

Noelle said, 'Please give us your take on the intelligence.'

Ann thought for a moment. 'The Deputy Minister called me this morning – I didn't call him. He knows, I think as well as anyone can, what the Prime Minister is actually up to. Being a dual national makes him an interesting agent. He has at least three loyalties: Cambodia, the US and himself.'

Noelle asked, 'Which comes first?'

'Himself. But that includes his scruples. He may be on the take, financially – who in this government isn't? – but if he can keep an innocent woman from being assassinated, he'll try.'

'And Prang?'

'I called him. I wanted to see what he could confirm. Sok told me Prang passed Mrs Ambler her instructions.' She shook her head. 'All he'd tell me was that she'd gone north to Siem Reap to attend a rally. There are several possible motivations for trying to cover up the operation, or trying to protect it. For me, he's confirming, at the least, that Mrs Ambler's picking up the monk.'

'Deria?'

'She confirmed that Prang told her he'd give her the inside scoop on a big story before the government made an announcement. She doesn't know what it is. That's what she's good for: confirmations. She isn't reliable as a sole source.'

'Why not?'

'In her normal work she's sometimes guilty of exaggeration. She may even be libellous.'

'Libellous?'

'Her article on Dr White. His conviction could have been

legitimate. Or it could have been political. It's difficult to tell after all these years. He could be a paedophile, but I doubt it was proven – to our standards – in '94.'

Noelle said, 'I see. Thank you, Ann. Do you have anything more?'

'No, except . . . I do have certain training, that Mike doesn't, that could be useful in a situation like this. I'd be happy to go with him.'

'I commend you for your zeal. However, I don't want to empty the embassy in this hunt for Mr Ambler's wife. His bodyguard's going with Michael; that should be sufficient. And this isn't an Agency problem.' She looked at me directly. 'It's a State Department problem.'

Ann got up. She wished me luck and left the office. As soon as the door closed, Noelle walked to the window.

'Michael, do you remember the discussion we had, about one's corridor reputation?'

'Yes.'

'Having an affair with the spouse of a foreign diplomat is the kind of thing you want to avoid.'

I said nothing.

'Obviously the government had Mrs Ambler under surveillance and they found you. I hope you realize that the main reason Mrs Ambler is in this trouble, or may be in this trouble, is your affair with her. The fact that you're responsible for this situation is the only reason I agreed to you trying to find her. This whole thing, so far, is completely off-record. If it goes wrong, and an official report becomes necessary . . .' She caught herself. 'Well,' she said, 'let's hope for Mrs Ambler's sake that nothing does go wrong. I want you to stay in touch. If your cellphone works beyond Sisophon, I want regular reports.'

'I'll do my best.'

'You know the reputation the Prime Minister's bodyguards have. Try to find her before they do.'

12

Traffic was heavy heading out of the city on a Sunday afternoon. Ambler's bodyguard – the ambassador's bodyguard – drove the Land-Rover. I'd last seen Scott Simmonds the previous December, during the ill-fated Christmas party. He hadn't changed. He was still quiet, well-mannered, in control. A better example than usual of the recently retired former SAS serviceman. I say 'better', because he appeared to harbour, as far as I could tell, no obvious or even vestigial anti-American or anti-foreign prejudice. Or perhaps he just remembered my attempt at assistance during that party, and was kindly disposed to a diplomat who wasn't afraid to wield a pipe in an emergency. I don't know.

Simmonds was as aggressive a driver as the Cambodians, but more skilful. We made good time, even through the little villages and towns on the way, where anybody and anything was likely to throw itself in front of you.

We reached Siem Reap before dusk and put up at the FCC Angkor, one of the fanciest hotels in town. The desk clerk told us that although the road north was greatly improved, they were still working on it, and we should plan on three to four hours to get to Banteay Chhmar. That kind of estimate is usually optimistic in Cambodia. We decided on an early night.

Over dinner Ambler called. He'd rung every hotel and guest house with a telephone. Zainab had checked out that morning – from the FCC Angkor. It was unreasonable, but I felt like we'd just missed her.

After dinner we had a couple of drinks and went to bed.

Early the next morning we ate a big, British-style breakfast, and were on the road by eight.

Just a few miles out of Siem Reap the population fell off. The land lay uncultivated, monotonous. Hour after hour we passed half-drowned bush, half-drowned trees, waterlogged forest. I don't think we saw an electric power line between Siem Reap and Sisophon – a three-hour drive with a fast driver at the wheel.

We drove straight through Sisophon, the provincial capital of Banteay Mencheay province. In the south, I'd seen tourist towns with smaller populations but better amenities. One thing it did have, however, was cellphone service. Beyond Sisophon it was questionable. So I called Ann and Ambler to see if either had news. They did.

Ann had more details from Mr Sok. Zainab was supposed to pick up the Burmese monk outside the ruin's main entrance on Tuesday morning. He didn't know exactly when. Ambler told us that Sovan had helped Zainab pack a backpack with canned goods, Thermoses of chilled juice, torches and clothes. This suggested she might be roughing it within the ruins.

Past Sisophon we crossed three rivers. Little more than streams in the dry season, they now flowed swollen and brown. On the first a bridge was awash but still passable, on the other two makeshift ferries carried us and the Land-Rover to the other side. It took time and it was past noon when at last we turned off the highway on to a clay road leading to Banteay Chhmar. As we approached the ruin complex we passed isolated shacks and paddy. Then we reached the moat.

Simmonds was up to date, and he'd brought along satellite photos of the site. It was perhaps two-thirds of a mile square, roughly aligned to the main compass points, surrounded by a moat fifty yards wide. The clay road turned right, following the moat's southern perimeter. Floating plants covered the water. According to Simmonds's photos, small bridges crossed on three sides, but the main bridge, a stone causeway, crossed the east. Opposite the causeway we came to a village.

We drove through. It wasn't much: a few little roadside

markets and restaurants that sold only Khmer food; a handful of modest government buildings; homes, some of them showing through their construction that tourism and conservation money was beginning to have a local effect. The usual dogs and farm animals. The afternoon sun baked the dirt road. Most people sheltered inside. There was no sign of anything like a hotel or guest house, however modest.

There were also no bodyguards or police, or at least none visible. We drove back to the causeway and proceeded slowly across the moat.

Halfway over we caught our first glimpse of the men who might have come for Zainab. At the end of the bridge three men dressed in the paramilitary uniforms favoured by the Prime Minister's bodyguards stood facing us.

Cambodian police are notoriously ill-trained and ill-paid and corrupt (but on a small, even tiny scale); the Cambodian Army is so incapable they are, practically speaking, non-existent. The Prime Minister's bodyguards are different. They are the closest thing the country has to a professional fighting unit.

These three representatives of Cambodia's professional fighting unit stood out. They were taller, heavier and fitter than most Cambodian men. They wore an air of physical confidence. Their faces held the blank, slightly sinister expression common to élite forces in the developing world. They watched our approach. We rolled off and Simmonds stopped the engine. Two men blocked our advance, while the other walked to the driver's window. He told us, in heavily accented English, 'Ruin closed. Closed for two days. Turn around. Go back.'

'OK,' Simmonds said, 'no problem. Why closed?'

'VIP come. Ruin closed. You turn around, go back.'

Simmonds nodded, and made a motion with his hand to indicate that he wanted to turn the Land-Rover around. The guard by the window shouted to the other two, and they stepped away.

We made a slow, wide turn. 'Look around,' Simmonds

told me, 'make note of what you see.' I took in as much as I could. Visibility was excellent: much of the shrub and the trees between the moat and the eastern wall had been cut down. We drove back on to the causeway, Simmonds waving at the guards. Once on the bridge I told him what I'd seen.

'There's a Cessna, it looks like a 172, to the north. There's probably a landing strip running up the line of the moat. Those things don't need much. Straight ahead were two new buildings and some huts. I imagine they're used by the conservation team. The remains of the eastern wall are just beyond. It looks like they're shoring up part of it. That was about it.'

'You were in the air force, right?' I'd told him a little of my background on the way up.

'Yes,' I said.

'Can those planes carry four?'

'Yes.'

'Then there's probably a pilot around somewhere. Might be taking a nap in one of those buildings. If they only made one flight up here, then that means we only have to deal with three guards.'

I thought his confidence misplaced. As far as I knew, Simmonds was unarmed; I certainly was. There were three of them, all, presumably, armed. I did not consider it a favourable ratio.

I said, 'Don't you think they probably have weapons?'

'I'm certain of it. First things first: we'll find Mrs Ambler. Let's talk to the locals. In a place like this a black foreign woman is going to stand out a mile. If anyone saw her, or knows where she is, so will everyone in the village.'

But the locals were keeping a low profile. We managed to find a restaurant with three customers. We sat down and ordered what they had, some kind of fish soup and a beer. The waitress knew too little English to be an informant; Simmonds introduced himself to the others and asked if they spoke English. We were lucky. Two had worked for the past year for the American conservation funder, and knew enough English to converse. One was a local villager.

They told us the guards had flown in on the Cessna that morning, they thought from Siem Reap. There were three of them and the pilot, a civilian. An aircraft seldom came to the village, and always it carried authority. The guards shut the whole ruin right down. They told the conservation workers to come back on Wednesday, and even ran out the people running the modest stalls selling trinkets and drinks to the occasional tourist. They appropriated the village's only policeman and sent him to the main road to warn off visitors. (I interrupted here, and asked Simmonds why he thought we hadn't seen him. He said, 'Taking a siesta probably, or a dump – remember where we are.')

We asked if anyone had seen a foreign black woman. Our informants hadn't, but such a woman had been spotted in the vicinity; they asked the waitress (who I'm sure was also the proprietor and cook); she said that a taxi from the city brought the woman to the village on Sunday afternoon. She didn't know where the stranger had gone. She was certain – she shook her head vigorously – that she wasn't in town.

There was no place she could be, other than the ruins.

Simmonds thanked everyone, and told them we were heading back to Siem Reap. No doubt we were a curious pair, with our questions, but at least we were just *Barang*, we weren't a threat. Back in the Land-Rover Simmonds pored over the satellite photos. I didn't put in my oar. He was a quiet man and having spent time with him I recognized certain characteristics of senior enlisted men which I remembered from my days as a young officer in the services. He was youthful rather than still young. He was extraordinarily fit, but, close up, he looked older than he was, as if too much of his life had been lived under too much strain – not the kind that breaks you, but the kind of quiet, daily strain that you get used to, so that you lose awareness that it's even there. But he was on the ball. He didn't say much but he observed, probed, calculated. He was a step or two ahead of me.

We turned back the way we'd come, along the south side of the moat, as if we were heading back to Siem Reap. The island on which the temple complex sat was rigidly square. Almost immediately the whole east side disappeared from view.

The clay road curved south at the moat's south-west corner, but an older, disused dirt road forked north. Simmonds slowed and turned on to the dirt road. It ran straight up the moat's west side. Halfway along, a low earthen bridge crossed to the temple complex. It looked barely fit for foot traffic. The Land-Rover was out of the question.

We found a solitary hut at the end of a dirt path on the edge of some paddy; Simmonds parked the Land-Rover behind the hut and offered a handful of dollars to a woman with firewood under her arm. With a smile and gestures, he indicated that he wanted her to keep mum. She nodded; it wasn't a transaction that needed much explanation. We removed our backpacks from the vehicle and headed back to the moat.

The sun burned down from a cloudless sky. No breeze disturbed the rice, the trees, the water of the moat. Flat green fronds floated still, covering the surface. The earth bridge ran low and narrow, a stretch of mud barely above water. We crossed carefully and made the other side without incident.

Back on solid ground Simmonds took out a compass. I asked him, 'What's our plan?'

'Our plan is to find Mrs Ambler and take her home. It's only mid-afternoon; we've got a few hours of daylight ahead of us. I'm pretty sure she's camping out somewhere ahead. My main fear is that she'll walk out and say hello to those guards.

'We'll strike out due east and penetrate the complex right down the centre as fast as possible. We'll continue until we spot the guards, probably from behind that outer perimeter wall. If we find her, we turn around and take her back to the Land-Rover. If we don't find her, we split up and head back slowly, one of us taking the north side, the other the south.'

It sounded like a good plan. But neither of us had been inside Banteay Chhmar.

The country at first was open. Grass and low brush and the occasional tree, and frequent irregular mounds, waist-high or less, the remains of foundations, I figured, or crumbled statuary. After a few minutes I turned around and realized we'd lost sight of the moat; we could have been in any unpopulated stretch of northern Cambodia. Simmonds proceeded in a steady march, counting his paces and glancing at measured intervals at his compass. I followed closely.

The temple complex was supposed to be enclosed by a wall, but all we found was mounds of thousand-year-old masonry: degraded, worn stonework, fallen in, fallen over, overgrown. Within, the trees grew so thick that we couldn't see more than a few yards ahead and the trunks and branches cast deep shadows. Beneath the trees the undergrowth rose like mushrooms in the dark: thick moss and tendrils rampant and voracious, engulfing everything.

The temple was a complete ruin.

Towers had fallen over, galleries fallen in, floors crumbled away. Only an archaeologist trained in Angkor-style architecture could have recognized the mounds of partially buried stone, and said: 'This was a gallery leading to an inner temple; this a wall covered with bas-reliefs; this corner tower overlooked a raised pool for purification.' To us it was one pile of unidentified stones after another. Rarely a bit of roof still stood, askew and insecure, between two leaning walls; rarely, columns still held up a window's lintel or a corbelled vault. Then we came across the stone faces.

Visitors to the temple of Bayon, at Angkor Wat, will recall the massive face towers. They are square, with a face of the Buddha on each side, each face surmounted by an elaborate crown. The faces are refined, strong, inscrutable. Although staring out, they give the impression of staring inward. They are both a realistic likeness, and at the same time a portrait so idealized as to be beyond a worldly state: it may be the abstract suggestion of the aspirant approaching Nirvana.

At Bayon the face towers are arranged in concentric circles and at different levels, so that they surround you at different points of the compass and both above and below. They look everywhere and they are everywhere you look. They are uncanny. If you are capable of a spiritual feeling, you are likely to feel it there.

But at Banteay Chhmar the face towers rise up from over-grown mounds of rubble, from an undulating sea of green, as high as but half hidden by giant trees. Some are clearly missing; they must have fallen over at some dim period, shattered into many pieces and swallowed by the jungle. Evidence of other masonry is fragmentary. The towers exist without an architec-tural context. And they are worn. We saw clearly, untouched by the restorer, what countless rainy seasons over a thousand years does to stone. They are monumental, they are recognizable – but they are decrepit. I recognized them for what they once were because I'd seen Bayon. Without that, ruinous and without context, they would only be half-engulfed, corroded stone, hinting at a significance lost, unknown.

We continued on. It was a slog. Finally, beyond a partial clearing we saw a broken wall and evidence of work. We crept forward. We'd reached the eastern boundary. Down a dirt path we could just make out the stone causeway we'd driven over earlier. The guards were out of sight. We saw no trace of Zainab.

'Plan B,' Simmonds whispered. There was nothing else to do. I chose the south side, he took the north. We split up.

The complex was longer than it was wide; it took only a few minutes to reach the southern perimeter of tumbled wall. I headed west. The terrain did not improve. I clambered up and down every mound I could find, crawled, carefully, into and out of every hole, and looked behind every tree. I made slow progress. Eventually I saw the top of one of the face towers in the distance, and began to wonder if we would find her.

Then I came to a gallery still partially intact, half shrouded by roots and creeper. I stepped carefully in. Someone, prob-ably the restorers, had partially cleared it of rubble and foliage and enough light filtered through the broken stone to light my way.

Within a few yards I felt – I don't want to say a presence, because I felt neither an actual presence nor a presentiment, and whatever I felt was dim – but I sensed a kind of concentration, or a feeling of intensity . . . It was subtle but definite, and I racked my brains to recall where I'd felt it before, for it was familiar. And then I remembered: it was the same intensity I'd felt in Wat Lanka, when kneeling cross-legged on the prayer mat, surrounded by Zainab and Sovan and the western lady Buddhists, all meditating in front of that garish statue.

I climbed a few steps as the gallery rose to a higher level, and there, meditating in the lotus position on a prayer mat at the end of the gallery, her back to me, facing one of the face towers visible beyond, was Zainab. I had to call her name twice before she straightened her legs, turned and rose.

I stood in shadow. It was a moment before she recognized me. I stepped forward and embraced her. She whispered in my ear, 'This is a good place.'

'Good for what?'

She leaned back and looked at me. 'For meditating. Michael . . . what are you doing here?'

That was the beginning of a long process. It continued for over an hour, first with me then with Simmonds. We had a hell of a time convincing her she might be in danger.

We had a hell of a time because I didn't want to tell her the whole truth: I didn't want to tell her about Westin Oil, and my involvement. I told her instead about our 'intelligence', such as it was. But she wasn't connecting; it was as if I were speaking Greek. She'd been alone in those ruins for twenty-four hours, for much of that time in solitary meditation. Seeing Simmonds – her own embassy staff – helped bring her down to earth. He suggested we have something to eat. He'd brought one hundred per cent non-organic, picnic-style provisions: cold fried chicken, cheese, crisps and Coke (I supposed one didn't drink beer on an 'operation'). They were delicious.

After the meal he took over trying to convince Zainab. He started by asking her how she'd spent her time since arriving.

She'd seen the pick-up at Banteay Chhmar as an opportunity. She was acquainted with the British conservator and she'd heard a lot about the site. She knew it was off the tourist track and the thought that (one thousand years previously) it had held a design resemblance to Bayon intrigued her. Zainab herself had put forward the name of the monk to be freed; years before she'd been slightly acquainted with him, and welcoming him into freedom appealed to her. It would be the perfect end to two days of silent, solitary, concentrated meditation. She told Sovan to pack a backpack for two days, and called a limousine driver whose card she'd kept for such a purpose.

She'd lived rough for a night and a day and looked forward to another of the same. Sovan had provisioned her well. Zainab was not the type to forget hygiene – an important issue in the tropics – and had taken a dip-and-pour bath on the shore of the northern moat that morning. As I listened my admiration grew. I'd known she was an accomplished and cultivated woman. I did not know she could also, with equanimity, camp out for two days in the Cambodian jungle.

But she ended her narrative by repeating that it was absurd to suggest she was in any danger. The Prime Minister himself had wanted her to pick up the Burmese monk – whom the Prime Minister was instrumental in expatriating to Cambodia. And, she pointed out, she was the wife of the United Kingdom's Second Secretary.

I explained that the Prime Minister saw her as the brains behind Prang's ever evolving platform. She was the one upping the ante, always upping the ante, and she had to be stopped.

She just looked at me as if I were dense. She repeated, 'I'm a diplomat's wife.'

Simmonds had an advantage I did not: he was British. They shared an understanding of the colour bar in the UK that an American has to be taught and that even then finds difficult to believe. He spoke to her more bluntly than I could have.

'Mrs Ambler, were you made aware of your colour, as a child in the UK?'

'What does that have to do with anything?'

'I'm trying to make a point, to make it easier for you to

understand the present situation. As a child were you made aware of your colour?'

'Of course.'

'Did it create problems for you, in school?'

'Not as a rule from my teachers.'

'By the other students?'

'By some, yes.'

'By some, or by many?'

'By fewer, the higher I went.'

'Even in university, did you find some prejudice?'

'A limited amount.'

'And later, when you practised law?'

'I never practised. I wound up joining the BBC.'

'Really? Was your colour a liability at the BBC – even a slight liability?'

'No. It was an asset. The BBC believes in equal opportunity.'

Simmonds smiled. 'How long have you and Mr Ambler been married?'

'Six years.'

'Do you think you've been an asset to him in his career?'

'I don't know. You've no right to ask that.' She was beginning to lose her temper.

'Mrs Ambler, I want you to try to make a comparison. I'm sure you're aware that Cambodians, like most Asians, value a white skin above a darker one. You know that, don't you?'

'Yes.'

'How many black-skinned *Barang* do you know in Phnom Penh?'

That stumped her. Finally she said, 'There's a security person at the US Embassy . . . all right, I don't personally know any.'

'Do you really think the Prime Minister, and the Cambodians beneath him, think of you as a white *Barang*, or as the mistress of the British Second Secretary, himself a *Barang* with a slightly twisted taste in sex?'

She'd done a lot of work for that country. For the opposition party, it was true, not for the government. The unspoken question was, how many others saw her as Simmonds suggested the Prime Minister did? Probably not Prang, he'd been brought up in the States. But how many others?

She asked, 'Even if what you say – what you've been told – is true, how do you think they'd do it? The monk's being handed over to me, by a group of Thais, tomorrow morning in broad daylight.'

'Before I answer that question, can you tell me how you planned to get the monk back to Phnom Penh?'

'The government's providing transportation. It may already be here. I'm pretty sure I heard a small plane land this morning.'

'Yes,' Simmonds said, 'you did.' He took a breath. 'I've been giving some thought, while tramping through this ruin, as to how they could eliminate you. I think the plane is the key.' He turned to me. 'Mike, you're sure that plane can carry four people?'

'Yes. Its primary limit is weight, but it's designed to carry four average-sized people: a pilot and three passengers. That's also the number of seats.'

'Well then, Mrs Ambler is right: they aren't going to do away with her in front of the Thais – or in front of the monk. I imagine they'll want to fly the monk out, to Siem Reap. Of course, they could fly you both out, but I don't think it's going to happen that way.

'I think they'll fly the monk out with one guard with him on the plane. The other two will stick around here, with Zainab, until the Thais leave. I expect they'll tell everyone that a government car is coming to take them and Zainab back to Siem Reap. In fact, after the Thais leave and the plane's taken off, I think they'll take Zainab at gunpoint to a secluded spot and bash her head in. They won't want to risk someone hearing a shot.'

'And what,' Zainab asked, 'will they do with my body?'

'They'll weight it down – there're a million suitable stones here – and slide it into the moat.'

'You've thought of everything.'

'It's only supposition.'

'How will the government explain my disappearance?'

'They won't. It'll be a mystery. How many similar mysteries have there been, during the past decade?'

She sat still for a moment, then nodded her head. She said, 'It's hard to keep count. All right. You've convinced me. That it's a possibility. But I'm not going to leave, not now. I have to make sure the handover happens.'

Simmonds said, 'My scenario's just a guess. We don't know what's going to happen, how it will play out.'

But she wouldn't budge.

Finally Simmonds said, 'Will you promise to stay out of sight?'

'No – I want you to promise that! But I won't show myself tomorrow until I have to, and I won't if it doesn't look safe.'

That's the best we could do.

It was getting late. Simmonds said it would be a good idea if we avoided having to use our torches, and suggested we find a place to spend the night, have an early dinner and turn in.

He led us to a spot he'd found a little further east of Zainab's gallery and closer in to the centre. Originally a kind of paved courtyard, the restorers had cleared it so it was a fairly level, fairly clean place to camp. But Zainab refused to sleep there. She intended to follow her original plan, and spend part of the night resting, part meditating, in the southern gallery in which I'd found her.

After dinner she rose to go, and told Simmonds, 'I'm going to appropriate Mr Smith, if you don't mind.' It took him by surprise but he could hardly say no. He did say that we needed to meet back at the courtyard at dawn. I didn't feel completely happy at leaving Simmonds. As a heterosexual I do not hesitate at abandoning a male bond for a female, but I also felt a little like I was putting an enlisted man in his place. I'd never done that in the services (as far as I recall) and I was uncomfortable at the suggestion of it now.

But I picked up my gear and followed her back to her gallery.

Once there she took my tent and unrolled it next to hers, forming a kind of double mattress. Then she undressed. She said, as she unbuttoned her shirt, 'So you're trying to save me again.'

'I suppose so.'

'It's an attractive role.'

I don't know why, but in the failing light, among those ruins, her darkness was even more desirable. But this time she led the way. A woman can lead and still give herself; she was passionate and in control but still giving; following her lead, I gave as well. We came almost together, her breasts hanging down, her nipples against my chest. It was one of our longest lovemakings and afterwards she rolled off into the night. I could smell our sex and feel her energy, her life force, but she was almost invisible to the eye, a shadow within the shadows.

After some time she said, 'I can believe that the Prime Minister would have little hesitation in making me disappear if I was a threat to him in any way. But I can't believe he'd do it just because of my work for Prang. I'm not that important. Don't you think there's something else?'

I'd hoped to avoid it but couldn't any longer. I said, 'Yes, there is something else.' And I told her, as briefly as I could, about Westin Oil, the letter of immunity, the Prime Minister's fear that she'd get hold of a copy through me and publish it – at the height of the election season.

It took a while for her to process that, and I lay there in silence. I say 'silence', but of course I mean mental, emotional or spiritual silence. The jungle, in actual fact, is continuously loud, full of sound. One doesn't notice it so much during the day, it's the background of one's own noisy clumping through the bush. But in the evening, lying silent, you become acutely aware: of the insects, the animals, even the jungle itself: the rustle of leaves, the movement of wind and water, the small sounds of growth and the sounds of death.

Finally she said, 'The fruits of karma rarely manifest themselves so clearly.'

'What?'

'Forget it. It must have been hard on you, Michael, pushing through that filthy deal while I kept pushing virtue, kept getting Reform to up the ante on the government. I wasn't purposely trying to drive you crazy.'

'We were both doing what we had to.'

'Yes, but I was happy doing it.'

I wanted to change the subject. I asked her, 'How did your meditation go this morning?'

'It was disappointing.'

'In what way?'

'I was trying to reach a certain level . . . I have a busy life and I'm seldom able to meditate regularly – I rely on the occasional retreat. As a result I've been slow building skill. I don't have very high ambitions, but I would like to get better, perhaps realize one or two things more clearly.'

'Like what?'

'Oh, like any of the basics. The four noble truths: suffering, meaning that everything in life is imperfect and impermanent; craving, meaning that suffering is caused by ignorance and desire; Nirvana, that there is an end to suffering; and finally, the middle path, Buddhism's ten commandments. If you follow them, and meditate well, you can reach a higher spiritual level. Maybe even, after many rebirths, Nirvana.'

'It sounds to me like you've got a pretty good grasp.'

'Intellectually. But I'm sure you understand the difference between knowing something with your mind, and knowing it with your heart, with your bone marrow.'

'Yes, I think so.'

'I already believe in, understand, karma and rebirth. And I'm utterly convinced there is no God, and no soul. But you can always have a deeper understanding. And so much of mine is still of the surface, cursory.

'That's where meditation comes in. It brings many benefits,

and one of the first, most serious benefits is deep understanding. Insight.'

Insight. A word that seldom cropped up in my vocabulary, or my thoughts. As Zainab said, it means a deep understanding of something, but I never associated it with deep understanding as a result of numerical calculation, or technical analysis. To me the word always had a kind of mystical halo. Something I didn't get, a place I didn't want to go.

She asked me, 'What do you believe in?'

It wasn't the first time she'd asked, but I'd always avoided answering. The truth is, what I believe or don't believe has never much worried or interested me. I'm without religious faith. Belief systems in general arouse my scepticism; increasingly, even belief systems in economics. I said, 'Like most people, I believe in what I understand, what I know. I suppose I believe in what I can fix.'

'What you can fix?'

'My first career was as a pilot. Years ago some academics did a study, trying to find out what it was that characterized professional pilots.'

'I expect they're all thrill-seekers, risk-takers?'

'Absolutely not. *Top Gun* and all that Hollywood stuff is pure bullshit. Tom Cruise wouldn't have lasted one day. Hell, he wouldn't have lasted one hour. The military's not like that and pilots aren't like that. The most desirable profile for a test pilot is a man or woman who has more flying hours than anyone else, is a few years into middle age, and who has a spouse, two kids and a mortgage. And the characteristic that nearly all professional pilots have, military or civilian, is that they like to fix things. Almost all of them have a tool shed or a tool room in the garage.'

'Maybe that's why you're always there to save me. To fix my situation.'

'Or maybe you're just unusually accident-prone.'

She laughed and rolled half on to me again, skin to skin; it was so warm we didn't need clothes and the mosquitoes weren't troubling us yet. She said, 'Why do you want me,

Michael? Is it the constant opportunity to play the hero? Is it my intriguing personality? My music lessons? Or is it simply sex?'

I gave it no thought before answering. Sometimes that's the way truth comes out: by accident, surprising everybody, including yourself. I said, 'I think you're my better self. The better me. I must be your worse self.'

She laid her head on my chest. 'If you're my worse self then I'm better than I thought. You're better than you know. This business with Westin Oil . . . I know it's been like a slow-acting poison in your blood. Why is it poison to you? It isn't to others. Why do you hate it so much? Why did you join the Foreign Service after Lehman Brothers collapsed? You were senior enough, I'm sure you could have found another job in finance, another desk on another floor in another building full of the same group of people who'd all drunk the same Kool-Aid.

'I think you joined the Service because you wanted to work for a greater good and a greater cause than just making money. You wanted your work to stand for something more important.'

I said, 'Maybe there's something to that. But there's also job security, and a rock-solid pension at the end.'

'That's so typical! You're the most out-of-touch person I've ever known! Out of touch with yourself. You're rock solid—'

I interrupted: 'I hope you mean dependable.'

'Oh, you're dependable, totally dependable. How many scrapes have you been in, to get me out of? And where are you now? Here, with me! But you're rock solid in another way as well: dense, as dense as granite.'

My eyes had adjusted to the darkness; I saw her shake her head and reach out her hand. She tapped my forehead with her forefinger. 'What else,' she said, 'what else in there aren't you consciously connecting with? What else is going on, of which you're but dimly aware?'

'If I'm that dense, how could I possibly know?'

She got up on her knees, then bent down quickly and brushed her lips against mine. 'You're right. Now, I'm going to get dressed. You shouldn't meditate naked.'

'Where are you going?'

'Just down the gallery a little way. The end of it's gone, and you can see right through to one of those towers. It's dark but you can make it out.'

'For how long?'

'I don't know. Maybe until dawn, depending on how strong I feel.'

'We have a big day tomorrow, Zainab.'

'I'll be ready. Think of me tonight. I'll be just a few metres away.' She stood up and stepped carefully into the darkness.

I rearranged my little tent and slipped in under the mosquito net. The net was high quality, cotton, not plastic, and the night air passed through. I did think of her as I approached sleep, and my thoughts, while carnal, were also gentle, loving. As I sank further into my own darkness the carnal disappeared, and I fell asleep holding an unfamiliar image: pure love.

13

I awoke just before dawn. The sun wasn't yet over the horizon but through the gaps in the gallery's roof I saw cirrus lit up at twenty thousand feet. It was that time of day when the air is still and even the jungle is, briefly, almost silent.

Without looking I knew Zainab wasn't there.

I slid out from under the mosquito net and rose stiffly. I wasn't used to spending the entire night outside, sleeping on thinly covered stone. It occurred to me that I must look like hell. I tried to straighten my clothes, rubbed my eyes and ran my fingers through my hair. The improvement was not marked.

I found Zainab as I'd found her before, sitting on a prayer mat in the lotus position, still meditating, still at her post (I don't know why the old services phrase comes to me). She faced away, out of the open gallery, to the ruined tower in the distance. The sun reached the top of the trees and, lit at an acute angle, the details of the stone face leapt into view. For a few moments it was again a serene, inscrutable Buddha.

I must have made some noise. She slowly unwound her legs and stood and turned. Her face held a sweetness I'd seldom seen: a combination of happiness with a hint of the serenity on the stone face. I said, 'Did you get any sleep?'

'No. I meditated straight through the night.'

'You must be exhausted. We have an intense day ahead of us.'

'I feel refreshed. I was meditating deeply, I think deeper than I ever have before. I reached a different level. I achieved a breakthrough, Michael. An insight.'

'An insight?'

'Yes. But – it's hard to describe. Have you ever read the Old Testament?'

'Not for some time.'

'There's a story about one of the prophets, I forget who; maybe Moses. He wanted to find God. God told him to go up a mountain, but at the top he found only a thick cloud. He was enveloped in a cloud of unknowing, he could see nothing, but was in the place where God was.'

'I didn't think you believed in God.'

'I don't. The story's a parable. Insight doesn't always come the way you expect. I don't think you attain it on a linear path, like aiming at a goal. It may come when you're so deep into meditation you're aware of nothing except your breath, the present moment. It may come when you're enveloped in that cloud.'

'What was the insight?'

'The reality of *Dukka*. The first of the four noble truths.'

'*Dukka*?'

'The Pali word for "suffering".'

I didn't know what to say. She'd discovered, apparently at some deep level, the reality of suffering. But she looked at me, that intelligent, discriminating woman, with a look of happiness almost simple in its purity.

A high, thrice-repeated whistle interrupted our conversation; it couldn't be a bird. I turned and there was Simmonds, holding all our gear, already packed. He said, 'It's dawn. A good time to leave.'

Zainab told him, 'I have a monk to pick up at Banteay Chhmar.'

'Don't you think they can hand him over without you?'

'Maybe I'm the guarantee that the handover will take place. Or maybe I'm the guarantee that the monk makes it to Phnom Penh.'

'Maybe it's happening right now. Maybe we're already too late.'

'I doubt it. But you've got a point. We should start walking to the east wall. But there's no reason why we shouldn't have breakfast on the way. Would either of you care for a granola bar?'

She was in charge and Simmonds and I just had to accept it. She handed out her bars and bottles of water, and we hoisted our backpacks and moved out.

Like most well-brought-up, middle-class Brits, Simmonds was a polite and fast eater. He finished his granola bar and asked Zainab, 'Tell me about this monk: who is he? Does he speak English? Is he able-bodied?'

'His name's Sayadaw Maung Thant. He's Burmese but he was educated at Oxford, so, yes, he speaks English fluently. He's been in prison for several years now so I don't know how able-bodied he is.'

'You know you're doing the Burmese regime a favour.'

'At least here he'll be safe from torture. And he can still be a voice for reform, for democracy.'

As we approached the east wall, Simmonds told me, 'Remember: these are Third World Cambodian bodyguards, not the SAS. If we have to show ourselves, display confidence. The more confident you look and act, the less likely they'll try anything.' We crouched behind a mound of fallen masonry while he scouted the place out. He was back in minutes.

'There're four of them, the three guards and a guy in civilian clothes – probably the pilot – sitting around drinking coffee with condensed milk and having a smoke. Waiting for the Thais to show up. No reinforcements yet.'

Zainab asked, 'Are you expecting any?'

'I've no idea. I wish I did. We may as well get closer, keep an eye on them.' He led us to a section of wall still in good condition, with a nearly complete window. We settled down on each side of it, watching in turns.

We watched and waited for two hours.

We were too far from the village to hear sounds of life, so we didn't at first hear the 4×4. Zainab alerted us; she was at the window when the approaching vehicle drove into sight on the causeway. It drove straight up to the ruin and stopped just short of the bodyguards, now standing close as if to form a better target. At that distance we couldn't make out the number plate, whether it was Cambodian or Thai; we saw no markings on the vehicle.

Two men got out. I hadn't been in Asia long enough to identify nationalities. I could identify a Filipino or a Japanese: they're racially distinct. But Thais, Cambodians, Vietnamese – they still looked the same to me. Simmonds pointed out that neither man wore a uniform, and they carried themselves like civilians. 'I don't think these are reinforcements,' he said. 'I think these are the Thais.'

The two groups stood and talked a little away from the vehicle. They looked businesslike, friendly. They must have been communicating in English, but they were too far away for us to make anything out. At one point one of the Thais raised his arm and gestured towards the ruin – towards us. The others turned and looked in our direction. We dimly heard their voices rise and fall. 'I doubt they're discussing Angkor-era architecture,' Simmonds said. 'They're probably discussing you, Mrs Ambler.'

She said, 'Do you think the monk's in the car?'

'I don't know where else he'd be.'

'Then they're waiting for me.'

'Let's just sit tight. Let's see how this unfolds.'

Presently one of the Thais went back to their vehicle and took out a Thermos and a couple of glasses. The 4×4 was parked nearly head-on and its windscreen was tinted, so we couldn't see who or how many might still be inside. The Thai rejoined the others. They all sat down to drink and smoke.

They drank and smoked for an hour.

At a quarter to ten the Thais stood up and headed back to their vehicle. Zainab watched at the window. She alerted us: 'I think they're going.' We crowded beside her; if anyone had looked in our direction, I'm sure they would have seen three heads.

Simmonds said, 'Don't jump to conclusions.'

The Thais reached their 4×4 and climbed in. We heard the engine start.

Zainab said, 'They're going. I've got to stop them.'

'They may just be heading into town, to see if you're there. Or heading to the west entrance.'

The vehicle was parked in a place where, to turn around easily, it had to first pull forward. The driver slipped it into gear and drove forward in our direction.

Zainab said, 'They're leaving because I haven't showed.'

The 4×4 continued towards us, past the Cambodians, before it slowed and began a tight turn.

I was between them so Simmonds didn't have a chance to grab her; by the time I took my eyes off the 4×4 she'd slipped away around the wall, then in front of it, in front of us, running towards the vehicle and waving her arms.

'Christ,' I said, 'what do we do now?'

He was reaching for his backpack. 'Stay put,' he said. 'See how it plays.'

The Cambodians saw her first. They waved the Thais down. Zainab slowed to a walk, pulled her passport out of her pocket and held it up as if she were displaying her police identification at a crime scene. I suppose we've all been influenced by American television crime dramas. The Thais got out of their car again and stood amazed; even if they'd been told who to expect, it must still have been a surprise to see this tall black woman, dressed in *Barang* khakis, running out of Banteay Chhmar. Her passport and her manner did the trick. Within a couple of minutes she was shaking hands all around.

So I was surprised when I saw Simmonds carefully pull out of his pack what took me a moment to recognize as a submachine gun. It was only about twice the size of a regular revolver. He pulled out a clip and snapped it in. The weapon had the shortest barrel and longest clip I'd ever seen. 'What's that?' I stupidly asked.

'Heckler and Koch MP5.'

'Do you think we'll need it?'

'I hope not. I don't see any arms on anyone. But Mrs Ambler is pointing in the direction of the plane.'

I looked back and saw he was right. She was talking to the Cambodian bodyguards, perhaps repeating something, while pointing with her outstretched arm towards the Cessna. The men nodded their heads.

Then the Thais brought out the monk.

At a distance he looked an old man, not, as Simmonds would have said, able-bodied. The Thais had to help him down. He was short, of medium build and stooped: he walked carefully, with the aid of a cane. He was dressed in a Burmese monk's maroon robe. Zainab greeted him in the traditional Buddhist fashion. I remembered her telling us that he spoke excellent English, and wished I could hear what they said.

The Thais had accomplished their mission. I don't know if they had any doubts about the monk's or Zainab's safety. (Simmonds told me later that the Thais probably thought she was safe: in Thailand she'd belong to the untouchable class.) In any case a doubt is not necessarily a concern. They wasted no time. They said their goodbyes, got back in their 4×4 and drove away across the causeway.

The group split up. The pilot, one bodyguard and the monk started towards the plane. The two remaining guards stood together near Zainab, and smoked. One of them offered her a cigarette; she accepted. They loitered and smoked while the other three slowly made their way to the plane. Once or twice Zainab cast a glance in our direction. As the monk passed behind a stand of trees, they quietly closed in on her. If she noticed she did not give a sign.

Then the tallest guard punched her in the solar plexus.

She dropped to her knees and bent over. He knelt down beside her and, fitting his arm around her neck, started to squeeze his elbow closed.

There was no way of knowing if he wanted to restrain, disable, or kill her.

Simmonds jumped out from behind the wall and started a steady jog, cradling the sub-machine gun. I followed him.

Directly in front of us pieces of masonry with catalogue numbers painted in white strewed the ground. It was like running over an obstacle course. We'd just passed the last of the masonry when the shorter guard looked our way. He exclaimed something in Khmer and the other released Zainab and stood, facing us. I don't think either saw, in the first instant, that we were armed.

Simmonds shouted, 'Mrs Ambler, move away. Move away.' But she was too stunned to move away; she sat down on the ground, holding her neck.

The guard realized his mistake and made a grab for her but Simmonds fired a short burst in the air. That froze everyone in place. The gun sounded both quieter and harder, more metallic, more sinister, than I expected. He shouted, 'Hands up,' and everyone complied, even Zainab. For a quiet Brit, Simmonds could be an authoritive character. He said over his shoulder, 'Get her behind me.'

I did as he ordered. In a moment Simmonds had the two guards on the ground with their arms spread-eagled. He reached into his pocket and withdrew a handful of plastic ties and held them out to me. I bound the guards' hands behind their backs. Simmonds told me to tie them tight, and not worry about blood circulation. When I finished he said, 'I'm going to catch the pilot. If one of these guys moves, kick him in the balls. Fucking hard.'

He ran in the direction of the plane. I knelt by Zainab and hugged her while keeping an eye on the men on the ground. In a few minutes Simmonds arrived back with his free arm supporting the monk. 'I took care of the pilot and the guard,' he said. 'They're not going anywhere.' He asked Zainab if she was all right.

She said, 'I'm OK,' but her manner was subdued.

He asked her what she'd learned.

'The Thais saw that the plane wouldn't hold all of us. They asked if we needed a lift to Sisophon – I think it was a little joke, or maybe even an insult, on their part. One of the guards told them that a car was coming soon. After they left, he told me the plane would take Maung Thant and I'd return to Phnom Penh with them in the car.' She looked Simmonds in the eye. 'You were right.'

'Which one told you that?' Simmonds asked. 'Point him out.'

She pointed to her assailant, now on the ground. Simmonds walked over, knelt by his head and rested the gun barrel on the man's skull. He spoke low so I didn't hear him clearly. In a minute he rose and rejoined us. He said, 'The car's supposed to be here by ten. That's five minutes ago. He said it was big – he probably meant a 4×4 – and would bring more men. He could be lying. There's no way of knowing.' Simmonds looked at the plane. It wasn't far away. He asked me, 'Do you think that could carry five?'

'It's a Cessna 172. It's not rated to carry five but it might. It would be a very tight fit and it would need more runway to get off the ground. I've no idea if that dirt strip's long enough.'

We stood and considered it. I was pretty sure I knew what Simmonds was thinking. The plane was the fastest way out, maybe the only safe way, but it could be counted on to take only three of us, and the pilot. Simmonds would want the three to be him, me, and Zainab. But Zainab wouldn't go without the monk. That meant he could either leave me, or volunteer to stay on the ground himself. But staying on the ground himself meant trusting Mrs Ambler to me, a lame Burmese monk, and a pilot working for the Prime Minister.

He asked, 'Have you ever flown that type?'

'Yes.' It was like admitting to an episode in your youth you would rather have forgotten. I said, 'We used to call it a T41, but it's the same aircraft.'

'So you think you could fly it?'

'It's been close to twenty years.' I thought back. 'It's been eighteen years.'

'You were a professional pilot.'

'I flew C130s. The T41 was our first trainer. Basic flight training. Twenty-five hours.'

He looked at his watch. 'It's eight minutes past ten. Can you fly us out of here, or not?'

'Do we have time for a little risk analysis? A crash on take-off in this kind of aircraft is usually fatal. What's the alternative?'

'If reinforcements arrive armed, the alternative could be a fire-fight. We must avoid that if we can. Trying to reach the Land-Rover with the monk is not an option.'

Put so baldly, it looked like I was the only game in town. But I hated to agree. I wanted to find a way out, but there wasn't time. I had to make a snap decision. 'All right,' I said. 'I'll give it a try.'

The four of us set off, Zainab and Simmonds on either side of the monk, helping him along. Simmonds told me to go ahead, and see if the thing was airworthy. It was a good idea. I started jogging and reached the two Khmers first, on the ground and bound like the others. I searched the pilot's pockets for the ignition key, but found nothing. I assumed he'd left it in the plane.

I reached the aircraft panting and strung up. One look told me this was one old, banged-up Cessna. It was a seventies model. I didn't immediately do an external inspection; I wanted first to make sure the batteries were charged and we had fuel. I opened the pilot's door and climbed in.

Plastic was all the rage in the seventies. People actually wore it: nylon shirts, polyester trousers and skirts. Car seats and even home furniture were covered with naugahyde. Aircraft were no exception. Fire-retardant materials were not yet high on anyone's list, and the most common injuries in survivable accidents in those days were burns caused by inflammable plastic.

Everything inside this plane except the actual dials on the control panel was plastic of one kind or another, and almost forty years of wear and tear had taken its toll. I expected signs of age but the duct tape on the seats and the interior door panels did not reassure. Any carpeting or rubber matting on the floor had long since disappeared: it was bare metal. The pilot was a short man and my knees scraped the bottom of the instrument panel; I fumbled for the adjustment and pushed the seat back as far as it would go.

The instrument panel looked complete – there weren't any holes where an instrument should have been – but it was also basic. Mechanical dials for everything, of course, in an aircraft this old. There was a lot to familiarize myself with after so many years, but first things first. The key was in the ignition. I pressed the master switch (coloured red, easy to find) to 'On'.

The needles on the two fuel gauges, one for the left tank, one for the right, both swung to the right. The left showed a quarter full, the other just under half. So we had electricity and fuel.

I looked out of the door. Simmonds, Zainab and the monk were on approach. I switched the master back off and climbed out to make a quick external inspection.

There were no chocks but the pilot had wedged rocks against the tyres to prevent the aircraft from rolling. I pulled them away. The tyres were inflated. I did a walk-around, looking for landing damage, anything obviously loose, any fluid leaks. There wasn't time to double-check the fuel tanks or the engine. The plane had flown in and landed the day before; I was just going to have to expect most of it to work.

The runway was a grass strip extending from an earthen water tank in the north-east corner due west nearly the length of the ruins. Occasional trees rose on each side and a stand at the end hid the western moat. I did not remember how long the take-off run was for a fully loaded Cessna 172; it would be longer on this strip than on a smooth runway. The pilot had obviously thought it would be long enough, or he wouldn't have put it down. In any case there was nothing I could do about it, except make sure we were at full throttle on take-off.

I pulled one of the rear seats forward and found two sub-machine guns and ammunition clips in the baggage compartment. By that time the rest of the party had arrived; I motioned Simmonds in and showed him the cache. I asked him what he wanted to do with it.

He said, 'Will the weight make much of a difference?'

'In an aircraft this size, on this kind of field, it all makes a difference.'

He pulled out everything, threw the guns in the grass and hurled the clips into the water tank.

Simmonds and I helped Zainab and the monk into the back seats and then took ours in the front. I reached over to make sure his door was secure, and made everyone belt up tight.

I turned my attention to the instrument panel. It was simple, old-fashioned, there was nothing to it – but it was my first for almost twenty years. And it was over thirty years old. It was an antique. Besides the pull knob for the throttle control there were pull knobs for an engine primer, the fuel mixture and two carburettor heaters. Electronic injection and ignition had replaced chokes and carburettors and distributors by the mid-eighties. There were a few electrics under our plane's cowling – spark plugs, points – but I don't think there was anything actually electronic.

I checked my seat pocket for a take-off checklist, but found only a couple of crumpled-up receipts. Simmonds's side looked empty too. He said, 'The thing stinks of oil like an old MG.'

'It's nearly as old as I am. Do me a favour and open that map compartment.'

He pulled open the little door.

'Anything inside?'

He reached in and removed a crumpled pack of cigarettes – a Cambodian brand – and a lighter.

'That's it?'

'What did you expect?'

'I was hoping for a checklist and a map.'

'I doubt their pilot used a checklist.'

I looked at him, but his face was expressionless.

'OK,' I said. 'I'm starting the engine.'

I pressed the master switch to 'On'. The fuel gauge needles jumped again. I turned the magneto switch – even the word sounds antique – to 'Both'. Proceeding through a combination of analysis and memory, I pushed the mixture control in to full rich and pushed the throttle in a finger's distance. Then I turned the ignition to 'Start'.

The prop jerked and swung and jerked and swung again. The engine coughed. I released the ignition, waited a moment, then turned it again. Again the prop swung a couple of times but the engine failed to start.

I released the ignition and examined the panel. I'd forgotten the primer. There was no way I could remember the suggested amount required to prime a cold carburettor, and besides, did eighty degrees Fahrenheit count as cold? I gave it two shots, pulling it out and pushing it in twice. Then, once more, I switched on the ignition.

The prop swung, the engine coughed and then caught. The whole plane – mostly thin sheet aluminium – juddered and swayed. I pushed the throttle in a hair and the juddering died down. The needle on the tachometer swung and steadied. Oil pressure pointed straight up.

I had no recollection of idle RPMs on this engine. The tachometer had a narrow green area between 2,000 and 2,500 RPM, with a red line above. It wasn't much of an indication. I wanted to warm up the oil, and concentrated on the tach while gently pushing in the throttle. It sounded pretty good at 800 and I was still staring at it when Simmonds said, 'We're rolling.'

Startled, I looked up. He was right. I slammed my feet into the rudder pedals, but nothing happened; of course, the brakes were in the toes. I lifted both feet and pushed.

The plane stopped on a dime. The landscape through the windscreen swung up as the nose bounced down on the front wheel. At least the prop didn't hit the ground. But it shook me. I was going to have to multi-task a hell of a lot better.

It shook Simmonds, too: he asked carefully, 'Are you sure you're up to this?'

I thought back. As long as everything was working and set correctly, taking off in these things was like falling off a log. Or at least it was when I was twenty-two. On a smooth runway. There were special techniques on a short, rough field; what were they? Flap, probably, a little bit of flap, and maybe keeping the tail down a bit. No, I thought, that last might be a bit fancy.

The engine sounded OK and the oil temperature was rising. I put both hands on the control yoke and, looking out of the windows, checked the ailerons. They worked. I pushed the yoke in and out – the elevators balanced. The rudder pedals in the cramped space below the panel moved freely. It took me a moment to figure out the trim controls; I set both the elevator and rudder trim tabs to the take-off position. I found the flap lever over to the right; it was set to zero degrees. I wasn't one hundred per cent sure, but I pressed it down to ten degrees and checked the inboard trailing edges. The flaps went down – they worked.

I needed only one flying instrument on the panel for take-off: the airspeed indicator. And then I realized I couldn't remember the most important figure of all: the required airspeed for rotation. The dial wasn't much help. A green band stretched from about forty-six knots to eighty-five. That must be from stall to maximum climb, but what was take-off?

Simmonds said, 'OK, cut the engine, we don't have to do this.'

I heard a laugh come out of me from somewhere. I told everyone, 'Hold on tight.' Then I pushed the throttle all the way in. The engine roared to an ear-splitting blare – I remembered now that we'd always worn headphones – and the aircraft structure vibrated until we shook in our seats. I checked the tach. The RPM needle was jumping but staying high; through the windscreen the prop had spun invisible. I focused my eyes alternately on the airspeed indicator and the airstrip ahead.

I let my feet drop out of the brake pedals and the plane leapt forward.

14

I remembered the take-off runs as being short – close to no time at all – on a smooth runway, in the dense winter air of Enid, Oklahoma, and carrying for load a skinny kid and an instructor pilot. Now we had a bumpy grass strip, hot and probably thinner air, and three grown men and a woman. After the initial leap we were slower picking up speed. It would be a longer run than I recalled.

The full load kept the wheels bouncing as we accelerated and the jolts shot right up through our seats. But there was no cross-wind to lift one wing prematurely, or push me off course. I didn't play around with the rudder. The plane started rolling in the right direction and with the smallest corrections I could make I kept it there.

The airspeed indicator's needle came alive at thirty and kept going, moving to the right. The wheels bounced a little less. The wings were generating some lift. I made a snap decision: if forty-six was stall speed, I'd try rotating at fifty-five. The conversion from knots to miles is about 1.1; fifty-five knots would be a bit over sixty miles per hour. It didn't sound much, but we were only just past stall speed and the clumps of brush and trees on each side tore by in a blur.

We hit fifty. My right hand was trying to push the throttle right through the panel and my left gripped the yoke. The trees at the end of the field were getting taller. I figured we'd used up over half the strip and there was no question we were beyond the point of a safe abort. I thought I heard Simmonds yell something above the din but I couldn't make it out and anyway I had no time.

It was unlikely the airspeed indicator was accurate to more than two or three knots at best; on the ground it could easily be out further. It hit fifty-five and I let the plane run on. At sixty I gently pulled back the yoke. The nose rotated, the nose wheel left the ground, the main wheels bounced one after the other and we were airborne. What usually happened at that point happened: the wings wobbled. I tried not to over-correct and pushed the yoke forward a tad: I wanted to gain airspeed.

Now off the ground and barely climbing, we picked up airspeed faster. The treetops rose straight ahead and closing; I pulled back and we floated right over.

We were flying.

But there wasn't time to take it easy. That's what I remembered during my initial twenty-five hours on this type: there was almost never time to take it easy. You had to fly the aeroplane constantly. I raised the flaps to gain more speed and put the plane in a shallow climb to about a thousand feet – enough altitude to manoeuvre. Then I levelled out, pulled the throttle until RPMs sank to the midpoint of the tach's green zone, and, using ailerons and rudder, wallowed through my first one-hundred-and-eighty-degree turn in almost twenty years.

Simmonds shouted, 'Congratulations!'

I shouted back, 'Thanks!'

He said, 'You turned around?'

'Yes. We'll head for Siem Reap, and see how much fuel we have left at that point. If we have enough we can try for Phnom Penh. But we don't have any maps. We'll get to Siem Reap the same way the Cambodian pilot got to Banteay Chhmar: we'll follow the road. That's why I turned around.'

'There's more than one road out of Siem Reap. Can you be sure of taking the right one to Phnom Penh?'

'We won't follow a road to Phnom Penh. We'll follow the Tonlé Sap.' Looking down I saw the moat ahead and the road leading off from the south-west corner. I looked over my shoulder to Zainab and said, 'Say goodbye to Banteay Chhmar.'

She smiled, staring out of the window, excited and happy as normal people are the first time they're aloft in a small plane. Then she turned and smiled at me and blew me a kiss.

Over the road I made too tight a turn to the right and sideslipped a little before recovering. The recovery gave me confidence but the sideslip did not; I realized I was going to have to take this seriously, develop not just a flight plan but a lesson plan for the flight: a plan to relearn and recover as much as I could – in maybe two hours.

I made a mental note of the time and the fuel, and then climbed slowly to two thousand. I told Simmonds he was my navigator; I'd keep an eye on the road we were following but I was also going to do some gentle manoeuvres, and I needed him to alert me if I went off course. If we lost the road we could go higher and try to find it again, but cumulus was forming above, I estimated three eighths scattered at about six thousand feet, and once lost the road might be harder to find than we thought.

The entire flight to the outskirts of Siem Reap, including the dog-leg to Sisophon, took about ninety minutes. I didn't break any speed records. I suppose many people would consider flying in a small plane at relatively low altitude over the Cambodian jungle an exotic pleasure, something the more adventurous would pay money for. I'm pretty sure Zainab enjoyed it that way; I don't know about the monk. I expect Simmonds knew too much to enjoy it. I did not enjoy it. Even if I'd been relaxed enough, I didn't have time. I was working too hard. I used every minute to get a feel for the aeroplane and for the controls and to get reacquainted with the flying instruments. They were all useful to varying degrees, but in an aircraft this size the seat-of-your-pants component was useful as well.

I said I didn't enjoy it, but thinking back I wonder if that's true. Certainly I didn't enjoy it the way a passenger enjoys a pleasure flight. But doesn't intense concentration, intense focus on a job or even an object, release the mind from a hundred other major and minor preoccupations and worries?

What did I think about for an hour and a half? Not my role as an enabler of criminal corruption. Not my adulterous affair. Neither business nor love alighted one moment on my mind. My only thought was flying. The techniques, the observations and calculations, the muscular responses needed for flying. My focus, my work, was for a good cause: to bring the woman I loved to safety. Maybe a Buddhist would say that gave the focus a special virtue because it wasn't selfish – I don't know, I'm very ignorant on the subject. But I do think that if mindfulness (which, if I'm correct, is intense focus), really does clarify one's mind and enhance one's life, then it's having a beneficial effect every working day on a class of men and women who have never and never will wear orange robes: the architects, the designers and engineers, the pilots and painters and the carpenters who – if they're any good – stay focused for hours at a time, because they have to, to do the job right.

Although I had neither time nor interest in sightseeing I couldn't miss the lake: it started as a marsh south-west of Sisophon but soon filled the windscreen. I used the line of the lake's horizon against the cowling to confirm my vertical attitude. The Tonlé Sap was at its flood and the waters covered the floodplain. The far shore receded to the sky but the near followed the road. It was unexpected insurance, another map, a second guide to Siem Reap and one that more altitude wouldn't lose. We flew over swollen rivers and flooded paddies and flooded forests while I practised accelerations and decelerations, gentle ascents and descents, mildly banked turns to the left and to the right. And always the sun shone between the clouds and flashed on the placid waters draining south.

The minutes sped by. Simmonds and I kept track of time and airspeed and I kept track of fuel consumption. The Siem Reap airport couldn't have been more than fifteen minutes away when I told him what I'm sure he already knew: that we had no chance of reaching Phnom Penh. Our left tank was empty, the right only a quarter full. The pilot had put in just a few gallons extra for the round trip. We'd make even

Siem Reap only by Third World cowboy standards, with no reserve.

He thought for a moment and then asked if the US Embassy had anyone in Siem Reap. 'Even,' he said, 'an honorary consul?'

'I'm afraid not. No consulate, nothing. Why?'

'It would be helpful if we had someone to meet us at the airport. Someone official. Someone who could do an end-run around the police.'

I just shook my head and concentrated on flying. We were probably within Siem Reap airspace and might be showing up on their radar and I hadn't even turned on the radio. Communications would be the next challenge.

Simmonds said, 'Do you think you could land it outside town?'

The question took me by surprise. 'Why?'

'There're going to be a lot of questions if we land at the airport. We need to keep the two in the back out of police custody. I was thinking, if you could land it out of town, maybe we could rent a car to get us to Phnom Penh.'

'Where do you suggest I put it down?'

'A road, maybe. Or a good-sized, flat field?'

I may have laughed. 'I'm sorry, it's out of the question. Landing is the hardest part of flying, and this will be my first for many years. It's going to be a challenge, even on a smooth runway.'

'Right-oh. Just a thought.'

That's when the engine conked out.

It gave a splutter and then resumed and I didn't think much of it: one splutter I could handle. But then it started missing and I felt the airspeed drop. Adrenalin shot through my skull like an injection of some wonder drug. I leaned the mixture and it got worse; I riched it and it didn't get any better. I gave it more throttle but now it was missing more than it was catching. I pulled the carburettor heaters on with no effect. The right fuel tank still showed almost a quarter full; I tapped the dial hard with my knuckles – and the needle dropped like a stone to empty. The engine gave one more splutter and ceased firing. The prop free-wheeled then stopped, its blades stark through the windscreen.

Simmonds said, 'What happened?' Without the engine the only sound was the rushing of the wind against the wings and fuselage; by comparison it was almost silent, and our voices sounded loud.

I said, 'The fuel gauge needle was hung up. We ran dry.'

'The pilot must have put enough in to make it back.'

'Maybe he got to Banteay by compass heading. I don't know.'

Zainab leaned forward and said, 'What happened?'

'We ran out of fuel. We're gliding. We're going down.' I focused on airspeed and rate of descent. We'd been going about eighty knots; we were down to seventy. Our rate of descent was six hundred feet a minute; I thought we could do better than that. Up to a point the flatter the glide the slower the speed: I pulled out the yoke to get the nose up a little and our airspeed down to sixty knots. At twenty-five hundred feet our rate of descent slowed to five hundred feet a minute.

We had five minutes left in the air.

I said, 'We're not going to make the airport. Everyone start looking around for a good place to land.'

Zainab said, 'How about the main road?'

'Too much traffic. I'd prefer to avoid it.'

Simmonds said, 'Can you ditch in the lake?'

'I'm not Sully Sullenberger. These things aren't meant to be ditched. If there's no other alternative I'll try, but I don't want to.' I told them: 'Look for a good, long, flat field. A dry field. Or a secondary road without obstacles, without trees on each side or overhead wires.'

Simmonds said, 'I don't think we have to worry about overhead wires out here.'

I let them do most of the looking and concentrated on keeping our rate of descent steady. I determined where the horizon should be above the cowling and kept it there, and followed the lake shore down. Five hundred feet a minute is a good, flat rate of descent for a glide, but it's still fast for landing. I'd have to try stalling it just above ground, and that low the altimeter wouldn't be helpful. I'd have to eyeball it.

Two minutes went by and the dead silence from Simmonds and Zainab was becoming ominous. I understood their problem: most of the land was flooded. We were under fifteen hundred feet and I was beginning to think about ditching when Zainab said, 'There, up ahead, do you see the road leading off from that village?'

I looked but it took me a moment to find. It was a narrow strip of red clay among the blue and green. I said, 'The one leading straight inland?'

'Yes, that's the one.'

I asked Simmonds, 'Do you see it?'

'Yes. It looks good.'

The road looked straight and unobstructed, with no traffic, but it was at right angles to our glide path. In another few seconds we'd be over the village – an accumulation of buildings and houses on stilts. There were two decisions to make and I had to make them instantly.

'OK,' I said. 'We're going for it.'

I let us sail over the end of the road, past the village, before I started a right turn over the lake. My plan was to turn two hundred and seventy degrees and come out lined up straight with the road. I hadn't practised turning that far and I knew I'd lose more altitude than in a straight glide. If anywhere between ninety and a hundred and eighty degrees I thought I was too low, or just losing control of the turn, I'd come out early and ditch near to and parallel to the shore. The water couldn't be deep that close in.

The turn started well but went wide. I wasn't aggressive enough. I'd got used to the different forces required to control the ailerons and the rudder – the first light on the yoke, the second hard on the foot pedals. I just didn't use enough of either. We should have lost altitude in the turn and gained speed; instead we lost both altitude and speed. At the one-hundred-and-eighty-degree point we were over water and it's always hard to judge how you're doing when you're low over water. I decided to continue the turn.

Coming out of the turn we were a little over five hundred feet and fifty knots and we hadn't even cleared the village. Controls were mushy. Airspeed was decreasing and rate of descent was increasing and we were dropping flat: all bad signs. We needed to pick up airspeed just to reach the road but we were too low. Then I remembered the flaps. I'm sure I swore. I pushed the yoke in to lower the nose and slammed the flap lever all the way down.

The three or four hundred feet that followed were the worst of the flight.

I pulled up before I wanted to – we were too close to the ground – but at least I'd increased our speed. I don't know to what because I didn't have time to look at any of the flight indicators. They're not very accurate anyway, in that type of aircraft, that low.

Everything considered, it was a credible landing. It's true we barely cleared a large building by the shore – we learned later it was the local school. Probably we cleared it better than it looked at the time. It took me a few tries to centre the aircraft over the narrow road because I had to simultaneously concentrate on bleeding off speed in the flare. The stall alarm sounded and kept sounding for longer than I remembered; with forty-degree flap we were floating, at the very end, like a kite.

We landed hard and tail low. We hadn't seen the road's washboard and ruts from the air and the little sheet aluminium aircraft rumbled and shook like it wanted to shake apart. I struggled with the rudder to keep it rolling straight, until I remembered the brakes. I shoved the brakes in and we bumped and shook and skidded to a halt, ending the flight the way we began, with the road through the windscreen swinging up as the nose bounced down on the nose wheel.

15

We all just sat for a minute, stunned. It was dead silent. Probably only Simmonds and I fully understood what a miracle had just occurred. Then Zainab came alive and thanked me, the monk said something and Simmonds just said, 'Well done.'

Everyone got out but me; to my embarrassment I discovered my hands were shaking too much to open the door latch. Zainab opened it for me. She asked if I was all right but after her first look she didn't need an answer. She and Simmonds had to help me out and the first thing I did was fall on my knees on the dirt road and bend over. While Zainab held my forehead I retched and heaved, bringing up the granola bar and what remained of the previous night's dinner.

So my worst ever moment in the public eye was shared with only three people on a stretch of deserted back road in Cambodia.

When I'd finished, Zainab helped me to the side of the road. I told her I wanted to go up a little ways, away from the plane. I wanted to get the thing in perspective. Maybe I also just wanted to put some distance between it and me.

I lay down on the grassy verge on my side, propped up against a tree stump that probably should have been pulled when they built the road. Lines of low brush ran each side of the road, and beyond stretched flooded fields, scattered trees and paddy. That tree stump felt comfortable. I was too exhausted to feel ecstatic, relieved or humiliated. Zainab and the others were happy to stand after more than an hour in a cramped cockpit but I felt capable of staying propped up against that stump for some time. I was staring into the distance when the monk knelt down beside me in his maroon robe. Seen close up his face looked younger – in his fifties, maybe – than his hunched and lame body. He smiled and his smile was sweet without being effeminate; it was avuncular. It sounds absurd but his face and expression reminded me of the newspaper obituary pictures I'd seen of Walter Cronkite.

He said, 'Mrs Ambler told me this was the first time you've piloted an aircraft in fifteen years. You're a brave and skilful man.' That's all he said. His English was accented but perfect. I was so surprised, he was back on his feet and limping away on his cane before I thought of thanking him.

Then Zainab knelt beside me and pulled a can of Coke and a pack of cigarettes out of her backpack. She opened the Coke and put it in my hand, then she put a cigarette between her lips, lit it, and offered it to me, saying, 'Here, aeronaut, have this.' Lighting that cigarette was a small gesture but it was intimate and kind and I think it was that gesture – and the Coke and the cigarette – that began to wake me up and calm me down, and got me on my feet again.

I was happy to hand the baton back to Simmonds. He looked ready to carry it. He waited until I'd taken a few puffs, then told us that news that a small plane had been seen going down in our vicinity would make it to the police in Siem Reap in minutes. We needed to get moving. The village we flew over upon landing might have a car, or at least a tuk-tuk. In town, surrounded by hundreds of other *Barang*, we'd be less visible. 'If we can get Mrs Ambler to a hotel room,' he said, 'we'll be okay. No one will notice the monk. For the Cambodian police, picking out Smith and me will be like a London bobby trying to pick out two Chinese on Gerrard Street.'

So the four of us walked back the way we'd flown in, down the dirt road to the village on the water.

We'd barely passed the plane when the village children ran up to greet us. We were all (except the monk) *Barang*, we'd dropped, literally, from the sky, but the kids – most of them probably ethnic Vietnamese – greeted us with the courtesy and respect that you generally find in the children and even in the teenagers of the underdeveloped Third World. It's odd that the phenomenon of the 'oppositional' child and teen, so oppositional that they wind up with clinical diagnoses and on prescription medication, is limited largely to the 'developed' world.

But nothing could keep those kids from the plane and to prevent any accidents I went back and pocketed the ignition key. I left them gawking and touching and probably planning to take pieces home for a souvenir. They were welcome to it.

Their village consisted of huts and miniature houseboats. Our road was the only dry ground around. Dwellings stood on stilts or floated. The building we'd nearly hit was the largest: the school. It stood on piles and was painted a bright yellow. It was the only painted structure; I'd never seen so much dead grey, weathered wood still in use.

A man, the village teacher, stood in the school's doorway. We waved and he waved back; we crossed a plank to the school's deck and addressed him. He spoke English. I let Simmonds do the talking.

The village had no cars or tuk-tuks. There were a couple of motorcycles but only one was running. Siem Reap was twenty-five kilometres down the road.

But they did have boats. Boats were their motos and their tuk-tuks, and the teacher himself would be happy to take us to Chong Khneas, where we could either take a tuk-tuk into Siem Reap, or a riverboat or cruiser south to Phnom Penh. We accepted on the spot.

The teacher led us along loose planks from houseboat to hut, until we stepped down into a narrow, flat-bottomed skiff. As is common on this type of Cambodian vessel an outboard motor drove a prop at the end of a long – in our case about six foot long – prop shaft. The practical effect is to enable directional control by very small movements on the tiller. The aesthetic effect is whimsical.

We chugged out of the village and down the lake, straying not far from the shore. The waters lay placid; this far north of the narrow funnel leading to Phnom Penh no current hastened us on our way. The lake, while not completely clear, was neither the silty brown of the Tonlé Sap; it reflected the colour from the sky. The only breeze came from our own forward movement. Small birds flitted over the flooded land. It was peaceful. I think peace settled on all of us; I know it settled on me.

But sailing always stimulates my appetite. My stomach was empty and by the time we reached our destination I was starving.

Chong Khneas is the largest conglomeration of houseboats, skiffs, riverboats and cruisers on the lake. It's the transport hub for people and goods between Siem Reap, the interior, and the capital. It is also for tourists a refreshing change, alive and full of life, after the spectacular but dead ruins of Angkor.

We wound our way through the vessels and the stores, the markets and municipal buildings. Everything was either afloat or on piles. Even here, on the lake, you could not escape the NGOs; we passed a couple of newly painted riverboats converted to offices with signs in English and Khmer. I remember one: The Colorado/Cambodia Sustainable Fisheries Initiative. The Tonlé Sap fisheries had somehow sustained themselves for two thousand years of recorded history, taking the medieval warm period and little ice age in their stride; I wondered what kind of help they needed now from Colorado.

Our captain chose a pier, cut the outboard, pulled the skiff in and tied off the bow. We disembarked and paid him off.

I suggested we eat. Simmonds scanned the area, crowded with locals, tourists and hucksters, for anyone in uniform. He gave the thumbs up. We chose one of the darker establishments, sitting inside rather than outside under an awning. We asked the monk to sit at a separate table; he understood and complied with grace.

Over the meal we tried to contact our embassies, but Zainab's cellphone was dead and neither mine nor Simmonds's could acquire a signal. We discussed our next move. We had several options: head into Siem Reap and, once there, either stay put until rescued by our embassies, or take a cab south; or just board a boat – one of the many tied up outside the restaurant – sailing to Phnom Penh.

Zainab wanted to board the first cruiser going south; Simmonds wanted to find a comfortable bolthole in Siem Reap where he could contact Ambler. They looked to me to break the tie, something I dislike doing in the absence of quantitative data. We'd done well relying on Simmonds's judgement so far. I sided with him.

But the moment we left the restaurant Zainab spotted a police jeep at the other end of the road. It had to have come from Siem Reap. Simmonds said, 'Let's turn around and walk back to the piers.' He told Maung Thant: 'Sayadaw' – for that is how Zainab had told us to address him – 'it would be a good idea if you followed us off to one side.'

So we sauntered among the tourists, for all the world like tourists ourselves, along the row of piers, looking at the collection of vessels, turning down the occasional offers of trinkets, snacks and of being photographed. Halfway down, Simmonds looked back, and said, 'Don't turn around. The jeep's moving in our direction. We'd better board one of these boats.'

As if he were reading our minds a Cambodian leapt from the stern of the nearest skiff and offered us, in practised but limited English, a tour of 'the floating village'. We could start immediately. Simmonds beckoned the monk and we boarded. The skiff was similar in size to the first but a canvas awning stretched from bow to stern to protect tourists from the sun. It hid us a little from the shore. The captain untied his boat and started the motor. I looked back as we pushed away from the pier. The jeep was parked a few dozen yards away but I saw no police. We might have given them the slip.

We motored out beyond the confusion of anchored and tied-up boats of every size and description, out to a narrow but open channel, lined with the things that tourists come to see: a forest of waterlogged trees, a string of houseboats. Our captain kept up a running tourist-guide monologue, long memorized and repeated verbatim. The roar of the outboard motor, thank God, drowned most of it out.

I thought, what a waste of time: after an hour and a half flying over this lake, we're now going to spend an hour floating on it to no purpose. The prospect was soporific. Fatigue, the heat, the tedium of the water rushing by, the monotonous roar of the outboard – it was too much. I began to nod off.

So at first I hardly noticed the small skiff far ahead, much smaller than ours, little more than a rowing boat. But it had an outboard: a line of foam streamed from the bow and the occupant held a tiller. It was heading straight for us, keeping a steady course. We were bow to bow, the rate of our approach the sum of our forward speeds. I clawed up from my comatose state as we closed, the other boat growing larger and larger, faster and faster, a collision every second more inevitable. I heard Simmonds yell something to the captain but it looked already too late. At the last moment the oncoming skiff swerved enough to just graze our side, throwing a splash of water in my face; I dimly saw an arm pitch something into the air. Then a clunk as a hook caught, the captain throttled right back and we pitched forward as our boat slowed to almost dead in the water. We had the other skiff in tow at the end of a short line, its grapple wedged firm in our hull. I watched in disbelief as a young Cambodian woman in shirt and shorts jumped like an acrobat from her own bow to our stern gunwale, stepped down and stood before us under the awning, smiling with her lips tight closed, excited but controlled. It was Sovan.

We were too incredulous to do anything but call her name.

For once with the *Barang* she was mistress of the situation. She embraced Zainab and bowed to the rest of us, her hands together as if in prayer; she bowed low to the monk. Then she told us: 'Mr Ambler send me here. You all come with me. I take you to Phnom Penh.'

Zainab asked, 'How did you find us?'

Sovan said, simply, 'Everyone know.'

I said 'Everyone?'

Simmonds asked her, 'You're from here, aren't you?'

'Yes.'

'That's what I thought. She means the bush telegraph. That explains the police back at Chong Khneas.'

Sovan said, 'I take you to a place no one know. I take you now, in my boat. Mr Simmonds, you give this man money. Twenty dollars. Then I talk to him.' She gestured to our Cambodian captain, who had watched and listened with equanimity, as if his craft were boarded this way on a daily basis. Simmonds opened his wallet and pulled out a bill and handed it over. Sovan spoke to the captain rapidly in their language and he nodded his head. I imagine the twenty dollars paid for his silence. It was a done deal.

She pulled her boat closer and held the line while the four of us boarded. Then she freed the grapple and jumped across. Her skiff was too narrow for anyone to sit abreast; Simmonds told us to sit steady. We were a full complement. The skiff had little freeboard left.

Sovan started the outboard and we motored into open water. None of us had an idea of where we were going. In retrospect I can't help but wonder what induced us to unquestioningly put ourselves in the hands of Ambler's young housemaid, an uneducated girl from a family of fishermen, who had previously passed a brief sojourn as a hospitality girl at Martini's. It might have been sheer fatigue, but Simmonds at least was trained to overcome the degree of fatigue we'd so far experienced; it might have been a perceived lack of alternatives, although we could just as easily have finished our 'tour', gone back to shore and tried to board a ferry south.

I believe it was Sovan's character. She was neither articulate nor expressive, but we knew she had our best interests at heart. She was a woman who, due to the circumstances of her life, had become a survivor, had learned how to do what it takes to survive. And in Chong Khneas and the floating villages and flooded forests and swamps around and in the lake itself, she was in her native environment – in her element. We could trust her motivation, her judgement and her knowledge. At least we were pretty sure we could. Who else did we have?

Presently she steered us towards a line of waterlogged trees. It was a small wood that normally grew on a slight rise or hill – judging from the trunks, I don't think the water was deeper than six feet. She throttled the two-stroke back (we left a thin trail of oily smoke behind us) and manoeuvred skilfully between the trees.

We came out into a narrow but deeper channel and turned back, I thought, towards shore – although by this time it was difficult to tell in what direction we sailed. Sovan did not increase our speed. Soon, even if we weren't sure where we were going, we did know where we were. The sunken bows and sterns just breaking the surface of the water on each side, then the half-sunken skiffs, houseboats and riverboats large and small, told the story. It was a vessel graveyard.

Simmonds queried Sovan and after several tries and partial explanations, we had the picture. Some vessels were owned by families who had moved to dry land for a season, meaning to return, but who, for one reason or another, had not. In this climate, without regular maintenance, they quickly decayed, began taking on water, and sank. Others, already in poor condition, were anchored with the intention of being repaired, but the funds were used for another purpose, the repairs would have to come later – decay had come first. The rest were just too old, too broken and too rotten to be any longer worth repairing; they'd been frankly abandoned.

Sovan turned into a tributary. As soon as we entered we saw it: a small riverboat, old, very old, but afloat – not even listing. 'There,' she said, pointing. 'There, the boat I rent for you, madam,' (she always called Zainab 'madam') 'Mr Smith, Mr Simmonds, Sayadaw. Boat's name, *Bayon*. This boat take us to Phnom Penh.'

She cut the engine and we coasted to the bow. She threw a line to the deck and jumped up after it, then tied it off and helped us aboard.

Later, Simmonds and I paced the deck to discover the boat's

length. The upper deck was short and the main deck ended at the wheelhouse, but we estimated the hull at about thirty feet. That is not trivial, but for a vessel meant to carry parties of people on two decks, it is not large.

The riverboat was free of furniture. The Cambodians would have little use for deckchairs and it was a long time since groups of *Barang* tourists, after a morning at Angkor Wat, had drunk and lounged and laughed on these decks. The decks and hull and railings were gayer then; a few patches of blue paint still remained. But the wood had weathered bare: an open-grained grey that came off in powder and flakes on to your hand. At least we had freeboard; without passengers or cargo (but, we discovered, with a foot of water in the bilge) we had a metre of hull above water. It gave us confidence being that high; it was like being on a ship.

At the stern the main deck was split-level: you stepped down a ladder through a short doorway into the wheelhouse. The ceiling was too low for anyone but Sovan to stand. Here were the wheel and windows (caked with grime) for the steersman. He or she and the whole Cambodian family that owned the boat would have had their meals and slept and socialized here while the *Barang* partied above.

Another ladder led to the wheelhouse roof, surrounded by a low rail; from there you climbed again to the upper deck. The weathered boards creaked beneath our feet and a section of the starboard rail was gone. After a brief inspection Simmonds and I climbed back down. He asked Sovan, 'How long has she been laid up?'

When she didn't understand she shook her head.

'I mean, how long has the boat been tied up here?'

'One year only. That why it still float. Not like others. I know owner. Mr Ambler rent it for very good price.'

Simmonds said, 'I bet he did.' He added, 'Where's the engine?'

For the first time Sovan sounded hesitant. She asked him, 'You know engines?'

'Yes.'

Her face, normally inexpressive, displayed relief. 'Come with me.'

We followed her down into the wheelhouse and then down again, through a smaller hatch leading forward beneath the main deck, to what passed as the engine room. At least we could stand, although our feet were in water. The only light came through the hatchway we'd just entered. Simmonds examined the underside of the deck and found an overhead hatch. Together we pushed it up and to one side. Then we examined the engine.

It was, as Simmonds described it, a six–cylinder, in-line petrol engine of ancient make, probably Japanese. He was sure it was older than the boat. He took an immediate and detailed interest and I left it to him. I asked him if he thought he could get it going. 'We'll know soon enough,' he said. 'A lot depends on the battery.'

Sovan peered down at us from the wheelhouse hatchway and must have heard; she asked, 'You need battery?'

Simmonds looked up. 'You have one?'

'Yes. Boat owner give me. In my boat.'

So we clambered out and fetched it. She'd thought of a lot, just about everything. In that little skiff she'd stowed a battery, a can of fuel, enough food to get us all through the rest of the day and night and even a box of hand tools. Simmonds gave a look of pure pleasure when he saw those. We'd both grown up just past the generation of teenagers who learned about mechanics by working on an old banger in the garage, but Simmonds's whole career had been in the British Army, the SAS, and he was expected to be able to fix things when they went wrong. Seeing him work on that filthy engine, ankle-deep in water, I realized that he enjoyed the challenge.

He did not work alone. The monk explained that he'd grown up on boats in Burma, and knew about engines. He asked us humbly if there was anything he could do. After turning the engine over without a sign of life Simmonds decided that the points and plugs were either oily or damp. The one thing we hadn't brought was rags, so I donated a spare shirt, and Simmonds and the monk, the latter with his robe tied up in a knot above his knees, spent an hour cleaning and drying the electrics.

Together they got the engine going, although very rough at first. A little more adjustment and it settled down, firing on all six cylinders.

Sovan retied her skiff to the riverboat's stern and Zainab and I raised the anchor. We motored slowly out of the tributary into the channel. Sovan manned the wheel while Zainab and I leaned over the top of the wheelhouse, cleaning the windows with her spare shirts. Simmonds hovered over the engine and the monk made his way forward to the bow where he sat cross-legged, perhaps praying for a safe journey, under the shade of the upper deck.

I'm not often very mindful of the wider picture, of the whole scene as it were, at any given moment. But for some reason I took it in then. I paused for a moment in cleaning my window and peered through it at the Cambodian housemaid, squatting on the floor of the wheelhouse with a confident hand on the wheel. I couldn't see the retired SAS warrant officer but I could imagine him, smeared now with oil and grease, bent over the carburettor, pondering an adjustment to the butterfly valve. Looking over my shoulder I could see, in profile, the doctor of law and present transparency consultant stretched out on her stomach, cleaning the wheelhouse's rear windows with one of her own shirts. And in the bows an Oxford-educated Burmese monk sat meditating, or perhaps praying – I hoped whichever activity was most likely to bring us luck. Or, as Zainab's NGO crowd would have said, the most favourable outcome.

The *Bayon* sailed slowly down the channel, making headway, its crew engaged in duties and chores . . . passing on each side the half-sunken and the drowned and sunken skiffs and houseboats and riverboats, some showing a bit of stern, some their bow, some the broken ends of ribs from a deckless and decayed hull. We passed them by, the only one still afloat.

I went back to my window, scrubbing harder, looking forward to the open water of the Tonlé Sap.

16

Once out of the channel Sovan gave the engine more throttle
and we picked up speed. Half an hour later the last sight of
land sank below the horizon. Wherever the shipping lane lay
in the lake when at flood, Sovan kept us out of it. We saw no
other vessels. I think everyone felt a sense of optimism, except
perhaps Simmonds, who was still below deck, concerned with
the engine. When Sovan wanted to open the throttle further
he put his foot down.

'You can't push it any harder,' he said. 'God only knows
when the oil was last changed, and we don't have a supply.
The piston rings are worn out – take a look at our exhaust.
You'd think this was a two-stroke, instead of a four. And the
bilge pump is only just working. I'm certain we're taking on
water. Going any faster threatens to open the planks.'

Sovan took it gracefully and settled down to steer. Zainab
gave her a hug that produced a repressed smile. Then
Zainab opened her pack, pulled out her sleeping gear and
made up a bed on the wheelhouse floor. She'd been up all
night and it was now past two. Looking at her lying on the
floor beside her housemaid, it occurred to me that an observer
might think we were going a little native. The idea wouldn't
have bothered Zainab and it didn't bother me.

Eventually even Simmonds couldn't do any more below
deck and he came up with a bucket and rope. He stripped
down to his shorts and washed himself as best he could with
the brackish water of the lake. The monk still sat in the
bows and to give him his privacy and us a little more breeze
Simmonds and I climbed to the upper deck. We leaned

against what remained of the railing and smoked. It was only our second day together, but it had been a fairly intense bonding experience, even, I think, for a former SAS warrant officer.

The US hasn't had a draft for thirty-five years. The results have been both positive and negative. On the positive side our armed services are much more professional. On the negative, most middle-aged and younger citizens are ignorant of the services and of service life. Nowadays most Americans under sixty, if they think of service men and women at all, probably think of them as violent risk-takers, possibly with anger management issues, and parochial in their everyday interests and tastes. Nothing could be further from the truth. Professional service men and women are, in my direct experience, temperamentally and professionally cautious. They shun risk whenever possible; risk is anathema to them. This is exactly as it should be, and will be obvious to anyone who gives it a minute of thought. Similarly, the armed services are no place for people with anger management issues. Those types do not last in such a heavily disciplined environment, where a high degree of tolerance is necessary to live and work for twenty or more years on rotating shifts, often under pressure, with people from different classes, countries, education and interests. Finally, service men and women travel. Typically at least a third of their career will be spent overseas, either in a war zone, or on a European NATO assignment, or at some other overseas military base. At these bases they interact with the locals professionally and (to a more limited degree in war zones) socially. Americans in the services travel far more than American civilians and, as a result, are the single most cosmopolitan and worldly segment of American society.

The situation is identical in the UK and as a result it took two days for Simmonds to open up, as opposed to the several weeks or months – or even years – required by the average Brit. And I'd spent four years in the services. It wasn't much compared to his quarter century, but it was another shared experience.

We began by talking about the engine and our chances of making Phnom Penh. He pointed out that, at a certain point, the lake would begin to narrow again, forming an ever tightening funnel to the capital, and from there on the current would increase. In other words if we could just make it to that funnel there was a chance that we could drift home.

Home. It's less likely to be a fixed concept for an ex-serviceman. I asked Simmonds about his, and it was as I expected. He returned to the Midlands town in which he'd been born and brought up only to visit his aged parents. His home now was that of his second wife: he had adopted Truro in Cornwall. He spoke of it with the pride of possession. I'd visited that small provincial capital years before on a holiday, and remembered enough to draw him out. One thing led to another and I learned that he had one daughter, still a child, from his second marriage (his wife, whom I had never met, was in Phnom Penh) and two grown sons from his first marriage at university in the UK. They were both studying engineering. The apples had not fallen far from the tree. I told him he must be very proud.

'I've not got much to be proud of,' he said. 'Their mother reared them largely by herself. I was away too much of the time. It was partly the demands of the services, but partly also my fault. I was a young man and I neglected my responsibilities. I try now to make up for it. I see them whenever I can, try to spend time with them, try to be a father. They'll be coming out here in a few weeks.'

I asked him, 'Do they get along with your new wife?'

'They do, thank God. It's my first wife's doing. She could easily have set them against her and against me. But she did not. It was I who grew away from her, I who wanted the divorce. It should have made her hate me. It didn't. I'll always be grateful to her.'

It was the admission of a man guilty (he didn't say as much, but it was given) of infidelity; but who admitted his failures, who was trying to redeem himself, and who was grateful to the woman who had, at least to a degree, forgiven him. His narration was so straightforward, so devoid of resentment or blame (except to himself), I felt it must be either naive or true. It rang true to me and I was moved to ask him, as if he were a monk instead of a retired SAS warrant officer, 'What do you do, when you've done something wrong, but that you can't regret; when it's inevitable that you're going to hurt someone – or cause someone to hurt another?'

He said, 'You do what it takes to put it right.'

The answer was so simple. So clear-cut. But the 'how' was missing – as it must be, for wouldn't the details be different in each case?

What did I have to 'put right'?

An adulterous love affair with the Englishwoman sleeping on the floor of the wheelhouse. How could I put that right? As far as I could see, there were three courses of action: keep on as we were; break it off; marry her.

I wasn't prepared to end anything with Zainab. I loved her, I wanted her, and she wanted me. Keeping on as we were was not a long-term option. It wasn't fair to her, to keep encouraging her abuse of her husband. Was I prepared to marry her? If I wasn't, what the hell was I doing on this boat?

I explained to her once how I managed to enter my fourth decade still single. I had as many reasons as decades, but the real one, clearly, was fear of commitment. What was the cause? Was it rooted in childhood trauma: some infant episode with my mother perhaps, or some fault in my parents' relationship? How should I know? As far as I recall, my childhood was perfectly normal; if there was trauma, I'd forgotten it. I've never been addicted to self-analysis. And it didn't matter. Sooner or later every normal person outgrows their childhood. It was time for me to outgrow mine.

She would have to get a divorce. I didn't think there would be guilt, but there would be regret on Zainab's side – it was inevitable. The kind of regret you can do nothing about. I hoped she'd be sensible enough to put it behind her. Were there practical considerations? It would be a blow to my career, but not as bad as a continuing affair. An affair garners opprobrium; a marriage, even to a recent divorcee, even to one's former mistress, approval. And experienced economists are hard for the State Department to recruit. The department's inclination would be to forgive and forget. The whole thing would blow over in a few years – long before retirement.

Sitting under a tropical sun on the upper deck of a gently rocking riverboat can lead to dreams. I'd fallen half asleep when I heard Simmonds say, 'I'd better spell Sovan.' I didn't want to stay up there by myself and anyway I was getting too much sun. I followed him down. He climbed into the wheelhouse and I unrolled my bedding on the lower deck and stretched out. It was far from my air-conditioned bedroom, or any idea of comfort, but I was more tired than I knew. In a minute I fell asleep . . .

. . . *and half awoke for the first time in hours, on my soft bed in my air-conditioned room on the fourth floor of the Himawari. Half awake, I was still half in my dream, asleep on the deck of the retired riverboat on the Tonlé Sap, and I knew the riverboat was the dream, a dream of the past, but I didn't want to leave: I wanted to stay on that deck and on that lake; the dream, as uncomfortable as it was, was preferable to the reality of the sterile hotel room, devoid of love, of hope. In such states, half dreaming, half awake, it's possible by an effort to retreat. Gently I slipped back, out of the present, back into the past . . .*

. . . and felt the thin padding and the hard deck, and smelled the fresh air mixed with the brackish odour of the lake, with the sharper whiff of burned oil from our narrow smoke-stack above the wheelhouse. I looked at my watch. I'd been asleep for over two hours. The afternoon was well advanced. Further up the deck Sovan was preparing to boil rice; incredibly, she'd even brought a miniature gas burner and the pot was already on the ring. Zainab and the monk sat beside her, talking together. When I sat up Zainab excused herself and joined me. She knelt and said, 'Michael, I have something to tell you. In private. Can we go to the upper deck?'

'Sure.' I had no idea what she wanted to say, but I was willing to follow her anywhere. Once above, we stood together at the rail.

She said, 'The day was pretty non-stop until we boarded this boat, wasn't it?'

'Yes, it was.'

'You must be exhausted.'

'I'm rested now.'

'So am I. I've had time to think. I've thought about what you told me last night, about your efforts with the oil company, with the Deputy Minister, about that letter . . . and about me, about us.'

She continued quietly, almost as if thinking aloud, but not about that damned letter – about our relationship. She spoke as if she were tying up the strands, trying to make sense of things. Her voice, when speaking intimately, was soft (she was English) and a late afternoon breeze that had come up over the lake blew a few of her words away.

Her idea was that we'd been moving in tandem, as our relationship progressed, but in opposite directions. The more our affair advanced, the deeper I'd got into enabling corruption and the deeper she'd got into promoting transparency. But only official, only governmental transparency: as far as our affair was concerned, she'd been going deeper into adultery, into betrayal. 'It's as if,' she said, 'the more we made love, the more I needed to up the ante on virtue – but only government virtue. The very kind' (she flashed me a half-ashamed smile, as if apologizing for my failure) 'you were trying to undermine.'

'I wonder,' she said, 'about my motivation.'

I interrupted: 'You wonder about your motivation for our affair?'

'No, no . . . that's clear enough – I think. Maybe we should both look into that. But I meant my motivation for getting Prang to sign on to all those initiatives. He wasn't all that keen, you know, especially towards the end. He was afraid we were pushing too hard, and he even said we might have trouble ourselves, in the unlikely case we won, keeping up to the mark. I had to convince him. Why did I? Why did I keep pushing the party up to a higher level of virtue? Was it . . .' But here the wind intervened. I thought I caught the word 'redeem', but I'm not sure.

Her last questions hung unanswered. I couldn't provide answers. I scanned the sky. The cumulus of the morning had dissipated and the sky was clear except for wisps of cirrus. The sun neared the horizon. The breeze over the lake was warm.

She said, 'Now I understand your anger.'

'Anger?'

'Yes. Almost every time we met, you were deeper into corruption and I was higher on my high horse of NGO virtue and transparency. I must have driven you crazy. Why did you continue seeing me, Michael?'

'You never drove me crazy.'

'I made you angry as hell. The day at Wat Lanka, remember?'

I remembered. 'A one-off.'

'How you must have resented me. That explains some of the sex.'

'The sex?'

'It wasn't all love, was it?'

I wondered if this was part of why I was still single. Not fear of commitment: fear of communication. But Zainab was worth it. She was worth the occasional discomfort, even the occasional resentment. She was worth everything. I told her, 'I've been thinking this over. We have three options, three directions for the future. We—' But I didn't get the chance to explain or enumerate.

She interrupted me: 'Michael, isn't that smoke, over there?'

She pointed off our port bow. A layer of smoke, dispersed but still heavy, floated a few hundred feet up. We followed it to its source: a smudge of a vessel halfway to the horizon.

We alerted Simmonds. He tied off the wheel and joined

us. Zainab said if the vessel was in distress we should go to its aid.

Simmonds took a long look. Then he said, 'There may have been a fire, but it looks over. I didn't bring binoculars. Did either of you?' We had not. He continued, 'That ship's east by south-east and we're heading south. If we change course we'll be going out of our way. We don't know if its drifting or making headway, or in what direction. For that matter, we don't know if it's even in distress.'

He might have saved his breath. Zainab was insistent. He went down and told Sovan to delay our dinner, climbed back into the wheelhouse and swung the bow east south-east.

We'd picked up some current. Coming from abeam it pushed us south towards the other vessel. It never moved off our bow. It had to be dead in the water.

Soot drifted down like black snow as we approached. I asked Simmonds if there was a radio channel on which we could try hailing, but he just pointed to an empty shelf on the wheelhouse wall. Sovan came aft and offered to take the helm. The rest of us joined the monk forward on the upper deck, above the bows.

Once close in, Sovan throttled down and circled the wreck.

Judging from the hull's size it had been either a ferry, or one of the larger, two-decked excursion riverboats. Enough of the superstructure was left to see that the first deck had been enclosed. Fire had engulfed everything from the bow to the stern and what remained of the collapsed decking still smouldered. Litter floated on the lake around, bits of structure that had burned and fallen off. We saw only two bodies, both face down and barely afloat. Zainab gripped my arm tight. Simmonds thought that most passengers and crew had got away in lifeboats. 'They've probably already been picked up,' he said, 'that's why there's no one around. The rescue's already been accomplished.'

Zainab said, 'Then why didn't they pick up the bodies?'

'The scene might have been different two or three hours

ago. A lot of fire, a lot of smoke, a lot of people to rescue. They might not have seen them. Or they might have run out of room.'

Zainab asked, 'Shouldn't we take them to Phnom Penh?'

Silence greeted her proposal. Then Simmonds went down and spoke to Sovan. I told Zainab to remain above and joined him. We didn't have a grapple and we were too far above the water line to reach the bodies from the deck. We drew Sovan's skiff up by its rope, climbed down and pushed off. We rowed to the corpses and tied them to the skiff – we were afraid of swamping if we tried to bring them aboard – and then rowed back. We tied the skiff to a stay and Simmonds climbed on deck. With me pushing and him pulling we got the bodies aboard the *Bayon*. We laid them on the lower deck in the bows. They were both Cambodian women, so the ship had probably been a ferry. Simmonds and I rummaged through our packs and covered their faces with our last clean shirts.

After that there was nothing more we could do. Simmonds reset our course to south. Sovan carried her cooking gear and food to the upper deck and resumed making dinner. She was like an insistence on life. The rest of us joined her. Once or twice I looked back. The wreck and the smoke receded and finally vanished astern.

Sovan's rice and fried fish tasted delicious. We were hungrier than we knew. She insisted on taking her own dinner down to the wheelhouse and taking over from Simmonds so he could join us above. It was getting on towards dusk, the sun setting from starboard, and although we couldn't yet see land we knew we were sailing in the right direction. Simmonds told us he thought we'd reach Phnom Penh in two or three hours, if nothing went wrong. He was certain the water level in the bilge was rising. 'I don't mind it reaching the sump,' he said, 'but if it reaches the block we could have trouble.' He looked in his element. After dinner he went back to his engine; he had what light was left from the sunset and a couple of incandescent bulbs hanging from their wires below deck. The monk excused himself and joined Sovan in the wheelhouse, I think to keep her company. She was a village girl and down-to-earth, but like many if not most Cambodians she was also superstitious. She took the two corpses in our bows more in her stride than Zainab, but I suspect she was also more worried about their spirits – about their ghosts.

Zainab and I were left alone on the upper deck. We stood together in silence for a while against the rail. The sun sank beneath the horizon and, except for a dim glow from a bulb through the wheelhouse windows, we were in darkness. The stars shone above.

Then, as if letting off a strong head of steam, Zainab began a rant on how pointless life, and how sudden and meaningless death, could be in the Third World (of course, even in her rant, she used the term, developing world). She presented a list of the pointless accidents and deaths she herself had either read of or actually witnessed, in little more than a year in-country. Not one but two poorly maintained, ancient Russian passenger aircraft, converted for cargo, crashing on their way north with the loss of all hands, due to engine failure. A French lady doctor working for one of the NGOs, an acquaintance of hers, struck down and killed by a motorcycle – the driver fled, never to be caught. On their way back from a visit to Koh Kong, she and Ambler narrowly missed colliding with a lorry that had just overturned – overloaded, a tyre burst, trapping the driver upside down in the cab. Unable to be extracted because the removal of a door would have weakened the cab to collapse, the driver hung stoically while petrol leaked from the engine, pooling in an inflammable puddle around his head. They were on a major road but deep in the country, and although many hands were available to help, there was no ambulance and no rescue crew. After half an hour neither Ambler nor Zainab could stand the suspense any longer and got back in their car and drove off.

'And here I am,' she finished, 'with all this pointless death, all this pointless suffering, a million practical, on-the-ground development things to do . . . and what am I, in fact, doing? Promoting transparency in government.'

'Well,' I said, 'it's better than promoting opaqueness in government.'

For a moment she glared. Then she laughed – and stopped, covering her mouth with her hand, looking towards the bow.

I said, 'It's all right. We could all use a little laughter. I think even Sovan and the monk would agree.' I handed her a cigarette. 'There's nothing to explode here.'

We smoked for a while in companionable silence. I used the time to get my courage up. My plan was to be direct, not to beat around the bush; although Simmonds had given us two or three hours, I felt for some reason as if I was running out of time. But a proposal needed more courage than I'd realized. Finally I threw the butt overboard and said, 'I want to make a commitment. A commitment to you.'

She looked at me with surprise. She said nothing.

This was going to be even harder than I thought. I said, 'I hope it's not too much of a shock. I hope you know how I feel about you, but maybe I haven't made it clear. I love you.'

'Do you really think this is the place, or the time?'

'Yes, I do. Who knows what's going to happen when we reach Phnom Penh?'

'Probably everything will continue as before. I'll go back to Robert – and to Prang. You'll go back to your embassy.'

'I don't want everything as before.'

'That's the way it has to be. For now.'

'Why? Is it my job? Am I on the wrong side?'

She shook her head. 'Of course not. I'm certain that most of what you do is admirable – or at least, harmless. I'm not really interested in the details. I don't even ask Robert any longer about what he does, what he's up to. We inhabit different worlds – different work worlds – just as you and I do. I don't despise your work, Michael. You have a good position. I admire you for it. Everyone has to make compromises in life. I chose a road where I have to make fewer. But I also have fewer responsibilities.'

'In that case, where's the obstacle?'

She said quietly, 'I love you. You must know that. But I have a legal and emotional commitment to my husband. And I love him, as well. Even if it's in a much different way.'

'A sexless way, you mean.'

'Platonic.'

'Isn't that reason enough to call it quits, to marry me?'

'No, that alone isn't reason enough. Many marriages get to that point; mine isn't unique.' With one hand she caressed and cradled my face. She said, 'I think, probably, you're reason enough. But I have to think.'

'How long?'

She turned away, saw something, and said, 'Look!'

I followed her gaze. An intermittent string of lights hung in the west; we turned and saw another string, fainter, to the east. Distant lights, but we saw them stretch away south. Land. The Tonlé Sap lake was becoming the Tonlé Sap river. We'd entered the funnel.

I repeated, 'How long?'

'I'll give you an answer after we get to shore. Can you stand that? Can you stand ambivalence for one more night – a few hours?'

'I guess I'll have to.'

'For heaven's sake.' She put her arms around me. 'You'll always have me, for ever, deeply – you know that.'

I said, 'I want you carnally. Not for ever. Just every night.'

She kissed me. When she withdrew she said, 'That's part of how I want you, too. Now, let's go down and tell Simmonds we're in sight of land.'

But Simmonds already knew; Sovan had informed him. We found her at the wheel, staring wide-eyed at the Brit, now shirtless and all lean muscle, as he tediously bailed the bilge with our one small bucket, filling it below deck, then climbing up into the low wheelhouse, further up to the deck, emptying the bucket overboard, then back down again. He stopped and told us, 'We're taking on more water. I think the planks are opening up. The bilge pump was leaking so badly I disconnected it. The pump ran off a pulley attached to the engine's drive shaft, but it'd become a passenger – using a couple of horsepower for nothing. So I'm bailing by hand.'

I asked, 'How's it going?'

He shook his head. 'I'm not keeping up.'

I offered to spell him. He rested on deck while I climbed up and down those little ladders, carrying that little plastic pail. It wasn't bad at first, but it became tedious, then hard on the back (it was impossible to stand straight in the wheelhouse), and finally, after some time, hard on the legs. I didn't keep up either: when I took over, the water in the hull was a couple of inches below the level of the engine platform; minutes later it lapped the bottom of the sump. Simmonds told me to rouse him after half an hour, or sooner if the water looked like drowning the sump; I became obsessed with the idea of giving him as good a report as I could. It was essential to get into a rhythm.

Three steps down the ladder to the engine room, bend and fill the pail, turn and three steps up to the wheelhouse, turn and four to the deck, turn and two good strides to the rail and empty the bucket overboard, then about-face (the marching manoeuvre drilled into my head at the age of twenty-two in air force basic training, still remembered), two strides . . .

. . . *one leg in front of the other. The dream merged into waking reality . . . or was waking reality intruding into the dream? Which was more real: the tedious rhythm of walking with a brain and legs still weak from jet-lag and a 'syncopal episode', walking stiff-legged in the heavy monsoon heat along the riverfront, up Sisowath Quay – or the tedious rhythm of carrying bilge water up two short flights of stairs, under ceilings too low to stand? Which was more real? The syncope, the monsoon, and no hope that I could see . . . or the struggle to stay afloat, with a lover on deck, and the bow – with two corpses – pointing towards Phnom Penh? I preferred the dream. Hope and love create their own reality; the past held more of each than the present . . . I squeezed my eyes shut and staggered forward. A motorcycle (they crowded the riverfront in the early evening) backfired and I was back . . .*

. . . to the lower deck, where I jumped to an explosive crack from below. Simmonds barely had time to sit up before the engine shuddered to a halt.

'That's it,' he said. 'It's packed up.' We descended. The water was halfway up the sump. The engine looked all right, but when we called to Sovan to press the starter, all we heard was a chunk and a groan. Simmonds inspected it top to bottom, finally running his hand under the sump. 'There's a hole,' he said. 'A big one.' His hand came away slick with oil. There'd always been some floating in the bilge; now there was more.

'It threw a rod,' he said, 'right through the sump. The connecting rod must have separated from the piston and the crankshaft.'

'Is that likely?'

'Likely? It's not likely that we got it going at all. The question is, did the rod do any damage to the hull? How far did it go?' We climbed to the deck and he gathered Sovan and Zainab and the monk around us. Simmonds wanted to put everyone in the picture at once.

He said, 'The engine's dead. There's no hope of repair. We're adrift. But the current's picking up as the river narrows,' (already I saw the lights on each shore closer) 'and we're near centre channel. We might reach Phnom Penh without doing a thing.

'We might be able to pick up speed and even steer if we can put the boat in tow. We still have Sovan's skiff. If its engine still works, we can tow the boat further in to shore or further out, if necessary. When the time comes to land, we'll drop anchor and make landfall in the skiff.

'Sovan, Mrs Ambler, I want you both to stay on the upper deck and keep watch for shipping. It's late but there may still be tankers heading north. Look out for anything afloat. If there's a chance we could collide, tell me.' Then he asked for my help with the skiff.

We pulled it in. I held the line while he clambered on board and started bailing. The riverboat, drifting now with the current, began a slow rotation. When he'd got the skiff reasonably dry he climbed back on deck. 'Do you see how much the boat's settled?' he asked me.

'No. I hadn't noticed.'

'You can see it clearly from the river. Let's go below.' We peered down the hatch. The battery was still alive; the two overhead bulbs still burned. But the engine platform was gone, the water lapped the top of the block. 'We've got to get this thing in tow now,' Simmonds said. 'There's no time to lose.'

He went to get Sovan while I untied the skiff. She jumped into her boat with a grace the *Barang* on board could only envy. I pulled the skiff to the bow and tied the end of the line to the post.

Sovan started the engine on the third pull.

In our rotation we faced east; she pulled us around heading south and put us in tow. The line wasn't more than twenty feet paid out; we could easily shout to her and she to us. With the narrowing of the channel the current picked up noticeably; with the addition of the skiff, modest as it was, we made better headway than before.

There was nothing for the rest of us to do but keep a lookout and monitor the rise of water in the hull. Simmonds went down and I joined Zainab and the monk on the upper deck. Both shores were now clearly visible. Entering the northern limits of the capital, the lights glowed brighter and separated into shops, homes, cars and street lamps like the lights of a city when you're in a plane on descent.

I'd hardly spoken to the monk during our trip, but now I welcomed him to Phnom Penh. He replied graciously. I asked him about his plans. He had a formal way of speaking that might look cold on paper but was warm when spoken. Although a man of the cloth, so to speak, his sincerity was unaffected, never unctuous. He said, 'My plans have been decided with the help of Mrs Ambler and her Cambodian friend. I shall seek shelter at the temple you call Wat Lanka. I am aware that I have the Cambodian government to thank for my release from Insein prison, and I expect to have the opportunity to express my gratitude. Other than that, I have little interest in Cambodian politics. I doubt the authorities will take a continuing interest in an ageing, itinerant Burmese monk. For the future, I will make myself useful to the *sangha*.'

Simmonds rejoined us. He said, 'We're sinking by the stern. When the water reaches the deck it will pour down the hatch, and that will be that, but we're not there yet. I think we'll make Sisowath, or very nearly. The question is, should we put off the monk and Sovan first?'

Zainab asked why.

'I suspect the authorities know by this time what we're up to. They may have the police, or more likely the Prime Minister's bodyguards, on the lookout. They'll be looking for three *Barang* and a monk. They won't notice a Khmer girl and a monk.'

It was a good idea. Zainab and I agreed.

Simmonds went down and forward to shout instructions to Sovan; after a couple of tries she got the idea and bent her course towards land, towing us downriver and closer to the west shore. The rest of us followed Simmonds down. From the main deck we saw with a shock how far we'd settled: we had less than a foot of freeboard left at the stern. We settled further by the time Sovan straightened us out on a due south trajectory, not a hundred yards from land. She throttled back and Simmonds untied her line and walked it down the deck to us, holding the rail. The bow was getting higher.

'The Japanese bridge is in sight,' he said. 'We're going to make it. Here's the drill: we'll load you, sir, in the skiff, along with myself and Sovan. She'll land the two of you. You'll be in good hands with her. Then I'll turn the skiff around and rejoin the *Bayon*.' He turned to me. 'There's one more thing to take care of,' he said in a lower voice. 'It occurred to me up at the bow. We have to carry the two corpses into the wheelhouse.'

'For God's sake, why?'

'Because they won't float for long. They'll sink before morning and they'll stay under for a few days. By the time they come back up they could be halfway to Vietnam.' He looked at our stern. 'The boat will probably go down in front of the tourist strip, certainly not much further south than the parliament building. They'll bring it up. I want them to bring those two ladies up with it.'

So the two of us carried the drowned Khmer women down the deck and into the wheelhouse. We laid them as far back as possible to minimize their chance of floating out of the hatch.

By that time we were so low in that the water the monk stepped right off our stern and into the skiff. Simmonds followed him and they pushed off towards shore. Zainab and I were left alone on the boat.

It sounds ridiculous but we both felt strangely light-hearted.

Or maybe it was light-headed. We climbed back up to the very front of the upper deck, over the bows and, almost without a care, or at least pretending we didn't have a care, devoted ourselves to sightseeing: to observing our entrance into Phnom Penh. We saw the first of the tatty but charming old French colonial buildings pass by on our right, and we saw the Japanese Friendship bridge, crowded with traffic, pass overhead – not far overhead, for it's a long but low bridge. The river reflected back the lights from the busy quay, busier as we approached our old haunts, the tourist and expat haunts. For some reason, maybe because we were now so low in the water, so waterlogged, the boat didn't change its orientation, but continued drifting bow first. So perhaps we didn't look too odd to anyone on a veranda or balcony, or just looking out from the quay, who might have noticed us drift by, bow raised and stern very low.

We were so entranced with our homecoming that we forgot about Simmonds, until we heard him hailing us somewhere aft of the stern. We ran back and saw him not far behind, alone in the skiff. But we couldn't hear the engine.

'. . . out of petrol,' we heard him yell, and, 'Throwing

you the line.' I climbed down to the wheelhouse roof and leaned over the stern rail as far as I could, but we were just too far. He threw it thrice and thrice it fell into the water, out of reach. He wasn't getting any closer. We were both of us adrift.

Zainab shouted out from the deck behind me, 'It's all right. We're home. Look!' She pointed to the shore. 'There's the FCC! We'll just have to swim for it.'

Silence greeted this, then I think I heard him swear. Then, I know I heard him laugh. Zainab laughed as well. I expect I smiled. He called out, 'Where are you headed, once you reach shore?'

'Home,' Zainab replied.

Immediately I thought, which one? I turned and asked her: 'Robert's, or mine?'

She seemed to consider for a moment, then said, 'First let's get ashore.'

Simmonds called again, now in a very calm voice: 'Your stern's awash. There will be some suction when it goes under. I'm taking to the water now. I suggest you abandon ship.' We saw him stand in the little skiff, with one foot on the gunwale. He said, 'See you on shore!' and stepped into the river.

The roof of the wheelhouse swayed gently under my feet. I told Zainab I was going to close the hatch door and climbed down.

But the river had beaten me; it flowed over the lower sill. The door opened inward and I couldn't pull it shut. It's harder than you might think to close a small door when a body of water is trying to enter. I was still pulling when the bow tilted and I lunged for support – I nearly fell forward into the flooding wheelhouse. The river swirled around the ladder to the upper deck and as I watched, the deck supports began to bend. I turned and started climbing towards the bow. Halfway up I looked back. The river, gaining speed, advanced towards me up the main deck.

I reached the bow and called to Zainab. She called down, 'I'm here,' and, leaning back, I saw her directly above, balanced barefoot, her heels on the edge of the upper deck, holding on to the railing behind.

'We're going down,' I told her, and she shouted back, not with alarm but with happiness, as if this were the high point of some party, or the successful climax of an adventure: 'Every man for himself!' She let go of the rail, raised her arms, and sprang in an arched dive into the river.

I hung back, hesitated, then dived in after her.

The water was ink black. In the light of day the Tonlé Sap is brown with mud, you can't see an inch into it, and I tried not to think about how much I swallowed. It was cold; the months in the tropics had thinned my blood. I tried to catch up. I swam freestroke and she only swam breaststroke – she'd never learned better. But she was strong. Twice I stopped to make sure she was in front: a head and shoulders bobbing rhythmically in the low waves. We'd entered the water not fifty yards off shore but I gained on her slowly. I was still in over my head when she made landfall at the tourist boats' concrete slipway. I trod water, watching her stand and walk, the muddy water pulling at her clothes, up the ramp and out of the river. With one more effort I swam until my fingers brushed the bottom, then planted my feet and stood up.

She stood on dry land below the road. She turned around to me, but the lights from the hotels and bars backlit her, so I only saw her silhouette. Her drenched clothes clung to her figure. She waved vigorously, like someone announcing her arrival at a destination much desired after a long, difficult journey. I waved back . . .

. . . *and in memory heard the shots again.* Now wide awake, standing on the same slipway but in the pouring rain, for the monsoon, seven months later, had broken. I heard them as clearly as I'd heard them in the same place but at a different time: seven months before, right here. Two shots. She was shot in the back by an assassin (no suspect apprehended) on the road, on Sisowath Quay. God knows how long they'd been following us. I couldn't see her face because of the neon signs behind. She dropped to her knees then fell forward on to the concrete slipway.

I dropped to my knees now, staring down to where she'd fallen. It was the beginning of the monsoon and the river had turned, reversed, flowing sluggishly north. And the turn of the river was like the turn of a key, unlocking memory; I remembered what it was I'd forgotten, what I'd repressed: the decision she'd made weeks later, before her death in Phnom Penh.

PART THREE

17

'I am glad you had this breakthrough in recollection, Mr Smith. But I wish you had found a less stressful method.'

It was Sunday morning. Dr White and I were exactly where we'd been twenty-four hours before: I in my bed in the Himawari, he standing beside me. The hotel management, alarmed at my condition upon returning from the quay the previous night, had helped me to my room, put me to bed, and called the doctor the next morning. He found me tired but lucid and alert.

When he asked why I'd been walking on Sisowath Quay in the middle of the night in the pouring rain, I told him that I'd spent the evening revisiting places in order to recall more vividly the past. At the end, I'd had a breakthrough: I remembered what I'd forgotten. He didn't ask me what it was. He just went about his examination and then methodically repacked his doctor's bag.

The thought that I could have forgotten something so important, or at least so bitter, disturbed me; it was like evidence of mental frailty. I asked Dr White, 'Is it common to forget something very painful, even traumatic?'

'Yes, very common. We don't call it forgetfulness, however. It's called repression. Sexually abused children, for instance, commonly repress memories of their abuse until adulthood.'

I did not care to be lumped in with abused children. I said, 'I didn't mean a physical trauma. I meant an emotional trauma.'

'All trauma is emotional, Mr Smith. That is the human condition.' He snapped his bag shut. 'Is there any chance you'll stay in bed for the rest of the day?'

'I'm not sure.'

'So many patients lie to their doctors. Thank you for being frank. If you decide to go out, then do not take any more of these pills. You know what the traffic here is like.' He stared down at me for a moment, then repeated something he'd said the day before. 'You knew Zainab Ambler, didn't you?'

'Yes.'

'And her husband?'

'Yes.'

'When did you leave Phnom Penh?'

'The day before Christmas, last year.'

He paused, then said, 'You knew of their deaths?'

'I'd heard.'

'You know he committed suicide.'

'Yes.'

He nodded. He said, 'Is there anything about them you'd like to ask me?'

My mouth was getting dry. 'No,' I said, 'at least, not now.'

He picked up his bag. 'Very well. After her operation in Bangkok, Mrs Ambler elected to make her recovery at home in Phnom Penh. She asked me to be her attending physician. She was a very loyal patient. I did attend her: I arranged nursing care for her and I brought in two consultants to help treat the infection she developed. Our treatment was unsuccessful. She declined further hospitalization and died at home. If there's anything about that time you wish to discuss, feel free to see me. You've visited my surgery – I live directly upstairs. Goodbye.'

After he left I lay back and closed my eyes, but not to dream. I'd done with dreaming. I remembered all I had to remember, and I'd learned from the doctor the cause of her death. There was only one thing left, but it was probably beyond discovery. How do you go about questioning the dead?

Forensics as a speciality has never appealed to me, but of course I had to study forensic methods in both my previous careers. Military aviation accidents are investigated by expert technical teams under safety investigation boards; suspected fraud in business is investigated by forensic accountants. Their methods are the same. They start by examining, in detail, the evidence at the scene of the accident, or the scene of the crime.

There was only one scene for me to investigate – if I could. The scene of her last weeks of life, and her death.

I got up and followed the routine of the day before. After a shower, coffee and a cigarette, I went down for breakfast. But I hesitated in front of the hotel restaurant. Instead I walked out of the open-air foyer and took a tuk-tuk to Flavours, my old breakfast haunt, and ate bacon and eggs and toast opposite Wat Lanka. This morning the temple's gate was closed, but a stream of white smoke, as usual, drifted from the crematorium's chimney.

After eating I hailed a moto and was driven the short distance to the Amblers' old villa. I could have been back in my dream. The guardhouse beside the front gate was empty. Even the narrow street between two tall walls, hardly more than an alley, was deserted at mid-morning – as in dreaming, where one forgets or omits characters extraneous to the action of the dream.

For some reason I didn't comprehend I hesitated to knock at the gate; instead I pushed it gently and when it gave, pushed it harder. It swung open, unlatched and unlocked. I walked through, down the driveway with the garden on my right. An open gate suggested new tenants at home, but the garden was badly overgrown, months overgrown. In this climate an unattended garden could revert to jungle within a year. The lawn looked like a rice paddy just before harvest. An encroaching tree obscured the gazebo. Dead leaves littered the empty driveway.

The front entrance was shuttered and locked. I ducked under a tree limb and pushed my way through shrubbery to the veranda, deep in shadow under the shade of the roof and trees. I walked to the door I'd entered a year ago, at night, in the pouring rain. The handle turned. I stepped inside.

I felt for the light switch and turned on the single overhead bulb. The room was unchanged: woven mats scattered over the floor, folded prayer benches against the walls, a wooden Buddha on a low table. A faint odour of dust. I crossed, opened the opposite door and walked into the living room.

Some light filtered dimly through the windows; they needed cleaning. Most of the furniture was still there, but the piano was gone. Probably it had belonged to the Amblers and was sold locally, or shipped back to some beneficiary in the UK. The furniture that remained came with the house. I stepped up to the dining area – the step on which poor Ambler had broken his leg – and started the climb to the first floor. Having just come from the States, I was surprised at how uneven the stairs were. In the near gloom I put my foot down on thin air; it upset my balance and I nearly fell. I thought, how ironic if I fell and broke my leg in this dark and deserted villa. Who, across the long living room, through the meditation room, across nearly a hundred feet of overgrown garden and beyond a solid concrete wall, would hear my call for help?

Upstairs, the glass doors to the balcony let in more light. But the former library/TV room was denuded of books and television. The empty shelves and, downstairs, the absent piano, more than anything brought home the reality of death and absence, that old phrase, 'dead and gone'. I felt an inner emptiness, a void. An emptiness that had nothing to do with self-pity, that was beyond sorrow, so deep it was like a disability; I could still walk, talk, probably work – but something essential was missing. I pushed the bedroom door open and walked in.

Lim Sovan spun around with a feather duster in her hand.

Her eyes gaped, her mouth opened wide and I think she tried to scream, but all I heard was a hiss. I've no idea what I looked like. I've no idea what, if anything, I said.

She remained as immobile as the biblical pillar of salt. I collected myself enough to say, 'Sovan, it's me, Mike Smith. Mike. I just got back. I got back Friday.'

We both started breathing again. The feather duster came

down. She said, 'Mr Mike,' (it was her usual form of address) and I nodded. She was Cambodian and I wouldn't have dreamt of embracing her. It would have been gauche.

I asked her out to the upstairs balcony, where there were still a couple of chairs and a table, and we sat down, but it must have reminded her of her former employment, for she jumped back up and asked me if I wanted coffee, I thought that anything suggesting normalcy was a good idea and said I did, and asked her to join me. The Amblers had used a French press and ground their own coffee, and the beans and appliances were still there. In a few minutes she was back up on the balcony, pouring us both a cup.

I asked her how she was and what she was doing there. She replied in monosyllables: 'OK', 'cleaning'. So I asked her to tell me about the past six months. I asked her to tell me what had happened since we last met.

She had little formal education and her life had not schooled her in connected narrative, I don't think even in Khmer. But she was intelligent and she understood what I wanted. Her spoken English was fluent, in that she almost never hesitated for a word or construction, but she sometimes chose the wrong word and her grammar and diction and pronunciation were all over the place.

She had remained with the Amblers as their cook and housemaid right up to the very end. The first two weeks, after the shooting, were uneventful for her, because Zainab and her husband were in Bangkok. The embassy airlifted her to a hospital there as soon as the local A&E got her stabilized. I remembered that period. There'd been nothing I could do but make the occasional call to Thailand.

They'd arrived back in Phnom Penh on 12 December and from that point on Sovan's every waking moment was devoted to her employers. Dr White arranged for a trained nurse to come for an hour every day and White himself attended Zainab regularly, but Sovan was the live-in nurse, housemaid and cook. I think she was nostalgic about that time, and I don't believe that is as strange as it might at first seem.

She was making a contribution, helping, to a degree she had never helped anyone before, someone whom I believed she loved.

The first eleven days home Zainab was recovering. Sovan was insistent on that. The rigor and importance of her work had impressed upon her the necessity of accurate time-keeping. On the twelfth day Zainab's condition worsened (I imagined this was due to the infection that Dr White had mentioned) and although two other doctors were called in, her condition continued to deteriorate.

I interrupted here, and asked Sovan why Zainab had not been readmitted to hospital. She said simply, 'Madam Zainab say no.'

The end came on 5 January. Sovan's English became even more confused, and I was left with the impression that during the day there were many people in the garden, praying. Who they were or why they should have been there I could not understand. Ambler and Dr White were the only two people attending Zainab at the time of her death, shortly before midnight. Narrating the very end, Sovan became calmer and clearer. Just before Zainab died, Dr White ordered Sovan to go to Wat Lanka and bring back the Burmese monk, Maung Thant. She didn't want to leave because she had seen people die before, and was sure there were only minutes left. But she obeyed. At the wat, waiting for the monk, she saw something. It was hard for her to describe it in English – I expect it would have been almost as hard in Khmer. As far as I could make out, it was a vision of light. Not in the sky. In her mind, or maybe I should say her mind's eye. 'I know then,' she said, her tenses fairly close, her meaning crystal clear, 'I know Madam Zainab died.'

Zainab had told me of Sovan's spirit world, a world shared, I am sure, by most Cambodians of her class and generation. She was a Buddhist, to be exact a Theravada Buddhist, but her Buddhism in some ways was closer to something even older, closer to animism. For her, the fields, the mountains and the rivers all teemed with spirits. So it was easy for me, on that veranda under the bright light of day, it was very easy to dismiss Sovan's vision.

But I did not want to be discourteous. I nodded my head and kept silent. After a few moments she continued.

Dr White had arranged for the body to be taken to Wat Lanka for cremation. Sovan skipped a few weeks, then – it must have been a depressive time – and told me that Ambler had gone to Hong Kong on a business trip of just a few days. He was very quiet when he returned. Two weeks later he gave Sovan the weekend off.

When she arrived at the house on Monday morning, she found Ambler dead in bed. He'd taken a massive amount of morphine, washed down with vodka.

I couldn't feel much for him, other than regret, but my heart went out to the young Cambodian woman.

On top of everything else, she was suddenly out of a job. But that didn't last long. In a couple of months Ambler's replacement, a bachelor with a much smaller house, arrived and hired her. And Ambler's old landlady, who was having trouble renting the place, asked her to come in on weekends and dust. That's what she was doing this Sunday.

I'd learned, I thought, all I could from her. I took down her cellphone number, so I could keep in touch. I thought of giving her a tip, but she was working, and I was pretty sure she would find it patronizing. I did not want to offend her.

Then she did something surprising. She told me to wait, and went inside. In a minute she returned and held out her hand. In it were two USB memory sticks.

I'd completely forgotten that she was computer literate. Ambler had sent her to classes, and bought her a used ThinkPad.

One memory stick was red, one blue. She told me the blue one was Zainab's and before she died she had given it to Sovan, and instructed her to give it to me, if I ever returned. The red memory stick was Ambler's. It was more problematic. Sovan said that Ambler wrote something every day and saved it there; I guessed she meant some kind of diary. When she found him dead the memory stick was on the floor; she thought it had fallen from his shirt pocket. Sovan was by now a member of the family and family business was private; certainly the police had no business prying into their affairs. She'd kept it.

I asked her if she'd read either. She had not. Zainab's was for me only. And Ambler's . . . She didn't finish her sentence, but I think I knew what she meant. He was a *Barang* and so was I. I, too, was almost a member of the family. If Zainab had wanted me to have hers, then I should also have his.

I thanked her and left. I told her where I'd be, and asked her to get in touch whenever she wanted. Then I took a tuk-tuk back to my hotel with Zainab's last letter in my pocket.

18

Back in my room I plugged the blue memory stick into my laptop and accessed the device. There was only one file, a word processing document. I opened it.

Dear Michael,

It's 16 December. I've been back from the hospital for four days and I'm beginning to feel like I'm going to recover from this. Robert told me the first night home I was on my feet in the bedroom, sleepwalking, in a morphine dream . . . We've been reducing the dose since then, and I can think, and talk, and even write, although it's easiest for me shortly before the next dose. It's interesting that now, for me, the time of greatest discomfort, sometimes pain, is also the time of greatest clarity. No doubt I should regard this as an opportunity for mindfulness practice! But it's almost time now for another dose, and I haven't even begun to tell you why I'm writing this, what I have to make you understand. It's . . .

18 December. I was interrupted by Robert with his dose – a little less each day. Today I'm feeling clearer and I'm starting earlier. My mornings are my best time, right after Sovan's breakfast. (I see I'm trying to avoid my main point – I'll get to it.)

Michael, by now you will have received the handwritten letter I sent you through Sovan yesterday. When was the last time you received such a thing? I did it because a written letter is more personal, more sincere, and, these days, more secure than electronic communications. I sealed it in the envelope myself, and there are no copies. You might ask, then, why am

I writing this? It's part of my weakness: I can't talk to you in person, so I'm doing it on my laptop – absurd, I know, but it's better than nothing. And, perhaps, one day you will read this, when what we felt for each other is cooler, more moderate, more under control. In the past.

I was sincere when I wrote in that letter that I didn't want you to call, or visit, or try to get in touch in any way. Let me make the first move. I will, once I've recovered, once I've found the strength to put the necessary distance between us.

I meant to tell you why; that was the whole point, but it takes me for ever now to write, and it's almost time for another dose. Tomorrow . . .

19 December. Better still. I'm able to sit in the sun, even walk a little in the garden. Too tired and still too drugged to enjoy reading. But clearer in the mind.

Michael dear, the word 'epiphany' is a very pompous word to use nowadays, but I don't know a better one to describe what I felt in A&E at the American Clinic in Phnom Penh (staffed mostly by Kiwis). It was before anyone had given me anything for pain, and after the initial shock of being shot – what a thing to alliterate! They were prepping me for the airlift and I wouldn't be that clear-headed again for weeks. I'm still not that clear-headed, even today, although I can remember how it felt, and what I was thinking.

I was thinking: I may be close to death. This is how it feels. Michael, I was observant, keenly observant, I was not eager to leave this life. But I already had one foot away, one foot off the ground, as it were. And suddenly I felt two things: I felt compassion towards everything, towards everybody. Towards the nurses who were trying to help me, to you, to Simmonds (you'd both brought me there, and were in the outer room). And also I felt, if not ready to go, at least not frightened. It was as if one thing cancelled the other out: as if compassion towards all reduced, weakened, attachment – what Buddhists call attachment – towards the people and things I'd wanted, loved. Towards you, even to life.

I've just reread this, and it hardly makes sense to me, so

how can it make sense to you? I'm getting tired, but I'll try one more time. I felt close to death, but calm. My heart went out to everyone. And at the same time I felt my desire for possession, for individual love, decrease.

And it seemed so simple, so clear, so easy. I thought, if I survive this, if I live, I have to remember.

21 December. I'm afraid I overdid it, tried to do too much. I spent yesterday in bed. But that didn't keep Robert from reducing the daily morphine dose. It's making a difference – good and bad. I have to take the bad with the good. I tend to be jittery around midnight, for an hour or two, unable to settle down, to sleep. But the mornings are clearer and clearer.

Dear Michael – I'm still going to call you dear, at least in this letter (When will I send it? When will it end?) – you've been very good, you haven't come over, you haven't tried to call. I appreciate that, I do. For who knows if I'd have the strength to turn you away a second time?

I'd intended to give you intellectual justifications for non-attachment. It's not that difficult. But it's all in a dozen books, many dozens, I have my favourites, of course . . . and I'm still too tired for intellectual justifications. Using my head is how I came to Buddhism, but, eventually, doesn't faith take over? I know you don't believe in faith, or rather, you don't believe in blind faith; neither do I. You once told me you believed in quantitative analysis! I do too – as far as it goes.

You're an atheist, of course, and I wish I had the strength to show you how Buddhism is the right faith, maybe the only faith, for atheists. I say faith, even though I came to it through my own critical reading and analysis. I made the decision to adopt Buddhism through reason, not faith. And it works for me. But for any modern, western person, I think certain elements of Buddhism still need a leap of faith. For me, rebirth was a leap. But if so much of the rest of the philosophy makes sense, and so much is demonstrably true (I've demonstrated a lot to my satisfaction), then that final leap is not hard to take. Aren't engineering and aviation similar, Michael? Maybe even economics – what you used to call technical analysis? If you have a specific goal in mind, an engineering goal, or some goal in business, and you adopt, through research and analysis, a procedure for reaching it, and the procedure works: your goal is being incrementally attained . . . isn't it natural then to have at least some faith that the procedure will work out to the very end?

And doesn't this encourage faith in yourself, in your own powers of reasoning, of problem-solving? Isn't this kind of faith something that we need and use every day, in our everyday life?

What a lot I've written, and how I look forward to sharing it with you, as soon as I can. But I've reread it, and I see I've given you, not an argument for non-attachment, but for faith. So perhaps my mind isn't as clear as I thought.

23 December. A trip to the local hospital yesterday, arranged by my nurse – and Dr White only discovered it today. It was the first time I've seen him really angry. He didn't look angry that night at the Café Musicum; he got rid of that drunken pianist almost clinically – do you remember how cool he was? But today he was furious with the nurse for arranging the hospital visit without consulting him. She should not have done it, of course. Even though all it was, was tests, examinations.

I wonder if he'll keep her on. She's an American Buddhist, but not Theravada – Mahayana, Tibetan. I wonder if White knows I'm Buddhist, and if so, if that's why he sent her. Her faith is not congenial. From a few things she's let drop, she's deeply superstitious, a kind of American fundamentalist Buddhist! But she's kind to me, and careful. If you only got along with people whose religious opinions were identical to yours, you'd have a pretty restricted circle.

I remember that I was going to defend to you the Buddhist concept of non-attachment, but I'm sitting now in the recliner that Robert has set up for me, and looking out of the window at the garden below, with the trees and flowers of all kinds – the whole Asian profusion. And I'm wondering how to explain that you can appreciate something without thinking you need it. It's human nature to want, to desire. It's even how we procreate, how we continue. Maybe an ordinary person like myself (for I am, in terms of spiritual or intellectual attainment, a very ordinary person), needs a near-death experience to finally understand, to appreciate non-attachment.

But it's so *practical*. That should appeal to you, Michael! It's practical because it leads to a more virtuous life. You have less desire, less attachment to what Buddhists call 'unhelpful' actions and desires. What we were taught to call 'sins'.

Of course, that's the negative side. What it helps you not to do. What's the positive side?

I think it helps you put things in perspective. Even a little detachment is, I think, a good idea. I know that doesn't sound passionate, and it's passion that makes the world go round – passion for all kinds of things. In the west we passionately believe in finding ways to go faster and faster from point A to point B. We passionately believe in finding better manufacturing techniques. We passionately believe in making movies. Bach passionately believed in composing and performing polyphonic music for the glory of God. Was that bad? Was that unhelpful?

I don't think so. I think we have to be practical: are we going to renounce ordinary life, try to become a saint? I know it's beyond me! The middle way. That's what we should strive for, that's the positive side of non-attachment. Unless we have a genius for something – like Bach did – striving for at least some degree of non-attachment can save us from unhelpful, unprofitable concentration, from obsession.

Oh, Michael, I've just taken a nap, a long nap, and woken, to find that poor Robert is asleep and has forgotten my dose! And so the pain is worse, but my head is clearer, and when I read what I wrote to you this morning, it seems as dry as dust, as dry as one of the pages of one of those dozens of dry books on Buddhism. Non-attachment! And here I am, thinking only of you, obsessing about you. Who am I trying to fool?

25 December. Christmas! A day for giving thanks and for being with those one loves. But by my own arrangement I can't be with you. Was that wise of me, or self-important, or just

masochistic – not that anyone's ever accused me of masochism. Robert is here of course and is doing his best. I try to appreciate him – I think I do. But how I miss my aeronaut, my aviator, my serial saver.

I'm weak today, Michael. Recovery is not, after all, a straight line. Yesterday a relapse and today not much better. Dr White put me on an IV for the first time since I left the hospital. Some kind of antibiotic. So it's an ill Christmas, as well as being a lonely one.

You might wonder what I've been doing, when I'm not writing to you. For the most part, I've been trying to be mindful. That probably sounds simple to you, but it's even harder than usual, not because of the pain (which isn't normally bad) but because of the morphine. It takes concentration to be mindful, and morphine eats into that. It's another reason why I'm glad that, with Robert's help, I'm taking less every day.

26 December. Worse still, mildly worse. Dr White told me today that I have to expect the occasional relapse, but he also took some blood; he wants to run some tests. He examined my dressings and changed them himself. He normally lets the nurse do that.

How difficult non-attachment is, when things aren't going as well as they might! And yet, in A&E, when death was a real possibility, it seemed easy . . . Perhaps I need another jolt, but I'd rather not.

In my weakness, how I wish you were here.

29 December. For two days, Michael, I've been poked and prodded and IV'd, and I've held out against a higher dose, held out successfully. But it's been hard. It hurts, now, when they change the dressings; it hurts most of the time. I'm trying to get beyond it, to deal with it mindfully, but it would be easier if they let me alone.

Dr White brought in two consulting physicians, one Frenchman, one an American/Canadian woman. Both very on the ball, but I think the woman more current. Dr White's playing it close to his chest, but tomorrow, if I'm not better, I'll demand to know . . .

30 December. Bad news. It's a resistant staph infection, almost certainly picked up the day the nurse took me to the hospital. Dr White's pumping me full of enough antibiotics to kill (or cure) a horse, but I can tell he's worried. I'm trying to beat the pain the usual way, without morphine, and usually it's working, to a degree.

I wouldn't be much for you to see, that's for sure. I haven't been out of this bed for days now . . . but how I'd love to see you. A kiss would be so lovely – for me, probably not for you. That's weakness, but it's hard to be strong when your body's this weak. I have to continue trying.

31 December. Dr White told me today that it doesn't look good. He expects blood poisoning to set in shortly, and he doesn't think I'll be very aware after that.

It's so unfair. So unfair.

I love you, Michael. I'm glad I sent you away when I was strong, because I'd never be able to do it now. Tibetan Buddhists say that you can meet the same souls you've loved over and over again, in future lives. I've smiled at that in the past (I don't really even believe in a soul) but I hope it's true. If you meet someone, in a future life, who calls you a serial saver, you'll know it's me.

1 January. Almost done with the morphine – only minimum dose. Nurse wanted to increase it, but Robert's taken complete control. Had a good talk with Dr White.

I've told Sovan to take this to you, after I've gone. Dying is hard. Nothing easy about it. Non-attachment comes and goes. Concentrating on being mindful. The sky's so beautiful out of the window.

Concentrating on mindfulness. No regrets. No regrets.

Thanks

The last entries were not dated.

Not once, to my recollection, had I broken down and wept for her. I did so now. I stood up and staggered from end to end, from wall to wall, of my luxury hotel room, blurting out the declarations that now she would never hear, the questions for which no one on earth has a satisfactory answer. That kind of display of grief is, I'm sure, a safety valve. It should not, in my opinion, last long. Maybe that's the unreconstructed, emotion-averse male 'me' speaking. Maybe if I'd wept earlier, given vent earlier and more often or more thoroughly, I wouldn't have broken down so badly. Maybe I wouldn't have suffered from 'repression'. I'll never know.

When I finished I lay down on the bed. I wanted to sleep, to escape, even for a short time. I succeeded. I slept without dreaming, or at least with no memory of having dreamt. I awoke in the late afternoon, calmer and refreshed. It was the monsoon and outside the clouds were already lowering. I'd fallen asleep without the air conditioning on and was wet with perspiration; I put on some coffee, stepped into the shower and then took the coffee and a cigarette out to the balcony.

Zainab died, according to Sovan, late on 5 January. Twenty days after she'd sent me the letter telling me not to call, not to write, not to appear. Twelve days after I'd left Cambodia, having been declared, quietly, non-publicly, persona non grata by a government still worried about my discretion.

I couldn't even remember when, exactly, I'd repressed her rejection. When I'd remembered only being declared, unofficially, an officially unwelcome person.

So now I knew everything. And understood almost nothing. The doctrine of non-attachment, at least at the first reading of her last letter, seemed as obscure as the doctrine the priests had tried to imprint upon me as a boy: that Christ had died for our sins. Neither as a boy nor as a young man had I been able to wrap my head around that: what on earth did it mean? I still didn't understand it, in my forties. Non-attachment belonged to the same category.

But it was the reason she turned me away. A rejection so

traumatic I'd repressed it completely for months. Didn't I owe it to myself, as well as her, to try to understand?

Inside on the table lay the other, the red memory stick. Robert Ambler's document . . . whatever it was, whatever it contained.

My laptop screen glowed on the desk as I swapped the memory sticks and opened Ambler's file. It was not a letter, it was his diary. He was a disciplined, if not ambitious, diarist: the document started on 1 January of the previous year, and there was an entry for almost every day, but most, as far as I could see from skipping along, were very brief – not more than a sentence or two. The diary stopped altogether when Zainab was shot and did not resume until she was back in Phnom Penh, recovering at home.

He resumed it for a specific purpose: tracking his reduction of her morphine. She had only been on it for a little over two weeks when he attempted to lower the dosage radically, at her request. It was a mistake. She no longer needed the higher dose for pain management, but her body, even in that short a period, had become addicted. The radically lower dose resulted in physical tremors and some mental agitation. So after consulting with Dr White he took her back up, and then gently, day by day, brought the dose down.

For this reason the previous short diary entries, which had consisted mostly of notes regarding work, or visitors, or his infirmities, were now devoted to his wife's condition, her progress, and her daily dose of morphine.

By the 15th he had her stabilized and on a downward trend. The next day she was strong enough to send me her letter.

His entries during this period were more detailed than previously. Although Dr White came regularly, and the nurse daily, Zainab's minute-to-minute care was up to Ambler and Sovan, under Ambler's direction and supervision. It was a 24/7 job and he took it as such. From the morning after her shooting he'd taken a leave of absence, and although of course he could not have foreseen it, he never went back to his office at the embassy.

He and Sovan managed Zainab's care in shifts, but unless one or the other was sleeping they were very often in each other's company and were never separated for long. In fact they were each other's companions as well as helpmates. As the days went by, it is evident, reading between the lines, that Sovan is becoming concerned about him, as well as his wife.

Zainab's near-death experience, if the shooting and the airlift and the emergency operations in Bangkok can be so described, affected Ambler profoundly. He was not a naturally demonstrative man, but his love for her began to show through. It showed through despite his difficulty in self-expression. I read with mixed feelings. On the one hand, I sympathized, even empathized – he and I, at least in certain ways, were more similar than I'd thought. On the other hand the very similarity bred irritation. His late recognition (or rediscovery) of his love had come even later than mine. His shortcomings echoed mine and I did not care to be so reminded.

Neither Dr White's nurse nor Dr White had large roles in the narrative, until Zainab's condition worsened. As early as the 29th, the day before the infection was diagnosed, the nurse suggested to Ambler that, in case the worst outcome became a possibility, he and his wife might want to discuss end-of-life issues, while she was still capable. My first reaction upon reading this was, what a morbid suggestion. That was Ambler's first reaction as well. However, after a little further thought he recognized it as a good idea, and on 1 January, although she made no mention of it in her letter to me, Ambler and Zainab had that discussion. Probably the most important decision taken was that, given the prognosis and the level of personal care available locally, she would stay in Phnom Penh. The other important decision was cremation, if possible at Wat Lanka. Both decisions were hers.

That discussion took place with the nurse in attendance, as a kind of facilitator. That evening Dr White came by, not just to check on her progress – he normally did that during the day – but as a kind of social visit. It was the last time she got out of bed, but it was not far: just into the TV room, with the

IV stand on rollers beside her. White was frank with her, and free of unction. He questioned her about her Buddhist beliefs, regarding karma and rebirth. Ambler, who must have heard it all before, did not document it in detail, but again reading between the lines it must have been a remarkable evening and I wish I'd been there. How common can it be, for anyone just days away from dying of blood poisoning, to have the strength, physical, emotional, mental, to have an intellectually rigorous social evening with one's attending physician?

That was the last serious interaction Ambler had with his wife. The next day she was much weaker and her physical condition deteriorated rapidly day by day. He and Sovan got very little sleep during the last two days. His entries, most of them, are short and to the point: brief records of hospice nursing care. Two entries, however, stand out.

The afternoon of the day she died, Sovan woke him to report that a delegation of monks and laity from Wat Lanka were outside the gate, with the request that he allow a number of people to come into the garden to pray. Sovan explained that Zainab was known in the local community as the woman who had convinced the government to free the Burmese monk, and in a way had given her life for him. The monk was still living at Wat Lanka, where he had already established a reputation. Among the religious and laity, Zainab was regarded as a *Barang* of unusual virtue, on the path to enlightenment. Praying for such a person, and being near them at their end, was good karma; to use Christian terminology (this was Ambler's own interpretation and his entry), they would be vouchsafed grace. He gave his consent. For the rest of the evening the garden was full of Cambodians, meditating, praying and chanting very low.

The entry for the death also stands out. Zainab had not been active or talkative during the day; she dozed most of the morning and was briefly sick in the afternoon; at this point also she had become incontinent; Ambler and Sovan together took care of her on a constant basis. The nurse arrived late in the afternoon and stayed for less than an hour; she told Ambler it was doubtful that Zainab would last the night.

Dr White arrived after dinner and settled down by her bedside. At eleven thirty he called for Ambler, who had been resting downstairs. Sovan came up with him. Ten minutes later he asked Sovan to go to Wat Lanka to get the Burmese monk; apparently the monk had requested that he be notified, if possible, when death was imminent.

Ambler's entry at this point became clinically specific. Zainab lay flat on her back in the middle of their bed. Her arms were raised so that her hands rested beside her head on the pillow, palms upward and open. Her eyes were open wide, staring straight up. Her expression, he wrote, was as if she had finally found something she had been looking for, and was now concentrating on it.

During her final ten minutes her expression did not change, and she did not respond to questions. Her breathing became rapid, then shallow, then gradually slowed until it stopped altogether. Dr White kept his finger on her pulse, which continued weakly for almost a minute after she stopped breathing. When he could no longer detect a pulse, he pronounced her dead. When Sovan returned, she and another Cambodian lady washed and laid out the body.

Ambler's record continued the next day. He went on recording. I gained the impression he was so habituated to his record-keeping he couldn't stop. It had become an almost automatic activity. Perhaps it had also become a way to avoid thinking too much about what he was recording.

Dr White provided a death certificate, and the head monk at Wat Lanka gave his permission for the cremation. However, a party official contacted the British Embassy the morning after Zainab's death, with the message that a government permit was required to cremate foreigners on Cambodian soil. The clerk on duty took the message directly to Ambler. He spent much of that day trying to get to the bottom of that message and the messenger. By the second day he concluded that it was nothing but a blatant attempt to keep him from cremating his wife's corpse in Phnom Penh. Even with air conditioning, the climate in Cambodia is such that bodies are cremated within twenty-four hours of death. On the morning of day three he called Dr White and had Sovan bring the Burmese monk over. He explained his predicament to them, in the hope that one of them had a string they could pull.

Both Dr White and the monk were struck by the condition of the corpse. The bedroom had never had its own air conditioner; the Amblers had relied on the wall-mounted unit in the TV room. Ambler had done his best to keep the bedroom cool, but it was, after all, Cambodia, and conditions were by any measure warm and humid.

Zainab's appearance was unchanged.

The monk suggested that they have the body carried to the wat, on a standard bier and under a sheet, as if she were a Cambodian. Handled correctly it was unlikely to rouse suspicion. Sovan and her family (which consisted only of one sister and two brothers, none married), would serve as pall bearers and mourners. It would appear as a standard, if somewhat small, Cambodian family funeral procession to the wat for cremation.

The head monk approved the plan that evening, and on the morning of the fourth day Sovan and her family, and three monks from the wat, took Zainab away.

They held the brief ceremony as soon as they arrived at Wat Lanka. Zainab was cremated directly afterwards. Ambler noted, without detail, that he 'broke down'.

At this point the entries, although still daily, became shorter. He and Sovan embarked on a major programme of house cleaning. There was correspondence to attend to, primarily with his solicitor in the UK. He was not besieged by callers. I got the impression that their friends had been mainly her friends. Perhaps they thought that leaving him alone at such a time was a kindness.

He did have one visitor: Dr White's nurse. She came back for a visit about ten days after Zainab died. She was a good woman and a professional nurse, doing her job, checking up on the spouse of her deceased patient. If Ambler was upset with her, he did not mention it. She was a western-educated

Buddhist, like his wife, and there were points he wanted to be clearer on. Zainab believed that rebirth happened immediately upon death, but Ambler had heard other opinions and he asked the nurse hers. She said, without batting an eye, that it took exactly forty-nine days. Ambler, whom I suspect was taken aback, asked her if she didn't think it possible that forty-nine days was metaphorical. She thought for a moment, and asked him if he meant it could be forty-eight.

The next day Ambler asked Sovan the same question. The unlettered Cambodian housemaid-cook, with little formal education, and a strong belief in spirits, replied, 'I don't know, the monks don't know, nobody knows.' It's clear from his entry that her reply impressed him.

Did his respect for Sovan make her more sexually attractive to him? His entries over the next few days, regarding the sex he had with her, were so brief, almost telegraphical, that the nature of his attraction, his feelings towards her, must be speculative. The sex itself was limited to fellatio – he used the clinical Latin term. It's my belief that it was, for him, an unconscious affirmation of life. I think for her it was compassion. Certainly she was closer to him, and was probably more aware of his condition, and his pain, than anyone.

Three weeks after his wife's death he attended a British Foreign Office meeting in Hong Kong that lasted three days. It was the first embassy work he'd done since Zainab was shot, and it would be the last. He returned very late on a Friday night, and was awakened in the small hours on Saturday morning by an 'olfactory hallucination' – his words. Zainab had become incontinent during her last day, and of course Ambler and Sovan cleaned her up. Weeks later, around two o'clock on that Saturday morning, a strong odour of urine woke him. The odour remained even after waking; he did not at first connect it with his wife: he thought he had wet himself. He got out of bed but saw that he and the bedclothes were dry. Only then did the odour begin to fade.

His last entries are suggestive of morbid obsession and depression. His obsessions were what he came to regard as the three 'miracles' – once again, his word. They were: Sovan's vision; Zainab's apparent ability to maintain mindfulness until the moment of death due to blood poisoning; and her body's apparent incorruption for four days after death. He also obsessed over the concept of rebirth. He spent most of his days and nights alone, reading, thinking, recollecting. He suffered from guilt over the various failures of his marriage. I believe he was racked by loneliness, and although I suspect he knew he was depressed, I am certain he was unaware of just how depressed he was.

He did not become a Buddhist. But he came to doubt his own disbelief. The future held no promise for him. He did not believe that he could look forward with any certainty to being reunited with his wife in the next life, should there be one. But neither did he feel that he could look forward with certainty to annihilation. He had come to consider rebirth as at least a possibility.

His last diary entry was a calm and businesslike checklist for suicide.

He had never disposed of the quantities of morphine in pill form that had been prescribed both in Bangkok and in Phnom Penh. Two weeks after returning from Hong Kong he turned the air conditioners in the TV room on full, sat down on his bed and swallowed two bottles of morphine, with two tall vodka gimlets as chasers. He then lay down and assumed the same posture his wife had taken at her death. His end must have been easy, for he was still in that posture when Sovan found him, on Monday morning.

19

So Ambler had gone, to use an old slang Brit phrase that he might have used himself, round the bend. I am aware that that is not a compassionate or even considerate way to speak of a man driven to suicide by loss, guilt and loneliness. I have my faults and a lack of compassion may be one of them. I was surprised, reading his diary, at the similarities between us; they made me recall that he and I had similar educational backgrounds in the rigorous, numerate disciplines. This made his 'suspension of disbelief' (as I believe a literary gentleman once called it), and his acceptance of even the possibility of miracles, even more disappointing. As far as I was concerned it was just credulity, another word for intellectual weakness. Once you open that door, where do you stop, at what point do you say, enough? Saints? Ghosts in Irish castles? Late Roman-era carpenters rising from the dead? The universe made in a week?

His diary, starting out so well, at least so accurately, degenerated into something like mysticism; in the case of Ambler himself, into clinical psychological illness.

Of the three main people who had been with Zainab during her last illness, I'd interviewed one, Sovan, and read the diary of another, her husband. There was one other, who had also been there at her death. Dr White.

He'd given me his card; I found it and punched his number into my cellphone. He answered. I identified myself and asked if I could come over for a few minutes, to talk about Mrs Ambler's death. He suggested I come after dinner for a drink.

I walked to a nearby restaurant I knew that served a good stroganoff, and afterwards took a tuk-tuk to his surgery. He lived above it. I rang the bell and he came down to open the door.

The architecture of Phnom Penh can surprise you. I expected to climb the stairs to a standard, pre-Khmer Rouge era, walk-up flat. Instead, we climbed to one landing after another, until I realized that we were going up and inward to a much higher level. The final landing opened on to a living area lit by a sky-light a floor above, and a light well, barred only by a railing, stretching from the roof to the ground. Two steps led to a raised kitchen and dining area, and a circular stairway wound to a balcony leading to the bedrooms. It was the sort of whim-sical architecture that makes you smile the moment you walk in. With all those stairs it also struck me as impractical. I would never have expected the dour Dr White to have been happy for years living in an apartment designed with such caprice.

He motioned to a chair and asked me if I'd care for a whisky. I said yes and he poured two. I noticed two Buddhas on a shelf. They were no indication of his religious beliefs, should he have any. Every expat in Cambodia has one or two Buddhas in their living room. Dr White sat in an armchair opposite me and said, 'What would you like to know?'

'Since we saw each other this morning, I've talked to the Amblers' former housemaid-cook, Lim Sovan.'

'So you decided against spending the day in bed.'

I smiled. 'I haven't been all that active.'

'Go on.'

'Sovan told me as much as she could about the Amblers' deaths.'

'It's a pity that she had to be so involved, particularly with finding Ambler's corpse. However, as far as I can tell, she's taking it with some equanimity.'

'She gave me a memory stick that had belonged to Ambler. It contained his diary. He kept it right up to the very end.'

'Did you read it?'

'Yes. I thought it might give me some insight into the circumstances of his wife's death, and into his suicide. The Amblers and I were good friends.'

A buzzer somewhere in the room sounded, like conscience catching me out in a lie. Dr White excused himself and walked upstairs, closing a bedroom door behind him. After a few minutes he came back down.

He said, 'My mother is dying of cancer upstairs. It's a slow process. I usually have a girl to help me, but she had to take the evening off.'

'I'm sorry.'

'So, was the diary useful to you?'

'It gave me more detail. Apparently Zainab was, at first, recovering from the gunshot wounds.'

'She was making a satisfactory recovery. Unfortunately, her nurse – an American who should have known better – on her own initiative took Mrs Ambler into hospital for some tests. It was almost certainly there that she caught the resistant staph infection that killed her.'

'Do you know why she refused hopitalisation?'

'I said she was making a satisfactory recovery, but in fact she was in a severely compromised state for a mersa infection. I treated her with intravenous antibiotics and fluids but she entered sepsis almost immediately. I explained to her what kind of treatment she could expect in Bangkok, and her chances of recovery. She did not want to become a biological specimen. She preferred to die on her own terms, with some level of dignity. I did not try to dissuade her.'

'You knew she was a Buddhist?'

'Yes. So did the community. The grounds of her house were full of Cambodians, praying, chanting and so on, the night of her death.'

'You were there, I believe, at the end.'

'I was. So was her husband.' He took a drink of his whisky and stared away at something. 'Her death,' he continued, 'was a textbook example of how there are so few textbook examples.'

I shook my head and said, 'I don't understand.'

'Every human being is different, Mr Smith. Even identical twins are not truly identical. In my career I have seen more cases of death by septic shock than I can count. But Mrs Ambler's case was different from them all.'

'In what way?'

'She was aware, I believe in a mindful state and perhaps even meditating, almost, maybe even up to, the very end.'

'That's very rare, in such a case?'

'It is unknown.'

The word was like a kick, a little kick on a door high up in that absurd apartment, a door leading to a mystery . . . I said, 'Ambler, in his diary, thought it miraculous.'

Dr White said, 'That is not a word I ever use.'

His assertion was firmer ground under my feet. I felt safer, more secure. Secure enough to keep pushing. I said, 'Ambler devoted several entries to the difficulty he had in arranging the cremation.'

'The government wanted the body shipped back to the UK.'

'But in the end she was cremated here.'

'At Wat Lanka.'

'It took some time to arrange.'

'It took several days.'

'Was there anything unusual . . . about the condition of the corpse?'

Dr White looked like a man holding tight to patience. He said, 'The corpse was in unusually good condition. Did Ambler also consider that miraculous?'

'I think he did.'

'Mrs Ambler asked me to discontinue her IV two, maybe three days before she died. I'd have to consult my notes to be certain. She was coherent and I followed her wishes. In any case she was able to take water by mouth until the end. However, she took little and, being septic, she perspired freely for days. In other words she was, at her death, dehydrated. That would have slowed decomposition.'

So there was an answer for everything. I said, 'Were you aware that Lim Sovan had a vision?'

'No, Mr Smith, I was not. However, it does not surprise

me. She is a young Cambodian woman, from somewhere deep in the provinces. I would be surprised if she did not have visions.'

There was only one thing left to demolish. I told him, 'Ambler wrote that the three of you had a long conversation about Zainab's religious beliefs, just a few days before she died.'

'It was a remarkable conversation; I don't remember it being that long. I wanted to be completely certain that she understood the gravity of her situation. She did. We then discussed her religious, or perhaps I should say, for she was an intellectual, even sceptical Buddhist, her philosophical beliefs. They were nothing that I had not heard before, but she was very articulate, even persuasive, despite her condition. As you would expect, she held to a refined form of Buddhism. She believed neither in the existence of a soul, nor in the continuance of one's personality in the next life.'

He paused, and I asked, 'Then, what does continue?'

'Karma. One's karma is reborn into a new life. It sounds somewhat arid. I wish you could have been there to hear her. She was persuasive without trying to be persuasive. Her faith, if you could call it that, was charming; she charmed both of us. She held her faith affectionately, as if it were a child, or someone she loved. But it was based on rigorous thought and analysis. And she was completely undogmatic. The last thing she said, before returning to her bed, was, 'But of course, I may be deluded.'

I said, 'I don't think that Ambler thought she was deluded. But I don't think he saw it in quite such a refined way. He thought there was at least a chance he would meet her again, recognize her, be with her, in the next life. He committed suicide to that aim.' I stopped and tried to get a grip on myself; my hand shook. I looked down and saw that I'd spilled my whisky.

The doctor said evenly, 'I did not see Ambler again after his wife's cremation. My nurse did. She reported that he showed signs of depression. Perhaps I should have seen him. I was busy with other patients. It would have been abnormal if Ambler had not been depressed. However, depression, even clinical depression, does not normally lead to suicide. It is usually no more than a contributing factor.'

I said, 'It was depression plus his belief in ghosts, the mumbo-jumbo — in karma, rebirth — that led to his suicide. It was swallowing all that hocus-pocus.' I sat back, too bitter to speak further. Zainab rejected me because she'd so affectionately swallowed that mumbo-jumbo. The superstitious nonsense that views love as an obstacle to some spiritual path.

Dr White finished off his drink. Then he asked me, 'How high's the bar?'

'I'm sorry?'

'Do you believe in spirituality?'

'I don't know what it means.'

'Then you haven't experienced it, or are unaware of having experienced it. Or you're in denial.

'I was present at Mrs Ambler's death. I have been present at more deaths than I could possibly remember. Mrs Ambler's was a spiritual experience; I think the most spiritual experience I've ever had.

'It was partly her ability to still be mindful, possibly even in a meditative state, while dying from multiple organ failure. That was the physical background. But the experience itself was beyond the purely physical. It was about her: her personality; her spiritual quality; the way she met her death. Observing her death, I felt close to something — something I knew not what, something ineffable. Not a presence, more like a state . . . Are you at all musical?'

The question threw me off kilter. Without thinking, I said, 'No.'

'Too bad. There's a kind of music — Bach composed several examples — which I'm sure Mrs Ambler was aware of, called canon. I no longer play, but many years ago I did, and one evening, while playing a Bach canon from memory, I felt, briefly, as if I were outside myself; I felt that I'd entered a musical stream, like the flow of a river, or the rushing of the wind, and that this flow – which was the music of the canon – was continuous: it came from I knew not where and continued I knew not whither. While I played, I was, for a short time, a part of that musical flow. This vision or waking dream ended the moment I finished the piece.

'Witnessing Mrs Ambler's death I felt something similar: as if I were observing a process that continued, beyond my sight or understanding, after her death. I feel certain that her husband also felt something of the kind.

'Of course, there was no phenomenon involved. I am speaking of a purely subjective mental or emotional state, brought on in my case by a patient's death. The corpse's apparent incorruption, four days after death in this environment, was a phenomenon, but can be explained . . . dehydration. Her housemaid-cook's "vision" can be easily discounted. She comes from a culture in which people commonly see, feel the presence of, even hear spirits. We explain this as self-induced hallucination.'

At that point I remembered an incident in Ambler's diary: his own hallucination, an olfactory hallucination of urine. He must have been under terrible emotional stress, even trauma. I asked White, 'What's your point?'

'It's simply this: how high's the bar? How many things do you have to find "scientific" explanations for, before you start to doubt your own disbelief? Is there a limit? Is it three things, four things, five?

'I think you should be kinder to Mr Ambler. He was lonely and depressed, possibly clinically depressed. I suspect, as you say, he had convinced himself that there was at least a chance that he would meet his wife again in another life. He could be certain that he would not meet her again in this. As a middle-aged physician, I could not begin to count the number of suicides I have seen who had weaker reasons to end their lives.'

I asked him, 'What do you believe?'

'Me? I believe in nothing, Mr Smith. Nothing. However, I do believe in trying to keep my mind open – just a crack.'

The telephone rang. He answered it. After he hung up he told me, 'I'm afraid I have to go. An Australian guest at one of the tourist hotels is ill enough to concern the management. It's probably just alcohol poisoning, but you never know.'

An uncharitable impulse made me ask, 'How's your practice?'

He gave a grim smile. 'You mean since Miss Goldstein's article?'

I nodded.

'The practice is recovering. I relied greatly on the NGOs and embassies, and although many of the embassies still use my services – several did their own investigation and found nothing that would hold up in court – most of the NGOs and UN agencies dropped me. They wanted nothing to do with a whiff of scandal, even if it was only in the *Phnom Penh Post*.

'So I've taken my practice to the tourist hotel industry. It is lucrative, but it's all on-call. The whole thing's been a lesson to me. In casual relationships, avoid ladies of the press.'

I rose to accompany him downstairs when the phone rang again. He picked it up, and with an expression of surprise said a few words in Khmer. He'd been in-country for many years. He put the receiver down and told me, 'Let's go. There's a friend of yours waiting downstairs.'

'A friend?'

'Sovan. She's brought you a message from Maung Thant, the Burmese monk.'

We found her waiting outside the door. She was dressed simply but in what I expected was one of her better outfits: white slacks and a long-sleeved cotton shirt. The doctor bade us goodnight and Sovan told me, in her thickly accented, diction-free English, that the monk had heard I was in town, and wanted to see me. I asked her how she'd tracked me down. It took me a minute to make her understand my question; the idea that she could have difficulty, in Phnom Penh, finding a *Barang*, particularly me, was hard for her to grasp. She'd simply gone to the hotel, talked to the doorman and then my tuk-tuk driver.

I saw little point in asking her what he wanted to see me about. We got into a tuk-tuk and drove to Wat Lanka.

Sovan escorted me inside. It was not yet late and lights burned in the dormitories and even in some of the offices. She took me to one of the older two-storey buildings and led me up an outside flight of stairs to a balcony. She stayed there and motioned me in.

The room was unfurnished except for a number of mats and cushions on the floor. Maung Thant was alone, sitting cross-legged; he rose and greeted me. He wore the yellow robe of a Cambodian monk. He insisted that we sit outside; like a Cambodian, he didn't believe that a *Barang* could be comfortable sitting on the floor, and the balcony had a couple of plain wooden chairs and a small table. Sovan bowed to him and slipped back downstairs to wait.

Phnom Penh is a small town and I'm sure there was little about me by that time that Maung Thant didn't know. He was concerned for me but was neither pressing nor intrusive. In a modest, quiet voice he asked me three or four questions regarding my plans, my health, and so on. His manner emanated peace and encouraged confidence. I asked him how he was doing and if he expected to remain in Cambodia long. He smiled and said, 'I am no longer news. The authorities have made it clear that, as long as I stay clear of politics, I am free to come and go. Probably I will travel; I would like to visit again the UK – as you know, I spent many years there. The Buddhist community in Britain is neither as large nor so well-established as it is in your country. I would like to help it, encourage it. I think Britain is today the most secular country on earth; only China comes close.'

I said, 'Mrs Ambler considered her form of Buddhism secular. She would have considered it as a philosophy, more than a religion.'

He nodded. 'I only meant that the UK today is so secular that even Mrs Ambler's form of Buddhism would be considered by most to be religious. She and I came from the same school: Theravada. What used to be called the Lesser Vehicle. I understand she was a very refined Buddhist.'

Suddenly I couldn't keep up speaking of her in the past, almost academically. I don't know if it was fatigue catching up with me, or the feeling of peace the monk engendered, or his empathy. I felt I could speak to him plainly, calmly. I told him, 'I've heard that over and over again, and maybe she was. I expect she was. But she was also a flesh and blood woman. She loved and was loved. At the end of her life, she rejected love. I know she rejected me.'

The monk thought for a moment before asking, 'When she knew she was dying?'

'No. Before. Shortly before.'

He nodded. 'The British have a phrase: to concentrate the mind. Don't you think that being shot, wounded, being flown to Thailand and hospitalized, then back here to recover . . . don't you think that that may have concentrated her mind?'

'On rejection?'

'On some degree of detachment. She may even have had a premonition, conscious or unconscious. For shortly after she made that decision, she did become aware of her imminent death, didn't she?'

'Yes.'

'How fortunate she was in having that knowledge. She had time to prepare herself. For a Buddhist that is a great boon.'

'Please don't tell me we should be happy for her.'

'Death is part of life. It is something over which we usually have little or no control. It sounds arrogant, but it is hard not to come to the conclusion that for most people the circumstances of their death are unimportant. From what I've heard, Mrs Ambler had a good death.'

'Complete with miracles.'

'We don't need to bother about those. At the most they suggest she was what we call a stream entrant. We may hope, for her sake, that is the case. But this is a very superstitious environment. The stories you have heard are of little account. What do we know, for certain? We know she had a mindful death. That is something for which we can be grateful; and from which we can learn. But the real test is her life: what can we learn from her life? In what way did she influence others? How may she influence us, now?'

He paused for a moment, and then chuckled. 'I beg your pardon,' he said, 'but I remembered an Englishman I once knew in London. His wife was very interested in Buddhism, but he was not. He was a good man, but of the earth, earthy. He was a professional salesman for a large corporation with an office in Berkeley Square. I remember one of his favourite sayings: "What goes around, comes around." A pithy phrase!'

It occurred to me then that the monk, an older man not in the best of health, and probably with a punishing daily schedule, might be even more fatigued than me. I thanked him, made my excuses and stood up – and nearly fell from sheer light-headedness. I sat back down and he called for Sovan to come and help me. She went inside and returned with a glass of water; in a minute I was fine. I stood up again, this time without incident, and bowed to him with my hands together. It takes no trouble to be polite.

As we parted, he said, 'People commonly ask me, Mr Smith, for a suitable subject for meditation. If you don't mind, I would like to suggest one for you.'

'I'm afraid I'm not a meditator.'

'That's all right. I'm not using the word in its Buddhist sense, but in its general English sense: to think about, to contemplate. May I suggest a suitable subject for meditation would be, Mrs Ambler's influence on you?'

20

The next morning I reported for duty at the American Embassy.

I greeted my fellow staff, none of whom had changed (the Political Officer had finally returned from emergency leave) and retired to my office until the 11 a.m. country team meeting. The office had been kept clean and some tidying up done, probably on Noelle's orders, but it was essentially as I'd left it six months before. It felt like six years, or maybe sixty: I felt like a ghost in my own life, revisiting after death the scene of the crime.

I took out my key and unlocked my filing cabinet, and found, still within its folder, my report to Noelle titled, 'Result of Proposal to the Deputy Minister, Ministry of Oil, Concerning Westin Oil', along with the copy I'd made of the ambassador's letter of immunity. I removed them carefully from their folder, placed both on my desk, and turned over the pages. I felt almost as if I should be wearing white gloves, examining a find at an archaeological site – perhaps a crypt. I slipped the two documents into my briefcase and relocked the filing cabinet.

The agenda for the team meeting was sparse. No guest speaker was on the list and the Sergeants Higgins were on leave, eliminating our security briefing. It looked at first as if my reappearance was the only real news, until Noelle dropped her bombshell.

She was resigning. She had accepted a position with a think-tank in Washington, effective almost immediately. She apologized for there not being time for a farewell party or function, but complimented us as a group and individually for our professionalism and contribution to the work of the mission. Me she complimented for my 'cross-discipline expertise and ability', and my willingness to take on 'urgent and sensitive' work.

After Noelle called the meeting to an end the other officers rose as one and surrounded her; everyone wanted to say a few words and I'm sure everyone wanted to know why she was leaving. She pulled away long enough to ask me to meet her in her office in twenty minutes.

When I walked in Noelle was behind her desk. I'd left the meeting without speaking; now I told her I was sorry to see her go. 'I'm not being conventionally polite,' I said, 'I'm sincere.'

'Thanks. It's not quite as sudden as it looks. I've been talking to the Asia Institute in DC for some time and I handed in my resignation to the ambassador three weeks ago. I haven't given general notice until now because I wanted a minimum of fuss. I'm flying out on Friday. How are you? You're looking a little tired.'

'It was a long flight.'

'Did the department pressure you to come back?'

'Not really. They preferred it. I wanted it.'

'Why?'

'Be frank with me, Noelle. I wasn't in very good shape when I left, was I?'

She looked at me coolly, appraisingly. 'No, Michael, you weren't. I thought you might be close to a breakdown. When the government let us know they considered you persona non grata – they never made a formal declaration – the ambassador and I thought it a good excuse to get you home for a while.'

'I was that bad?'

'We thought so. You'd gone through an extremely traumatic experience. We thought some professional help would be a good idea.'

It's not pleasant to be labelled damaged, even if it's true. 'Well,' I said, 'I'm better now.'

'Good.'

'In fact, coming back was the last step towards recovery.'

She said nothing.

'I'm going to try to publicize the Westin case, Noelle.'

She sat back in her chair. 'You mean, the letter of immunity that the ambassador signed?'

'Yes. And the report leading up to it.'

'Why? And why now?'

'You once told me that we hang on to this career because of the expectation that, during twenty or thirty years, we'll be able to do more good than harm.'

'I remember.'

'I'm not willing to take that long a view. I don't have that expectation.'

'You know Westin has yet to sink a well. The practical effect of going public with those documents will be to kill Westin's concession dead, and most likely to promote China's position.'

'There are other practical results that I'm more interested in.'

She nodded. 'Well, I sympathize. When do you intend to go public?'

'Not until after you've left. And I'll try to keep you out of it.'

'Thank you. You know of course this means the end of your career.'

'Yes. I've decided to resign.'

'You came back to resign?'

'No. I made the decision last night – or maybe this morning, I'm not sure.'

'You've thought it through?'

'I'm certain.'

Noelle thought it through herself for a moment. She said, 'I'm exiting as Chargé d'Affaires; the ambassador's in Hong Kong on business until Monday. If you don't mind, I'd prefer we keep this conversation confidential, and that you hand in your resignation directly to him, upon his return.'

'That's fine with me.'

'How much notice do you intend to give?'

'None.'

She smiled and said, 'Given your intention to blow the gaffe, I think that's reasonable.'

It was an old-fashioned British phrase, and it triggered my memory. I asked her if she knew what had happened to Simmonds.

'He stayed on for a little while, but the Brits thought he'd made enemies – which was undoubtedly true. The Brits aren't quite as high in the untouchable category as we are and of course Simmonds wasn't a diplomat, just an embassy employee. They sent him back to the UK, I think, pending further assignment. I haven't heard from him.'

'At the meeting this morning you didn't give a reason for your own retirement from the Service.'

'Oh, it's a lot of things.' She tapped her finger on the polished desktop. 'The Westin affair left a bad taste in my mouth, too. It was going to be a skeleton in my closet. And the monk handover . . . The concept was Mrs Ambler's idea, for the Reform Party, but the details – it was supposed to be a confidence-building measure – were mine.' She said heavily, 'You can't foresee every disaster.' She looked up. 'And I have personal reasons. We talked about them that night we discussed careers.'

Ethics and guilt. We had a lot in common. Even loneliness. She didn't want to face a future alone. Neither did I. She said, 'You'll have to leave almost immediately to withdraw from diplomatic status. Where do you think you'll go, what will you do?'

'I haven't given it much thought yet.' I was only half kidding when I said, 'If we both wound up in DC . . . we might be a good match. At least I might be a good date.'

'It wouldn't work, Michael. Only newspapers welcome whistleblowers. You'll be beyond the pale, even for an associate of the Asia Institute.'

We got up and shook hands. I said, 'I'm sorry to hear it. I always admired you.'

'And I you.' The Chargé mask, the professional carapace of office, descended upon her. 'But we'd each be a constant reminder to the other of the whole affair. And we'd have so much to try to forgive, of ourselves and of the other.'

'So much?'

'We both share some complicity, even if inadvertent, in the death of Mrs Ambler.'

The following morning I sat by myself, finishing my breakfast of bacon and eggs and toast and coffee and fresh-squeezed orange juice (for the equivalent of five US dollars) on the veranda of Flavours, opposite Wat Lanka. The sun shone in an as yet almost unclouded sky. Happiness is often to be found in the conscious enjoyment of the present moment, and I was aware of being solitary but happy over the remains of my breakfast, on the edge of the awning's shade, across the street from the newspaper and magazine vendors and the tall white temple wall.

It was important to enjoy the moment because I expected it to be soon interrupted by the arrival of Deria Goldstein.

I'd telephoned her the previous afternoon and met her that evening, after dinner at her apartment.

She lived, oddly enough, on the same street as the apartment that Zainab and I had shared, but two blocks further down. The further down that road you got the more decayed it became. I use the adjective in its most concrete sense: as I swung open the small gate leading to the stairwell of her apartment, it dropped off its hinges in my hand. I propped it against the wall and entered.

Her apartment was on the top floor, three storeys up. I still didn't feel completely back to normal and I waited for a minute on the landing to catch my breath before knocking.

She asked me in with distant courtesy, as if I were a salesman peddling something for which she had little use. Her apartment was a spacious but seedy bedsit. An ancient sofa bed and a low, rickety table sat in the middle of an otherwise unfurnished room. On the table lay a laptop and wireless modem, the modern equivalent of the typewriter. Two open suitcases sat shoved against a wall. They contained clothes, books, papers. A tiny kitchenette and a balcony completed the picture. I was certain there was a bathroom somewhere but it wasn't in sight.

Deria herself was as thin as before, if not thinner. She was dressed in a shirt and jeans. I saw no air-conditioning unit, and the apartment was so hot her shirt stuck to her flat chest. She asked me to sit down on the sofa bed in a tone that suggested she had a lot on her plate, and was doing me a favour by agreeing to see me at all.

I was about to offer her the scoop of her life.

The deal was simple. I offered her the Westin story, with my documents to back it up. A story of the State Department contravening US law, and encouraging an American company to corrupt a foreign power. I'd give her whatever additional background she needed. I had three conditions. The story had to come out, at least initially, in a major US or UK or European paper. It couldn't come out for at least two weeks. And neither Noelle nor her position could be mentioned in any way.

Deria attempted to dig in her heels at that, but I cut her off. I told her it was a deal-breaker, period. I threw her a couple of sweeteners: myself and the ambassador – a political appointee I'd never thought much of in any case. I knew I'd landed her when she pulled out a digital recorder from one of the suitcases and asked if we could get started immediately.

I talked and answered her questions for forty-five minutes, until I couldn't take it any longer, and insisted that we take a beer break. I was dying of the heat. Her larder was bare but she didn't want to let me out of her apartment and insisted on going out herself to bring back beer and cigarettes. We went on for almost another hour after that. She said she'd Skype an editor she knew at the *Times* in New York at one that morning. Might as well start at the top.

She would report to me at ten for coffee at Flavours. If her news was positive, I'd hand her my documents.

★

At two minutes past ten a moto drew up in front of the restaurant and Deria slipped off the back. I waved to her and she waved back and sat down at my table. She had on a clean shirt and had made some effort with her hair. Her smile for once looked neither condescending, louche, nor calculating.

'The *New York Times* is interested,' she said. 'I've already negotiated a deal with them. You and I didn't discuss—'

'Forget it. I'm not interested in money.'

'I have to be. This is my job.'

I opened my briefcase, took out the documents and handed them over. 'I won't be around much longer,' I told her. 'If you need any further information or clarifications, call me soon.'

'I don't think I'll need anything more. Where are you going?'

'I'm not sure yet.'

'I won't be here much longer, either. This is the biggest story I've ever had, and it'll pay me enough to get out, back to New York. The government won't want me here, anyway, once the story breaks. You know the Prime Minister's party won by a landslide.'

'I'd heard.'

I thought: I've seen her as unattractive at the best, contemptible at the worst, ever since I first met her – the same night I first met Zainab. Now, in a way, she's doing Zainab's work, and she already looks better: a more whole person for it. Or was it just the result of success?

I told her, 'I'm glad it's working out for you.'

She looked at me suspiciously, and I was reminded of how corrosive gratitude can be. I thought I'd better nip it in the bud. I said, 'I didn't know any other journalists here who had the right connections.'

She stood and held out her hand; I stood and shook it. Then she said, out of the clear blue sky, 'I admired Mrs Ambler.' A passing moto stopped on the road beside us; she waved to it, got on and drove off.

I sat down and ordered another cup of coffee from the young Cambodian waitress. A crippled beggar eyed me from the street. I indicated to him to stay and wait; I'd give him something when I left, but didn't want to be besieged before I'd finished my coffee. I felt tired; it had been a long flight back and a difficult weekend, and I had no idea what the future held or even where it was to be.

Then for some reason I remembered what I'd read in Ambler's diary, what Zainab had told Dr White on that special evening before her death, with the three of them sitting together in the television room in the House of Usher. She'd told them that the passage from this life to the next is but a thought moment, and is like the flame of a candle that burns through the night: the flame of the morning is not the same as the evening flame, but neither is it another.

I sat back and looked across the street. The gate was open and an empty bier, its white sheet flapping in the breeze, lay on the ground in front of the crematorium. White smoke drifted from the tall chimney, puffs of smoke that were soon lost among the white clouds, already building, of the monsoon.

Calgary, 31 October, 2009

Acknowledgements

I am indebted to Dr Brian Unger and Dr Sheila Robinson for their hospitality and introductions in Phnom Penh, but most of all for their characters, as friends and as expatriates. I also wish to thank Dr Joyce Neal of the Center for Disease Control for her kind introductions, which proved both useful and inspirational.

John Sanday, OBE, the Project Director for Banteay Chhmar, introduced me to the ruins over an excellent Christmas dinner at his house in Phnom Penh.

This book was developed and outlined in residences kindly made available by Rachel Louise Snyder and Paul Burton in Cambodia, and Dr Liliane Bartha in Olympia, Washington. Dr Bartha was also my first reader and editor.

I want to thank Sheryl Chantler for renewing my interest in flying and for getting me again behind the control yoke of a light aeroplane.

Oum Nimol, in Phnom Penh, helped me in many practical ways, as well as providing inspiration and insight into Cambodian culture.

Finally, I would like to thank the senior officer (who does not accept Buddhist non-attachment) of the US Foreign Service, who was so knowledgeable and helpful – and discreet.

Read more . . .

John Lathrop

THE DESERT CONTRACT

**A novel of sexual obsession, the danger of innocence and
one man's attempt to redeem himself**

Businessman Steve Kemp is looking to make his fortune in the
Arabian Gulf when chance reconnects him to his former lover, Helen.
Married to an older man, she must choose between loyalty and
desire. Kemp is focused on cementing their love and financing their
escape – but he needs a major deal.

The perfect client finally arrives, but time has run out. Jihadists are
seeping across the desert and the regime looks set to crack. Everyone
looks to their own escape plan, while Kemp chases his deal as far as
he must.

*Order your copy now by calling Bookpoint on 01235 827716 or
visit your local bookshop quoting ISBN 978-0-7195-6854-1*
www.johnmurray.co.uk